RESISTING MAXU

THE CLECANIAN SERIES: BOOK SIX

•

First paperback edition November 2022

Cover design by Mayhem Cover Creations

ISBN: 978-1-958397-99-2

www.victoriaaveline.com

RESISTING
MAXU

THE CLECANIAN SERIES: BOOK SIX

VICTORIA AVELINE

Prologue

D ead.
  Meg stared at the black screen of the ancient iPod clutched in her fist. She'd found it cold and wet on Jeremy's outdoor weight bench. Whirling through the patio doors and swallowing bitter tears, she headed toward where Jeremy would be. Where he always was. His office. If you could call a stale-aired, wood-paneled game room with a dedicated energy drink fridge an office.

But had Meg batted an eye when he'd pushed to remake the guest room she'd spent months scouting yard sales and curbs to furnish? Nope. She hadn't raised a word of objection when she'd had to sell the DIY tufted headboard or the upcycled solid wood nightstands she'd fought over at the VanBuren Street Goodwill. Because he'd told her all the money they'd spent on his fancy microphone and gaming computer were the beginnings of a dependable streaming career.

And she'd believed him. Again.

But now…her iPod?

Meg didn't ask for much. Not out loud anyway. She didn't splurge on fancy new phones or push to go out to extravagant dinners. What she did hold dear was her music. Years and years of carefully curated playlists for every mood, every situation. And Jeremy had left it outside in the rain after one of the four times a year he used the rusty workout bench. Nice weather will make me want to work out, he'd said when she'd argued against leaving the bench outside. She might snort if she weren't so angry.

But it wasn't just anger for his thoughtlessness. Or his laziness. Or his utter lack of regard for her things. It was anger with herself.

One balmy late spring day after school, she'd made the colossal mistake of going to Jeremy's house to watch a movie. They'd both been hormonal seventeen-year-olds, and she'd ended up flat on her back, virginity gone, with Jeremy's holier-than-thou sister looming over them.

To say her religious parents had been upset was the understatement of the century. The words harlot and damned had been all but stamped across her forehead. They'd pushed for her and Jeremy to get married as soon as they turned eighteen, and his parents had been just as adamant.

Meg hadn't put up a fight then either. Fear of being kicked out of her house had held back any arguments she might have had. They lived in a small town and she had nowhere else to go. No other family that would take her in. Her parents had done a marvelous job of selecting her friends for her— meaning the shallow acquaintances she'd had were all just as strict and pious as her parents were.

So, ten years ago, three weeks after her eighteenth birthday, she'd married Jeremy. A boy with whom she'd only ever exchanged a few sentences and flirtatious looks with before their five minutes of fumbling sex.

Now, grinding her jaw, Meg took in a calming breath, then pushed open the office door. She cringed as warm, stagnant air rushed out. How long had he been sitting there? It was close to six p.m., yet Jeremy was still clothed in the frumpy workout sweats he'd been wearing the day before. He gave an annoyed grumble and his right eye squinted at the light pouring in from the hall. His gaze didn't stray from the screen in front of him, his fingers clicking and flicking the greasy game controller in his hand.

"Did you use my iPod?" she yelled, hoping he could hear through the weighty noise-canceling headphones. She held up the waterlogged evidence and waited.

After a beat, his gaze flicked to her, then the device, then back to his screen. "Yeah. I thought that workout mix might make me power through some reps, but it sucked. All girly stuff."

3

Meg lifted a brow at his pale, thin arms. In high school, he'd been lean and tall. She could remember staring at him from across her desk, eyeing the cornflower-blue button-up school uniform and daydreaming about how he'd look as a man. Exactly the same, as it turned out. He hadn't filled out in the shoulders like she'd thought. His messy blond hair had never deepened in color. He was stagnant. Just like the air in this room. Just like her.

"You left it outside, and it rained this morning." She seethed. Of course, all her songs and playlists should be up there somewhere in the cloud, but that wasn't the point. She'd bought this over ten years ago with money she'd scraped together. The device had been there for her, giving her relief when she'd needed it most.

It was sentimental to her, not to mention well used. At any given hour, she could be found puttering around the house, cleaning, or doing chores, and she always had her earbuds in, iPod securely tucked in her pocket.

He knew how important it was to her, and he'd just...just left it outside.

"Huh?" Jeremy curled his tongue over the left corner of his mouth and angled his body to the side as if doing that would prevent his avatar from being killed. When he successfully avoided the oncoming attack, he shot another glance at her and she could see her complaint register in his brain. "Oh, sorry, babe. I must have forgotten."

Obviously! He didn't say another word, and it took a moment for her to comprehend he didn't plan to. He was already focused on his game again. Just like that. He'd destroyed her most cherished possession and all he could muster was a hollow "Sorry"?

Her eyes burned from lack of blinking.

Seeming to realize she was still standing there; he finally paused his game. "You can play the music from the laptop, right?"

Meg's jaw clenched. He was not trying to give her solutions as if she'd come to him with a problem. "I can't carry the laptop around everywhere with me, can I? The battery only holds a charge for, like, ten minutes. It has to stay plugged in. My phone is on its last legs, but maybe I could buy a new one." Meg took a tentative step forward. "If I got a job too, we could—"

"No. No job. What'll happen when we have a kid? Besides, where would you even get a job? You've never worked a day in your life. I don't want you to have to worry about all that."

Meg wasn't surprised at his answer. Apparently balancing their accounts, doing their taxes, and keeping their house clean inside and outside were not skills that could be put to use in a "real job," according to her gopher of a husband. Her parents, in-laws, and Jeremy were of the same mind on this. She was to stay at home like a good wifey and have babies.

The one and only time she'd gotten a job behind their backs, Jeremy had found out and sent her stern father to harass her at the deli counter until she'd finally thrown off her apron and allowed herself to be led out.

Good women listen to their husbands. Good women are modest and obedient. The entire way home, she'd been treated to an endless lecture filled with passages from the Bible illuminating her father's arguments. Did it matter to him she and Jeremy barely even went to church anymore? No. Hypocrisy was alive and well in her father's household.

Her lack of children was a continual disappointment to her family, and though they never said it outright, she knew her father's critical gaze was always assessing what she was doing wrong. How she was failing to be worthy of the blessing of a child.

Still, him thinking she wasn't being devoted to Jeremy enough was better than the truth. If they knew she'd been sneaking two towns away to get birth control pills, her dreary life would get a lot more exciting, but not in a good way.

A ping sounded from the screen, and Jeremy's eyes zoomed toward it. He kept his body facing her while sitting in the chair. Somehow, it still felt like he was turned away, though. She was a pesky annoyance. Like a gnat he couldn't catch but was always trying to swat away.

As she stared, some of her anger vanished, replaced by the hopeless resignation she'd come to recognize. Jeremy never pushed her to become pregnant. He never questioned why she hadn't gotten pregnant yet either, not that they had sex all that often. Though he claimed he wanted a child, he spoke about it without much enthusiasm. As if it was an inevitable thing they had to do since they were married. The next phase of life. But what phases had there been already?

Being controlled in her parents' house, then being controlled in Jeremy's house? She'd roll over and die before she let her child be controlled too.

Besides, in many ways, Jeremy was just a boy. A big, lanky, twenty-eight-year-old boy. Neither of them had wanted to get married then, and neither wanted to be married now. They'd been amicable for the most part, but these roles they'd fallen into...this person she'd become...she hated it. A part of her that her bitterness wouldn't acknowledge knew he hated it too.

She was a coward.

Her shoulders slumped, shame leeching away the rest of her ire. If she were braver, she'd leave him. Damn the consequences. But every time she came close, apprehension weakened her resolve. She had no money of her own. No family or friends that would take her in. As Jeremy so kindly pointed out, she'd never had a job. No actual life experience. She hadn't ever even been outside of Indiana. Her arms dropped, the iPod dangling from loose fingers.

She'd had so many dreams as a bright-eyed teen. She'd wanted to travel and meet people from all over. She'd wanted to eat new foods and see amazing sights.

How was this her life? How had she let this be her life? How had she let herself care so deeply about a decade-old iPod—an inanimate object—that when it was gone, it felt like her world was crumbling around her?

Something in her broke a little at that realization. She cared more about this iPod than she did about anything else in this house, including Jeremy. Meg took a step back into the rust-colored seventies carpeting of their hallway. As soon as she'd cleared the room, Jeremy swiveled back to his screen. Husbandly Attention Given to Hysterical Wife mini game...complete.

She floated through rooms like a ghost until she was outside. The tips of the tall yellow grass tickled her fingers as she shuffled into the overgrown fields that surrounded the house on all sides. Pale and full, the moon hung overhead in the early evening sky.

She plopped onto the ground, clutched her iPod to her chest, and closed her eyes. All was silent except the gentle chirping of insects and the rustle of prairie grass as it swayed in the breeze. By all accounts, she should be relaxed, zen. She supposed she was something akin to that.

No, not zen. Numb. She'd grown so damn numb to the world. It was the only way to survive, really. If she let any of her disappointment in, it would bury her.

Next time, she told herself, as she so often did. If reincarnation exists, then next time let me be braver. I'll do things differently. I promise.

Her lids were squinted so tightly shut, all her concentration focused on her wish that she didn't see the shadow blocking out the dying light. Hearing the rustling behind her, she turned. "What do you want, Jer—" She gasped.

Not Jeremy.

A lizard the size of a man loomed above. Her mouth fell open on a scream, but the lizard pointed something at her. The last thing she remembered before the world went dark was wet mist hitting her face.

1

Nine Months Later

"And you'd pay me?" Meg gazed at the elegant older woman across from her—the Queen—and tried not to let her bubbling excitement show on her face.

Not only was she speaking with the ruler of Tremanta but also three other high-ranking officials.

Metli, the Queen's right hand and self-proclaimed protectress.

Vila, a contrary woman. Meg couldn't understand why Vila was invited to these types of meetings since she tended to spend her time questioning every word out of the Queen's mouth. Unsurprisingly Metli and Vila didn't get along.

The last woman present was Asivva, an Intergalactic Council representative who'd made it her business to see to the humans, always making sure they were comfortable and understood the complicated world they'd been dropped into.

She was gorgeous, with dark hair swept into an elegant bun, pale skin, and periwinkle eyes. Her plain outfit did nothing to detract from her beauty. She wore a simple beige jumpsuit outfitted with a large golden kite-shaped pin. The pin contained five circles of varying sizes organized vertically through the middle—the planetary symbol of Clecania.

Meg still couldn't believe it. Not nine months earlier, she'd been praying for another chance at life, and now look at her. Swept into an adventure so incredible, she half thought she'd died and gone to heaven.

The Queen raised a manicured white brow, and the faint dark circles under her eyes hollowed. "This is very important. More important than your trip to Sauven. You may find some enjoyment on the tour, but it's also a job. I have expectations. It will be difficult at times, and I want to make sure you're compensated for those"—her lips thinned ever so slightly—"challenges."

Meg's instinct was to shrug off the ominous comment, but she forced herself to think through the warning. If the Queen of a freaking alien city was urging her to take the opportunity of a lifetime seriously, she probably should.

Since being abducted from Earth, Meg had been through the wringer. She'd been kidnapped by a radical group of aliens set on finding reproductively compatible females, locked in an underground bunker, rescued from said bunker by non-radical aliens, and shown a whole new world that clashed with most of the beliefs she'd grown up with...and she'd never been happier in her entire life.

The only downside of her time here was that apart from a four-day trip to the forest city of Sauven, she'd been confined to Tremanta. Shortly after her rescue, one of the other human women who'd been abducted had mated with an alien man and become pregnant. The magical event of mating had been lost to these aliens for hundreds of years, so when the Queen had found out one measly human had made sacred and elusive mating marks appear on the hands of a guy named Theo, well...it had been a big deal.

Concern that the citizens of the planet would find out and tear down the city of Tremanta in search of the other humans had forced Meg and her fellow rescues to remain cooped up in hiding until the Queen had been able to figure out how to best announce their exciting discovery without causing a riot.

Earth was considered a Class Four planet. This planet, Clecania, was a Class Two planet. Class Fours were off-limits in a big way. Like, intergalactic laws that wouldn't affect one rule breaker but an entire planet of people big. From what Meg could tell, the process of getting Earth's status switched to a Three would be a delicate political chess match. Having a slew of desperate Clecanians illegally flock to Earth to pick themselves up a mate of their own would not help their cause one bit.

As of now, Class Four meant no one was allowed to make contact with Earth. They couldn't even fly close to it. Humans were still developing, and there were strict laws in place to keep that development happening at a natural pace.

Meg had read one account of interference from eons ago, where the primitive species went mad after being introduced to a visiting species of aliens keen to make contact. Yet another account had shown how dangerous the uneven power dynamic was when advanced races with advanced weapons showed up on a planet and took valuable resources. Countless interactions like this had resulted in a law that clearly forbade interference with planets whose species had not yet evolved to the point of deep space travel.

Meg didn't care if Earth was ever switched over. It'd take them a million years to get to evolve to a Class Three status if she had it her way. It left a tight knot in her throat to know that her old miserable life was still out there, waiting. She didn't want it back.

On Clecania, they provided for her. They gave her housing and clothing and food. And not just the bare essentials. Good stuff. They'd offered to train her for whatever career she wanted for free. The first step had been learning to read their language.

Implanted translators had made it unnecessary to learn the spoken language, but Meg had leapt at the opportunity to master Clecanian writing. Studying each vertical loopy symbol into the wee hours of the morning, she'd picked up on the written language faster than anyone else. For the first time in her life, she was proud of herself.

Unlike some of the rescued humans who spent their days shuffling around drearily in mourning for their old lives, Meg had flourished. At least within the confines of the Pearl Temple, where all the women lived. But now she wanted to flourish elsewhere too. After months of studying, she felt like she'd been kept in a holding pattern. Stuck in limbo between moving away from who she'd been and discovering who she was.

A few months ago, when the announcement had been made to the planet that humans existed, the Queen had started dropping hints that she wanted to schedule a tour of sorts for a select few humans. A trip around the world, where curious Clecanians could meet humans and ask questions. Meg believed the Queen hoped that having a taste of the humans would help tide the surging discontent running through the planet.

From what she understood, many cities were furious that Tremanta had sheltered a large portion of the humans for as long as they had. They felt the Queen was keeping the humans to herself, hoarding them for her citizens alone and not allowing other cities' residents their chance at recognizing a mate.

Many discussions of how a tour like this might be accomplished had been held over the last few months, all of which had actually included a group of interested humans. Meg had been thrilled and baffled to be invited to these talks. At first, she'd felt out of place. She'd barely graduated high school. She'd never had a job or any practice with the complicated political maneuverings of a city with a highly sought after resource.

But after a few meetings where not only the other women but the Queen herself had listened to Meg's suggestions, her confidence had been bolstered. She'd promised she'd be a different person in her new life, and by God, she would be.

She'd be brave and confident. No one knew her here. It was an opportunity to remake herself. Who'd know the difference? Opinionated, well read, and—hopefully—well traveled. She'd started dressing the way she'd always wanted. Showing off more skin than would've been allowed back home. She experimented with dying her hair blonde before changing it back to brown and chopping it off. Now she styled it to look sexy and a bit rumpled, like the carefree French exchange student, Monique, who'd gone to Meg's high school for a year and driven all the boys to distraction.

Drinking and cursing had been next on her list of things to try, and she'd found she liked both. Meg had even begun testing out her flirting abilities on a few of the men in town who'd approached her. Her skills were rusty, to say the least, but the men seemed to find her charming anyway. It made Meg feel powerful and confident to know that she could turn a head, even if she didn't want to take it any further than that quite yet.

Though she mooned over all the gorgeous, perfectly sculpted alien men in Tremanta, she knew most were far more interested in recognizing her as a mate and building deep, meaningful connections than they were in having no-strings-attached flings. So flirting was all she could do without getting their hopes up too high, and she was fine with that. Ten years stuck with Jeremy made the mere idea of being married again as foul as rotting fish.

This was her time to learn who she was and live life to the fullest. No slipping into old habits.

With a start, she realized the Queen was still studying her, seeming pleased with the long time she was taking to give her answer. Meg lifted her chin and nodded as if she'd thought it over carefully and come to a well-reasoned conclusion.

In reality, she'd started reading everything she could about every single city on Clecania as soon as the Queen had mentioned her tour idea. If anyone was getting picked to take an all-expenses-paid trip around the world, she'd make sure she was prepared enough to be on a shortlist.

"I think even with the challenges, this trip will be fantastic for everyone. Other cities can have some of their curiosity lessened and hopefully learn a little more about Earth and why swarming the planet might be a bad idea." Meg tried to keep her focus on the Queen and not on Metli, whose nails were clacking against her screen as she took notes.

Vila folded her hands in front of her. Meg chewed the inside of her lip. How could someone with a bright blonde pixie cut, a frilly high-collared mauve shirt, and warm honey-yellow eyes look so severe and intimidating? "You've declined participating in every marriage ceremony. Is that right?"

Meg straightened in her seat, taken off guard.

Though the Tremantian marriages were temporary and less disagreeable than the "till death do us part" Earth marriage she was used to, a cold sweat still broke over her chest at the thought of them. They were geared toward finding a man worthy enough to have a child for, and one thing Meg did know about herself was that she did not want to have a child right now.

Marrying some random guy and having him shower her with attention and gifts and fine cooking sounded heavenly, but she wouldn't do it. Not when she was one hundred percent certain she wasn't ready for a kid.

She didn't explain all of that to the women staring at her, though. "That's right," she said instead. Her toes curled in her shoes, her body stiffening with every thunderous tap of Metli's nails on her screen.

Would they think she was rebuking their customs by not taking part in the marriage ceremonies? Would it ruin her chances of being picked to go on this trip?

Suddenly, this felt far more like a job interview than it had before. Meg's mouth went dry.

"There is a possibility that you may be recognized while abroad. Are you comfortable with that possibility?" Vila pressed, her painted lips turned down.

Meg's gaze flitted to Asivva, who gave her a reassuring nod.

"Oh, yeah. Sure," she said, smiling. She waved her hand.

Metli paused her typing to peer up at Meg. Had her tone been too flippant?

When the Queen's purple eyes narrowed on her as well, Meg explained. "It's just, I've been studying matehood and how people are recognized. In the past, it seemed that it could happen whenever or wherever. After just a smell, even," she added. "But I've also been researching how it's happened for the humans, and everyone I've contacted has said they were with their guys for a while before they were recognized. I believe…" Meg could hear her own tone and wanted to cringe. It was true she'd done a lot of research on this very point, but was she really trying to lecture her case to a Queen? She cleared her throat and when on. "I believe that since humans are more distantly related to Clecanians, it takes longer for us. You have to be around a person for a while, maybe even be intimate with them for recognition to occur. The shortest time I heard about was with Alice. Luka recognized her in only a few days, but…" Her knee bounced under the table. "There were extenuating circumstances there."

Asivva, Luka's sister, nodded with understanding, and Meg was beyond grateful she didn't have to further explain that the drugged-out primal state Luka had been in when he'd recognized Alice had probably helped his mating instinct along.

Wrinkles appeared between the Queen's eyebrows as she mulled over Meg's argument.

"My plan is just to not spend more than a day with any new person if I can help it. No one will recognize me, then," Meg added in a rush. Perhaps she was trying to assure herself as much as she was these women. If she thought for a moment this trip would result in a lifelong commitment to one man, a veritable stranger, she'd have to seriously reconsider going. But how could she pass up this opportunity? Denial and delusion. That's how.

The Queen tipped her head at Meg, studying her with slightly bloodshot eyes. Concern leaked into Meg's mind. Over the last month, the Queen had been looking more and more stressed. Meg couldn't even imagine the amount of pressure this powerful woman must've been under. How to keep an entire world happy while also being fair to the humans. It was a balancing act that required far more care than Meg could dream of.

Suddenly, she felt sorry for wasting this impressive leader's time. Did she really deserve a face-to-face interview with someone who had that much on the line? Not even a little.

"It'll be okay," Meg assured. She let out a slow breath, hating the words about to come out of her mouth, even knowing they needed to be said. "If I am recognized, I...well, I understand what that means and what I'll have to do." If—

and that was a big if—she was recognized as someone's mate, she'd need to stay with that person. Anything else would be cruel. Once recognized, a Clecanian would slowly wither if not near their mate. Whether it be physical or mental illness, it was a torturous thing. Since the Clecanians all recognized each other, she'd only ever read accounts of mates being separated by death. She couldn't imagine how much worse it would be if a human chose not to be with their mate.

"I'm glad to hear that," Vila commented, not sounding glad at all.

The Queen eyed her for a moment longer. "I believe we've asked all of our questions." The women rose from their seats.

Meg shot up from her chair with far less grace than the Queen. "So…do I have the job? Officially?"

An actual smile formed then. "Yes. I'd be delighted to have you represent our city and your planet."

She wanted to squeal. But that would be weird and immature, right? Instead, she just grinned like an idiot and, through a tight throat, said, "Thank you."

Metli stayed behind as the Queen, Asivva, and Vila swanned out of the room. "You'll leave in one week. As I understand it, you've requested Daunet to be your escort?"

Her eager nod would rival any bobblehead. Daunet had accompanied her to Sauven six weeks ago. They'd bonded while sharing a small two-room nest, though she was sure Daunet had wanted to strangle her by the end of their trip. Apart from their excursions to watch the famous Sauvenian marriage games, Meg had complained constantly about not being allowed to tour the rest of the city.

"I'll make the arrangements and send her your official itinerary in a few days."

Itinerary. I have an itinerary! Meg couldn't remember ever hearing a more exquisite word. She could only hope the skyscraper-long list she'd made while researching each city on the planet would coincide with at least a few things on her itinerary. She covertly chewed the inside of her cheek and recited the word in her head a few more times.

"I have to say, it's wonderful to meet a human who's so excited to explore our world. The shock of being abducted has dimmed most of your people's curiosity. I don't blame them, but…it warms me to see your enthusiasm."

"You have no idea," Meg all but shouted.

With a last nod that made Metli's cool-blue hair bounce, she crossed to the door and left Meg to celebrate the second successful job interview of her life.

2

The cruiser Maxu was watching paused in the middle of the road once more, and the corner of his mouth curled upward. He scanned the dozen or so other cruisers, whose progress had stalled as their safety functions kicked into action and they waited for the erratic one to clear off the road.

What they didn't know was the cruiser wouldn't be moving. He'd made sure that the transport would be harmless—yet irritating—for as long as it took authorities to show up, disarm it, and trace it back to him. It shouldn't take long since half the guards in the city were on this very street today.

They wouldn't be able to prove much. Maybe that he'd hacked into a control panel. He expected a few weeks in jail. A slap on the wrist. Then he'd be out and ineligible for marriage for another year.

On second thought, the Queen might be exceptionally angry about him pulling this today. After all, this was the start of her much-lauded human tour. Honestly, if he'd remembered it was happening today, he'd probably have picked a different location. Or done it another time. As it was, his little stunt was blocking the road so thoroughly that the waiting line of extra-large cruisers ready to transport humans across the world were all stuck in place, halted until his mess could be cleared.

He couldn't bring himself to feel too bad, though. Parading the humans through secretly selected cities of Tremanta was offensive. Like these aliens were walking pieces of art for Clecanians to take in.

The crowd should've been annoyed the street was blocked in the direction the departing humans needed to go, but all he could see from his wall-leaning stance fifty yards away was smiles. Between a short break in the crowd, he spotted a tall female with dark curls and deep brown skin smiling and waving. A blonde followed behind, grinning just as broadly.

Maxu found himself squinting through the Clecanian swarm for glimpses of the humans despite his aversion to the parade. His Traxian half, a species far more tumultuous in their emotions and actions than his other half, Lignas, pushed him to feel reluctant curiosity about the humans.

Well, not about the *humans* specifically but about the possibility of a mate. He'd learned from an early age that temporary marriages weren't for him. Trying to convince an emotionally distant female that he was worthy of attention was hard enough. But when his Traxian instincts kicked in and he found himself vehemently against letting his wife go at the end of their contract, he realized that he wasn't compatible with *temporary*. He'd only been married once, but it had been enough to show him he never wanted it again.

Sure, he could have flings of a sexual nature with females. He enjoyed those. But when he connected with a female, when he smelled her on him for too many days in a row, something in him railed against seeing her move on with another male.

Matehood would be different. If he recognized a mate, they'd be bound together for life. He could be as possessive as he wanted since everyone would chalk it up to his mating instinct.

A cruiser flying high above the rest, indicating an authority vehicle, swooped above the throng of traffic. Maxu produced a wanget fruit from his bag and bit into it. How long would it take this time?

The device in his pocket could be traced quickly if the guards weren't incompetent. He watched as one lanky guard barely out of husbandry school scratched his chin and stared at the malfunctioning cruiser now slowly twirling in the center of the road. He might be here a while.

He could go home and wait there, but then he'd have to disarm all the various snares he'd set in place to prevent forced entry while he was locked away. No, he might as well just wait.

His body tensed when a throng of guards rushed past him. In the epicenter of their circle strode Metli, the Queen's right hand. Flaunting six-inch platforms and a skirt high enough to barely cover her ass, Metli glided among the guards, her pale blue brows slashed downward as she surveyed the mess of cruisers in front of her. Voluminous fabric puffed out from her neck and waist, giving her the appearance of a fluffy cloud with sculpted legs.

Vondalese. He smirked. Metli might have left her home city of Vondale half a century earlier, but she still dressed with the vigor of an ostentatious Vondalese socialite.

As if sensing his hard gaze, her eyes swiveled in his direction. Her frustrated glare flitted to the traffic jam ahead and then back to him, and suddenly a fire lit in her gray irises. She'd always hated him for the way he blithely undermined the Queen and the marriage ceremony.

But what was he supposed to do? The Queen hadn't given him another choice. Males all over Tremanta were able to successfully exempt themselves from the marriage ceremony, yet since his parents had had six children, a staggering number by Clecanian standards, he was forced into it every year.

"You!" Metli hissed, charging toward him while her guards backtracked in order to follow her abrupt route change. "You did this! Today of all days?"

"Careful, Metli. That was dangerously close to a screech," Maxu drawled, taking another bite of wanget.

Metli angled her face to the sky, slammed her eyes closed, and let out a slow breath before leveling him with a stare cold enough to make anyone shiver despite the dry heat of the day. "You don't respect our Queen. You don't respect our traditions. But are you really so thick as to not realize what this tour means to our *world*?" She spread her hands wide. "Do you know how many threats the Queen has received? Invasion. Murder. Beatings. Not just to her but to our people for supposedly hiding the humans away. You know what made the threats stop? Announcements of this tour."

Metli spoke her words slowly, as though he were an imbecile. His wanget became pulp in his hand. "Empty political moves from a sly leader. This tour is a piece of cloth over a sliced artery," he spat.

If there was a person more loyal to the Queen than Metli, he couldn't fathom who. The ruffling of her slicked-back silvery-blue hair was the only indication she wasn't completely frozen. Finally, she whispered, "Search him."

Quelling the instinct to fight, he allowed two guards to grab him by the arms while a third rifled through his clothing. He held Metli's stare until one guard rooted around his pants pocket and found one of the small devices he'd pinched from the cruiser manufacturing site in Braghon.

Metli held it to the sun, examining the small buttons and metallic prongs that fit perfectly in a cruiser's control panel.

He doubted she recognized exactly what the device was, but she was smart enough to guess.

Without a word, she nodded toward a guard. In an instant, Maxu had a magnetic cuff around his throat. The guard placed a similar cuff around his own arm, and as the guard stepped away, Maxu was pulled toward him.

"I'll make sure you're locked up for months this time," she said, dangling the device between two fingers and waiting for a guard to take it.

Doubtful, he guessed to himself. All they could prove was that he'd used the device. They had no proof that he'd stolen it. And they wouldn't. He was too good, and stealing had always been laughably easy.

As his hands were cuffed behind his back, Metli turned on her heel and marched toward the crowd in the direction of the Tremantian prison. Maxu couldn't help but feel a slight sense of satisfaction. One more year without having to worry about the marriage ceremony. At this point in his life, these stunts had become more than just a way to circumvent marriage.

Though not normally a political person, Maxu hated being controlled. Every time he discovered a way to make sure he wasn't paraded in front of waiting brides like a piece of meat with a set of grades tied to his collar was an achievement. The rush of that triumph would follow him to prison and bolster him for as long as it took the Queen's ire to cool.

The scent of sweat and crushed ground moss filled his nostrils as he neared the group of gathered Clecanians. Cheers erupted, and his escorts paused, peering around for the source of the excitement.

Just like that, his cruiser had been cleared. The tour would be underway any moment. He watched a timid brunette with tanned skin, silky straight hair, and heavy bangs board one of the cruisers. The magnetic band on his guard's arm forced him forward into a denser area of the crowd as he watched on. Before she disappeared into the black interior, she waved, and cheers sounded once more.

A burly guard with a scowl on his face joined her. Through the mass of onlookers, he could just make out what he assumed was another human female and guard boarding as well. Then their door slid closed.

Flashes of light glinting off the metallic surface of the cruiser lit the crowd as it pulled away. Another appeared in its place. Maxu's eyes were focused on his steps, careful not to slam into people as he was forced along, but then a scent caught his attention. His shoulders and neck began to tingle, making him shiver.

The smell engulfed him, the spice of it settling on his tongue and reminding him of a steaming confection he might drink in the dead of winter. Sweet and warming. The scent crept down his throat, and he twisted his head to figure out where it was coming from.

Maxu hadn't realized his steps had paused until he was wrenched forward by his neck and stumbled. He closed the distance between himself and the guard, a sudden panic making his heart ram against his ribs. He bobbed his head, trying to peek through the gaps in the shifting crowd.

What was happening? Where was the smell coming from? He closed his eyes and inhaled. Between the tinge of perfumes and sweat wafting from the gathered people, he smelled it. His mouth watered.

"Stop," he said quietly, a buzzing in his ears making it hard to think. "Stop!" he repeated in a shout that carried over the crowd.

Metli swung around. Irritation oozed from every clenched muscle in her body. "If you wanted to watch the send-off, you should have…" Her words died out as she caught sight of his wide-eyed, frantic gaze sweeping over the crowd.

Heat raced under his skin, perspiration evaporating in the dry air and leaving him clammy. For some inexplicable reason, his shaft stiffened in his trousers. The scent of sun-warmed nectar and sweet spice pulsed through the air now, overwhelming his mind and weakening his knees.

"Are you…?" Metli began. Maxu spared her a glance, then did a double take at her slightly parted lips and awestruck expression.

He couldn't keep his attention from darting back to the crowd as he asked, "What?" Suddenly, a dark head popped into view between the shoulders of two men. His eyes latched on to the limited sight of soft black hair as if everything else were out of focus.

"Oh, Maxu." There was far too much joy in Metli's voice. He darted a look to her and found her giving him a wide grin, hiking a thin glitter-coated brow. "Have you recognized someone? Your eyes say yes."

He blinked. The mask of indifference he liked to don was lost beneath utter shock. Had his eyes changed? A crack echoed from his neck when he jerked his head over his shoulder. He spun in a small circle, trying to catch sight of his hands. "Are they there?" he barked, whirling and presenting his back to Metli.

He didn't need to elaborate on what he meant by "they." Every Clecanian who'd caught even a bit of their conversation would know what he was asking. Had his marks appeared on his hands? Had he fully recognized the person the universe decided was his? Had he just found his mate?

Gasps sounded from a few of the guards, but a light chuckle was Metli's only response. He rounded on her but was yanked back when his guard took a step away from Metli. "Looks like you have a mate out there," she said.

Maxu's pulse roared through his ears as his desperate gaze scanned the crowd for that short, dark-haired head. His mate was somewhere near the center, but that meant... Maxu's breath caught in his chest and, without thinking, his arms strained against his cuffs.

She had to be human. And if she was human, that could mean she was *leaving*. Heading away from him on a three-month-long tour. The crowd closed in as the last cruiser pulled into place. He strained against the collar holding him back and leapt to see over the onlookers. Brighter and more clear than anything else in sight, his focus was immediately drawn to the back of a female's head. A flash of short dark hair and a slender, pale neck were all he could make out before she moved forward and disappeared behind the crowd.

"Move!" he barked. A few of the Clecanians in front of him jumped and scurried out of the way, but most hadn't heard his command over the din. His collar kept him from advancing into their vacant spots, so he snarled and whirled on the guard with the armband. But the male was ready for him, and Maxu's collar forced him to stop as if he'd run into an invisible barrier, the magnetic tension both pulling him close and keeping him far enough away to not cause harm. Maxu roared at him. To his credit, the guard only flinched.

"Let me go. My mate is there," he snapped at Metli.

Her grin faltered, then fell. "You've been balking at finding a wife for as long as I've known you. You've publicly disrespected the Queen again and again. And now, after you've slighted her on one of the most important days of her career, you expect us to just let you go?" Bitterness dripped from every one of Metli's words. "You'll serve your time, and then you can go find your mate. It'll teach you an overdue lesson."

Even now, Maxu could feel his mate moving farther away, as if a string connecting her to him was tied to his gut. It tugged uncomfortably in her direction, though he couldn't see her. A dangerous growl reverberated through Maxu's chest as he glared at Metli.

When he finally got out of these shackles, he'd tear Metli limb from limb. He began to tell her as much, but before he could get a word out, a guard to his left held up a canister of sleep spray. The fine mist burst into his mouth and nose.

He staggered toward the cruiser in a last-ditch effort to stay conscious. Grunts and squeals reached his ears as he crumpled into the crowd, asleep before he hit the mossy ground.

3

❧

"First stop. Are you ready?" Daunet, Meg's personal guard, peered at her from across the cruiser, leaning close, elbows on knees.

Meg rubbed her palms on her thighs and tried to shift her focus away from the somersaults in her stomach. "Are you sure *you're* okay?" she countered when she took in Daunet's pallid complexion. Most of the cruisers back in Tremanta didn't have windows, but the long specialty cruisers they'd been given had optional windows, allowing occupants to choose whether or not to look outside.

It wasn't until halfway into their ride that Meg and the other human in the cruiser, Sophia, had noticed their Clecanian guards growing a little green around the gills. Apparently, watching the scenery zoom by at a hundred miles an hour made most Clecanians sick. After learning this, Meg and Sophia had had no choice but to close the windows for fear of wearing their guard's lunches on their chests before they'd reached their first stop.

Cribus. The city in the sky.

She'd spent a good portion of the ride rereading everything she could about the city. It wasn't really in the *sky*. Rather, it rested at the edge of the sea atop enormous cliffs. The city had earned its nickname because of the fog and mist that often rolled in off the water and covered the ground. The entry she'd read had described the fog as so dense the grass and water were completely blocked from view, giving the illusion one was walking through clouds.

She'd also read how incredibly dangerous the fog was. Many had been so entranced while strolling through the sky that they'd stepped right off the treacherous cliffs. It hadn't happened for a long time, of course. Barriers had been placed so even if you made it to the cliffs an invisible wall would stop you from tumbling over, but the odd phenomenon had shaped the culture of Cribus nonetheless. The people of the city were notorious for what Meg called their "feet first" approach.

Once the windows in the cruiser had been closed and she could no longer gaze in wonder at the pastel fields and sparkling turquoise rivers, she and Sophia busied themselves with extending their feet and pointing their toes in what was the traditional Cribusian greeting. Meg felt like some kind of shoe model every time she attempted to stretch out her leg and rest her pointed foot in front of her. Sophia said it made her feel like a ballet dancer. After an hour of practicing, though, both had had to stop due to cramping in their arches.

Meg had been confident in her knowledge of the city on the four-hour ride. Confident that she'd learned about all the faux pas. What was polite to say and do, and what wasn't. But now, as she opened the window and stared at a small crowd, growing larger by the minute, she second-guessed everything she'd learned.

They'd arrived at what looked to be a large amphitheater built right on the edge of the cliffs. There was no fog today, and the wild blue-green ocean was visible past the steep drop-off of the theater.

She'd seen some pictures of Cribus, but it had never looked quite like this. The rolling hills were greener than she'd thought they'd be. The round topped houses in a rainbow of colors were different too. Taller. More *real* than when she'd "awed" at the quaint, brightly colored buildings on her trusty reading screen back in Tremanta.

And the amphitheater? The picture she'd seen had been an empty, beautifully carved outdoor seating area with intricate mosaicked flooring. But now? So many people crowded inside that she couldn't even see the floor.

Daunet had tried to prepare her for this. She'd warned Meg and Sophia that though no one knew which cities the humans would arrive in during their tour, as soon as the specialty cruisers showed up, the citizens would flock to them.

Meg's heart crawled into her throat, and a hollow dread settled in her stomach as the Cribusian people filed into the theater. Most were varying shades of pale blue with long, graceful legs. All were stunning.

Was she really qualified for this? The people, the buildings, the orange sun hanging above the white-capped sea. It was all so lovely. It was what she'd been looking forward to for months. But in this moment, it was terrifying.

"Wow. It's true," Sophia said, gazing past Meg through her window. "They really don't wear shoes."

Meg squinted at the feet of the nearest Cribusians, and a small glimmer of excitement cut through her nerves. The two women, who kept shooting curious glances toward their cruiser as they shuffled into the theater, wore no shoes. Meg hadn't noticed at first because there was something covering the tops of their feet. She all but pressed her face against the window to make out what it was and grinned. "I think they're feathers."

"Really?" Sophia scooted as close to Meg as she could to get a clear view. Her long black hair brushed over Megs' arm, and when Meg tipped back in her seat and lifted her hands, Sophia leaned over Meg's body to squint through the window. "Oh, wow, they are! Do you think they glued them on there, or do they have feathers on their feet?"

"The people of Cribus decorate their feet to be fashionable."

Meg and Sophia both turned to see Heleax, Sophia's guard, had spoken. Daunet agreed absently with a nod, while patting down her uniform and adjusting the weapons strapped to her shoulder and chest.

Meg had read about that. All kinds of things could be used to dress up their feet. Jewels, feathers, plants, paint. Meg now realized reading and experiencing were very different. That was the beauty of this gift she'd been given. To *experience* a place and its people, not just read about it. This was what she'd wished for. Meg continued watching as more and more Cribusians filled the stadium, and incrementally, she let her awe and gratefulness wash away the worst of her anxiety.

She didn't need to be a scientist or well traveled. The people coming to see them just wanted to know about humans. Meg was qualified enough for that at least. She could answer whatever they threw at her. She turned to Daunet with a grin. "I'm ready."

4

〜

Meg hadn't been ready.

Of the six women onstage, she'd been the one to bungle her answers most often. She couldn't be too hard on herself, though. Most of the questions they'd asked had been about romantic relationships and sex and things she'd never in her life been so open about with anyone. Not even her husband.

What was courting like on Earth? Did females generally guide the courtship? *How should I know? I've been married since I was eighteen!*

What positions did humans prefer? *Out of the two positions I've ever tried, I prefer missionary.*

Which party was responsible for child rearing? *Well, in my screwed-up family, the women are invariably in charge of that.*

Why did humans kiss? Were they not worried about mouth bacteria? *I tried to kiss my husband as little as possible, so I couldn't tell ya.*

How would humans feel learning about other planets? *They'll go apeshit and point missiles into space.*

These were all the answers that had popped into her head when she'd been asked these questions, but instead of speaking them aloud, she'd goggled at the crowd like a fish, grappling for something, anything to say that was even remotely informative.

The women with her—Sophia, Lucy, Rita, Tara, and Camille—had all taken turns answering questions. Some had done better than others—*some* being Lucy, Camille, and Rita. The rest had stumbled through, just like her, while fidgeting in their seats and looking as if they'd just been asked to feed a starving lion.

Luckily, Lucy, Camille, and Rita had been angels incarnate. Whenever Meg had tripped up on one of her answers or Tara had gone off on nonsensical tangents completely unrelated to the question asked, one of the three would gently jump in and take the reins.

Occasionally, the political representatives of the Tremantian Queen, Kel and Malinu, would elaborate on the human's replies, but mostly they'd remained silent, only stepping in to answer questions pertaining to the current plans for integration between Clecania and Earth.

Each city on Clecania had their own rulers and their own ideas for how to deal with the arduous task of convincing the Alliance to reclassify Earth, but the Queen of Tremanta was the *planet's* representative. Out of all the rulers here, she'd been elected as the one to meet with the Intergalactic Alliance and argue Clecania's case to have Earth's classification changed.

Meg had also learned through the icy tones of many questioning civilians that they didn't particularly like the power the Tremantian Queen wielded.

But even though the inquisition portion of the day had been rough, the rest of the evening was shaping up to be spectacular. Their whole traveling party had been dressed in the finest Cribusian clothing in preparation for a lavish party at the Gilganti Menagerie.

The Menagerie, as Meg understood it, was an old building constructed against the side of the cliffs. It had once functioned as a sort of zoo but was now more of a museum and event space. The person who'd built it had designed the three connected buildings to resemble the three egg bundles the female Gilganti arachnids laid. Three glass globes connected by thin passageways dripped down the bluff like massive Gilganti egg sacs.

Gross. Meg grinned dreamily. She couldn't wait to see it.

While puffing her hair in the mirror, Meg gave herself an internal pep talk. *Okay, so the interview didn't go great, but this will be my time to shine.* A party. A *real* party. Her smile widened.

Sure, she'd never actually been to a sophisticated party like this unless you could call her small, solemn wedding a *party*, but *new* Meg—the person she wanted to be—loved parties.

She was a sexy, flirty, interesting party girl on the inside where it counted, and she'd finally let that side of herself out tonight.

She'd been given the choice of several outfits—all gloriously beautiful—and had selected a light pink gauzy number that made her feel more fashionable than she ever had in her life.

Tiered layers of diaphanous pink fabric wrapped loosely around her body from her shoulders to her upper thighs, almost like a cape or a poncho. Though the horizontal strips of fabric overlapped each other slightly, they were still very see-through.

She'd been so close to saying fuck it and wearing nothing under the odd outfit, but then the voices in her head had gotten the better of her and she'd requested a skin-toned bodysuit.

Still, anyone looking might *assume* she was naked underneath the translucent material unless they looked closely. How would they know?

The outfit was a masterpiece so short she'd worried about bending over. Of course, she needn't have worried. Like every other wonderful creation in this city, the dress was both gorgeous and functional. Loose shorts were hidden under the final layer of fabric and disguised as the hem of the dress. No gusts of wind would have her flashing anyone tonight.

Unsurprisingly, heels were uncommon here. Instead, a captivating man with sparkling teal eyes named Lito had come and designed everyone's foot décor based on their outfits. His assistants had glued fresh pink-and-white blossoms and glittering rhinestones to the tops of Meg's feet in a gorgeous design that crawled up her calves. They also applied makeup to her feet, contouring until she barely recognized her own toes. Had they ever looked that graceful before?

The foot accessories were hard to get used to, but the more Meg studied herself in the mirror, the more like a mystical forest dryad she felt. Even the gold symbol of Clecania she and all the members of her traveling party were required to wear while in public shined happily on her shoulder where it was pinned. Her gauzy dress had little sparkles embedded in the fabric, and when the light hit the cloth, the curves of her silhouette looked sensual and elegant against the glitter.

"Wow, you look incredible," Meg breathed as the silky blue fabric of Daunet's dress swished into sight. In uniform, Daunet was beautiful, but out of uniform, wearing a form-fitting sky-blue gown with strips of fabric crossing over her shoulders and wrapping around her torso, she looked like a Greek goddess.

Daunet ran her gaze over Meg's outfit, and instinctively, Meg's jaw clenched, her shoulders curling forward. *She hates it. It's too revealing. I can't pull this off.* Maybe she could get another one-piece in a bright color, so it was clear she wasn't naked underneath.

Daunet smiled. "You look absolutely enchanting."

"Jeremy would never let me out of the house looking like this," Meg said while calming the heat that had crawled up her cheeks at the compliment.

"Who's Jeremy?" There was an edge to Daunet's voice, and her golden eyes narrowed. "You've never mentioned him before."

Meg stilled, holding back the suspicious gulp lodged in her throat. She hadn't told anybody about Jeremy. What would the Tremantians do if they found out she was a married woman? They wouldn't take her back, but would they try to limit what she could do? Would they contact Jeremy as soon as Earth was reclassified?

This was a constant worry in the back of her mind, and despite how selfish it was, Meg prayed Earth would never be introduced to the larger universe so she wouldn't have to find out. "He's nobody," she said a little too quietly. Rather than holding Daunet's critical gaze, she turned to the mirror and pretended to fiddle with her hair.

"Alright," Daunet said slowly, clearly not fooled by Meg's response. She extended one long leg, pointed her toes, and rested her foot in front of her. "Have you practiced your greeting?"

With a jolt and a nod, Meg imitated. She pointed her toes and dropped them next to Daunet's, copying the woman's slight bow. Bowing hadn't been mentioned in her research, but if Daunet was doing it, it was probably right.

She let out a gasp. "Your foot is gorgeous, Daunet!" Pearls of varying sizes swirled over Daunet's foot and wrapped around her ankle. Holographic blue shimmer was strategically dusted over the high points on her foot, making it look like her natural skin. Suddenly Meg understood why people did this little bow. When she angled her body forward, she found her focus automatically shifted to both of their feet. It was a chance to admire the art everyone took so much care to create.

"Thank you." Daunet admired her own foot before straightening. "I was going to remind you that you have to remain in my eyeline all night, but with that dress, I won't have a hard time keeping track of you. It commands attention."

Meg twirled in place. "I know, right?" Her spin stopped short, and she gave Daunet another once-over. "Even if there is trouble, though, you won't be able to do much in that." She gestured to the tight bodice of Daunet's dress.

The woman chuckled. "We're about to visit a building dedicated to the female Gilganti, a creature who entices male partners with her smooth fur and patterned wings before devouring them whole. A female can be both deadly and beautiful, and I am no exception. I have everything I need to keep you safe."

"Yes, ma'am," Meg agreed with an impressed nod.

Once the other humans were ready, they set off. When they reached the Menagerie, they were instructed to stand in front of horizontal ground-level notches in the building wall. Meg jumped when a metal tray slid through the opening in front of her, almost bumping into her toes. The man guiding them into the building lifted one leg and placed the sole of his foot into the foam on the tray. When he lifted it, an almost indiscernible clear layer was molded to the bottom of his foot like an invisible second skin.

Meg followed suit, dipping both of her feet into the foam and coming away with a thin layer that she could barely feel.

"When you leave the building, you can peel off the coating. We ask that everyone change their coating before entering each section of the Menagerie."

He waited for the group to nod their assent before leading them inside. Meg's nod was a little jerky, her excitement making her giddy. Each human's guard stayed close to their charge as they walked down the long spiral staircase and out onto a landing overlooking the first globe of the complex. Meg's breath caught. The whole building was made of glass, and the view before her was magnificent. A teal sea glittering with fiery orange sunlight.

The group descended a set of stairs to the left that curved downward along the wall to the open main floor below. Her pulse thrummed through her body as the waiting crowd came into view. All eyes turned to their small group.

Meg had been expecting some kind of direction once they'd reached the party, but there was none. The humans dispersed, making their way into the crowd and letting small groups of polite Cribusians approach and talk with them.

After a glass of strong, clear alcohol that warmed her insides and a few minutes of small talk with the two feather-footed women she'd noticed outside of the amphitheater, Meg relaxed. Though Daunet stayed close by, she never interfered with her conversation. No one was telling her what to do or who to be.

Her family would have dropped dead of mortification if they saw her traipsing around on her bedazzled feet, grinning at men and women. But all she felt was happiness. Freedom.

People came up to her and chatted in an inquisitive way, similar to the interview from earlier in the day but much more relaxed and friendly. As she drank another glass of burning clear liquid, the grin she shot at the people who came to talk to her grew larger, her eye contact bolder.

Some people she smiled at kept their expressions neutral, but many grinned back. She was flirting, she knew she was, but she couldn't help herself. She *wanted* to flirt. She hadn't had many opportunities to flirt as an adult. And she'd never looked this good.

Not only did she feel beautiful on the outside, she felt important too. Like she was actually doing something that benefitted her fellow humans.

Zeleph—a tall, broad-shouldered male who'd been giving her space yet returning to her when there was a lull in conversation—approached, holding one of the small candies she'd been snatching up from the floating trays circling the room.

He was beautiful, with a warm, broad grin and bright robin's-egg-blue skin. Unlike in Tremanta, the men of Cribus sported well-groomed facial hair. Zeleph's beard was a lovely shade of creamy white. Small gems were scattered throughout it as well as his hair, which was short and slicked away from his long, pointed ears. It was like someone had taken clouds, blue sky, and muscle and sculpted them into a perfect man.

Her eyes caught on the candy in his hand. She'd never tasted anything like them before. A mix of cherry and something undefinable, like icy air or fog. Something she'd never known *could* be a taste. She didn't love the flavor as much as she loved the extraordinariness of it.

He offered the candy to her. With a little blush, she accepted. "Thank you, Zeleph."

He smiled, flashing a set of brilliant white fangs that were a bit out of place amid his otherwise kind features.

"You are most welcome, Meg. I noticed you enjoyed them." Mouth already full of the chewy candy, she gave a sheepish grin and nodded. Her jaw grew sore with the effort to chew quickly as he stared. "May I speak with you a little longer? You look so radiant. I'm having trouble focusing on anything else."

Warmth dripped down her spine, and she melted. He didn't leave her side for the rest of the night. Meg didn't mind. They flirted and talked. She'd learned about so much from her studies, yet as she carried on a conversation with Zeleph and immersed herself in the party, Meg realized there were so many things about a culture that could only be learned through experience.

They strolled together through the three buildings of the Menagerie. The second was almost identical to the first. Plain glass all around, but when Meg finally remembered to look down, just like everyone else was, she froze. Though the walls and ceiling were bare, the floor was anything but. Layers of clear glass spotted with sculptured plants and paint made it look like you were in a cloud walking over a forest from above. They sauntered over the art installation, commenting on the delicate way the artist had placed the leaves so it looked like they were blowing in the wind.

By the time she and Zeleph had reached the final building, her cheeks ached from smiling. Drink in hand, he guided her into one of the dark glass tunnels that burrowed through the cliffside.

Her palms grew sweaty. Was he going to kiss her? Why else did men lead women into dark corners?

Meg swiped her tongue over her lips when his head was turned and tried to remember how to breathe. Did she even know how to kiss well? She'd only ever kissed Jeremy, and from the amount of moisture she'd had to wipe off her mouth after every kiss, she assumed he was bad. But she might be just as bad. How was she supposed to know? It wasn't like they'd ever talked about it.

He won't know if you're bad at it anyway, she reminded herself with a rush of confidence. Then she recalled how unnatural most Clecanians found kissing and frowned. Well, maybe he was going to kiss her neck or something, then. Whatever the equivalent was here.

She could make out the pale rock of the cliff against the glass as they walked and marveled at how difficult it must have been to mold the material to the curves and points of the cliffside.

"So, why did you bring me in here?" Meg whispered in a flirtatious tone, brushing her arm against his and thankful the tunnel was too dim for him to see the furious blush heating her cheeks.

"The Gilganti," he whispered back. His gaze dropped to the floor, and she followed suit.

Spiders as big as her head scurried over craggy ledges in the cliff right below her toes. Waves crashed violently against rocks a thousand feet below the creatures. She let out a shriek and jumped back against the glass wall, her drink tumbling to the floor.

Zeleph rushed toward her with concern creasing his brow. "Are you alright? They can't get in here. I'm so sorry. I thought you'd like to see them."

When her heart finally lifted from where it had dropped into her belly, she grinned. A slow chuckle built until she was all out laughing. "I'm fine. I'm fine. I don't know why I'm laughing." She wheezed at his stupefied expression.

Taking a deep breath and clearing her throat, she stared down at the spiders again. Thick hair covered their bodies, almost obstructing their legs from view. If it weren't for the four delicate fairy wings protruding from their backs, they would have looked like severed heads scuttling around the rocks.

Meg peered up at Zeleph, who was still gazing at her with a worried expression. She crossed to him, pressing a hand to his arm. "I'm good now. They really are...something. Thank you so much for showing me." She held eye contact, keeping her hand in place on his arm. *Kiss him now, dummy.*

Before she could build her courage, he gave her a gentle smile, swiped her glass off the ground, and guided her through the remainder of the tunnel. Daunet was waiting on the other side. She raised a brow at Meg.

During their time together in Sauven, Daunet had come to understand just how ready Meg was to experience everything her new life had to offer. Including men.

"It's time to go back to the housing," Daunet announced. "I'll be over there." She motioned toward the entrance to the building, and Meg nodded.

"It was wonderful meeting you, Meg. I hope you'll come to Cribus again very soon." Zeleph stood with his arms clasped behind his back. The inner corners of his pale white brows curled up, showing his disappointment.

Gathering her nerve, she lifted to her toes and pressed a kiss to his lips. Zeleph's eyes widened, and his mouth remained firm. Fire raced over her skin. An odd pain stabbed through her belly.

This was awkward. She didn't know why she'd assumed it wouldn't be. She wasn't exactly a master of seduction, and nobody here kissed. Falling back to her heels, she quickly murmured, "Thank you for showing me around and keeping me company." Without waiting for a response, she sped away.

Once she reached Daunet, she heard an amused, "How did it go?"

"Shut up," Meg chuckled, embarrassment still heating her entire face. She darted a last glance over her shoulder and found Zeleph staring after her, brows drawn in confusion. "Please, can we just get out of here?" she groaned.

It was probably for the best that she'd crashed and burned. Baby steps. She'd kissed somebody new. That was something to be proud of at least. She'd put herself out there. It was a good thing he hadn't wanted to take it further—or at least she tried to convince herself of that as she and Daunet silently wound through the party until they met with the rest of their group at the entrance.

After all, she'd only been with one man—more like one guy—her whole life. Her knowledge of sexual relationships was meager at best. She knew how things had worked between her and Jeremy and knew she didn't care for it, but that wasn't much to go on. She wanted to learn, to experiment, to figure out who she was and what she liked, but even as the idea of being intimate with someone thrilled her, it also made her jittery all over.

"Hey, lady! I'm surprised to see you here." The soft southern accent came from Meg's right. Camille, gorgeous in her slinky magenta gown, fell into step beside Meg. The gown's high slit exposed the gold star-shaped gems running up her shin. Gold had also been dusted strategically over her collarbones, shoulders, and cheeks, enhancing her umber complexion.

Lucy, who'd donned a bright yellow ballerina skirt, strolled next to Camille with a knowing grin. She was the picture of summer itself, with bold yellow flower petals covering golden-tanned legs. "Yeah. What happened with Mr. Blue Eyes? You two seemed real cozy when you went in that tunnel."

"Can't have all my fun on the first day, right?" Meg lied with a playful shrug.

Daunet snorted next to her. Lucy began gushing about some other hot guy she'd chatted with, while Camille marveled over the Gilganti. Meg's mind remained lost in memories of the night.

Before she knew it, she'd stepped into her small, comfortable room on the second floor of a bright red domed building. The layers and layers of fluff that had been built right into the floor and made up her enormous bed called to her, and before she'd even heard her door zoom shut, she'd collapsed onto them.

She replayed the evening in her head, wanting to capture the memories in amber so she could relive them forever. Maybe it was the alcohol still working its way through her system, but even her embarrassing exit from the party no longer bothered her.

What would have happened if she'd just stayed? Let Zeleph get over his shock for a moment? Would he have smiled down at her? Taken her hand and led her back into the dim tunnel?

She kicked her feet up in the air in front of her, admiring her legs and the delicate flowers flowing down her shins. They swirled with the sparkling gems placed ever so carefully on her skin. She ran her hands over the velvet-soft petals, then grazed them over her knees and up her legs. The fabric of her dress ghosted against her upper thighs as she brushed her hands over the material. The scratchiness of the cloth against her skin made her break out in goose bumps. Would that be what his beard felt like?

When her fingers lingered on her low belly, she bit her lip. She rose and, with as much nonchalance as she could muster, searched the room. She didn't know why she was always so timid about this, but she was. Even now, contemplating *it*, heat rose to her cheeks. When she was certain there was no one hiding in the bathroom or behind the freestanding clothing rack, she tiptoed back to the bed.

Masturbation had always been secret, shameful, and yet she loved it. Loved knowing that feeling of release. Loved losing herself in a fantasy for a few blissful minutes. Zeleph's wide blue eyes and fanged smile appeared in her mind as she sank to her knees on the bed.

Meg scooted toward the wall and grabbed a few of the fluffiest pillows she'd ever seen, then straddled them, bunching them between her knees until they felt just right. She pictured Zeleph walking backward, pulling her into the tunnel.

The slow rocking of her hips started up as, in her mind, he pressed her against the cool glass wall and began kissing her neck, running his soft, pale blue hands over her arms, down her back. She pictured him stripping off her delicate outfit and sliding her thick underwear down her ass and thighs.

Heat pooled deep in her belly as the friction of the pillow rubbed against her clit. He gripped her hips and spun her around, forcing her forward until her naked breasts were pressed up against the glass. A frown pulled at her mouth and her brows furrowed.

That didn't feel right. It was what she wanted, but it didn't fit with Zeleph. He was too sweet. He wouldn't do it like that. In her mind, he gentled, pressing soft kisses to her shoulder and whispering how beautiful she'd looked in her ear.

The heat in her core cooled a fraction, and she struggled to hang on to it, grinding her hips harder against her pillow. He wrenched her hands above her head and ran his fangs over her neck. She squinted her eyes open. The heat still pulsed in her low belly, but nothing built.

The idea of Zeleph being rough was too incongruous, so why did her mind keep going there? She *wanted* to picture him. Right? Maybe this was her mind's way of telling her she'd wished he'd made a move, been more assertive, that was all.

She closed her eyes again and stopped trying to force her fantasy. *On the ground.* The gruff voice giving the command sounded nothing like Zeleph, but his words shot through her like an electric current. Slowly, she sank to her knees in the dark tunnel.

On your belly now. Spread those pretty knees for me. Pressure built in her sex as the rocking of her hips sped up, and she pictured herself lying on her belly on the glass floor of the tunnel. Luckily, her mind edited out all the spiders, but not the thousand-foot drop to the crashing waves below.

She tried to turn her cheek to the glass, but suddenly the man came down on top of her, his naked body molded to hers, one firm hand around her throat, forcing her to look into the glass. She could almost make out his reflection in the floor as he loomed over her shoulder and his cock slid over her ass.

The man holding her down and forcing her legs wider apart with his knees wasn't Zeleph. He was too broad, too heavy. The hand on her neck was too rough. Her breaths came in deep pants and sweat ran down her spine.

One of her hands glided up her body to cover her breast over her dress as the other fisted into the pillow between her thighs. The man's mouth locked on her neck as he prodded her entrance. He bit down on her shoulder, and her hips bucked.

She was rocking faster now, her movements jerky and shallow, hitting just the place she needed. One hand still at her throat, his other snaked down and wrapped around her hip. He gripped her there so she couldn't move as his cock slid inside in one smooth thrust of his hips.

Meg bit her lip to keep her noises from coming out. She wanted to moan and say the dirty things in her head out loud. But she'd never done that before, always too afraid of being caught. So instead, she said them in her head.

Yes! Fuck me, please. Make me come. The man obliged, slamming hard into her like she imagined this kind of man would. Her knees shook and tensed around the pillow, the lips of her pussy and her clit pulsing as her orgasm built.

In her head she chanted, *I'm coming. I'm coming. Please don't stop.*

His mouth rested on her ear, and his thrusts grew so, so deep. *Never.*

Heat rushed through her. Her back bowed and her whole body tensed as her orgasm crested. She let out a strangled whimper.

Then the heat under her skin grew molten and gentle, turning her limbs to jelly. She ground against the pillow once, twice, then curled forward, falling onto the bed with a moan of contentment. Shoving a few new pillows under her head and pushing the old ones away, she stretched and grinned.

Though the night hadn't ended with who she'd thought would pleasure her in her head, it had still been the best night she could remember. Meg drifted to sleep with a smile on her face. Sated, a little buzzed, and still wearing her risqué, sparkling pink dress.

5

They'd healed him. Again.

Maxu stared at his unblemished knuckles and gritted his teeth. For the past week, he'd been locked in this damn cell. Each day, he spent his time yelling at the guards, presenting them with his mating marks, and when they ignored him, using his fists to pound against the unbreakable clear barrier in front of him.

He was losing his grip on reality and rationality. Could feel it in his mind whenever his thoughts grew disjointed and confusing. The inability to search for her was tearing at his insides. His skin itched. His stomach roiled. He couldn't eat. Couldn't sleep. The only thing that felt better than the constant ache was pain. Like when you smashed your hand in something and the only relief was clutching it as tightly as you could. Pain on top of pain.

The guards had to gas his room every so often, knocking him out so they could heal him before he did too much damage to himself. The only way he could keep track of how much time passed was the holographic clock high in the corner of the room. But even his time unconscious was no reprieve.

Every sleeping moment he was running and running and running after this mysterious female. Her short black hair skimmed the back of her neck, and her hips swayed gently as she walked away from him. But no matter how fast he ran, her slow gait never failed to carry her out of reach. And she *always* walked away. He could never see her face. No matter how loudly he called out to her, she never turned.

He ran a finger over the bright blue markings swirling around his knuckles. They were distinct from his brothers'. Three of his siblings had them now, and they were all slightly different.

His oldest brother Theo's markings were curlier and a bit darker than his. Thicker too. Luka's were slim, without as much movement. More precise, though not geometrical. Auzed's were similar to Luka's in design, but they were thick like Theo's.

Maxu's swirled over his knuckles in small spirals, then circled his fingers as if he were wearing rings on each digit. They then curled down to his forearms and wrapped around his wrists in thick bands.

Would *she* like them? His body stirred. The reminder of her brought on painful, aching stabs in his gut and a cold sweat on his skin.

The urge to claim her. To see her and inhale her and taste her was driving him mad. His sparse cell was in shambles. The small cot that'd been bolted to the wall was now ripped away and lay in a mangled pile.

His smell permeated the air, since he hadn't even had the mental energy to bathe. His hair was shaggy and greasy, and all he could do to forget about the sickening gut feeling of being trapped in this room was to rage. To let his Traxian side free. So he did.

He picked himself off the floor where he'd crumpled when they'd filled his room with sleeping gas, and flew at the wall. He hammered his fists against the glass, and when he heard a crack in his hand, he threw his body at the glass wall instead, roaring with each battering ram of his shoulder. The wall only shuddered and made his bones reverberate with the percussion, chattering his teeth.

The growl in his throat rumbled out on each deep exhale. His chest heaved, and a new layer of sweat dirtied his week-old clothing.

An image of Metli popped into his head, and fury exploded through him. He ran into the glass as fast as he could, and rather than stumbling away on impact, he hit it so hard that he bounced off and lay sprawled on his back, his shoulder warped at an unnatural angle.

He stared at the ceiling before sliding his eyes closed. Nectar and spice. He sniffed, trying to conjure her scent, but only smelled himself and the grime of the room.

"I've heard you've been making quite a fuss." A calm, smooth voice he recognized floated to him. He bolted upright and stared through the glass at the regal, stiff posture of the Queen.

"Let me out," he growled.

"I'd like to have a conversation first." As if on cue, a guard rushed over with a plush black velvet chair. Without looking at the guard, she sat, spine as straight as ever.

A chat? He could barely remember what day it was. Images of black hair and the delicate curve of a neck were the only things he could focus on.

The Queen didn't wait for him to nod his ascent, though. "You recognized one of the humans on my tour?"

He'd told Metli as much. The Queen would already know his answer. Despite the irritation in him and the pain flaring from his shoulder, he ground down on his molars and nodded.

"Who?"

If only he knew who. He shook his head. "I only smelled her and caught a glance. She had short black hair. Not very tall. Slender, if I had to guess."

Suddenly, every bit of his focus was on the Queen's face, scanning, examining, searching for any hint of recognition. He didn't need to study too hard. As soon as he described the female, the Queen's brows rose and the corner of her mouth quirked up. "I know who you mean, and I believe you may have a challenge on your hands."

Before he knew he'd moved, he was at the glass, pressing his hands against the smooth surface. "Who is she? What's her name?"

"Her name is Meg. She's…an interesting one."

"Meg." He rolled the name around in his head and had to quell the purr building in his chest. She was so far away. His body could sense the distance between them. Told him constantly that he wasn't close enough through pain.

So why, then, did merely hearing her name calm the queasiness plaguing his gut for a second? He waited, his breath caught in his throat, for the Queen to continue to tell him anything else about his mate. But she didn't.

"What will you do when I let you out?" she asked, surveying him with pursed lips.

In his mind, she'd always been an opponent. He understood why she forced him into the marriage ceremonies every year and why she afforded him so much leeway when he broke the law. It wasn't because they were close or because she liked him. It was because his genes were good for breeding, and that was good for Clecania.

The Queen, who both carefully and carelessly guided her people.

He couldn't blame her for it, but at the moment, this cell and the Queen were the only things standing in the way of his mate, and he hated them both. His hands slid down the glass, his palms leaving smears of rusty blood.

"I will find her," he said simply. What was she expecting him to say? This female, Meg, was his mate. *His.*

The Queen's chin tipped up. He could see her thoughts almost as if they were his own. She wanted to tell him how to act. What to do. Who to be, just like everyone else on this damn planet. But he also saw in her lavender eyes that she knew the futility of lecturing him.

"Get yourself in order. Meg will need a delicate hand. She'll need to be won, not secured or collected or stolen like you're used to. I suggest you start with a bath and a good night's sleep."

"Let me out," he barked again. She was already standing when Maxu gave a sharp slap of frustration on the glass. "Wait!" The Queen didn't even flinch at the rumbling of the glass, just turned her head. "Where is she?"

The news of humans traveling around the world, sitting down with members of different cities, answering questions and socializing had caused a spark of excitement everywhere. Excitement and a fervor that could prove dangerous. So, it'd been decided that each city stop on this tour would be randomly selected in a lottery, and to prevent hordes of Clecanians from showing up in great mobs, none of the selected cities had been announced publicly.

If the humans showed up in your city, you were lucky. They'd only stay for a couple of days, and then they'd leave. In and out quickly enough that races from across the world couldn't swarm. As such, he had no idea where she was. He could, of course, learn where she'd been, learn where she was right now, but by the time he got there, she'd be gone. On to the next city.

"Tell me where she's going next," he tried instead when the Queen just looked over her shoulder at him and didn't answer.

She clasped her hands together behind her back. "You know, Metli pushed for you to be locked up for a year this time. I didn't even know what had happened until yesterday when the guards came to me, concerned with your deteriorating state." She held his glare for a second longer. "I'll let you out, but I won't tell you where she is. I think your mind needs time to recover first. As you get closer, you should get better."

A low growl rose in his throat, his skin going icy.

She lifted the corner of her mouth. "Shouldn't be a problem for you. You're the male who can find anything, aren't you?"

Though his growl didn't ebb, a dark smile spread over his face.

Yes. I am.

6

Saying the last two weeks had been a whirlwind was not a strong enough word in Meg's opinion. Seven cities in fourteen days and she was exhausted.

The second city they'd stopped at had turned out to be the one other city she'd visited before, Sauven. Though slightly disappointing, it had been interesting to visit the massive palace treehouse and reconnect with a few friends from the city.

They'd then spent the next week touring fabric factories in Linadety, sweating their asses off in the desert city of Mithrandir, and admiring the gold-flecked rock of the Tygestian Mountains.

A highlight of the trip for Meg had been their stop in the farming city of Gulaid. Massive skyscrapers used to vertically grow enough food for the whole continent dominated the otherwise flat landscape. The Gulaidites were a friendly people, intent on feeding their visitors unbelievable foods every moment of the day. Meg guessed she'd gained about ten pounds during her two-day visit, and every single ounce had been worth it. She'd already decided a longer, more leisurely trip needed to be taken if only to visit a few more of the world-renowned restaurants in the city.

Currently, she was recovering with the rest of her traveling companions in a large, round hearth room on one of the icy islands of Kitibard. They'd been here for two days now and were set to leave the next morning.

Early in the trip, the group had been boisterous during their few hours of downtime each night, chatting incessantly about the city they were in. But as the days had gone on and the go, go, go of their schedules had started to wear on them, the mood at the end of the night had become more relaxed. Tonight, though, the energy of her friends slumped on hard cushions around the fire was withdrawn.

"Leaving in twenty minutes," Nirato announced, earning him a chorus of groans.

"Can't we skip the party just this once? We went yesterday, and I'm not recovered yet." Camille moaned as she stretched to reach for a glass of water set just a little too far out of the way.

"No," he said simply.

Meg released a sigh and let her head drop back against the hard upholstered wall.

Though the mountainous charcoal landscape of Kitibard was breathtaking in a rather ominous way, this city had been her least favorite by far.

Their arrival had somehow been leaked, and by the time they'd arrived on the island, three times as many people as they were used to had swarmed the interview space. It hadn't helped that the people of Kitibard were as cold as the frozen ground either.

The Clecanians' questions were normally intrusive and direct, but the Kitibardians took it a step further with their harsh tones and unsmiling faces. One woman with fine white hair covering her pale body had almost brought Sophia to tears, finding her answer to How many tysentrics into the surrounding universe have Earthlings traveled? to be lacking.

Malinu and Kel, the Tremantian representatives, had tried to intervene and help answer the scientific question, but the Kitibardian women, in particular, were less inclined to listen to the two men than they were to the collection of humans before them.

Sophia sat with her third cup of a warm drink made from pressed root vegetables that Tara had wisely spiked as soon as they'd returned to the small sanctuary of their housing. "I'm not sure I want to show my face tonight after that interview," she sniffed. "They all looked at me like I was a complete moron."

"You were perfect. Fuck them," Camille assured, finally stretching far enough to nab the rim of her glass with a finger.

"Yeah," Tara agreed. "What did they expect? You're literally from a Class Four planet. By definition, we don't know what a tryptoglyph is or what it measures. It was stupid of that woman to think we would."

As if on cue, Meg felt Daunet shift next to her. She tried to hide her grin by pretending to scratch her cheek. Supposedly, Daunet was Meg's guard, but after spending two weeks together with all the humans, Meg had noticed Daunet watching Tara far more often than she watched Meg.

"A tysentric," Daunet corrected, gazing at Tara across the room.

Meg raised her arms in a stretch, subtly nudging Daunet with an elbow as she cushioned the back of her skull with her palms. "Smooth," Meg said low enough that only her guard could hear. Daunet's exhale of annoyance had Meg biting her lip to keep her grin from showing.

Daunet added in a rush, "Though you're right. I barely know what the distance of a tysentric is. It was unfair to think any of you would."

Tara gave her a grateful grin. "See?" she said to Sophia. "It was a terrible question."

Meg shot Daunet, who'd begun fidgeting at Tara's smile, a glance. Her tight jaw and unblinking stare straight ahead told her Daunet wanted to look anywhere but at her in that moment.

The interview portion of each city's visit wasn't Meg's favorite thing either, but she'd gotten better at it and felt more confident in her answers. It was mainly due to the fact that most people asked the same questions. They all wanted to know about human relationships and how the humans believed Earth would react when they learned they weren't alone in the universe.

And always, always, one specific question would be asked by an eager man in the crowd. "What do females who prefer males look for in a partner?"

This question had landed on Meg three times now, and she always had the same response. "I can't answer for all women, but I can tell you what I look for. I want a man who treats me like a goddess."

She always grinned when she said this, so the audience knew she wasn't being completely serious. But a part of her *was* serious. She'd been ignored and made to feel less than for so long that the only way she could see herself settling down again would be with a man who treated her like the sun shone out of her ass.

"I think this is the first time I'm not looking forward to the party," Meg chimed in, staring down at the furry white collar of the comfortable suit she'd been given to wear tonight. It wasn't ugly by any stretch, but it didn't feel like *her.* It was large and shapeless. On a six-foot-tall model who had the innate ability to make anything look good, it would be fabulous, but on her? She looked like a fluffball who'd just fallen out of a knotted bit of Yeti fur.

"Can you believe that guy who asked about how to find women who wanted the most children?" Lucy said with a raised brow. "I mean, I know there's a population crisis here, but Jesus. It's like he was looking for a broodmare, and he just would not let it go."

Meg giggled along with the other people in the room. Uthen, Camille's personal guard, slung an ankle over his knee and grinned. "Looking for females who want many children isn't an uncommon kink," he said without any show of discomfort.

Most of the Clecanians she'd met talked about things like sexual preferences and kinks as if they were talking about favorite soda brands. She wanted to be that comfortable talking about those topics, too, and was attempting to do it more often so it would feel easier, but her damned cheeks burned at Uthen's words all the same.

Lucy pursed her lips and shook her head. "Well, he ain't looking for me, then."

"Or me," Tara said, gathering her dirty blonde hair into a high, messy bun.

"I bet there are people here who have dispositions we've never even imagined back on Earth." Rita, a dreamy older woman who never seemed to have a care in the world, added in her smooth voice. "With all the repression going on, sexual and emotional, I can only imagine what your heads have dreamed up. Marvelous," she added with a grin. Rita was the only one among the group to have a permanent Clecanian partner back in Tremanta, and as her gaze grew far away, Meg was sure Rita was thinking of something very specific and very personal.

"I think you're right, Rita, but I also think that it's crazy how everyone is so open about sex, yet they act like kissing is the most perverted kink of all," Sophia said, brushing her fingers through her thick bangs.

"Very true," Tara nodded.

Meg cleared her throat. "But it would be interesting to kiss someone who's never done it before, right? I mean, surely not all Clecanian's think it's gross. What do you think, Daunet?"

Daunet's head turned to meet Meg's innocent gaze. To anyone else, Daunet's impassive stare would seem innocuous, but Meg was sure that if Daunet could have figured out a reasonable excuse for whacking her with a pillow, she would.

She grinned back at Meg. "I'm not sure. How did it go for you when you tried?"

Meg's grin dissolved in an instant.

A chorus of "whats" echoed from around the room. Daunet tipped her head and furrowed her brows as if to say, Oops. Was that a secret?

Meg turned to the group and waved it off. "It was just a peck. I'm sure I could do better with a little more time and a little less cockblocking from my guard here."

"What is cockblocking?" Heleax asked from behind them suddenly. He'd been absorbed in a conversation with Gamso,

Atolicy, and Nirato, but all the male guards had paused and were staring.

"It means she was ready to take that guy home, but Daunet stepped in and prevented it from happening," Sophia explained with a smirk and a slight slur.

"Nonsense!" Daunet's voice was a few octaves too high. She cleared her throat. "She could have brought him back to her room. I only told her it was time to leave. As you all know, you're welcome to invite anyone you'd like to join you here as long as you clear it with us, but you can't go off to some unsecured location by yourself."

Meg was about to argue, even though she knew she'd scurried away from Zeleph like a scared puppy, but Gamso cut in, "Well, in terms of kissing, I would like to point out that most Clecanians are very open to experimentation. It may not be everyone's preference, but I wouldn't be shy about requesting it." The man paced around the perimeter of the room like a damn anxious dog. He did it wherever they went and at first, it had driven the humans crazy, but after a while, they'd gotten used to it.

"Is that an invitation, Gamso?" Lucy grinned and leaned forward, elbows resting on her knees, chin resting in her hands. When Gamso slowly turned to her, she shot him a wink. He faced forward again, pacing a little faster than he had before, a slight blush creeping into his cheeks.

Camille gently shoved Lucy's shoulder. "Stop it. You know your flirting makes him uncomfortable."

"I think he likes it," Lucy said when Gamso's gaze flitted back to her. "Besides, humans flirt. Meg flirts too," she said defensively, gesturing to Meg.

It was true. She did flirt in each city, and for the most part, she enjoyed it. The problem was she hadn't met anyone she was drawn to, or at least no one she liked enough to want to take back to her room, despite the almost constant ache she had between her legs. Night after night she'd make herself come, all while imagining rough hands squeezing and scraping their way over her skin.

You'd think for a girl who could barely keep her mind off sex, she'd be able to find even one guy that caused a pulse of heat between her legs, but no. No one in the room knew this—not even Daunet—but she'd tried to kiss another man back in Tygest.

She'd pulled him into a dark alcove, pressed her body to his muscular one, and kissed him. It'd gone better than it had with Zeleph. The man had at least understood what she'd been trying to do and attempted to kiss her back. He'd actually been pretty good at it after a few minutes of practice. But she'd barely felt a flicker. Weeks of flirting, yet despite all her efforts her vagina remained frustratingly unimpressed.

"I'm just doing what I was brought here to do. Teaching our culture. Lots of women flirt," Lucy continued. She caught Heleax side-eyeing her from his chair perched by the window and wiggled her fingers at him.

Heleax didn't turn away with a blush like Gamso. He slid his body on the chair until he was facing her fully. "You should know by now that in *our* culture, many will follow through when a female flirts."

Lucy straightened a bit. His tone wasn't playful, but it wasn't angry either. "Promises, promises," she muttered into her glass.

***

A few hours later, Meg was ready to go back to her room to hide. For the second night in a row, Kitibardians and eager citizens of neighboring cities alike had stuffed themselves into a grand hall located in one of the city's many giant ancient ice tubes. As soon as the humans had arrived they were jostled into waiting groups, who growled questions at them.

Normally, Daunet hung back, keeping a watchful eye but giving Meg space to socialize. But not tonight. She'd been attached to Meg's hip from the moment they'd walked in, and Meg was happy for it.

"What do you mean, none of your people have fur? What about the ones who live in cold climates? Are there only bald humans to choose from?" a man who hadn't bothered to give his name asked. He was quite handsome, the short white fur covering his muscled body only enhanced his alien hotness. But his brash attitude completely obliterated Meg's initial impulse to snuggle into his cozy chest.

"I told you," she said with a slur and as much politeness as she could manage in her intoxicated state. "We have hair. It's just not as thick as yours. Some people have thicker body hair, but not a ton more. It's not like Clecania. We all look pretty much the same."

"Where is your hair?" he grumbled. The woman next to him angled her head to peek down the front of Meg's shirt as if expecting to find her chest hairy, and Meg took a clumsy step away.

"I've removed it," she grated. Despite the intention of her scowl, both the man and woman seemed to perk up. Apparently being bitchy was the equivalent of blowing a kiss in this city.

In a different situation, on a different day, Meg might find these people interesting. She might even enjoy donning the bratty attitude that was the cultural standard, but she was tired. She peered around at the other humans she could spot in the crowd and recognized the tight-lipped expressions of fatigue and irritation on their faces too.

All except for Rita, that was. Meg swore nothing ever fazed that woman. Currently, she was deep in conversation with a furious-looking gray-pelted woman.

"Come back to our rooms and show us." As though she'd already accepted their invitation, the Kitibardian woman grabbed Meg's wrist and pulled her along. The man swiveled toward the exit without a word as well.

"No!" she screeched with irritation. Meg rolled her eyes when her two suitors only looked confused. "I'm not going with you." She tugged her wrist out of the woman's hold and stumbled back into someone.

"Hey," Lucy squeaked. She turned toward Meg, then stared around the group, instantly aware of the tension. "You okay?"

Meg gave her a shrug.

"Why won't you come with us?" the man asked. "You've been speaking with us all night. You've made your interest clear."

Daunet's posture was tight, poised to strike, but the two weren't doing anything other than being pushy, which all the humans had known to expect.

Meg gaped at them. "No...I...I was being polite."

The couple glanced at each other, then the man peered at Meg again. "But you are attracted to me. I've seen you admire my fur. I'll bring you back on my own, then." His hand extended toward her, and she jumped back again.

Heat rose to her cheeks, words failing her. She turned to Daunet, pleading without words for help. Daunet gave her a funny look, furrowing her brows as if she didn't understand. Meg leveled the same look on Lucy, and in less than an instant, Lucy's blue eyes hardened.

"Sorry. She's not interested," Lucy snapped, pulling her away from the group without another word.

Meg's gut churned. Everything in her wanted to turn around and apologize. It was rude to just walk away from someone like that, but…but no, it wasn't. She'd told them no, and they'd ignored her.

"Can you believe—"

A new man with blinding white fur stepped in front of them, blocking their path. "Hello. I saw you were interested in Nuphan, but he failed. I'll please you tonight instead." He turned to Lucy, his frown never altering, "Or you."

Lucy and Meg exchanged bewildered looks.

Daunet appeared, pressing a hand to the man's chest and forcing him back a step. Rather than speaking to him, though, she spoke to Lucy and Meg. "Remember, this is how courting works here. They say what they will do, they don't ask. Be firm if you aren't interested. Hit him."

The alcohol in her system made a laugh bubble out of her. She eyed the man, who hadn't even blinked at Daunet's advice. He wasn't much taller than a normal human, but he was broader, denser, and outfitted with claws that could turn a block of ice into a snow cone.

Lucy leaned close to Daunet. "You want me to hit—"

"Hello."

"I'm getting really tired of being interrupted." Lucy hissed.

The man from before, Nuphan, was in front of them again. "If it's a matter of attraction, I'm sure I could see past your baldness."

The other man scowled. "I don't mind your baldness, female."

"I'm not interested!" Meg clutched her head as it began to spin. The crowd in the room was pressing in on her. The atmosphere was too heavy, and no matter which way they turned, the intense heat of a hundred muscular hairy people made the air thick and warm.

"I know," Nuphan said, brightening. "We'll fight, and you'll be enticed again." Without waiting for her response, he squared off with the other man.

Another Kitibardian spun from the table he was seated at. "If a selection brawl is occurring, I'd like to enter as well."

"Stop! She doesn't want anyone," Lucy yelled.

"Why?" Nuphan said. Ridiculously enough, he looked sincerely confused.

"Because…because…" Lucy glanced around, brain whirring behind her pretty blue eyes.

Meg balled her fist. She supposed there were worse things than hitting someone and breaking her damn wrist to get out of this bizarre situation.

Lucy blurted, "Because she's already been recognized."

The scowls vanished from all three men's faces, and silence settled for a moment.

"Isn't that right, Meg," Lucy urged with a bump of her hip.

"Yeah? Yeah!" She nodded finally. "He… My potential mate's eyes changed right before we left Tremanta. We expect his marks to appear when I get back, but I'd already agreed to this trip, so…'" Meg swayed a little on her feet as she scrambled to think up the lie. She described a broody, dark-haired man to the rapt group around her, embellishing little details about his imaginary appearance here and there.

A shout of pain echoed from across the room, and all eyes turned. Heleax appeared through the crowd, escorting Sophia, who cradled her fist against her chest.

"It's time to go," Daunet said from her left. Meg turned and withered at her guard's icy stare.

***

"I can't believe you said that," Daunet fumed while stomping down the deserted hallway.

"It's not like you were helping! I panicked. And, news flash, it worked. Did you see how quickly they left her alone after that? They even apologized," Lucy argued.

"Daunet, she's right," Nirato agreed. "The Kitibardians are normally forward, but I've never seen them like that. They weren't listening."

"Why didn't you hit them?" Daunet's glare flashed to Meg.

Meg crossed her arms over her chest. "I've never hit *anyone* before, and did you see them? They were made of rock. Sophia freaking broke her hand trying to hit them."

"Besides they were so desperate to see signs where there weren't any, they would have probably seen her punch as a come-on," Lucy added.

"No more from you today," Daunet snapped.

They reached Meg's room, and Nirato urged Lucy to keep walking forward, though her glower said she wasn't happy about it.

Once they were out of earshot, Daunet slid her eyes closed and took a deep breath.

"Look, I'm sorry, but we were frustrated and tired, okay? We've been adapting to a new culture every two days with no breaks, and I think, apart from this, I've done a pretty good job. We finally ran out of steam tonight, and so we told them something we knew would get them to back off. You can't hold it against us."

The woman eyed her for a moment with a clenched jaw.

Meg could see her softening. "Would you really have liked to see me punch that guy? I'm guessing I would have succeeded in knocking myself over."

"With how much you drank, I'm guessing it's more likely you would've missed." A tight smile threatened to break over Daunet's lips, then she let out a long sigh. "Next time, just tell me you are overwhelmed. I could've stepped in for you if I thought you couldn't do it on your own."

Relief had her shoulders relaxing on an exhale. "I did tell you! I gave you the look." Meg activated her room's lock and shuffled inside.

"The look? What look?"

"You know. The girl-code look that says, *Help. I'm really uncomfortable, and I need you to come rescue me.*"

Daunet's head jerked back slightly. "You never gave me a look like that."

"Oh, yes, I did." Meg laughed. "Remember?" She imitated the wild-eyed nonverbal message she'd sent to both Daunet and Lucy earlier.

"That?" Daunet all but shouted. "That doesn't say anything."

"It does to human women." This was the first time Meg had ever had the opportunity to use the silent SOS call, yet Lucy had understood it no problem.

Daunet waved her off. "I'll see you in the morning." But Meg noticed she wasn't walking toward her room.

"And where are we headed?"

Without turning, Daunet answered, "I'm going to make sure no other humans are opening their eyes slightly more widely than normal."

"Uh-huh. Sure. Tell Tara I said hi."

7

Hours. He'd missed her by hours. Maxu wrenched the steel-and-stone doors open, stomping down the steps into the half-buried building his mate had been housed in. For the last week, this had been his life. Racing after some faceless female and arriving just a little too late.

He thought since the location of this tour stop had been leaked to the surrounding cities, he might have been lucky enough to catch her before she vanished, but no. Now all that was left for him was whatever scraps of evidence he could find in her room. Pulse ticking upward at the hint of her scent, his steps quickened. He'd learned which building had housed her by listening in on hushed conversations in the tavern, but he needed no further guidance to figure out which room she'd occupied. The grinding pressure in his chest carried him to a metal door and, without a second thought, he glanced down the deserted hall and started working on the lock.

His breaths evened as he assessed the security of the door. This had always calmed him. Focusing on a task like this. The shot of serotonin he got every time he broke through a puzzle fed his ego and reminded him of who he was. A male that didn't let anything stand in the way of what he wanted. He pulled out the print of Meg's hand he'd found on a side table in Sauven—the only other room he'd broken into that hadn't been cleaned yet.

As the whir of mechanical locks sliding out of place sounded, he thanked himself for deciding to sacrifice a few hours of travel time to infiltrate that lab and print a usable dupe for his mate's palm.

He slipped inside the dark room and stilled. She was everywhere. Her scent, the ghost of her activity. Gaze zooming around the space, he took in the half-empty drinks scattered on every surface, the rumpled sheets of the bed, and the extra sound orbs floating around the ceiling next to the dimmed lights.

As there had been back in Sauven, the sounds orbs were more plentiful than normal. She must have been adamant about listening to whatever it was loudly to have requested additional orbs in not one but two cities, possibly more. His brows furrowed. What had she listened to?

Taking a chance, he slapped her printed palm onto the controls by the door and commanded. "Repeat."

Nothing happened for a moment and Maxu assumed the system must have purged itself of its memory already, but then a soft note built in the room. Music. She liked music.

Maxu didn't usually play music, preferring instead the silence of his home. How would he hear his trip alarms sound if he was blaring music? But something about the gentle yet dramatic notes of the stringed instrument harmonized with the ache present in his chest since he'd recognized Meg.

He lowered onto the blankets that she'd so recently twined herself in and closed his eyes. The throbbing in his chest grew unbearable, so he fisted her pillow, burying his face in it and inhaling until he saw spots. His gut tightened, but not with the usual nausea he experienced as he chased after her.

This was different. He was the closest he'd ever been to her, and his body knew it. Maxu couldn't decide whether he wanted to tear the pillow up or clutch it to his chest until the pain stopped. It was like his body was sparking. Every powerful emotion he had flashed through him.

He needed to find her. Needed to claim her.

Maxu flipped onto his back and stared at the ceiling. He'd stay here for just a little while longer. Maybe if he did, her scent would follow him and he could imagine he'd wrapped her up in his arms. It would be a few hours at least before he knew her next location anyway.

He cleaned himself up using the foam shower, ate a few scraps from his bag, then collapsed back into her blankets. No more than five minutes had gone by before he could no longer remain still. He shot up, pacing the room, and made his virtual rounds.

Maxu probed every one of his contacts for bits of information. Had there been any sightings of the three cruisers? Any whisperings from any city? Nothing. Not even a picture for him to moon over.

The cruisers had licenses to fly high enough that their metallic surfaces disappeared against the sky and, from what he could gather, the cities who knew they were getting a stop didn't even know when the visit would occur—probably to keep people like him from tracking down the humans. It was working.

In lieu of learning where she would be next, he maximized his time by learning everything he could about her. In each city, he made a point to interrogate the locals and anyone else who'd spent time with the humans. It'd taken immense self-restraint not to rip apart every single person who'd described a human matching Meg's description as a bright, beautiful thing who'd sweetly flirted with many of them.

Maxu hadn't questioned the Kitibardians about Meg yet, and he seethed just thinking about it. *She doesn't know she's mated*, he reminded himself again as a headache—a result of him incessantly grinding his teeth—built at his temples.

He stalked around the room, searching every nook and cranny he could, but as always, she'd left little behind. He'd just pulled all the bedding from the mattress when a different scent hit his nose. It was her again, but *more*...different. A purr pulsed out of his chest as he lifted a pillow from the ground to his face. Rumbling growls mixed with his purr when the scent of her arousal invaded his senses.

Cock as hard as stone, hand white-knuckling a dainty pillow, he scooped up his bag and charged out of the room. He needed to find his female. Now.

The bitter wind slicing over his face as he stomped to the nearby tavern did nothing to cool the fire in his veins. It was time to question the citizens of this dreary city. A group of Kitibardians spilled out of the tavern and slogged toward a patch of carved out snow to relieve themselves. He lowered his hood over his face. They were too drunk to be of any use, and if they so much as uttered an incoherent word to him, he was afraid he'd throttle them just to let out some of this tension. He couldn't afford any more time locked away.

Before he could brush past, one male shouted, "Did you just come from the grand round house? That's off-limits." Maxu ignored the slurred accusation. It was obvious where he'd come from. There were no other buildings in that direction, and his deep tread marks in the snow were evidence enough.

He kept walking, but the male backtracked and caught up with him, grabbing him by the arm. A grin broke out over Maxu's face as he spun, slamming his fist into the male's face and watching him collapse. His face tipped toward the sky, and he let out a breath of relief. That felt good.

He was about to turn and continue on his way when another male spoke. "Are you mated to that human?"

Time stopped. His bag's strap across his chest stretched taut with his inhale. Ice and snow scraped under his boots as he slowly rotated on the spot.

"You have the marks," the male said, staring at Maxu's fingers, still clutching the pillow in his left hand.

Was he dreaming this? There must've been another human with a mate because unless he was very mistaken, Meg didn't know about him.

"Elaborate." Maxu's tone was bitter enough to make even the scowling Kitibardian male lean away.

"One of the humans made a scene last night with a few of my kin. Word spread. The human said her male had only initially recognized her, but she described someone who looked like you. Your dark hair. Your build. Did your marks come in after she left?"

She'd described him? Maxu's mind raced. Did Meg know she was mated? He ground his teeth and managed to grate out, "What did she look like?"

"Short, dark hair. Bald everywhere except for her head. Pale." The man studied Maxu's face with eyebrows slashed downward. As if the universe itself were trying to cool his temper, snow began to fall. It clung to the white fur on the male's cheeks. The flakes sizzled off Maxu's skin. "Did she know your marks had appeared?"

She knows! That little... He pounded away a few paces without a word, then halted. Where the fuck was he going? He had to find her, and yet he couldn't find her. *Because she's hiding from me!*

Without realizing he'd moved, he found his nose buried in her pillow, inhaling as if the ghost of his mate could grant him some sense of control. It didn't.

Torture. He'd been tortured for weeks, and she knew. His fists shook.

"I know where they're going next." As though from a great distance, the male's voice reached him.

A humorless smile cracked over his face. She'd made a mistake, and he couldn't wait to torture her right back.

8

Camille and Meg sat at a floating table with two gorgeous Vondalese men, yet Meg couldn't keep her attention from flicking over her shoulder. Daunet grinned back at her while she reclined against the wall. Meg frowned.

Apparently, Daunet and Gamso—who'd also been offended by Lucy and Meg's lie concerning matehood—had taken it upon themselves to tell any party interested in either woman that they were mated. Punishing them for lying by telling the same lie. Hypocritical? Yes. Effective? Undoubtedly.

Meg had almost been attracted enough to a man yesterday to invite him back to her room, but then Daunet had casually announced that Meg's mate was attempting to reach her. The guy she'd been talking to was so taken aback that he'd barely had time to shoot a look of disgust in her direction before sprinting away.

Her armed guard had learned what cockblocking was only a few days ago, and yet she'd mastered it.

Meg refocused on the man in front of her. Navy skin, a square jaw, and intricate tattoos running over his scalp rather than hair. He grinned at her, his fangs flashing along with his glittering purple irises.

"Your eyes *are* really beautiful," he repeated. She'd come to realize there were many differences between the Clecanians, but one thing the men in particular had in common was a penchant for rote flattery. At first, she'd basked in it, never wanting the praise to end. But after the fortieth time her eyes were vaguely complimented and after hearing the same accolades uttered to all other women in the room, the words had lost their charm. The compliments weren't specific to her, they were more a courtesy like "good morning" or "have a nice day." Polite, but shallow.

As if to mirror her thoughts, the man across from Camille scooted closer and said, "Yes, and yours are a shade I've only seen in the most beautiful flower."

Camille rolled her eyes and smiled. "Really? Do you hear that, Meg? Apparently his favorite color of flower is brown." Meg held in a chuckle as the two men exchanged a confused glance.

Still, neither Camille nor Meg was repelled. The men were sweet and flirting the way they'd been taught to. It wasn't their fault their methods weren't exactly working on humans.

"Try harder." Camille leaned forward and shot the man across from her a teasing smile with just a hint of a challenge. "Tell me something I've never heard before."

Meg's suitor, Bantio, listened, and his gaze became far off as he, too, tried to think of a unique compliment.

Camille's man—Rikad, Meg thought—straightened at her challenge. A true grin, one that was different from his charming, practiced smiles, spread over his face and he seemed to study Camille with renewed interest.

"I enjoyed watching your dimples appear when you spoke of your job working with Earth beasts during your interview this afternoon. I wonder how I could make you smile so they deepen even more."

Camille's grin widened at that, her dimples pulling in.

"Marvelous," Rikad breathed.

"Okay. You have my attention," Camille said, propping her chin on her hand.

"Shall I show you the flower I was speaking of?" He lifted a large palm to her.

Camille glanced at Meg and whispered, "You good?"

"Fantastic." Meg smirked back and watched as an eager Rikad shot to his feet.

"Do you guys use your fangs for anything specific?" Meg asked Bantio while taking another swig of her drink.

His eyes lingered on the retreating backs of Camille and Rikad. "Huh?"

They were seated on the top floor of a three-story event space. It wasn't exactly a restaurant or a bar or a club, although food and drinks were available and rhythmic music pulsed from the floating sound orbs above. Vondale was a city of people watchers, and this space seemed to be designed for just that.

The two lower levels were filled with birdcage-like structures that boasted elegant inset seating and curated lighting. They hung throughout the two floors, and fashionable attendees of the party chose their spots based on illumination and position. Those who were the most extravagantly outfitted chose rooms near the center where they could be seen from every angle. There were even little paths circling all the enclosures where people could walk and admire everyone without ever speaking to them.

Meg had asked to be seated on this higher level because it was an open space. Everyone still gawked at each other, including her, but the floating tables and chairs scattered throughout this quiet level made her feel a little more comfortable and less like a human in a display case.

"Your fangs. Are they functional?" Meg already knew the answer, but she'd found that not everyone she'd met appreciated how much she'd already learned about their culture. They seemed to prefer the idea of an uninformed Class Four–planet human who they could dazzle with alien knowledge. Meg didn't really mind pretending not to know things. At least it gave her topics for conversation.

Bantio smiled and launched into a heated explanation of how his people used their fangs. She half listened. The music had changed, and she couldn't help but concentrate on the interesting beat being created by some kind of percussive instrument she was unfamiliar with. When it wouldn't feel like she was interrupting or uninterested, she'd have to ask for the name of this song so she could listen to it later.

Meg liked Clecanian music, yet she couldn't help but miss her playlists. Music on this planet was mostly instrumental, and when there *was* singing, the background melody was soft or nonexistent. Many places felt that combining singing and instrumental music lessened the impact of each rather than enhanced them both.

A loud crash from below had both her and Bantio jumping. She craned her neck to look down the revolving staircase but couldn't see anything.

Bantio pulled his chair forward until their knees were brushing together. "I can show you," he rasped, his light purple gaze heating.

It took her a moment to recall what he'd been talking about. *Fangs. Right...oh.*

Despite the slight boredom she'd felt while talking with Bantio, her heart thrummed in her chest and heat crept into her belly.

A part of her thought, *This guy? Really?*

He was gorgeous, but she'd met a lot of gorgeous men who were far more charismatic and suave. As unexpected as her reaction might be, she was just happy she felt *something* finally.

This is it. I'm going to see what it's like to be with another man. She took in a shaky breath. "Yes. Uh. I'd like that."

"Oh, Meg. I forgot to tell you—"

Meg nearly fell out of her chair in an attempt to stop Daunet from saying what she'd crept up behind her to say. "Damn it! Don't! I told you I'm sorry."

Daunet had plastered a confused look on her face. "Oh, I was just going to remind you that your mate had called." Without a care in the world, her guard flounced away.

Meg's lids slid closed, and she let out a slow breath through her nose. When she turned back around, Bantio had leapt three feet away and was staring with wide accusatory eyes.

"You have a mate?"

Another crash and a few heated shouts echoed from downstairs. Who was fighting, and what had set them off?

"No. She's joking. I don't have a mate."

The man narrowed his eyes at her. "Why would she joke about that?" he asked.

"Because she can't get the girl she wants into bed and she's taking it out on me," Meg shouted loudly enough for Daunet to hear in her spot across the room.

Bantio peered over his shoulder when a deep bellow echoed from downstairs.

Meg stood and crossed to him. Dammit all if she was going to let the only man who'd caused a twitch of excitement in her belly from falling prey to Daunet's silly payback. She clasped Bantio's hand, and his attention shifted back to her. "I promise, I don't have a mate."

"You!" Both she and Bantio jumped when a deep voice echoed through the crowded space, bouncing off the glass and metal walls.

A man with dark hair, black eyes, and a murderous expression stood at the top of the revolving staircase, legs planted apart, hands balled into fists.

Damn, she was glad she wasn't "you." That person was about to have a very unpleasant day if the bulging stiff muscles of this man had anything to say about it.

Meg glanced over her shoulder, trying to figure out who was about to be murdered. When she saw no one making a run for it, she looked back.

Hair rose on the back of her neck, Bantio's hand slipping from her palm. She couldn't see the enraged man's pupils past the complete blackness of his eyes, but she somehow felt his gaze on her. Two guards from the balcony below suddenly collided with his back. Rather than be tackled, he only stumbled forward a step. She moved to the left, then to the right, testing a theory she couldn't bear to voice. His face rotated, following her progress. *Crap.*

Meg crept backward slowly, cursing as she bumped into a chair. Daunet appeared at the edge of the room, pulling a knife, but her movements slowed when her eyes locked onto something, and widened.

"You said you didn't have a mate," Bantio shouted while scrambling away, palms raised toward the dark-haired man who'd just flung one guard off his arm as if they were a fly. The other guard went tumbling down the stairs when the man spun out of reach and slammed a boot into his chest.

He sprinted toward Meg, dodging floating tables and clearing furniture with a leap. Shock kept her feet rooted in place, though she should've been bolting out of the way like everyone else.

The wild man closed in, and she slammed her eyes shut. *This can't be how I die.*

He crashed into her like a train, knocking the breath from her lungs with an *umph*. The two steel bands of his arms locked around her middle, and he lifted her above his eyeline. She was still trying to suck the breath that had been knocked out of her back in when his face disappeared into the crook of her neck. He inhaled so deeply that his expanding chest forced a last wheeze to escape her crushed lungs.

The world around her was still, everyone staring in their direction rather than helping. The man began trailing his nose and parted lips over her throat, her hair, her ear, and her manic gaze landed on Daunet in the crowd. "Help me," she gasped.

Daunet blinked, then motioned for the other guards to follow as she edged closer.

What the hell was going on? Meg tried to wiggle her arms, but they were welded to her sides under the man's bulky biceps. Hot and wet, his tongue laved a spot under her ear, and Meg shivered. His answering purr shot sparks through her belly, and she was suddenly very aware of a hard bulge pressing into her hip.

"Maxu?" Daunet called from a few feet away.

All at once, the man's body tensed.

"You know this lunatic?" Meg coughed as she fought for air. Spots danced across her vision. "Is that why you've all just been standing there?"

The man loosened his grip at her gasped words and pulled back enough to peer into her eyes. The most beautiful seafoam-green eyes she'd ever seen stared back at her. Though he'd relaxed his hold, Meg found her breath still caught in her throat.

Scraggly black hair covered his jaw and fell in knots around his ears. His eyes were bloodshot and weighed down by dark circles, but Meg's pulse sped up all the same. He was striking, beautiful…dangerous.

"You don't recognize your mate?" he rasped in a harsh whisper. His gaze narrowed, his lip curling in accusation as though he were furious at her.

"You must have me confused," Meg tried after swallowing hard. "I don't have a mate."

His glare lingered on her mouth when she spoke. "Don't toy with me, female."

"Maxu, put her down and we'll get this sorted."

Meg's head and hanging legs flapped in the wind like a ragdoll when the man—Maxu—spun toward Daunet. "She's mine, Daunet. You see my marks."

Meg had been taken aback by Maxu's actions, surprised, scared even, but as she heard the tone of pure ownership in his words, anger flared hot and visceral.

"But...she doesn't..." Daunet's words were weak, which only spurred on Meg's rage.

She began struggling with all her energy, kicking and baring her teeth. He only met her gaze and lifted a brow.

"I don't belong to anyone, asshole. Put. Me. Down."

The corner of Maxu's lips quirked up at her struggling, which resulted in little more than a vibration under his strong hold. "You know, little mate, I've been dreaming about you since you abandoned me in Tremanta."

"Abandoned you? What are you—"

"And," he continued, raising his voice over hers, "I'm glad to find you have some fire in you." He removed one of his arms, but the other remained in place, somehow keeping her pressed to him just as immovably as before. He held his hand up to her face, and she stilled. Bright blue marks circled his wrists and curled around his fingers. Meg's throat went dry when she took in the broken, bloodied skin underneath the swirling blue marks on his knuckles. "But make no mistake, you *are* mine."

Red invaded her vision. His imperious tone, his possessive hold—and what made her even angrier was the heat easing through her sex as a result of his imperious tone and possessive hold. She would not go back to being trapped. Never again.

His hand was still flexed in front of her face, and she glared at the marks. His smirk widened, turning her feral. Before she realized what she was doing, she lunged forward and sank her teeth into the meaty area below his pinky until she tasted blood.

9

∽

"So now that we've all calmed down—" The male officer glanced over his shoulder when Meg sniffed from the far corner of the room.

Four Vondalese officers and Daunet had positioned themselves between Maxu and his mate, even though he'd agreed not to touch her for the moment. They wouldn't be able to stop him if he really aimed to get to her, but touching her, smelling her, tasting her had calmed the mating instincts raging in him. And in any case, his pretty mate was ready to spit fire at him. Some cooperation wouldn't be the death of him. For now.

Across the room, Meg slipped a supple thigh over one leg and continued to stare at the ceiling, her nose turned up, her arms crossed over her chest.

Damn, he wanted to wrench those thighs apart. He balled his fists and grinned inwardly at the pulse of pain from his right hand. He couldn't wait to bite her back.

"Maxu, you claim Meg is your mate?" the male said while darting glances between them. The other guards sat quietly doing the same as their superior spoke. The poor male looked as bewildered as everyone else in the room. It was unthinkable that authorities would need to keep a mated female from ripping out her mate's throat with her teeth, but here they sat.

"She's mine. I recognized her back in Tremanta."

The officer nodded, then shot a tentative look at Meg.

She scowled back at him. "Why do you keep asking him that, then looking at me like the matter is settled? Just because he claims it's true doesn't mean it is."

She turned her head away again and her leg bounced.

It was true, what she said. All the officers had done was repeatedly ask whether Maxu was lying about being mated, then arrive at a loss when Meg didn't accept his response. It was a miracle that he'd recognized her, something every person on this planet wished for and something that couldn't be undone. Her pushback had every senior member of the Vondalese authority at a loss.

"They aren't going to do anything, sweetness. Matehood is sacred, and the fact that you knew about me yet left me behind doesn't do you any favors." Sharpness cut into his words, and the murmuring buzz in the room told Maxu all Clecanians present were on his side.

Her dazzling blue eyes narrowed on him. "I don't know what you're talking about. I told you I've never seen you before in my life."

101

"That's not what the fine people of Kitibard said." Her lips parted and her throat bobbed, making him salivate. The delicate curve of her neck had tasted better than she smelled. His voice a little more hoarse than normal, he continued, "You told a male there that you'd been mated. You described me to him so well that his kin recognized me when I was searching for you."

Meg gaped at him. "No…I didn't… That wasn't this. I didn't know about you."

"She lied," Daunet, who'd been silent and a shade paler than normal, finally stepped out of the corner she'd been stewing in. "There was a cultural misunderstanding, and she felt she had to make up a lie to get a few interested males to lose interest. I've been with her this whole trip, and I know Meg. She didn't know you existed."

"Thank you!" Meg blurted, pointing to Daunet and then to the officers. Triumph washed away any hint of her earlier surprise, and she shot Maxu a smug smirk. The grin he returned was savage and full of unspoken promises. Her brows furrowed and her foot began bouncing again.

She refused to break their silent staring contest, though he could tell she wanted to. His insides fluttered at the show of bravery. He held her gaze, heat racing to his dick at the stubborn set of her bottom lip as she glared back, unwilling to lose this silent battle of wills.

"So," the lead officer began, "Maxu recognized her in Tremanta, and you, Meg, didn't know he'd recognized you?

Yet you were moved to lie about having a mate and you happened to describe a male that looks like Maxu?"

"Right," she said, pursing her lips.

"Wow. You knew him before ever even knowing he existed. You described him so well that others recognized him from just your words. May the Goddess bless us all as you have been blessed." Awed intakes of breath and murmured prayers ran through the room.

"Right. Wait! What?" Meg's face fell, and her head whipped around. "No! That's not what I'm saying at all. I described a guy similar to him, but not him. It was just a coincidence."

Maxu couldn't contain the smile beaming from him. They were right. Even if she hadn't known he'd recognized her, something long buried in her brain had.

"I'm sorry. There's nothing we can do. He's your mate. We couldn't possibly keep him away from you. It would be cruel to you both." The guard reached out a comforting hand toward Meg, and Maxu snarled at him. The male immediately recoiled with an apologetic glance in Maxu's direction.

He shouldn't take as much pleasure in the absolute outrage plastered on his mate's face as he was, but he couldn't help it. He'd suffered for the past two and a half weeks, and the sooner she understood she had no way out of this, the better.

Daunet approached her, squatted down, and started speaking in a whisper Maxu couldn't quite pick up. His mate's soft skin flushed pink around her forehead and chest.

"No!" She suddenly shot up from her seat. Daunet rose as well, pinching the bridge of her nose with her fingers.

Maxu's legs tensed. *Run, little mate. Make me chase you.*

"Everyone out. Give them a minute alone together." Daunet swung on Maxu. "Behave. Talk to her the way you would a wife."

Maxu scowled and crossed his arms over his chest but said nothing. If this female got him time alone with his mate, he wouldn't argue, but he sure as fuck wouldn't speak to her like a wife—empty compliments laced with desperate pleas for acknowledgment. Never.

The officers filed out of the room, unconcerned with the boiling human in the corner.

"I'll escort you back in five minutes. Just give him a chance," Daunet pleaded in a soft voice.

Meg's teeth ground together. She remained obstinately silent.

When Daunet had slipped the door closed, Meg's gaze stayed fixed on the wall in front of her.

"Did you dream about me, vahpti? Is that how you were able to describe me so well?" Maxu slowly rose from his seat.

"Don't flatter yourself—" She turned, rolling her eyes at him, then paused when she spotted his slow movements. "Stop. Stay over there."

He rounded the table. "Because I dreamed about you."

That got her attention. She watched him warily as he took another step closer. "You're lying."

"I was only able to see the back of you, of course. Only what I saw that day in Tremanta." Maxu leaned back against the table and hooked one ankle over the other. He took his time running his gaze down her body, not hiding the heat that invaded his blood as he took in the swells of her hips and breasts. Blessedly plumper than he'd guessed. Perfect.

All spirit and emotion packaged in the most luscious body he'd ever laid eyes on. The blush of anger that had colored her chest ran up to her cheeks at his obvious leering.

"Shall I collect your things?"

"My things?" she parroted.

"I could be showing you your new bedroom in a matter of hours." The sooner he got her into his space, the sooner she'd submit to him. He just needed patience, something he'd always sorely lacked. "I'm sure you'll love our home."

"No!" A loud incredulous laugh erupted through the room, raising his hackles. "I'm not going anywhere with you." Her thick dark lashes fluttered, her eyes wide and unseeing as she whispered, "This can't be happening."

He pushed off the table. She noticed and scurried back a step. Maxu called on every ounce of willpower he had not to inch closer.

"Stop," she yelled, even though he already had. "This isn't happening again. I've made a life for myself. This is my job. It's important! I have a plan. I'm going to travel the world and meet people, men, live the life I never—"

A growl erupted from his chest at that. "No other men."

Meg only glared at him and continued on as if he hadn't said a word. "And now just because some pushy, controlling asshole with a chip on his shoulder comes in and tells me I'm *his*, I'm just supposed to be okay abandoning everything *I* want?" She ran a hand through her short hair, making it stick out around her ears. "For the rest of my life, no less?" She added in a croak. "No! I refuse."

His temper was simmering at the surface now. All the confidence he'd gained knowing authorities wouldn't keep her away from him dissolved under the weight of her words. Just because no one would hold him back didn't mean she'd accept him, and to his disgust, the mating instinct making his stomach roil seemed to need her acceptance just as much as it needed her proximity.

"You liked it when I touched you," he shot at her. He wasn't going to bring it up, use her own body's responses as a weapon, but he couldn't help it. "You say you don't want me, but the scent wafting from between your legs painted a different picture."

Her mouth actually fell open then. Her eyes bounced around the room, and she emitted an enraged sound, not unsimilar to a whistling pot. Swiping a nearby research screen, she hurled it at his head. He caught it with one hand.

"My body had a response the same way it does when I see a cheese curd double bacon burger on the menu. I may like it, but it doesn't mean it's healthy for me to eat. You are exactly the type of man I *don't* want." She moved to the door, and he blocked her way.

"This argument doesn't matter!" He bellowed, her words sinking in and stinging more than he cared to admit. "You're my mate! We belong to each other now."

"I don't belong to anyone," she hissed in a voice gone deadly calm. "Now get out, or I'll scream, and they'll come drag you away."

He had to give his mate credit. She stood her ground as he closed the distance between them. His neck ached from staring down at her, but he wouldn't crouch. He'd bend for no one, especially not a little spitfire wrapped in lush curves who refused to grasp the way this world worked.

"There's a lot of slack they'll grant a newly mated male who's being spurned, I guarantee it. You have no idea how much these marks mean to the people out there." Maxu flashed his hand toward her to show her the marks once more, but she flinched. Not just with her eyes but with her whole body, as if she expected him to hit her. The growl that burst out of him at the thought had her backing down, and the acrid scent of fear hit his nose.

This wasn't what he wanted. Yes, he aimed to conquer her, but not from terror. When he lifted a hand to touch her, he wanted a very different scent to leak from her pores. At the moment, though, the emotions swirling inside him were too strong. Hurt, lust, longing.

A line of wetness welled over her dark lashes, and Maxu felt like someone was attempting to tear his heart out through his ribcage. She turned away, swiping at her tears but disguising the movement by tucking her hair behind her ear.

He couldn't win her tonight. Not in his current state. He needed to clear his head, finally get a few hours of sleep, if possible. "I'll leave you for now. Give you some time to come to terms with this, but believe me, I'll be close by."

He ground his teeth when she didn't look up.

It was a stupid thing to do, but Maxu couldn't stop himself. He gripped her by the chin and forced her gaze to meet his. Fear flared in her wide eyes and the sour scent invaded his nose once more. She tried to pull away, but he kept her head in place with his other hand on her nape. "I may be rough, Meg, but I will never strike you." Her lashes fluttered, her gaze bouncing between his eyes. "Never." He repeated as he released her chin and stalked through the door.

Daunet waited at the entrance, leaning against a wall. He paused, eyes trained on the floor and his insides revolting at the direction he was forcing his feet to carry him. "Make her understand," he grunted at the female guard.

"I think that's your job. Do better," Daunet answered without an ounce of warmth in her voice. She held out his bag, which they'd confiscated.

Maxu swiped it and pounded away, intent on finding something he could rip apart.

"Where are you going?" she called after him.

"The doctor." Maxu held up his injured hand without turning to look back at Daunet. "Need to make sure my vaccinations protect me against rabid humans."

***

Four hours later and Maxu lay awake, staring at the ceiling of the room he'd threatened his way into. All the rooms in this wing of the Vondale housing, except for those reserved for humans and their guards, had been left vacant for the safety of the tour group. But after a drawn-out argument wherein Maxu insisted that if they didn't give him access to a room near his mate he'd simply knock down whatever door he pleased and stay in the room anyway, they'd acquiesced.

They'd done it not because of his snarled threats but because of the damn marks on his hands. Every employee here had either witnessed or heard about the poor male whose mate denied him. He should've been thankful for their sympathy, really. After all, without these marks, his behavior would have landed him in a prison within minutes. But their pitying gazes made him want to tear their eyes out.

She was just down the hall now. Two doors away. Might as well be a thousand miles. His whole body was aware of how close she was, how easily he could break into her room and wrap her up in his arms. He'd walked up to her door so many times already, in fact, that every chip and scratch in the heavily polished wood was burned into his brain. His gaze caught on her manufactured handprint tossed on his small table. It would take no effort to open her door.

He'd barely slept since leaving Tremanta in search of her. Between his fevered dreams and his determination to stay awake and keep his ears peeled for news of her current location, sleep had been the lowest priority. He'd even taken injections to keep himself conscious.

They'd worn off now, but sleep still eluded him. The frenzy of not being near his mate wasn't so bad anymore. He'd seen her, smelled her. But his insides were still as twisted up as ever. She was his, but she wasn't his. She hated him. Wanted nothing to do with him.

Maxu rolled on the hard mattress with a grunt and pulled her pillow up to his nose. The heavy scent of her arousal that had clung to the pillow when he'd stolen it had faded, but his dick still filled with blood at the faint scent. He groaned into the pillow, picturing her wide, expressive eyes and lush pink lips. How deep his fingers would dig in when he gripped her thick hips.

As he had every night of his recently cursed existence, Maxu took his shaft in hand. He imagined Meg underneath him, her small teeth sinking into his hand again, but this time to keep from crying out as his hips drove into her. His fist pumped over his cock until ropes of hot cum seared his abdomen, all the while his face remained buried in her pillow.

When his breathing evened out but his dick remained hard and unsatisfied, he let out a moan of frustration.

His hand wasn't enough anymore. He should be feeling the hot, slick grip of her cunt around his cock, not the rough callouses of his palm.

He needed a drink. Or a tranquilizer. Slowly, he rose in a daze. Exhaustion was catching up with him. His mind couldn't focus on anything for more than a few seconds. Even his thoughts about Meg were chaotic. What he actually needed, besides *her*, was sleep.

From his bag, he pulled out two bottles of mott. Dragging a chair from the small table nestled under the window, Maxu trudged outside his room. He set his chair in the middle of the hallway facing Meg's door, twisted off the top of one bottle, and collapsed onto the groaning wood.

He scowled at the shining door at the end of the hall. How dare it gleam more than any of the others. His gaze remained unblinking as he downed half his bottle.

What might she be doing behind that door? Thinking of him? Cursing him, probably. How was it that she'd described him if she hadn't known about him? Perhaps it had just been a coincidence. Even so, it meant she at least found males that looked like him attractive. Maxu shifted in his chair. What if she'd been describing someone else?

He lifted the bottle to his lips, only to find he'd emptied it. The mott coursed through his bloodstream, making him drowsy and sluggish. When he set his empty bottle down, he accidentally knocked the other over. It clanged on the stone floor and echoed down the hall.

His attention flew back to his female's door. Would she come out to inspect the sound? A few silent moments passed. Nothing. A rumble rose in his chest. Swinging his hand over the arm of the chair, he knocked over the other bottle and scowled at her door. She had to have heard that. Was she refusing to come out because she knew it was him?

He brought his second bottle of mott to his lips and sipped as the door next to Meg's opened. Daunet stuck her head and a tranq gun out into the hallway, spotted him, and pursed her lips. Without a word, she disappeared back into her room.

His eyes refocused on their target, vision more blurred around the edges than normal. Maybe he was overthinking everything. She might be in her room fast asleep, not giving him a second thought.

That idea brought a few choice curses to his lips, but they stalled in his throat when her door slid open at an excruciatingly slow pace.

Meg's silhouette appeared in the doorway, and Maxu's breath caught in his chest. Her large eyes spotted him immediately. She frowned. "What are you doing here? You said you'd leave me be."

Her chin-length hair was mussed, and her feet were bare. Pleasure oozed over his shoulders at the view of pale lavender lacquer on her delicate toes. She was wrapped in a soft, Vondalese sleeping robe. It was short and gaped at her neckline. He'd never appreciated a piece of clothing more.

Victoria Aveline

"I haven't knocked, have I?" It'd taken all his restraint not to, but he hadn't. Limbs heavy from the alcohol drugging his system, he draped himself over the chair, spreading his knees and relaxing his head on the tall wooden back, making it clear he was prepared to enjoy this unguarded view.

That ruddy pink blush stole over her cheeks, and his cock hardened. He'd only known her for a few hours, yet she'd tied him in knots without an ounce of effort.

"No, but I wouldn't say camping yourself outside my door and making a racket is leaving me alone either."

"I apologize if I interrupted your dreams of me, sweetness." Maxu lifted his bottle. "Care for a drink?"

"I wasn't dreaming about you," she hissed, flashing a glance between the two other doors.

He took another sip, reveling in the slight pinching of her lips. Was she lying? "Ah. So you must have been lying awake thinking of me."

The door across from Daunet's opened then, and an older human he vaguely recognized stepped into the hallway. The females exchanged glances.

Meg's nostrils flared as she huffed out a breath. "Everything's fine. I'm going to sleep."

"Pleasant dreams, my little vahpti," he crooned, forcing his legs to remain still and not stalk her into the darkness of her room.

With a final glare, she disappeared into her sanctuary.

His eyes lingered on the smooth wood for a moment longer before he noticed the other female still hovering in the hallway. He donned his usual mask of cold indifference and stared back at her. The look should have cowed her into vanishing, but rather than retreat, she smiled.

Finally, she disappeared into her room. Maxu grumbled his approval, but before he could feel too pleased about the effectiveness of his intimidation, she'd reemerged from her room with a chair.

"Maxu, right? Mind if I join you?" She pulled her chair alongside his and settled into it. His mind was so slow that he only watched her with a slack jaw, his bottle frozen halfway to his lips.

The female crossed her legs and let out a contented sigh while staring at Meg's door. Maxu lowered the bottle and straightened in his chair. Now that there were two of them blocking the hallway and scrutinizing someone else's room, he suddenly felt awkward.

"Congratulations on your marks." She nodded toward the hand currently gripping his bottle. Maxu hated the way his chest bowed with pride at the acknowledgment. Yes, he'd found his mate, but the amount of emotion tied to these damn marks was overwhelming. He was hanging onto his old, calloused self by a thread.

"Do I know you?" he grumbled through clenched teeth.

"We've met. I'm close to Alice, your brother's mate." The female smiled gently, causing the faint lines around her mouth to deepen.

He narrowed his eyes and managed to place her. Rita, he believed her name was. He'd met her a handful of times when visiting his brothers. And if he remembered correctly, she'd coupled herself with one of their old family friends, Zikas. He didn't say any of this, though, he only gave a grunt of acknowledgment and turned back toward the door where his future hid.

Rita remained quiet for a moment, but not uncomfortably so. The relaxed sway of her legs and faint smile made *him* sure as fuck uncomfortable. What did she want? And why were humans so damn difficult?

Finally, she spoke. "What's your plan here?"

"What?"

"Your plan. You made an…interesting first impression. Not quite off on the best foot with our Meg, I'd gather. How do you intend to make it right?" Rita's gaze held something he couldn't place. Her warm brown eyes weren't critical, exactly, more hinting, as if she were trying to get him to arrive at some conclusion she'd already reached.

He inhaled through his nose and took a long pull from his drink. "Splendid. Another blasted female telling me how I should behave." He gave her a harsh grimace and added, "With my own mate, no less."

Rita hummed thoughtfully, not even a little put off by the obvious dislike he was aiming at her. "You don't like being told what to do?"

"No."

"Or controlled, I imagine?"

"No," he growled again. Buzzing in his head from the mott and his fatigue had his temper pulsing under the surface rather than flaring to life. Maybe that was why this human wasn't scrambling away.

"That makes sense. I believe Meg feels the same way. It could be why she didn't fall upon your cock when you showed up, made a scene, and told her she belonged to you."

"I—" Maxu's head jerked toward Rita as soon as her blunt words settled in his mind. She gazed at Meg's door with a vacant smile, somehow knowing he needed a moment to compose himself. He turned away, mulling over her words. All he could think to say was, "She's my mate."

"Indeed." Rita angled her body toward him. It must've been the mott toying with him, but he found he was eager to hear what she had to say. "Zikas has talked about you a little, you know." Maxu clenched his jaw. "Nothing bad, I promise," Rita added. "He told me you don't want a wife. That you find ways to get out of the ceremony each year because of your dislike for the practice. Can I ask why you hate it so much when most men would kill for the chance to be picked?"

"Zikas should keep his mouth shut," Maxu muttered. With a sigh, he tried to form an explanation. "I… My instincts run too hot. I get angry and I'm possessive. I do things incorrectly and want more than I can have. It doesn't fit with how a husband is supposed to act."

"Hmm." She raised a brow, considering. "You sound very human to me."

Maxu eyed her again. He couldn't decide whether her words were meant to be reassuring or insulting.

"I know you don't want advice from *another blasted female*, but can I give you some advice as a human?" Rita's gaze held no superiority or condescension, so despite years of ignoring everyone else's opinion, Maxu gave a quick nod. "Meg is one of the few humans I've met that is excited to have been taken from Earth. She knows more about Clecania than any of us. She's studied all the cities and cultures of this planet. She learned to read your language within a few months even though she could just as easily use a translation glass. Meg is a smart, adventurous ball of light, and if your goal is to take her away and snuff out that light because *she's yours* and because you can, you're going to have a very hard road ahead."

Maxu didn't want that. He'd only just met her, yet the fire in her soul called to him on a level surpassing his mating instinct. He wanted to stoke those flames, bask in them. But he knew Rita was right. If he didn't change his approach quickly, he'd burn to ash trying to tame her.

"How?" he asked without elaboration.

Rita's smile widened as though she were pleased with her student. "I'd start with getting to know her. Did you even bother introducing yourself?"

"Yes, I…" Maxu thought back to their brief interactions. Fuck—no. He hadn't even told her his name. Daunet had provided it. As it always did, his frustration morphed into anger. "She's the other half of my soul! Formal introductions are trivial."

Rita chuckled. "I would have thought you'd be eager to *know* the other half of your soul."

Goddess, was that ever true. Even now he wondered how her laugh might sound and which city she was most excited to visit after all her studying.

Maxu jerked in his chair when Rita laid a hand on his forearm. "One more piece of advice?"

He fought back the impulse to pinch her middle finger and lift her hand. "What?"

"Clean yourself up. You look like you've been lost in the woods for a month. And get some sleep."

Maxu let out a humorless chuckle. As if sleep was that easy to manage. As if a buxom brunette didn't dance behind his lids every time he closed them.

"Here. This might help." Rita reached into the pocket of her navy robe and produced a small vial of sleep spray. "I have trouble sleeping most nights. Zikas gave it to me to help on the trip. It's illegal for civilians to have, but I'm assuming you won't rat us out." Her smile widened. As if she couldn't hold the words back, she added, "He's such a thoughtful man."

He didn't know how to express his thanks, not when he was simultaneously irritated, exhausted, and lost, so he took the vial and muttered, "He's very lucky to have found you as well."

Rita beamed and rose from her seat. "He is. I think I'll call and remind him."

Maxu remained in the hall long after Rita had left, brooding. Meg was his. It wasn't a claim of ownership, it was a fact. Simple as that. His body, heart, and mind were in agreement on this. But if he forced her, she'd hate him and his heart would lose out even if his body was satisfied.

The Queen's words floated back into his mind, hardening like cement. *Fuck*.

He had to win her.

10

Nothing about this day had gone according to plan. Meg averted her gaze as yet another pair of angry eyes landed on her. According to the Vondalese, she'd gone from fun-loving single girl to mated, heartbreaking bitch in less than twenty-four hours.

Camille was trying to say something to her, but she couldn't concentrate. For the zillionth time, she glanced over her shoulder, scanning the crowd for *him*.

Maxu, the hulking ghost of the hallway, had set up permanent residence in her mind. She'd been jittery all day, always searching for his scowling face around every corner. Each second she'd been sure he'd pop into whatever room she was occupying and haul her away while everyone watching did absolutely fucking nothing. And what was worse? He *hadn't* appeared.

By midday, Meg's nerves were so worn that she'd almost wished he'd show up. Just so she knew where he was. The suspense was too much.

On top of the constant paranoia that she was being watched, she'd also received crappy treatment from the Vondalese people. News of Maxu's appearance and of her blatant dismissal of his mating claim had rallied the city against her. Their interview this afternoon had turned into nothing more than a thinly veiled roast of her morals.

What reason would a human have for disparaging the sacred honor of matehood?

Are most humans selfish?

She'd taken the blows through gritted teeth. Remained stony faced as the Vondale citizens leveled her with dirty looks. It felt like everyone was against her again. The pressure raining down on all sides was bringing up memories from her past that she wished would stay buried.

Neighbors at her church shooting her dirty looks after news had spread of her dalliance with Jeremy. Their pastor coming to her house to urge her to do the *right* thing. But it wasn't just a small Midwest town looking at her as if she were garbage now, it was an advanced alien city.

How had this happened again? How had her hesitance to devote herself to a man, a stranger turned her into a cruel, selfish brat in everyone's eyes? Their accusing stares and harsh whispers were breaking her apart little by little. The only thing keeping the tears at bay was the layer of anger she wrapped herself in.

She just had one more night in this fucked-up city. Tomorrow morning they'd leave, and she'd finally get a reprieve…from them at least. She didn't know what she was supposed to do about her so-called mate. She took another deep swig from her glass and inhaled a thick breath. *Just get through tonight.*

At least she looked killer in the ruby-red frock she'd picked. The dress, with its mid-calf length, high collar, and long sleeves, might almost be called modest compared to the other outfits she'd been wearing. But the boning around her hips and waist, paired with the armpit-to-thigh slits held together by red laces, gave her a femme-fatale look that emboldened her. Well, that and the hard liquor she was downing like water on an empty stomach.

Does he like red?

The errant thought had her small sense of pride fizzling to nothing. No. She didn't care what he liked. She hoped he hated red. She glanced around the party again, pointedly ignoring the sneer coming from Bantio, the man she'd flirted with yesterday before Maxu had dropped into her life like a grenade.

On some level, she knew he was her mate and that she'd have to acknowledge that reality sooner or later, but she couldn't deal right now. She was too raw. Too panicked. She was a dog being backed into a corner, but this time, she wouldn't cower and show her belly. She'd bite.

"Woman, hello?"

Meg peered up and found her human entourage staring at her. At least she had them. They'd been so supportive of her at the interview. Defending her actions and explaining the correct ways in which a Clecanian should approach their mate if they recognized them. Her heart had hurt with gratitude at their efforts. But she'd told them to stop before they'd left for the party.

Their defense of her was sweet, but it had only seemed to turn the Vondalese people against the rest of the humans in addition to Meg. They couldn't accept that *any* human might defend the rejection of a mate, and her friends' arguments only served to paint humans in a bad light. As creatures without understanding or compassion.

Yup. She was over Vondale and its judgmental citizens. If Maxu showed up right now, lifted her skirt, and bent her over this table, they'd probably cheer.

Meg downed the rest of her drink and scowled into her empty glass. Why the fuck did she keep visualizing scenarios like that? And why the fuck did it continue to send a flutter through her belly and a pulse through her core?

"What were you saying?" she asked, trying to force herself not to give into the impulse to glance over her shoulder again.

"What did you talk about after you were escorted from the party?" Sophia asked.

She hadn't yet explained everything to her travel companions. Some of the women hadn't even seen the ruckus yesterday, and she could make out the curiosity burning in their expressions. She relayed everything with a slight slur, wobbling on her heels.

There were a few moments of silence before Lucy whispered, "Did you feel anything? Like, does the mating instinct exist in you at all?"

What a complicated question. One her brain was not currently functional enough to tackle. She felt…something. A pull that forced her to think about him more than normal. "So back in Indiana, there was this diner me and—" Meg cleared her throat. She'd been a breath away from mentioning Jeremy. "That I used to go to, and this one time I went, the waiter handed me my check and it was wrong. I told him it was wrong. That I hadn't ordered a side of hashbrowns, but he kept insisting I did. We argued about it until finally the manager came by and spoke to the kitchen. I was right, but that damn pimply waiter didn't apologize or anything. Just said he'd take the charge off and left."

"Okay," Camille said slowly. She and Tara exchanged a worried glance. They must've thought she was losing her mind.

"It'll make sense, I promise," Meg assured. She frowned as she caught herself scanning the crowd again and continued. "Well, that happened, like, six years ago and it still sometimes pops into my head randomly. I'll just be living my life and suddenly boom, this sour-faced waiter appears in my head and totally fucks with my mood. I end up thinking about what I should have said and how embarrassed I felt." How Jeremy had just sat back and let her argue for him rather than defending her. Not even to corroborate the fact they hadn't ordered the extra side. "It was so stupid and it doesn't matter at all, but my brain keeps bringing it up. Do you guys have anything like that?"

Tara snorted. "Do I replay old fights in my head and torture myself over how I should have done them differently? I'm a woman. Of course I do." The other women in the group chuckled.

"Well, that's what it's like. He keeps popping up in my thoughts, but not in a positive way. It's like the connection is there, and every so often my brain just wants to remind me that he exists and that I'm in this shitty situation. It's like I can't not think about him or stew about him. It isn't fun or romantic. I don't feel like I've met my soulmate. I feel like I just discovered an inoperable tumor." Meg's words grew more heated and harsh as she spoke, her throat constricting with each word.

"Don't hold anything back now," Camille chuckled.

"So, you don't like this guy at all?" Sophia asked in a higher pitch than normal. "You don't find him attractive at least?"

Meg scowled down at her toes. "No," she lied. "How can I like a tumor?"

"If you manage to stay strong on that, I'll sell my right tit," Lucy murmured.

Meg's face scrunched in confusion. "What?" She found all four women staring at something behind her, and goose bumps flared over her neck.

"Your boy is here, and he cleaned up reeeeaaaal good." Lucy's gaze was fixed over Meg's shoulder, and she was practically salivating.

"I'm a lesbian, but...I get it." Tara's brows just about disappeared into her hair line as she tried to take a drink while keeping Maxu in sight.

Meg froze. She'd stay strong. It didn't matter how he looked. He'd been the world's biggest asshole yesterday. *He wants to take me away. Control me*, she reminded herself firmly.

Awareness skittered over her back a moment before someone's body heat invaded her personal-space bubble and melted against her spine.

"Hello." His deep baritone slipped over her skin. Meg's pulse picked up speed.

A few breathy hellos floated out of her so-called friends. *Traitors*, she grumbled to herself.

Taking a deep inhale, she gave a quick nod over her shoulder. Two seconds, if that. She only let herself look for two seconds before facing forward again, and yet her mouth had gone dry.

He was clean shaven. His dark hair combed, trimmed, and styled into a slick side-parted masterpiece that both showcased the thickness of his hair and his widow's peak. With his chiseled jaw, full lips, and unfairly light eyes, he looked like he'd just stepped off an old Hollywood red carpet.

Meg concentrated on her glass, curling her toes to keep her reaction to him in check. How fucking dare he look so damn hot. It was unfair.

He must've realized she had no intention of turning around again because he stepped to her side and held out a glass of the exact liquor she'd been drinking. "I noticed you were empty."

She wanted to accept the glass. Her dry throat sorely needed some lubrication, but she'd let her windpipe crack and blister before taking it. It was a crazy comparison, but something in her drunken emotional mind likened accepting this drink to accepting him. And she couldn't do that. "No, thank you."

His long thick fingers and the blue markings circling them held the glass out for a moment longer. "Very well." There was a slight grunt to his voice, as if he were annoyed with her refusal. She darted an irritated look at him to show the feeling was mutual, and she was snared.

Maxu lifted her glass to his perfectly formed lips, slid his eyes closed, and tipped the amber liquid into his mouth. The high black collar of his shirt climbed halfway up his tanned neck. Bright white birthmarks crept out of his collar and came to a point along his jaw.

Meg couldn't stop her gaze from fixating on the thick muscles of his throat as they worked to swallow the liquor in one gulp. Spine straight, he lowered the glass, looked down his nose at her, and released a slow rumble of approval.

She didn't know if the sound was meant to praise the quality of the drink or her, but Meg shivered all the same. Inky black crept into the corners of his pale eyes as they traveled over her face and rested on her mouth.

Meg slammed her lips together, only now realizing they'd been parted in awe as she watched Maxu simply exist. She turned back to her friends, hoping for some sympathy, but all wore identical mischievous half grins. Like her life was some gasp-worthy reality TV show they were watching play out before their eyes.

She needed to get ahold of herself. Put him in his place. She aimed a saccharine smile his way and jiggled her glass between her fingers. "Looks like I need a refill. I'm going to go get *myself* a drink."

A hushed "oooh" that raised in pitch near the end echoed from one of the women behind her as she turned on her heel and power walked to the automated bar. *Don't trip. Don't trip. Don't trip.*

She managed to make it to the machine without too much tottering and programed in her drink of choice. She could sense him closing in even before he brushed against her arm. "Meg. Will you face me?"

Her jaw tightened. Was he asking? Calmly?

"Please." She could almost feel the effort it had taken him to push that one word out.

Taking a drink to steel herself, she turned and tipped her chin up so she could meet his gaze. His jacket buttoned on his shoulder and hugged his wide chest. The tailor had known what they were doing. It was simple yet angular. Cut in such a way that Meg's primal brain screamed to see if the body underneath could possibly be as wide and thick as the lines of the jacket made him out to be.

"Yes?" she croaked.

A muscle ticked in his jaw. "I…" His heavy brows slashed down over his eyes. "Apologize for yesterday."

Her focus caught on a vein throbbing in his throat. "Really?" she said with a raised brow, taking in the hard set of his jaw and the rigidness of his stance. "Because it feels like you're apologizing with a gun to your head."

His gaze shot to the sky, searching for patience. When he peered back down at her, he'd placed a terrifying smile on his face, though she thought he might mean it to be reassuring. "I am. I shouldn't have approached you in that way. I'd been searching for weeks, and I'd been locked up before that…" His words died and his Adam's apple bobbed. "Let's just say I was a little out of my mind."

Locked up? Could this get any worse? What had he been locked up for?

He took a step closer to her, hands raised on either side of her arms. She tensed instantly. His nostrils flared, and he licked his lips, rubbing them together in a slow movement full of frustration. His hands dropped. "I'd like to start over with you. If I—"

"Hello." Bantio walked up and grinned at Maxu. "I wanted to come introduce myself and congratulate you on your marks."

Bantio refused to look her way. She took another sip to hide her glower. Maybe Maxu had done her a favor. She'd almost taken this asshole back to her room without ever knowing what a dick he truly was.

Meg glanced back at Maxu, who'd become as still as stone. She didn't know whether to be worried or chuckle at the scene. Dark warning radiated off her mate as he continued to stare directly at her, his head slightly bent as it had been when he'd been interrupted. The vein in his neck bulged and the muscles in his jaw worked as if he was gathering every ounce of willpower he had.

She tucked one hand into the crook of her elbow and let her drink dangle loosely at chin height. With a curious brow lift to Maxu, she waited to see what he would do. His eyes raced between hers as if he was trying to gauge what she expected from him.

Finally, a mask descended over his features, and he straightened. He gave a small smile and nod toward the man, who was wildly unaware of the thick tension rolling off Maxu in waves. "I appreciate that. Thank you." He turned back to Meg determinedly, but Bantio didn't take the hint.

"Yeah, I also wanted to apologize for yesterday. She told me she had no mate. She insisted, actually."

The urge to argue rose in her throat, but she'd tried and tried over the course of the day with no success. These people believed what they wanted to believe. For the first time, though, Meg didn't feel overlooked because she was a woman. It was clear his poor opinion was due to her humanness. She couldn't decide if that was a step up or not.

"I understand," Maxu rasped, the rumble in his voice dangerously close to a growl. "Now, if you'll excuse us, I'm trying to have a conversation with my mate."

"Of course! Of course! And for the record, I really hope things improve for you. I mean, to be locked together with a female who lies like that—"

Meg hadn't yet had the opportunity to be offended by the little leech's words when Maxu's fist flashed out and connected with the man's throat. She stared in horror as Bantio collapsed, clutching at his neck and making pitiful gurgling sounds.

Partygoers nearby rushed over to help, staring between her and Maxu with thunderstruck expressions. When she finally tore her gaze away from the man still struggling to get air through his windpipe, she found Maxu's eyes closed again. A slight wince on his face, as though he knew he'd made a mistake.

"Nope." Meg downed the rest of her drink, dropped the glass onto the table and hustled toward the exit. She heard a strangled roar behind her and picked up her pace. "I'm out," she called to Daunet, who'd watched the entire conversation escalate while chatting with Heleax.

"Okay. Let's—"

"I'll escort her," Maxu's harsh growl interrupted Daunet, and Meg skidded to a halt. She spun and eyed her guard, her *friend*. Daunet's gaze bounced between them before finally settling on Meg. She wanted to shriek at the apologetic look Daunet was giving her. Her guard nodded to Maxu and remained in place, allowing the last person on this planet she wanted following her home to follow her home.

Meg power walked as quickly as she could on the five-inch heels she'd been so excited to wear yesterday. Heels were rare on this planet but common in Vondale. On Earth, she'd seldom had the opportunity to wear flashy heels, so she'd jumped at the chance to strap on the sexy red shoes. She regretted her decision now as the point caught on an uneven bit of ground. Her ankle twisted before she caught herself and continued stomping away.

"Wait. Please."

Meg scoffed without turning around. "Only you can make the word *please* sound like a command, I swear."

He huffed at her back and fell into step beside her. Cheeks already flaming from her almost fall, they burned even hotter when she caught his slow gait. She was almost out of breath, practically sprinting, and he was moving at a stroll. Pushing her shoulders back, she tried to walk faster.

"I couldn't help it. He insulted you."

"So you crushed his windpipe?" She wheezed out a laugh.

Out of the corner of her eye, she saw him shrug. "I would've preferred to tear it out, but I assumed you'd be unhappy about that."

Meg lurched to a halt. He gripped her elbow when she stumbled backward, but she wrenched it out of his hold. "That doesn't make me feel better." Her chest heaved and beads of sweat dripped down her spine. "What are you going to do? Throat-punch every guy who's a dick to me?"

"I'm not unreasonable, female." His eyes narrowed at her and a stubborn frown darkened his features. "Please, let me know where you'd like me to punch him instead, and I'll be sure to aim there next time."

"Ha-ha," she said without humor. She caught enough of her breath to walk again, but he grabbed her arm before she could start down the hallway.

"You're going to break your ankle." He grunted. She squawked as he scooped her into his arms and set off in the direction of her room.

"Put me down." She wriggled in his hold, but it was of no use. His grip on her thighs and rib cage was unbreakable.

"Stop flailing, or I'll throw you over my shoulder."

"You wouldn't."

He shot her a dark grin. "Wouldn't plant your pert ass right next to my face? It's all I want to do. Just give me a reason."

The words had heat coursing through her belly, and a small part of her wanted to keep squirming to see what he'd do. But that must've been the alcohol talking. Instead, she crossed her arms over her chest and stared ahead.

He carried her through the halls silently, but she could feel his gaze searing her. Meg tried not to notice the warm muscles of his torso rubbing against her side as he walked. She breathed through her mouth to keep his scent from making her dizzy. Musk and earth and something herbal she couldn't place.

"You look beautiful tonight. I didn't get the chance to tell you before."

She wished he would stop rumbling his words like that. Each one shot sparks through her bloodstream, making it bubble like champagne. His stupid voice. She was sure that was why his compliment almost made her want to grin. "What about my silly shoes?"

"Are they silly?"

She'd hoped her comment would make him spew something about how ridiculous the heels were. How it was just like a woman to wear something so painful and then need to be carried home. "They're pretty impractical," she pushed. *Just say something annoying so I can remember not to like being carried by you.*

His hand flexed on her knees, and one fingertip found bare skin under the hem of her dress. Meg inhaled a deep breath when he brushed his thumb over the side of her calf. *That's an erogenous zone I didn't know I had.*

"Well?" she prodded when he didn't answer.

He glanced down at her, the side of his mouth curling upward. "You don't want to know my thoughts on the matter."

Some of the heat pooling in her core cooled at that. "Yes, I do."

"Well, to me something impractical serves no good purpose." He cleared his throat. "I watched you walk away from me several times tonight, and I can tell you from where I was standing, they served a very useful purpose."

It took Meg a moment to understand what he was saying. When she did, the heat between her legs and on her cheeks rushed back.

He let out a short growl and grinned. "Or maybe you *did* want to know my thoughts."

"What do you mean?"

He met her gaze, and she was transfixed by the devastating combination of seafoam-green eyes and even white teeth. He bent his head, inhaling, then brushed his nose with hers before retreating an inch. "I can smell you. Remember?"

Meg could only blink at him, heart thundering in her chest a mile a minute.

No. No. No. She forced her gaze away. Stay strong.

They'd reached the last turn before her hallway, passing the curious guards keeping all other people trying to visit the humans wing at bay. Maxu's steps slowed. He was stalling.

"I could walk faster than this on my own."

Rather than respond to her complaint, he slowed even more. "I won't force you back to Tremanta with me."

Her thinned lips relaxed as she searched his expression. Was he being serious?

"I realize it wasn't right of me to demand you abandon your work simply because I want you to." His jaw was tight, features stony, but she sensed it was because he was uncomfortable, not disingenuous. How often did a man like this concede defeat or apologize?

He'd stopped moving altogether, and Meg realized they'd reached her door. The muscles of his throat worked, and he squeezed her against his body for a moment, as if fighting with himself to let her go. Finally he did, setting her on her feet and taking the smallest of steps away.

"I really appreciate that." She rested a hand on his arm and tried to inject her tone with the gratitude she felt. A weight had lifted at his words. If he was telling the truth, that meant she could stop flinching every time a new person appeared in the room. She wouldn't have the constant worry that at any second, she'd be spirited away.

Maxu's gaze riveted to her hand where she touched him. Black crept in at the corners of his eyes.

With a cough, she let her fingers fall to her side. Now that the threat of being carried off like a cavewoman was gone, something about Maxu softened. Her panic had clouded it before, but he wasn't so bad. He had a temper. In all honesty, so did she. He was handsome and broody and handsome and willing to admit when he was wrong…and handsome.

"I'm sorry I bit you," she grumbled with a half smile. "I hope I didn't cause too much damage. Is it all healed now?"

The hard slash of his brows relaxed as she spoke. He lifted his hand, and she could just make out a half moon of pale scars. She winced. "Oh no. They weren't able to fix the scars?"

Wait, that didn't make any sense. The doctors and technology here could fix almost anything.

His gaze turned heated as he studied the teeth marks on his hand. "I asked them not to. I enjoy seeing them."

Meg's breath caught in her throat. Was that hot or psychotic? Her mind couldn't quite decide. Her heartbeat, now pulsing warmly between her legs, told Meg her body had made a choice, though. "You're an odd duck, aren't you?"

With one smooth step, he invaded her bubble again. His head dipped, and he brushed his cheek against hers, pointedly inhaling. Tingles broke out over her scalp, her breaths shallow.

"I don't know what a duck is, but if I *am*, then so are you." His hot breath brushed over her ear.

Heart racing and cheeks hot, Meg dug her nails into her palms. It would be a bad idea to reach out and pull him down for a kiss. Sure, he was her mate, but he'd just told her he was going to give her some space. Running her hands up his shoulders would only send the wrong message.

It was a good thing he was going away. Meg didn't know how she'd keep herself from pouncing on him like an animal in heat otherwise.

"Um…so, when are you leaving?" she breathed, trying to ignore the forward sway of her body when he straightened away from her.

"Leaving?" A flash of something akin to hurt altered his calm expression for an instant.

Her brows furrowed. "Yeah. I think it's a good idea we take some space from each other. I realize you're my mate and we'll have to figure out some system to deal with that in the future, but you offering to leave me for now really takes a load off my mind. I feel like I can breathe, you know?"

He let out a dark chuckle that made her hair stand on end. "I'm not going anywhere, vahpti."

Meg blinked at him. "But…you said—"

"I said I wouldn't force you home with me. I didn't say anything about leaving you." His tone was firm, gruff. "You're my mate. I'm not going to let you out of my sight."

His words came down on her like a boot squashing her moment of relief under its heel. Anger bubbled in her stomach. How could she have been so stupid? Of course he wasn't going to give her space. "What are you going to do? Stalk me around the world?"

"Yes," he answered simply.

Meg took in a long breath. Maybe this could still be salvaged. He'd been reasonable a minute ago. A man who could admit when he was wrong was the kind of man who'd listen to sense, wasn't he?

"Look," she forced a smile, "I understand it will be hard to ignore the bond. Maybe you could come see me once a week. That would relieve those side effects while also giving me the space I'm asking for."

His chin lifted, and for a moment she thought he might consider it.

"No." The single word was as hard as cement.

Meg stomped her foot. "You can't just say no! Does it matter to you at all what I want?"

Maxu considered her for a moment. She wanted to scream when he took in her outraged glare and grinned. "It matters very much to me what you want. But how am I to learn what you want—what you really want—if I'm gone?"

Meg jerked her head back. "Is my translator broken or something?" She tapped her ear sarcastically. "Testing. One, two, three."

"We're mated now, and I don't believe acting as if we aren't is beneficial for either of us. Besides, I need to stay close by to make sure you're safe."

"That's a bullshit excuse. I have guards, and every city provides guards as well."

He shrugged and took a step back. "Even with all your guards, I was able to get to you."

"That's different," she sputtered, following him as he continued to back away. If he thought he was getting out of this fight that easily, he had another thing coming. "They saw your marks, and Daunet knew who you were. If you'd been a stranger, they would have never let you through."

"I'll be able to ensure that's the case if I'm nearby."

"I'm not... You're not..." Meg huffed a muffled scream. With a deep breath, she studied Maxu. So damn confident. "Just because you're here doesn't mean I have to acknowledge you."

"Going to ignore me, are you?" His face lit with an amused smile, and the stupid butterflies in Meg's stomach took notice. Why did he have to be so bone-meltingly hot?

"And what's so funny about that?"

"We're mated. I don't think you could ignore me if you tried."

Her teeth vibrated together as she slammed her mouth shut. She turned on her heel and stomped back toward her room. *I can't ignore him? Yeah, right. Just watch me, jackass.*

His gaze burned into her back as she clumsily activated her door and squeezed through. Once inside, she paced, fuming. Who was he to tell her what she did and did not want? It wasn't like she was turning down their bond. She just needed some time to come to terms with it. Time *without* him.

Meg undid the fastenings of her shoes, plopped them off, then sunk on her bed with arms and legs crossed, staring daggers at her door.

11

A few minutes of muttered bitching alone ensued before Meg finally jumped up and walked out of her room. Her steps faltered when she spotted Maxu sitting at the end of the hall again, bottle in hand.

A wide grin spread over his face when he saw her. "That was fast."

Sticking her chin into the air, she crossed over to Daunet's room and knocked. No answer. Maxu was visible in her periphery. She put her hand to the side of her face to block him out and knocked again. Nothing.

Of course Daunet wasn't here yet. What had she been thinking? They'd left her at the party and hadn't seen her pass them. Meg had access to Daunet's room in case of emergency. This wasn't really an emergency, but close enough. After all, she was in *serious* danger of murder at the moment.

Placing a palm on the door, she let herself in and waited. An hour passed. Two. Meg paced and sat. Then stood and paced before sitting once again, all the while fuming. Finally, bolts scraping from the door made her jump up from her seat. Daunet's gaze found her immediately.

"What are you doing?"

Hiding. "I was waiting for you. We need to talk about Maxu."

Daunet released a heavy sigh, her shoulders falling as though she were mentally preparing herself for a long fight. "He's your mate, Meg. I can't keep him away."

"Why not? Aren't women supposed to make the rules on this planet? If he were my husband and I didn't want to see him, you'd keep him away."

"That's true," Daunet responded in a tone meant to soothe, "but he *isn't* your husband. He's your mate. And he hasn't done anything to threaten your safety. I've already upset the Goddess by lying about matehood. I won't do it again by keeping you two apart."

Meg's eyes widened. "Is that why you've been so quick to be on his side?" A sour taste invaded her mouth, knowing Daunet's decisions were based on yet another higher power who had more of a say in her life than she did.

Daunet only smiled at her helplessly. "Meg, you're being stubborn. You told the Queen that you'd accept your mate if someone recognized you."

Meg knew, *well, that was when I was sure no one would recognize me*, wasn't a mature response, so she held it back. "I'm not *not* accepting him. I just need time to sort my thoughts. Alone. I can't do that with him setting up camp in the hallway outside my room. All you have to do is not tell him where we're going next. He can't follow the cruisers if we put their shields up."

"I don't understand." Daunet shook her head. "You act like finding your mate is the worst curse in the world. Maxu is rough around the edges, but if he's anything like his family, then he's a good male. Give him a chance."

Meg's pulse buzzed in her ears. *He's a good kid. He'll make a good father. Give him a chance.*

She'd heard these arguments before. Her throat constricted around a lump. No one was on her side, and that was what really hurt and terrified her more than anything else. She'd come to this world free, thinking she finally had a say in her own life.

As it turned out, that freedom was just an illusion. Tears sprung to her eyes, and she bit down on her lip, trying to reclaim her composure.

"Meg…" Daunet's eyebrows furrowed. "It's really not as bad as all this. I think you'll like Maxu once you get to know him."

Meg sank into a chair. She held Daunet's stare. "I know. But…I don't want to like him."

Her friend cocked her head in confusion.

It was time for Meg to come clean. "There's something I haven't told you about my life on Earth."

The weariness slumping Daunet's shoulders vanished, and she straightened. "What do you mean?"

Meg explained everything. Her family, Jeremy, how she'd been bullied into a marriage once in her life already and how the sudden appearance of Maxu paired with the shame being heaped on her by all the Clecanians had brought back all the emotions she'd believed she'd successfully suppressed.

By the time Meg was done explaining her life on Earth, she was dizzy and the fabric of her red dress was covered in dark wet splotches from her tears.

"You have a husband on Earth?" Daunet's eyes widened. "That's why you've never been interested in returning."

"It's been over nine months. I *had* a husband. He probably moved on a week after I went missing." Meg sniffed.

Sympathy shone from Daunet, but she also appeared conflicted. "Meg, I understand now where you're coming from and my heart aches for the position you've been put in, but I don't know what can be done. Do you really want me to send Maxu away? He'll suffer—you know that. He didn't ask for this either."

"I know, I know. I just need some time." Meg rushed forward and knelt in front of Daunet. "You haven't told him where we're going next, have you?"

"No," she grunted.

"So, just don't tell him. We're supposed to be in Adenelas for three days. Just give me those three days alone. And then you can contact him and tell him where the next city is. I'll have a plan by then." Meg held her breath. Hope floated in her like a rain cloud ready to burst at any moment.

Daunet stared, a deep crease appearing between her brows. "He won't let you go with us unless he knows what our next stop is. You know that. I'm positive he'll insist on riding with us, and I have no good reason to give as to why he shouldn't. The other guards will insist as well. Unless..." She gave her a defeated look. "You could tell them what you told me. They might have more understanding if they knew."

"No." Meg shook her head. She didn't want anyone's pity. She hadn't wanted to tell Daunet either, but she hadn't seen another choice. As much as she could, she wanted her shitty past to stay in the past. She lowered to sit on her knees and wracked her brain. How could they leave without Maxu knowing?

An idea formed in her mind. She winced toward Daunet, but it was all for show. In her heart, she was rather excited to see this plan through.

***

Maxu tugged Meg's pillow under his head and smiled. She wasn't exactly pleased with him at the moment, yet he couldn't help but feel a mild rush of satisfaction. His mate was close by. They'd be headed out to a new city tomorrow. And he'd have all the time he needed to slowly win her over.

It was true they'd clashed a bit. Like him, she had a hot temper, but he only felt that would translate into passion when he finally made her fall for him. A long night and half a day of sleep had worked wonders for his clarity.

He'd awoken with Rita's words fresh in his mind. He'd cleaned himself up until he was polished enough to be nearly unrecognizable and set out to win his female.

Though there'd been a few missteps at the party, he was rather proud of the amount of control he'd exercised. He hadn't murdered the man who'd insulted her, even though he'd wanted to. And when he'd carried her back to her room, he hadn't pushed his way inside, though he suspected she would've allowed it if he'd tried a little harder. Not even she could say she wasn't physically attracted to him. There was no disguising it.

Her affection and acceptance would come in time. He didn't doubt it.

A knock rang from his door. His instinct was to frown, but after one sniff of the air, the grin spreading across his face had his cheeks hurting from lack of use.

Maxu leapt across the room and waited for the door to slide aside.

There she stood, still clad in that red dress but with bare feet. He grinned. "Told you you wouldn't be able to stay away."

She shot him a tight smile. "I thought we could try talking again."

It wasn't at the top of his priority list, but if it equaled time near her, he'd take it. "Alright." Maxu stepped aside, but she didn't enter immediately.

A hint of worry filled her gaze. Was she worried about being alone with him in his room? He took a few steps back so she wouldn't feel crowded.

"Sorry about this." She winced. From behind her back, she produced a Pearl Temple guard's tranquilizer gun. Before Maxu could react, a click and whistle sounded and a sharp pain jabbed him in the thigh.

He swiped at the small dart.

"Did you...?" His words slurred as they left his lips. Fury erupted through him, and he lunged for her before collapsing onto his face.

12

There was no other word to describe Adenelas but stunning. White sandy beaches and turquoise ocean for as far as the eye could see. Meg was in an exceptionally good mood today. For one thing, the weather was hot yet dry, with the perfect amount of soft breeze rolling in off the water. For another, the people of Adenelas were so open and welcoming, none of them knowing the drama that had taken place in Vondale.

She'd been scrubbed, buffed, wrapped in layers of voluminous, airy white fabric, and was now staring at the ocean and scrunching sand between her toes. The small twinge of guilt she felt at having tranqued Maxu couldn't compare to the lightness her temporary freedom brought her.

Something about reclaiming a modicum of control had felt soooo good. Like finally finding that one piece of proof that allowed you to win an argument you'd been in for hours. Shooting him hadn't been the healthiest way to deal with her issues, she could admit that—but damn, had it felt good to take control.

The other humans had known something was up. Her Cheshire grin had given them hints enough, but she waited until they were all safely on their way to Adenelas before revealing that she'd tricked him into staying behind. She didn't reveal how, though. Daunet was the only one who knew, and though she'd been on board last night, she seemed regretful today. Meg couldn't bring herself to feel too bad.

They'd just emerged from the first round of interviews and were heading toward their housing's eatery. Meg hummed "I'm Walking on Sunshine."

"You know he's gonna be furious when he finds you again," Tara warned while smoothing her wet hair. She'd seized the opportunity to jump into the ocean the first moment she could.

Daunet had been chastising Meg for not having a plan two hours after arriving in the city, but the image of Tara emerging from the water wet and sparkling had rendered her guard a wistful puddle.

"What's he gonna do?" Meg grinned as they caught up to Camille, Lucy, Sophia, and Rita. "Barge into a party and claim his ownership? Oh, wait, he already did that."

"True," Tara muttered, unconvinced.

"Look," Meg started, "it's not permanent. I know he'll catch up and I'll have to deal with his wrath, but for now all I want to do is concentrate on having fun. We're free for the night since they're not having a party, there's a gorgeous beach just waiting for a group of humans to sit and drink on, and I don't have to even *think* about that pompous ass for the next three days."

They rounded the corner to the eatery, and Meg tripped over her feet. Sitting in the center of the room, legs extended on the table while he relaxed back against his chair, was Maxu, looking as carefree as a person could.

"Uh-oh," Sophia muttered.

Meg's shock was slowly replaced by steam. He was dressed in a thin, clingy shirt, light pants, and was holding a screen in front of him. Reading, as if he'd been here on vacation for weeks. He didn't even glance up as they entered, apparently too enthralled with whatever he was reading to be bothered.

"What are you doing here?" she hissed as she stomped over to his table. A few nearby patrons shot looks toward her.

Without glancing up, Maxu grinned. "I'm researching the human clitoris."

His cheerful announcement was loud enough for the whole restaurant to hear. Meg's brain short-circuited.

She was frozen in place for only a moment more before the snickering of her friends floated to her. Maxu relaxed his shoulders and resumed reading. Meg couldn't even imagine how red she must've been at that moment. Her skin burned from embarrassment. The stares of everyone in the room were heavy on her.

How had he found her? And with enough time to lounge around like this? Her eyes narrowed. *Daunet.* Fists clenched, she spun and charged toward the small group of guards who'd been following at a respectable distance. Rather than stopping to have it out with a wide-eyed Daunet, she flew past, spitting mad. "I can't believe you."

Meg had only taken a few steps in the direction of her quaint, beautiful, lonely room when she halted. Why was she running again? Why did she have to go and hide away from the rest of the world when that was the opposite of what she wanted? *He* should be the one to leave.

Fat chance of that.

Strangely enough, she peeked over her shoulder and found he wasn't following her. He'd been here for who knew how long, yet he hadn't approached her or sought her out. Maybe this was his way of giving her space? Maybe he wouldn't talk to her if she just ignored him.

She could feel all eyes on her as she walked back into the eatery and joined her friends at a lacquered flat surface that looked like it'd been ripped off the largest piece of coral she'd ever seen and repurposed into an irregular table.

The word clitoris floated toward her from somewhere nearby, and heat spread over her face once more.

With a careful half smile, Camille shrugged. "At least he's not mad."

Meg forced a grin, letting her gaze fall everywhere except on the one spot it wanted to. The other women exchanged concerned looks, which she also ignored. From the ceiling a cylindrical food synthesizer lowered, and the women took their turns typing in their orders—or rather, they took turns telling Meg what they wanted and she typed in their orders, since none of them had remembered their translation glasses.

Sophia, Rita, Tara, Camille, and Lucy ruminated on the interview they'd just left and chatted happily about this and that. Meg listened since she was a lousy conversationalist at the moment. She tried to follow along, laughing at appropriate spots and nodding at others, but Maxu was like a damn beacon in the room and her gaze threatened to land on him whenever she let her guard down.

More frustrating than that, he seemed to not notice her, still immersed in his reading. She brooded on that for a moment. *Pfft. Researching the human clitoris,* she grumbled to herself. He had attempted to embarrass her with that little announcement. Payback of his own for her unceremonious escape. He probably wasn't even reading about that.

Meg discreetly studied him under her lashes, ready to glance away at any second. He was gorgeous again, of course. As if nothing had even happened last night. She'd worried he'd broken his nose when he'd fallen. The boom of him hitting the floor had made remorse flare in her until she'd rolled him over and found him to be perfectly intact.

She hadn't wanted for things to go that way. Hadn't wanted to shoot her new mate in the leg. But what choice had she had? She hadn't gotten anywhere in life by asking, so now she was a woman of action.

Looking at him now, she might've thought he'd fallen directly into a mud mask among a pile of pillows. His shirt was crafted from a light fabric that rested against his muscled torso so perfectly she could make out every hard bit of him. It had no sleeves, so she could also see his thick arms and the white birthmarks running over his skin like opalescent tattoos. When the markings reached his wrist, they started shifting from bright white to blue.

The mating marks curled over his knuckles and fingers, taunting her with their beauty. The delicate designs somehow complemented his strong hands. Meg bit her lip. Big hands. Big arms too. She was preoccupied with examining the veins running over his forearms when she noticed he was staring at her.

She jerked her gaze away, reaching for her glass and knocking it over. "Fuck balls," she cursed under her breath as the women gathered napkins to clean up the spill. When a large, white cloth appeared, dangling in the center of the table, she didn't have to look up to know who was holding it.

Meg hesitated, her spine stiff, but when the drip drip drip of her drink hitting the floor echoed in her ears like a drum, she snatched the cloth from his hand and mopped up the rest of her mess.

"I'd like to speak with my mate, if you are all finished eating."

The splat of the wet cloth hitting the table preceded Meg shooting up from her chair. "Alright, guys. I'm all done. Are you? Let's go."

"Sit down, Meg, or I'll plant you on my lap and hold you there."

Meg leveled him with a glare. The women all rose slowly, not sure whether to leave *with* Meg or leave so Meg could talk to Maxu, but knowing with certainty it was time to leave.

Annoyance soured her insides. He could have just asked her to speak. Maybe she would have agreed if he'd been even a little pleasant about it, but now?

Meg rushed away from the table, hoping to call his bluff. She hadn't made it halfway across the room before muscular arms were wrapped around her torso from behind and she was being hauled over to a smaller table on the outskirts of the room.

The patrons of the eatery stared as though this were entertaining. Maxu settled on a bench placed within an enormous shell, and just as he'd promised, she was forced onto his lap.

"Don't test me, vahpti. I do what I say."

Her friends approached the table, drawing even more attention. Heat crawled to the tips of her ears. Between gritted teeth, she hissed out, "Fine. I'll talk to you. Let me go."

To her surprise, he did—and quickly too. Maxu stood, lifting them both, set her on her feet, then crossed to the other side of the table and relaxed into the large domed shell bench identical to hers.

He sent a glare toward her friends waiting nearby, and it warmed her to witness them scowl right back.

Meg gave them a thankful smile. "Meet you at the beach soon."

Once her friends had left, she asked "Did Daunet tell you where I'd be?" She darted another frown toward her guard, who didn't notice as she was preoccupied with Tara. If she weren't so pissed, Meg might've thought Daunet's deer-in-headlights expression as Tara spoke to her was cute.

"No," Maxu said.

She turned her glower on him instead. "Then who?"

The table's dedicated food synthesizer lowered from the ceiling, blocking their silent eye contact, and Maxu punched in a few commands. Without a word to her, he passed her a plate of bright seafood, a pair of delicately patterned ivory eating gloves, and a tall glass of something clear. It could've been water, but she'd been fooled before by drinks that looked strikingly similar to water.

When the column raised back into the ceiling, Meg eyed him with a lifted brow. "I'm not hungry."

His expression remained stony. "You didn't eat your food before."

So he *had* been watching her a minute ago. Just much more covertly than she'd watched him. "Being stalked from city to city makes me lose my appetite."

Maxu shrugged and pulled her plate toward him with a grin. "Well, stalking makes me rather hungry. We're a perfect pair." He popped a piece of spiny fish into his mouth with a crunch, foregoing the gloves which were much too tiny for his hands anyway.

She fiddled with the anemone-style design spanning the palm of one glove. *Ignore. Ignore. Make him so annoyed with you he won't want to spend time with you.*

Maxu let out a slow breath, a muscle ticking in his jaw. She could see that temper flaring under the surface again. "Tell me about your life on Earth."

She couldn't help but let out a chuckle. The question was just so out of place. As if they were on a normal date. A date she'd attended willingly. *I've never been on a real date,* she reminded herself. Dates with Jeremy had always felt more like family outings. Quiet, awkward affairs where one or both of them were on their phones and he criticized how many drinks she ordered.

Under different circumstances, was Maxu the kind of man to orchestrate a romantic date? Pick her up, bring her flowers, take her to a nice restaurant where they could get to know each other better while gentle candlelight set the mood? An odd, nervous tingle crept between her shoulders. She took a sip of the water and choked, nearly spitting it out. It *was* water this time. Salt water.

She wanted to ask why he'd given her a cup of ocean or criticize him for acting as if they'd both agreed to sit here and get to know each other, but talking would ruin her plan to make him frustrated enough to leave her alone, so she went back to toying with the fingers of the eating glove silently.

"You will talk to me without all this…" He swept a hand over her. "…hostility."

Her mouth dropped open, argumentative words ready to fly free, but she slammed it shut before they could get out.

Maxu's broad shoulders hit the back of his shell seating alcove as he leaned away, crunched on another bit of seafood, and studied her tight lips. "You'll talk to me—because if you do, I'll leave you alone for the rest of the day."

Meg crossed her arms. How could she stay silent with an offer like that on the table? "Really? You won't follow me around?"

The patronizing sigh Maxu released made Meg want to walk away right then, but she knew he'd just pull her back. "I'll still be here, but…I'll do my best not to approach you."

"Do your best—"

Maxu ground his jaw. "This is fair, Meg. You're my mate. I don't have to make these exceptions. I could drag you back to my home and no one would blame me, but I'm trying to compromise."

"How romantic," she drawled. "You really know how to make a girl feel special."

"I won't offer again," he snapped.

"How long?"

Maxu glanced through the wide, arched entrance to the eatery where the waves could be seen rolling back and forth over the soft sand. "Until the tide hits that boulder." He pointed toward a sparkling white rock made of a material similar to quartz.

She could survive until then, couldn't she? An hour maybe? He was her mate, suffocating though the fact might've been, and eventually she'd have to spend more time with him. "Fine."

"Earth. What was your life there like?"

Shit. Now she'd have to make something up. She hadn't planned to have a truly honest conversation with Maxu. How could she? Her mate had throat-punched a man for vaguely insulting her not a day ago. What would he do if he found out she already had a husband back home?

Maxu couldn't find out about Jeremy for no other reason than Jeremy's safety. Her human husband hadn't been the best, but he hadn't been the worst either. He didn't deserve to be maimed by a homicidal alien when travel to her planet was finally legal.

"I...was a home decorator." Well, she was...kinda. Maybe not professionally, but she'd shined her turd of a house into something admirable and had enjoyed doing it.

Maxu narrowed his eyes. "That was your job?"

Does he know I'm lying? He looks like he knows. But how could he? Meg stilled her bouncing leg with a palm to her knee. "Mm-hmm." Damn, why didn't this guy blink? Was he trying to stare into her soul? Wait…could he? Some races on the planet had special abilities, but she couldn't recall any who could read minds.

He rested his elbows on the table, leaning toward her in a move that was meant to be casual yet felt anything but. The sharp cut of his jaw looked extra appetizing when he tilted his head like that. Meg tried not to notice. "How long did you do that for?"

"Five years." She held eye contact.

"Lie." The word was hard and devoid of emotion. "Did you enjoy your job?"

"Yes," Meg breathed out. Her knee was hot from where her sweaty palm rested against it. Why did she suddenly feel like she was hiding a body under the table?

"Lie." Maxu didn't even seem phased by the idea he was being lied to.

Meg scrambled. Did she have a tell she didn't know about? She took another sip of water to stall before remembering it was pure salt. This time she did spit it out. Luckily, she was able to catch it with one of the eating gloves.

"Do you miss Earth?" Maxu asked as he called down the food synthesizer and produced two new drinks. He handed one to Meg, and she eyed it warily.

Heck no, she didn't miss Earth. But she couldn't say that. He'd want to know why. What kind of person who was abducted and plopped on another planet without the hope of ever seeing their family again wouldn't miss their home? "Yes, I miss it."

"Our time won't end until you speak to me honestly, vahpti."

All her instincts told Meg to capitulate, to behave, but then that nickname stuck in her mind. *Vahpti.* He'd called her that the first night they'd met. Her translator identified it as some kind of insect. When she'd gotten back to her room, she'd dug a little deeper.

Vahpti were tiny gnat-like bugs who flew in little swarms and sought out small, dark areas to keep warm in cold climates. Ear cavities were a particular favorite.

Meg was an annoying buzz in his head. She supposed that was fair. After all, she'd likened Maxu to a tumor. Regardless, the word struck a sensitive chord.

She'd been a vahpti to Jeremy and her family. An annoying pest flitting around and buzzing in their ears. Was that all Maxu thought of her too? Why did that make her so…sad? It wasn't like she'd given him much reason to feel differently.

"What did you really do back on Earth?" His gaze was expressionless, but his blue-green eyes were sharp, probing.

Meg wasn't that lonely girl from Indiana anymore. She'd changed. She'd made sure of it. Her hair, her clothes, her comfort zones. Talking about the person she used to be was not only counterintuitive to her mission of leaving the past behind…it was painful.

She took an experimental sniff of the drink he'd selected for her and wrinkled her nose. The strong liquor reminded her of Pine-Sol. She took a substantial gulp anyway.

"Maxu, the *real* truth is I don't want to talk about Earth. I'm not ready to share those kinds of things with you."

His chin lifted at that. Meg studied him and arrived at a loss. He gave nothing away. How could someone who'd displayed their emotions so violently for the last few days also have the ability to hide them so successfully?

Maybe he wasn't hiding them. Maybe he truly felt nothing in this moment.

***

A thousand questions swam through Maxu's mind. His mate was a puzzle he couldn't solve. He'd never encountered anything more vexing. Why had she lied about something so innocuous? Why had her whole demeanor shifted when he'd called out the lie? And where the fuck had the dejected sadness dimming her blue eyes come from?

She fiddled with the glove in front of her while Maxu attempted to mask the frustration building in him. How was he supposed to learn about his mate, like Rita had suggested, if she wouldn't talk to him? And why did it make him so damn upset that his mate didn't *want* to reveal all her troubles to him?

He wasn't the kind of male to care about such things. It was true he had possessive inclinations he couldn't quite control, but never before had he wanted to possess someone's trust, their vulnerabilities. He'd never felt the pull to comfort or be comforted in return. He hated it, this fragility.

She spun the drink he'd gotten her on the table. At first, he'd ordered her the preferred beverage of the Adenelas people as a trick, something to appease the bit of ego she'd damaged last night. But the second time he'd gotten her a drink, he'd actually attempted to select something she might like. Though there was no reason it should, it grated to know he'd picked wrong. As if he was still failing her.

She winced as she took another gulp, forcing the liquid down. He laced his fingers together to keep from calling down the synthesizer and ordering her one of every beverage available so he could discover which she preferred.

Meg broke the silence first. "What do *you* do for work?"

His fingertips tightened where they were twined. "I'm mostly retired. I used to work as a mercenary." His job had always been a source of pride for Maxu. His eldest brother, Theo, had moved into mercenary work when Maxu had still been in husbandry school and had helped him gain contacts early in his career. Maxu had excelled and now only took side jobs that interested him when life became dull. He'd been accepting more and more jobs before Meg had crashed into his every waking thought.

"What does that mean, exactly?" She tipped her head at him. "Do you do illegal things? Is that why you were locked up before?"

Maxu's shoulders straightened at that. Was there judgment in her voice? Or was he imagining it? "I chose to be locked up."

Her brows furrowed. "Who'd *choose* that?"

"Someone who doesn't want to take part in the marriage ceremony and knows that having a recent incarceration on their record is the only way to get out of it." The terse bite to his words had her mouth curling into a frown.

"Why don't you want to participate in the marriage ceremony? Aren't most guys dying to be picked?" Her tone had tightened in response to his, the temporary amicable conversation they'd been having threatening to turn sour again. He might be able to recover it with his next words, but he was defensive and pushing her back to a combative state felt far safer than explaining the truth. That he hated being judged and tested.

He couldn't open himself up and explain that since his parents had had six healthy children—a miracle five times over—he'd been raised with the knowledge females wanted him mainly because he had more potential to father children.

He let his temper take over, and though he knew he'd regret not trying harder in the long run, the immediate sense of his guard being raised was a relief. "It may surprise you to know that not all males want a wife to bow down to for three months."

"I didn't say *all males*. I said most guys. And sorry if you chasing me across the world and claiming I was yours forever gave me the false impression that you actually wanted to have a relationship with a woman," Meg snapped back.

Maxu relished the fire warming her gaze. Fighting was familiar. Easy. "A *marriage* is not a relationship. It's a test. I have no interest in being tested and judged."

"Oh, right? That's why you announced to the entire room that you were studying up on the human…" Meg had been leaning forward, immersed in their sparring, but her words faded out as if she hadn't meant to say the thought aloud.

He'd assumed his announcement might've been mildly embarrassing, but he hadn't predicted she'd be this shy about such a thing. Maxu smirked as red spread over her cheeks. She avoided his gaze, taking another pained drink. How wickedly adorable.

"I was just curious how a human could find pleasure with something so soft," he rumbled, leaning forward even more.

Her fingertips on her glass tightened, her body going still. Meg squinted up at him. "What are you talking about?"

"A Clecanian female's pleasure center is deep inside. They need long…instruments"—he continued, grinning at the blush traveling to the tips of her ears and down her chest—"to reach their orgasm. But when I was searching your old rooms to find you, I noticed you only needed a pillow. So I researched why that might be."

Meg's eyes were wide and horrified, her skin growing redder by the second. He didn't quite understand why this topic made her so uncomfortable. Were humans one of those prudish species? Or was his mate particularly shy about such things? Either way, he was enjoying teasing her immensely.

"You...you found...? How...?" Her mouth closed, and she swallowed. "That is such a violation, and it's none of your business how I..."

Her gaze darted to the ocean and locked on the still-exposed boulder. He only had a few more minutes before the rising tide reached it.

"I'd argue that as your mate, it very much *is* my business. I believe I understand how it works now, though I'm going to inspect the pillow again later to make sure I can picture the process."

As intended, Meg's eyes flew to his. How far down could he make that flush spread? If he was shocking enough, would it reach her nipples?

"What are you talking about? Inspect what pillow?" Her words were hushed. She scanned the room, ensuring no one was listening in.

"Your pillow." He grinned, not matching her low voice in the slightest. "From Kitibard."

Her thunderstruck expression held for only a moment before her lip curled. "You kept it, you freak? Why would you... It doesn't matter. Give it back."

Maxu tipped his head back and forth, making a show of considering her demand. "No. I've grown quite fond of it."

"Give. It. Back," she whisper-shouted. "It's not yours."

"Well, to be fair, it's not yours either. It belonged to the Kitibardians, and then I stole it. Really, it's mine now." Maxu rose from his seat and tipped his head toward the water as it splashed across the pale white boulder. "Looks like our time's up. I'll leave you alone for the rest of the day. I think I'll head back to my room to...rest."

Meg's mouth was hanging open as Maxu turned to walk away. After a moment of stunned silence, he heard her scramble out of her seat. Unfortunately, she didn't follow him, instead bolting toward her guard, but he didn't mind. Meg would seek him out eventually if only to tell him off once she regained her composure, and he couldn't wait to see how she'd retaliate.

13

∽

Meg slid into a short yellow dress and ran her palms over her hair and the frizz that had sprouted in the humid weather.

A headache was building in her temple from the harsh clench her jaw had been set in since leaving the eatery. He had her pillow. One of the ones she'd...

She still cringed with embarrassment every time she thought about it, though she knew she shouldn't. It was a perfectly natural thing for a person to do. Women were sexual creatures, and she should feel no shame.

But even after Maxu had sauntered away and she'd stomped up to Daunet, intent on filling her in on the situation and asking her to force Maxu to give the pillow back, the words had stuck in her throat. In order to ask for Daunet's help, she'd need to explain...everything.

Masturbation wasn't something she'd ever talked openly about. Sex had warranted conversations with her mother since it was something a married couple did *together*, but when you were alone? That wasn't something she'd heard discussed outside of a handful of scandalous conversations with girls at her school and a woefully unenlightening Sex Ed class.

The few conversations she'd had with Jeremy about it were no better. Early in their marriage, when she was still full of hope for her life with her husband, she'd asked him whether he ever jerked off when she wasn't around.

He'd blustered about, assuring her he'd never disrespect her in that way and how she was more than enough for him. When he'd turned the question back on her, she'd felt trapped. Would admitting she touched herself when she was alone make him think he wasn't enough? Did it mean she was being unfaithful?

Hiding and finding pleasure by herself had become so personal, so private, and so dear to her that having Maxu comment on it as if it were nothing was making her brain go haywire.

Meg straightened her dress in the mirror and frowned at the damn heat glowing red on her cheeks. She was an excessive blusher. Always had been. She hated it. And when she knew she was blushing, it only made her more embarrassed and in turn blush more. And it wasn't a cute pinkening of the apples of her cheeks. It was a full red face.

The mid-length sleeves of her dress had her searching the room for temperature controls, so she slipped it off. Another reason she hated blushing—it was always accompanied by sweating for her. *Sooo not attractive.*

Meg pulled on a skimpier sky-blue dress and tore herself away from the bathroom. She was only going to the beach. There was no need for five more outfit changes.

"Will you just tell me what's wrong?" Daunet asked from a chair that looked like it got stuck halfway between morphing into a beanbag.

"Nothing, nothing. He was just trying to embarrass me. He succeeded, but I'm fine." If she thought Daunet would actually help her get her pillow back, she might've found the courage to explain the situation, but most Clecanians were so much freer with things relating to sex. Daunet probably wouldn't think it was a big deal. And she certainly wouldn't help her break into someone's room because of something so silly.

"I still don't know how he learned where we'd be," Daunet assured once again.

Meg gave her a smile. Her guard had been making a great effort to prove she wasn't the one who'd leaked their location.

"I know. It was probably Gamso. He's been giving me the stink eye since we left Vondale. I bet he sent a message back, telling Maxu where we'd be."

Daunet gazed into space, a skeptical wrinkle to her nose. "Possibly." Her attention shifted back to Meg, who hovered near the door. "I could speak to Maxu. Maybe help him understand your needs."

"No, that's alright," she rushed out. *Apparently he understands my* needs *just fine.* "Besides, if you're going to be speaking to anybody, it should probably be Tara, don't you think?"

Daunet's gaze bounced around the room. "I don't have anything to talk to her about," she said, avoiding Meg's eyes and rising to her feet.

Meg laughed. "Is that because you swallow your tongue every time she tries to talk to you? Why don't you just tell her you like her?"

"I can't, or…I won't. Not until this tour is over. It would be unprofessional."

"Unprofessional to talk to her?" Meg prodded, enjoying the shift in conversation.

"No, but I want to do more than talk to her, and I know that feeling will only grow stronger the more I get to know her. It would be best to wait. Then I can present myself more favorably."

"I don't get what the big deal is."

Pursing her lips, Daunet joined Meg, and they strode out of the room toward the beach. "The big deal?" Daunet arched a brow. "There are very few females on our planet, and of those females, a minuscule amount are attracted to other females. And of those, an even smaller amount are solely attracted to females. Many of my fellow guards already believe I should be working with the implantation center, trying to get pregnant since I won't be taking part in any marriages. I'm not going to give them any more reason to think I'm unsuited for my role by flirting with a human when I'm supposed to be guarding another."

Meg bowed her head, staring at the floor, suddenly ashamed for acting so flippantly. "You're right. I'm sorry I didn't think about that. I know most women feel all this pressure to be married and reproduce, but I just assumed…"

"You assumed that because I wasn't forced into marriages with males that there weren't other expectations placed on me. We all have our duty, and we all must decide how much of ourselves we can sacrifice to fulfill those obligations. I worked with the implantation center for a very long time before finally taking a break. I've done what I needed to do, and I may feel like I have to try again at some point, but for now, I like my job. I like protecting the females that are making those sacrifices, and I refuse to give anyone any reason to doubt my abilities."

"I get it. I won't tease you about it anymore." Meg smiled and gave her elbow a nudge. "But you better believe that when this is over and it *is* time to talk to Tara, my jokes will resume."

The corner of Daunet's lips lifted, though she tried to hide it. "As long as you're open to me coming to you for advice on the strange creatures that are humans."

They navigated the spiraling hallways of the building, talking about the days ahead and carefully avoiding the topic of relationships until they were outside. Though it'd just come in less than an hour ago, the tide was already going back out. Something about the season and the two moons forced the ocean to change more often than on Earth. Or so Meg assumed, since she'd never actually been to an ocean on Earth.

As someone who'd only ever swam in lakes, rivers, and pools, the ocean still made her quite nervous. The expanse of it and the hidden currents that could drag you away—not to mention whatever creatures lurked within. There was no part of her that wanted to discover what the alien version of a shark looked like. No, she was content sitting on the sand and letting the sound of crashing water lull her into tranquility.

The voice inside that had started to feel more nagging than aspirational argued that *new* Meg would go swimming. She was so free with her body that she'd probably go naked like the Adenelese too.

Constantly pushing herself past her comfort zones was growing exhausting.

Odd indentations of varying sizes were strewn across the beach. They were concave, reminding her of the craters on Earth's moon. Inside some depressions was a cushioned floor, perfect for lying around and sunbathing. Others had tables and chairs. And a few low ones closest to the ocean were even filled with the warm water that had been left behind from the tide.

She caught sight of a crater raised slightly higher than the others, and though she couldn't yet see who was inside, she knew exactly who it had to be. Nirato, Uthen, and Heleax circled the crater, guarding the humans inside but ironically looking like sharks.

When Meg reached the stairs and joined the other humans, Daunet took her break, heading for the eatery. Though Meg understood that the guards were there to do a job, she sometimes still felt bad. They were in this beautiful place, lounging at the beach, yet her Clecanian friends had to work.

The women gave lazy hellos as she collapsed onto the soft floor. She scanned the sandy beach as if merely scoping the area, but really she was looking for one dark-haired masterpiece. He'd said he'd leave her alone, but she wouldn't put it past him to lurk.

What would Maxu wear to go swimming? She squinted, searching a little harder.

"We haven't seen him," Sophia interrupted Meg's casual, not-so-casual survey of the beach.

Meg was about to ask, "Haven't seen who?" in her most spot-on impression of a nonchalant person when she caught the knowing stares of her travel buddies. Her shoulders dropped, and she groaned. "This is like a disease, I swear. Why am I even looking for him?" Meg waved her hand in the air. "How can I be so annoyed every second that I'm with him and still want to see him go for a swim?"

"Any straight woman with a libido would like to see that man go for a swim," Lucy murmured, one hand draped over her eyes.

Meg grabbed what passed for sunglasses on Clecania. An object shaped like a headband that sat horizontally across your forehead. When it was activated, a holographic shield lowered over your eyes like a garage door coming down.

"Where's Rita?" she asked.

"Oh, she went back to change. Said she wanted to do some yoga on the beach."

"What have you guys been up to?" Meg asked as she pulled out her reading pad, curious to learn more about these odd craters.

"Relaxing. Those guys came over and flirted a little." Lucy pointed to a smaller crater where two men sat, peering in their direction every so often. Their warm, light purple skin, spotted with brown designs, covered broad shoulders and tapered waists; the men had the most fantastic examples of a swimmer's build that Meg had ever seen. "Everyone was told they were allowed to come and meet us one by one, but not many have come over here."

Meg nodded. "Yeah, that makes sense. I read that beach time is a very special bonding experience for the Adenelese. Like family time on Earth. It's generally considered rude to barge in on other groups. I'm surprised they came over at all. Were they nice?"

"Yeah, really nice, but I'm kind of over it." Camille turned onto her belly so she could grin at Meg. "Remember that guy that we were talking to back in Vondale who said that line about my eyes looking like his favorite flower?"

Meg chuckled, "Yeah."

"Well, it wasn't bullshit." Camille's smile widened. "He took me to this crazy garden on the top level of the building, and sure enough, there were these gorgeous brown flowers growing over the rocks of this waterfall fountain thing."

Meg's brows knit. She sighed. "That's so cute."

"I know! Totally unexpected. He's been sending me holo-messages since we left. I might be into him."

"That's awesome." Meg tried to keep her grin genuine, but a small ounce of jealousy made it hard.

Someone sweet. Someone who gave her compliments and found flowers that matched her eyes and sent her romantic messages. That was what she wanted. Instead, she'd ended up with a temperamental demigod who did little more than growl at her, issue commands, steal her sex toys, and plow through every boundary she erected.

"What are you gonna do?" Meg asked.

Camille shrugged. She piled her coily dark brown hair into a bun, stretched out, and dropped her chin onto her crossed hands. "See where it goes for now, I guess. I've never talked to a guy like that. He wanted to know everything, and he didn't even try to take me back to his room or ask to come to mine."

"Well, if you do ever fool around with him, just get your bites healed quickly. Mine were so itchy on the ride this morning. I was mad at myself for not waking up early and going to the doctor to get them healed."

All eyes turned to Sophia. Out of all of them—with maybe the exception of Rita when she lost herself in her head—Sophia was the quietest. The most sensitive. So hearing she'd let one of the fanged Vondalese bite her was more shocking than if Lucy had shown up in sweats with last night's makeup on.

"What?" Tara asked, a wide grin spreading over her face. "You've turned down everyone who's flirted so far. Why this guy?"

Sophia bit her lip, grinning back. Clearly, she'd been waiting to divulge this for a while now. She gave a tiny coquettish shrug. "What can I say? Back home I was really into vampires. I even had a…" She reached for her bicep, and her grin fell instantly.

Meg leaned forward, placing a hand on Sophia's arm. The other women stiffened as well. "A tattoo?"

"Yeah," Sophia smiled sadly. "A really rad design of Nosferatu I drew."

"That's so fucked up," Camille whispered under her breath.

None of the women liked to talk about their abductions. Some, like Camille and Sophia, didn't even remember it. They'd been stolen from Earth and kept in sleep pods until the Insurgent bunkers had been discovered and raided.

Apparently Sophia had been covered in tattoos on Earth. As an artist and graphic designer, she'd taken pride in designing most of them herself.

Whoever had taken Sophia had registered the tattoos as scars when they'd scanned and healed her. When she'd woken up, it was to find herself on an alien planet, her skin clear. Meg still remembered how hard it'd been for Sophia, for her mental health.

"It's alright," Sophia said, brightening. "I've come to terms with it, mostly. It's one of the reasons I wanted to go on this tour. I want to feel inspired again. I know there are a few cities here where tattooing is common, and I'm excited to see how it's done. Maybe I'll even be able to tattoo some marks on my hands if I'm ever recognized."

"You know what would be cool?" Camille pointed to her neck. "If you got two little puncture wounds on your neck here. You know, for your love of vamps and to commemorate the night you popped your fang cherry."

Sophia's eyes widened with excitement. "That is such an amazing idea! I'm totally doing that."

"Did it hurt?" Lucy propped herself on her arms behind her, soaking up the sun.

Sophia shook her head very slowly, her coy grin reemerging. "Nope."

They all laughed.

"I can't even imagine that. To be honest, Rikad's fangs kind of freak me out. I've been bitten by one too many dogs to want that." Camille winced and brushed her hand over the unblemished brown skin of her forearm where Meg assumed scars had once been.

"Oh, that's right. You owned a dog daycare, right?" Tara asked.

Camille nodded with a warm smile, her dimples popping. "Yeah. Barks 'R' Us." She rolled her eyes, and her smile turned mildly annoyed. "I didn't name it. My partner thought it was the funniest thing in the world. He took care of the daycare and grooming side, and I ran all of our training programs." She shook her head with a distant look. "I could whip even the most aggressive dogs into shape like that." She snapped her fingers.

Meg melted against a triangular pillow and listened as the women talked about their lives back on Earth. The good, the bad. What they missed. What they loved about Clecania.

It was wonderful. Diverting. So it took her a while to figure out why her chest had grown so tight. Why there was a frog lodged in her throat as Tara described the ridiculous conversation she'd gotten in with an Adenelese man earlier that day in which she'd tried to describe a Guinea pig.

Each woman was her own person, with her own interests, goals, and flaws. Tara was sarcastic and caring. She loved the outdoors and was the first to notice when someone was upset. But she took on too much, never allowing herself to have as much fun as she wanted everyone else to have.

Camille was intelligent and honest, always willing to look at things from every perspective, but she was also stubborn and a little lost. She'd prided herself on her work. Then "the

Raleigh dog whisperer" had been brought to a planet with no dogs.

Bright, bubbly, and overtly sexual, Lucy lit up every room she walked into, and yet there was a sadness there, something hidden, as if she wanted to make everyone believe she was perfect.

Sophia was quiet and introverted yet had the kind of artistic mind that saw beauty in everything. She tended to retreat into her own head far too often, though, and overanalyzed everything.

And Rita. Meg didn't know if she had the words to describe Rita. The woman seemed like she had answers for everything. Like she knew what life was about. What made her happy and what didn't make her happy, and somehow always existed in a state of perfect equilibrium. The problem was that she could often detach herself from others. Meg supposed it was a way to maintain that equilibrium.

Friends. Meg finally had friends. Friends who weren't picked for her or the people she tried to force herself to like because they were the only ones of her age left in her small hometown. And maybe this tightening in her chest was because she could see them all so well. Their positives and negatives. She could appreciate their personalities and how confident they were in their own ways.

But if they had to describe her, what would they say?

Meg. The girl who doesn't know who she is.

She sometimes felt like Peter Pan, except she'd *wanted* to grow up and just never had. She'd thought she'd known who she wanted to be, but when she imagined someone describing her as the words she'd tried to embody—exciting, sexy, vivacious, spontaneous, wild—they didn't feel right. She had a mounting fear that she was trying to force her square self into a round hole.

Still, she smiled as her friends chatted, hiding the miserable knowledge that they didn't really know her either. How could she feel so full and so hollow at the same time? So excited to be where she was, and so nervous to go back to her room and be alone with herself.

"Wait, what did you do on Earth again, Meg?" Tara asked.

Her throat tightened even more. She shot to her feet while speeding through a nonanswer. "A little of this, a little of that. I hadn't really settled on a career yet."

She squinted up at the sun. Since watches were uncommon in many cities on Clecania, she'd gotten pretty good at figuring out the time by the sun.

"If I had to guess, we have maybe three hours till sunset." And she was going to pull herself out of this internal pity party and have a good time if it killed her. "I'm getting drinks. Who wants one?"

Sophia and Tara raised their hands.

Lucy shook her head. "Not for me, thanks. I don't want to be puffy for tomorrow."

"Maybe in a bit," Camille answered while picking at her nails.

Meg gathered an escort—Nirato—and a floating tray of drinks at the eatery.

When she returned, climbing into the crater, no one turned to look at her. She passed out the drinks, then crawled forward on her knees, curious to see what had captured their attention.

"I can't tell if you're about to be happy or angry," Camille murmured without glancing at her.

"Huh?"

Camille, Lucy, and Tara all pointed to an area farther down the beach, and Meg squinted.

"Oh," she breathed, letting out all the air in her chest. She grasped behind her blindly for her drink, almost knocking it over.

Rita was doing her yoga, happy as could be in a lime-green amorphous piece of billowing clothing. And next to her, following each movement as if he were a celebrity having a private lesson on the Malibu coastline, was a shirtless Maxu.

Slow as could be, Meg lowered into her seat and activated her sunglasses. The warm, salty breeze had grown hotter in the late afternoon, and beads of sweat collected between her shoulder blades as she watched Maxu's glistening, powerful body lower into warrior something or other. "How is he a yoga guy?" Even Meg had never had the patience for yoga.

"Yeah. He read more boxing to me," Lucy commented, one side of her face scrunched up as she stared.

"Do they know each other?" Tara asked over her shoulder. She picked up her own reading pad and turned away from the spectacle making Meg drool.

"Rita was the only human not hanging out here near Meg." Lucy shrugged. "Maybe he's thinking she'll put in a good word or something?"

"Or maybe he's just over there showing off his six-pack 'cause he knows I can see," Meg grunted.

"So you *are* into him." Camille grinned, flipping around to face her.

A moment of confusion washed over Meg. "Did I say that out loud?"

The women all laughed, and some of the tension bunching her shoulders relaxed.

"Look, I never said he wasn't attractive. Obviously he is. From this distance, he's even hotter because I can't hear him bossing me around."

A soft snore echoed from Sophia, fast asleep on her stomach.

"But he's keeping his distance like he said. Doesn't that count for anything?"

"He's just playing nice until he gets what he wants. If I let my guard down—poof, six months will have gone by and I'll be stuck in his house following all the rules he's sneakily incorporated until I have no control left."

All eyes turned to her, curious and concerned. "That's kind of a stretch. Is that a personal example, Meg?" Tara asked.

Crap, she'd said too much. They'd only look at her like a sad little weakling if she explained, though, so she brushed it off. "Just a guess."

They appeared unconvinced, but Lucy moved on anyway. "Yeah, but what are you gonna do? It's not like he's gonna be content standing one hundred feet away forever."

"I don't know," Meg groaned. "I was thinking about it last night, and I wondered if maybe he might be open to some kind of platonic relationship. I did some research and it seems like the mating bond makes you feel like you have to be near the other person and protect them, but that doesn't necessarily mean we have to be romantic. Couldn't we just live in the same house and lead our separate lives?"

"What about sex?" Camille asked. "Don't mated couples feel this intense urge to be with their mate?"

"The text I read was not super clear, but yeah. It was implied," Meg grumbled.

"Do you have something *against* having sex with him?" Lucy asked, tipping her head to the side as Maxu got into a plank, the curves of his abs and the muscles in his forearms all rigid while he held the pose.

"I don't like him. And I don't trust him. He's controlling, and he doesn't really care what I think or how I feel."

Lucy chuckled. "It's been a few days. How do you know if you like him or not or if you could learn to trust him if you refuse to talk to him?"

Maxu and Rita stared at each other, and Rita waved her arms around, trying to explain something. She made a diving movement with her body, and he listened, hands on hips, impressive chest reflecting the sun.

Meg was feeling more and more like a petulant child with each reasonable word out of her friends' mouths. The truth was it was easier to paint him in a certain light. If she hated him, she wouldn't trust him. If she didn't trust him, there was no way he could let her down.

"No." Meg shook her head. "You guys don't understand. I need to be with someone who values my feelings, and after what he pulled today…"

"What did he pull? You mean forcing you to talk to him?" Meg froze. Crap. "Yeah," she lied.

Tara rotated, and Camille's eyes narrowed.

"What else did he do, Meg? You're a terrible liar."

Despite her years of hiding everything she wanted to say and do, Meg was beginning to learn how bad of a liar she was. She'd always thought she was a good liar, dammit. Why hadn't anyone ever told her before?

Her heart clenched a little at the idea that maybe they hadn't told her because they hadn't cared enough to call her out. "It's nothing. I don't want to talk about it."

"Was it bad?" Camille sat up a little straighter.

Tara's playful grin was suddenly replaced by thin lips at Camille's words. "What did he do?" This time, her words weren't curious. They were firm.

Was she going to have to say this? Really? "He..." She peered around the group, already feeling the heat rising on her neck. Meg downed the rest of her drink in one painful gulp. "I used...something...in my room to..." She swallowed. "Show myself a good time...and he...took that thing."

"Huh?" Lucy's brows were furrowed and one side of her mouth curled down.

Camille peered up to the sky and pointed back and forth with her finger, as if attempting to solve a riddle in her head.

Still looking stern rather than angry, Tara's eyes widened in realization first. "Oh."

"Oh?" Camille asked, propping herself up on one arm to peer back at Tara. She took one look at Tara, whose lips had disappeared into her mouth to hide her grin, and whirled toward Meg. "Oh," she repeated in a deeper octave.

Lucy clicked her tongue. "Hello? Fill me in, please?"

Camille flashed her white teeth in a grin. "Meg got freaky with something in her room, and Maxu stole it."

"What?!" Lucy laughed loudly enough that Sophia bolted upright with a gasp.

"What's wrong? What happened?" she croaked, head spinning as she tried to hold open her eyes while they adjusted to the bright sun.

Lucy patted her calf, giggling. "Nothing. Sorry. Go back to sleep. I'll tell you later."

Apparently, Sophia's Vondalese fling had sucked out all her energy because she only grumbled and plopped back down.

"He told you he stole it?" Lucy whispered. Leaning in close. "For what?"

Camille focused on the ground, a line forming on her forehead. "Is that hot? Or creepy? Or is it both?"

"What was the thing? Was there a gift basket somewhere I missed?" Tara joked.

"That's beside the point!" Meg waved her hand and glanced back over to Maxu, who was now holding a perfect handstand. At least he wouldn't see how red she was.

"What do you think he's doing with it?" Camille whispered to Lucy with a scrunched nose, as if they were having a private conversation.

Lucy grinned back. "I think it depends on what it is, no?"

"Focus!" Meg clapped. "Anyway. It seemed like he told me about it just to embarrass me. He doesn't care about my feelings." When the girls still looked unconvinced, Meg tossed her hands up. "He broke into my room and took it without permission! It's…a really serious breach of privacy, and it upset me."

"Okay, okay." Tara used her best calming voice, hands raised ahead of her. "I hear you. And if it's that important, why don't you ask him to give it back?"

"I did," Meg all but yelled. "He said no! He said it was his now."

"I'm leaning toward hot, to be honest," Camille added quite unhelpfully.

"Then, steal it back." Lucy shrugged.

All eyes turned to her. "Steal it?" Meg asked.

"Yeah," she shrugged again. "Clearly you can't play normal games with this guy. Asking didn't work and he doesn't seem too respectful of authority, so it's not like you could get a policeman or something to intervene—not that they would 'cause that makes no sense. So beat him at his own game. Steal it back."

Meg's mind caught on that, lingering for a long time on how delicious it would be to know he'd gotten back to his room to find it missing. She grinned, then faltered. "I've never broken in anywhere. How would I even get into his room?"

"Honey," Lucy started with a devious grin, "take a leaf out of his book. Both cities have now bent over backward to accommodate his requests because he keeps explaining he's your mate, right? Well…" When no one caught on, Lucy rolled her eyes to the sky. "Just tell the housing guy you need your print added to his door. He's your mate. I bet they won't even blink."

Lucy was right. This whole time she'd been approaching this situation like a human. Arguing the way a human would, without ever considering the newfound power she had as a recognized mate.

A small smile played across Meg's lips.

14

The icy wind whipped over Maxu, making him sway back and forth above a hundred-foot drop. The Xeric Tower wasn't the tallest he'd ever climbed, but the blustering wind threatening to toss him off the side of the building ensured his muscles would be stiff tomorrow.

It was exhilarating.

Maxu raised his palm, using a small device he'd affixed to his glove to scan the airspace above, searching for any lingering security measures he hadn't accounted for. *Nothing*—he scoffed.

When the humans had been discovered in Insurgent bunkers across the planet, their rescuers hadn't just found a new compatible species sent directly from the Goddess. They'd also found stores of Earth items. And what had his city done with the valuable alien objects that had once belonged to the abducted humans? Locked them in a secure facility where the rarest of Clecanian treasures were kept and guarded? No. To Maxu's amusement, he'd discovered last night that they'd all been sent to a group of biological and cultural scientists for study.

The idealistic pishots weren't prepared for a break-in by someone like him, and why would they be? From what he could gather, they were studying the chemical compositions of old clothing, mostly.

He braced his feet apart on the narrow ledge, spotting the window the bribed guard had told him would be the best point of entry. Squatting as far as he could, he leapt.

He flew past the window, jumping much higher than he could before, and barely caught a ledge a half story up from where he needed to be. He hung from his fingers, grinning toward the ground below. The mating marks had changed not only his mind but his body as well. He was faster, stronger, and could jump higher than before. Suffice to say, it was taking some getting used to.

Maxu swung from side to side until he had momentum, then released the ledge, dropping onto a beam just above the window. He pressed a machine he'd acquired from an undersea city on the planet of Chado and programmed it to emit the highest amplitude and frequency it could. Within seconds, the glass had shattered, and he swung inside, landing without a sound.

Floor-to-ceiling metal cabinets lined both walls, and he groaned. This would've been much easier if he knew what he was looking for.

Trying it Rita's way hadn't failed *per se*, but it also hadn't worked. Maxu wasn't the kind of person who could have relaxed, open conversations. He wasn't used to revealing information about himself to strangers—especially females, no matter how luscious they were.

So yesterday, as he'd run through Rita's silly exercises—which he'd never admit had actually made him sore in a few spots—they'd brainstormed an alternative approach. Well, he'd brainstormed and she'd tried to push him to speak with Meg again instead. Rita had also claimed that joining her in some prolonged meditation might help calm him.

Ultimately, Maxu had decided his problem was he didn't know enough about humans. Before he could learn more about his mate, he had to learn all he could about her species. The free information listed in the Intergalactic Alliance directory was fine if he wanted to learn about their basic physiology, but when Rita had vaguely mentioned a catalogue many of the humans were contributing to, he'd known it was exactly what he needed.

The only problem? It hadn't been published yet. Troves of valuable information directly from the humans themselves just sitting in a data bank somewhere, waiting for him to steal it.

The trip to the tower had only taken an hour or so. Meg had been wrapped up with the large beach party Adenelas was hosting, so he was sure she was being guarded at least.

And yet the twitches of pain in his stomach were becoming more frequent by the hour, regardless of his logical mind arguing that she was fine. He hated being away from her this long. What if she somehow escaped again?

He checked his communicator and took in a calming breath. His partner in crime was on his side. He was sure of that at the very least. When he'd awoken, bleary and furious after Meg had knocked him out, he'd been about to tear apart his room in a rage when he'd noticed an odd, folded message on his floor.

Using his reading glass to translate the clunky written language, he'd discovered his new accomplice—Rita—had explained where the next stop of the tour was. Given their talk yesterday in Adenelas, she hadn't seemed the least bit regretful of going behind Meg's back.

When he'd asked why, her simple response had been, "You two are like coconuts and pineapples." With a lazy smile at his confusion, she'd added. "Once you get past those tough outer layers, you're both delicious and even tastier together."

Though Maxu didn't know exactly what the fruits Rita mentioned looked like, he had to disagree with the point of her analogy. He'd followed Meg around all day today, and the only person she seemed to don a shell with was him. To everyone else, she was happy, carefree. Though there were a few instances that confused him.

With his heightened hearing, he'd listened to her gush over every detail of the famous Adenelese Dimples, as they were affectionately known to the citizens of Adenelas. But later in the day, when she'd been approached by an older male and he began describing the formation of the craters to her, she didn't interrupt. She'd let him teach her something she already knew, and Maxu couldn't fathom why. The male would have been beyond impressed with her knowledge of his beloved home.

During today's interview, Maxu had also noticed the rigid set to her smile and the way she'd bunched her toes beneath her thin fabric shoes when one citizen had asked her what her family structure had been. Her answer had been innocuous enough—a mother and father who she'd lived with—but the way her eyes had changed had him tying himself in knots.

Keeping his distance annoyed him at first. Why should he stay away from his mate? But when he'd decided to think of his time observing her as recon rather than surrender, their separation became much easier to swallow. He was gathering intel. Instead of discovering the best way to breach a building, he was learning all he could so he could breach the defenses she'd barricaded around herself.

Keeping his senses on high alert in case a late-night visitor happened by, Maxu found the drive in which the partially complete human-built resource was compiled. He copied the information and then began searching through the cabinets.

Stained clothes reeking of body odor made up a majority of the collection. Most were negligible pieces. Just underwear and small shirts.

He bared his teeth as he examined a long loose dress that had been ripped down the front. His blood raced through his veins and a snarl built in his throat. Logically, he'd known the humans had been stolen from Earth, but seeing these scratched, dirty things painted a bleak picture. What had his mate gone through? Had she been forced to wear her clothes for days on end?

Had she been dragged out of her home in the night wearing next to nothing? Terrified? Crying?

As someone who'd always resented the laws and customs of his planet, he'd had a certain ambivalence about the Insurgents. Wasn't it a good thing that they'd broken the law and searched the universe for a compatible species?

Now, seeing this, Maxu's mind was forever changed. The sour scent of fear clung to each item as if haunting it. For the rest of his days, he'd use every skill he'd acquired to hunt down all living Insurgent members and ensure this same smell clung to their clothing as they died.

One hour passed before he moved on to the second wall. The bag he'd brought with him was almost full now. He didn't know what he wanted with the items he'd stolen specifically, just that he needed more time to examine them alone without this gnawing feeling in his chest distracting him.

A buzz ran through the implanted chip in his arm, and he stilled.

"Who?" he growled.

As someone who'd spent his life getting into places he wasn't supposed to, Maxu was a master at protecting his own space. The only time this chip was activated was when one of the traps he'd laid at his home was tripped. Slowly, he lifted his communicator. Whoever it was would be alive and would have to be dealt with.

A side trip back home to Tremanta was the last thing he needed at the moment, and even before bringing up the camera feed, he knew this person would be in for more ferocity during his questioning than normal.

His brows knit when he saw the attempted break-in hadn't occurred at his home but rather his room, back in Adenelas. Though he always set up a few snares wherever he stayed— his Traxian half territorial no matter where he went—they rarely got any use. His breath caught in his chest as he pondered who it might be.

A live feed lit up in front of him. If Maxu had ever smiled harder in his life, he couldn't recall when. There was Meg, battling fruitlessly against his restraints.

Stowing his phone, he headed back through the broken window. He couldn't waste any more time here. He had a mischievous female to see to.

15

Dammit! Dammit! Dammit! Meg wrenched her hands every which way but couldn't break free from the wall, no matter how hard she pulled. She'd been stuck for what felt like an eternity now. How utterly mortifying.

Everything had been going so well too. During the middle of the party, Lucy had speed-walked over to her and informed her that she'd seen Maxu loading into a cruiser and leaving. Meg had immediately made a show of getting drunk, swapping the alcoholic drink she'd ordered with a visually indiscernible nonalcoholic one Camille had continued to order.

When she'd complained to Daunet that she hadn't been feeling well and needed to go back to her room to sleep, the woman had escorted her back without batting an eye. After she'd been deposited in her room, she'd waited a few minutes for Daunet to return to her own room, then snuck out.

Just as he had in Vondale, Maxu had ensured his room wasn't far from hers, and though she'd had an excuse ready for Heleax, whose turn it was to patrol the hall, she'd ended up not needing to use it. All she'd had to do was tiptoe a few doors down and enter Maxu's room using her print, which had been laughably easy to get. Yesterday evening, on their way back from the beach, she'd stopped an eager-to-help housing services worker, and he'd been all too happy to give her access. In fact, he'd been a little shocked she hadn't had access to begin with.

What an idiot she'd been.

Meg had even grinned triumphantly when Maxu's door had slid closed behind her. She'd gazed around the room, victorious for all of ten seconds, before gold pieces of metal had flown at her out of nowhere. A half shriek and raised palms were all she'd managed before the metal locked on her wrists and soared toward the wall behind her, dragging Meg along with them.

When she'd hit the wall with a thud, a third piece of metal had zoomed toward her neck. She'd screamed, thinking she was about to be decapitated, but the metal merely circled her throat, attaching itself to the wall without touching her skin. It was immovable, forcing her head to remain plastered in place, but at least she was still alive.

Since then, she'd remained pinned like a bug in a display case. She'd tried to scream eventually, conceding that it would be far less embarrassing to be found by Heleax than Maxu, but a slight shock had hit her neck when she did. She'd tried again and hissed in pain. The second shock had been stronger than the first, as if it was a warning that intensified every time it had to remind its prisoner not to speak.

She'd resorted to banging against the wall with her feet after that, but it was of no use. No one came. Meg scowled. None of her friends had accounted for this nonsense when they'd plotted on the beach. But it made perfect sense now that she thought about it. Merely locking your door was something *normal* people did.

She rested her chin against the cool metal at her throat and sulked while glaring at an inanimate object. The black pillow he'd stolen from Kitibard stood out against the dreamy pastels of the Adenelese bedding, perfectly placed in the center. Mocking her.

How long will he be gone? Anxiety had her pulse racing. What if he didn't come back all night? She knew her friends would figure out where she was if she didn't show up in the morning, but that would be hell. Standing like this all night. Not to mention she'd probably end up wetting herself before she was ever found.

Calm down. Calm down. Meg took a slow breath in through her nose and out through her mouth. "You're gonna be fine," she whispered low enough that her electric watchdog collar wouldn't get upset.

To distract herself, she scanned the room, studying everything she could see. Best-case scenario, he had some embarrassing item lying around that she could throw in his face. At least then this nightmare wouldn't have been for nothing.

Her mate wasn't interested in keeping a perfectly clean space. Empty bottles, rumpled bedding, and a few scraps of food sat on various surfaces throughout the room. But when it came to his personal things? Those were all organized.

A bag on some kind of purple undersea-mushroom shelf gaped open, and she could just make out the various neatly packed compartments within. A few electronics she didn't recognize were placed horizontally on a table a little too perfectly to be accidental.

Every one of his things looked brand new. No scuffs or dings. The metal even shined as if he regularly polished it.

Was that how Maxu treated things? Only giving items that belonged to him any care?

Meg's skin warmed. Did she now fall into that category? Was she one of *his* things?

Her gaze landed on a line of products set on the irregularly shaped window's ledge. Meg's eyes narrowed. She pressed her throat against the metal band, craning as far forward as she could to ensure she was seeing things properly.

There were five items. The first was very familiar, and Meg's fists clenched. It was an old notebook from her room back in Tremanta. It'd been near impossible to find since Tremantians rarely used paper products, but she'd gotten her hands on it when her reading lessons had begun, intent on practicing her writing with actual paper.

He'd been in her home at the Pearl Temple too? It was becoming clear that her mate enjoyed stealing things. Great. She'd been spiritually hitched to a kleptomaniac with no concern for boundaries.

The next item on the ledge—a delicate lilac sculpture of a small bird—was also familiar, but she couldn't quite place why. Where had she seen it before?

Oh yeah, it had been in her room at Linadety.

A creeping realization had her chin growing lax. A bright red silk cloth she'd used as a hair tie and had lost at some point on the trip. The golden stemless glass twinkling in the glowing anemone light had been on her table in Vondale. A dainty eating glove…from yesterday. Had he swiped that off the table without her seeing?

Meg stared at the items blankly. How was she supposed to feel about this? He'd stolen these things—all of which she'd used or touched—and then meticulously set them out. There were a few other flat shelves in the room, but he'd picked the rounded, uneven surface of that window for his stolen trinkets. A spot, she realized, that would be directly visible while lying in bed.

A flutter invaded her belly, and she gulped.

No. This wasn't cute or whatever emotion her brain was attempting to assign. This was creepy and intrusive and…sweet? No. He probably glared at them while falling asleep to fuel his possessive determination.

Meg continued to languish, tossing back and forth arguments in her head until she was more unsure than anything else. When the door finally slid aside and Maxu stepped in, for a split second she forgot she was chained to his wall. She studied him with furrowed brows and an erratically beating heart. Then he threw her a smug grin, not the least bit surprised to see her. Annoyance and hot embarrassment lit her nerves in an instant.

"What a pleasant surprise," he began, crossing the room to hang an overstuffed sack on the wall next to his bag. He was wearing all black in a slightly stretchy material. Like a wetsuit. The thick fabric top covered him from chin to fingertips, the shirt acting as sleeves and gloves in one. "Have you been enjoying my room while I've been away?"

Meg didn't answer, knowing the metal around her neck would zap her if she spoke.

Maxu retrieved a bottle of mott from the small refrigeration box installed in the wall above the table. "Don't worry. I disabled the shock. You can speak."

"Let me out of here."

He ignored her. "I spent all day yesterday and today leaving you alone like you wanted, and how am I rewarded? You truss yourself up like a delightful present and await my return? I have to say, your instincts of what type of gift I might love are spot on." He shot her another dark grin. "Unsurprising, since you're my mate, I suppose."

His attention traveled over her raised wrists and the metal circling her throat. Black invaded the corners of his eyes, and another unwanted flutter started up in her belly.

"Why are you dressed like that? Where did you go?" Meg questioned. What sort of trip would require the strange outfit?

Maxu followed her gaze, examining his clothes, but didn't answer. He smirked at her again. "Why? Did you miss me? Is that why you broke into my room?"

"Take these off," she demanded again, wiggling her hands.

He had the gall to chuckle at that. His gloved fingers traveled to his collar, and he began unfastening some metal clasps she hadn't noticed before. "It would be counterproductive to release an intruder as soon as you've caught them, vahpti." Maxu stripped the fabric away from his chest. He let out a relieved groan, whereas Meg's breath stuttered out.

The tanned skin of his chest pulled a little as the tight fabric he'd been wearing was peeled free. When it was gone, he folded it neatly and draped it over a chair, then stretched his arms behind him. It required an embarrassing amount of willpower for her to keep her gaze trained on his face and not to admire every rigid muscle of his abdomen or the tattoo-like birthmarks curling over his pecs and biceps.

He swiped the bottle of mott off the table and drifted over to her. His confident smile and easy gait made it clear he was relishing this. "I chose these," he said, moving in close and tapping a finger against each piece of metal at her wrist, then around her neck, "so that I'd have the ability to question trespassers."

The black shirt must have been sweltering, judging from the scalding body heat drifting off him. She tipped her head back as far as she could to peer up at him. Why, oh why did he have to smell so good right now?

His eyes ran over her face at length. The heat in their depths made a shiver run down her spine. Maxu noticed. His lip curled up on one side. "So. Why did you break in?" he questioned, stepping back until he hit the bed, then sinking onto it. Not a care in the world. His knees were parted slightly, one hand planted behind him, making him recline at an angle that did wonders for his chest.

He took another drink while waiting for her to answer, his eyes still roaming over her as though she were placed there for his enjoyment alone. Meg's skin buzzed under the sheer appreciation in his gaze as he admired the white pleated fabric covering her breasts in a shape reminiscent of two large shells. Her thin, long skirt would do nothing to hide the scent of her arousal if he kept up that searing appraisal. Disguising the movement as a simple shift from one foot to another, she pressed her thighs closer together.

"I came to collect my things," she finally answered. Her gaze strayed toward the pillow for a split second, and when she looked back, he was grinning. His smile was softer, though. Less teasing than usual. It appeared more affectionate, as if he found her attempt charming.

She took in his posture. His spread knees, stretched torso, and wide strong thighs making for a dangerously comfortable-looking lap. What would it be like if she had the nerve—and ability—to crawl over and straddle him while he was sitting just like this? Would he lean up, his free hand coming around her waist to mold their bodies together?

She chewed on her lip and gave her head an internal shake. Her outrage should've been mounting every second he didn't let her go. "I told you why I came in here. Now, take these off?"

Maxu twisted, snatching the black pillow off the bed. "You came for this? Why? What makes you so embarrassed about this?"

"I'm not embarrassed," she argued, lifting her chin and praying her cheeks wouldn't turn red at that exact moment.

"Lie." He flashed his teeth in a grin before lifting the pillow to his face and inhaling.

Heat flared over her face, her body tense and flustered. "Stop that!"

He raised a brow at her and stood. "Why?"

"Cause it's…" Meg grappled for an explanation. "Weird." Never in her life had Jeremy done anything like that. Why would that smell good to anyone? And why was the heat turning her skin pink not just from embarrassment?

"It's weird to enjoy the smell of my mate coming?" He tipped his head with a smile, and damn it all, he knew exactly how flustered he was making her.

"Uh." Meg shuffled from one foot to the other, pulsing warmth invading her core at his words and his growing nearness.

He pressed on, lifting the pillow back to his nose. The rumble of a growl mixing with his deep inhale had her breath coming out shakily. He released a murmur of pleasure on his exhale, now standing only a foot away.

His hand, still gripping the pillow, came to rest casually on the wall between her head and hand. She turned to look at it, and the icy metal pressed against the scalding skin of her neck. A gasp escaped her lips.

He murmured something she couldn't make out, then lifted a hand to her neck. "Let's get this off, sweetness."

Her wide eyes met his as he transferred his mott into his pillow hand, held his thumb to a spot on the collar, and after a quiet beep, threw the innocuous piece of metal over his shoulder. More gently than she'd have imagined, he gripped her chin, tilting it up as he examined her neck. Meg swallowed the sigh building in her throat.

"You didn't take the cuffs off," she said in a low voice.

He lowered her chin. "I have more questions for you."

Meg huffed out a breath. "What do you really want? To have sex? Fine, let's do it so I can get out of here."

His mouth curled down in pleased surprise and he straightened. "Sounds good to me."

"Wait! No. You're not serious." Meg gaped at him. "You're supposed to turn me down. Like a gentleman."

He lifted a sardonic brow to her, as if she'd said something incredibly foolish.

"Well…maybe not a gentleman," Meg stammered. "But you know I don't have feelings for you. I don't like you. I clearly don't love you."

His lips fell at that. Seafoam-green eyes glided over her body, assessing something, but she didn't know what.

He tipped his head, seeming to reach some conclusion. His hand and her pillow returned to rest on the side of her head, and he leaned in close.

"I bet I could fuck your love into reality, little mate."

Meg sucked in a gasp and stopped breathing. She had no idea how to respond to that. Her pussy was throwing a damn parade at his words, while the rest of her was short-circuiting.

Noticing it had been hanging open, she slammed her mouth shut and licked her dry lips.

"Mmm, are you thirsty?" he rumbled. His strong, deep voice slipped over her.

Was she thirsty? Meg gave a small nod.

Maxu lifted his mott bottle to her lips and tipped it back. The liquid stung her dry throat and some splashed out, running down her chin and neck. He pulled the bottle away, and she tried to wipe her chin against her shoulder.

The mott hit the carpeted ground with a thud as Maxu dropped it and gripped her chin once more. This time, his hold was firmer, his motions harsher as he forced her face up until her neck was exposed.

Meg's heartbeat slammed against her ribcage when she realized what he was about to do. On the first touch of his tongue to her throat, a whimper escaped her. Maxu let out a rumble of satisfaction. Then before she could clear her mind, he began purring against her skin, cleaning off the mott with one heavy swipe of his tongue.

Liquid heat raced straight to her core. The vibration of his purr mixed with the heat and wetness of his tongue was making her sex throb with need. Why didn't she feel upset? Outraged? Embarrassed?

She'd been trapped in his room for over an hour now. Strapped to his wall without apology, and now he was doing…this? She'd felt so cornered whenever she'd thought of him, that claustrophobic tightening of her chest making her act scattered and petulant. So why now, when she was actually trapped, did she feel so excited, so eager…so safe?

She was falling down a rabbit hole, confusion and yearning battling against each other, when he forced a knee between her legs and hiked her upward until the weight of her body rested on his thigh, her toes just barely reaching the ground.

The hand from her chin disappeared, and before she could register its absence, it had snaked behind her low back. A white spark lit up behind her eyelids when he bit the flesh of her neck just behind her ear.

Meg's eyes flew open when she felt something soft cushioning the hard muscle of Maxu's thigh. Her pillow.

He pulled away, his gaze wandering over her warm cheeks and wide eyes. One of his palms came up to her jaw, and he ran a thumb over what must've been her bright red blush. A bead of sweat trickled down her back, her embarrassment rising.

"Show me. Let me see what you like."

Meg's throat was swollen shut. She couldn't do that in front of him, much less *on* him. She was fully clothed, yet she'd never felt more naked. More vulnerable. She shook her head.

Maxu stared at her for a moment, his jaw clenching and unclenching. "Why don't you want me, vahpti?" His question was like a knife through her heart. The rawness of it reflected in his gentle gaze.

He wasn't asking why she didn't want to show him how she liked to pleasure herself or why she didn't want to have sex. He wanted to know why she kept him at arm's length.

There was no good reason that the truth should've bubbled up in her throat, but it did. "I... It's not you... I can't be trapped again."

The wrinkle between his brows softened. He pressed a kiss to her temple. "That's good enough for now."

Meg's head swam as his mouth dipped and he licked his way to her ear, his hot breath making goose bumps sprout all over her body. He rocked his thigh against her sex, and Meg had to bite her lip. She was still, but she knew exactly what it would feel like if she moved. Heavenly.

The cream glove on the window caught her attention, making her heart pound faster. "Maxu, why did you take those things?"

As soon as the words were out, Maxu stilled, his mouth freezing on her skin. At length he gave her neck a slow press of his lips, then pulled back until their eyes locked. His brows weren't knitted in confusion concerning what items she was talking about. They were turned down in thought.

His lips tightened, as did his fingers gripping her hips. Then something unexpected happened. The harsh slash of his brows softened, lifting a bit. Was he nervous?

"They're..." His voice died out, and he let out a long breath before continuing. "They make you feel less out of reach. By being surrounded by your things, I can imagine I'm surrounded by you."

Meg blinked. Emotion tightened her heart. Was this truth or manipulation? She studied the rigid set of his jaw, his hard stare, and the stillness of his chest. *Is he...?*

Warmth spread through her. Yes. He was holding his breath.

She leaned forward, holding his gaze until their lips were an inch apart. Her lids slid closed, and she kissed him. His fingers tightened on her hips while his lips over hers parted slightly but otherwise remained unmoving.

She canted her head to the side, gave his lower lip a swipe of her tongue and sealed their lips, leaning as far forward as she could with her wrists still glued to the wall. Finally, his body came alive, his breath whooshing in through his nose as a loud purr rumbled out of his chest and caused a lingering vibration to pulse through his body.

She loved the way their mouths fit. How the edge of her chin fell perfectly into the dip of his as she kissed his upper lip.

He was slow at first, experimental, letting her take the lead, but when she finally allowed her hips to move over his thigh, he changed. His mouth widened and his lips grew firm, demanding.

She rocked against him, trying to hold back her sighs and moans, but it felt too good. Arousal dampened her underwear, and the delicious, even pressure made that ball of need in her belly tighten. Tired of holding back—tired of hiding her reactions for fear of judgment—she let out a moan.

Maxu's answering groan emboldened her, and she rocked against him faster. His palm clutching her hip tightened and loosened as she moved. Like he was learning her pace and studying how her pelvis tilted when she hit the right spot.

A strangled cry rang through the space when Maxu palmed her breast over her shirt, digging his fingers into her ass as he spurred her on. "Yes, little mate, let me hear you."

Meg wanted to smile. Why had she been so embarrassed to do this? Maxu was desperate for her to come, maybe even more than she was. Her breaths were raw gasps. Her feet lifted off the ground completely and her thighs clenched either side of his.

Maxu's purr took on a rougher edge. He buried his face in her hair, holding her chest against the wall with his upper body. "That's it, beautiful. You're doing so good. Almost there."

The sounds that escaped her at his praise had never passed over her lips before, but she couldn't seem to be embarrassed. All she could feel was the weight of him, holding her down and urging her on, the frantic grinding of her pelvis as her orgasm crested.

Her muscles tensed, wrists pulling down in their cuffs almost to the point of pain as she came. An elongated cry built and ebbed in time with the waves of her climax until she slumped against Maxu, trying to slow her racing heart.

She let out a gasp of surprise when he deactivated the cuffs and she collapsed fully into his arms. "You're breathtaking, vahpti."

He murmured things she couldn't make out against her skin, peppering kisses along her jaw as he set her on her feet and held her until her legs supported her.

Breaths still heaving out of her, she took a step back and peered up at him. The split second of regret she had vanished at one glance. His chest was rising and falling as fast as hers, his eyes completely black and a little wild. A large bulge pressing against the thick fabric of his pants caught her eye, and she couldn't help but grin.

She'd done this to him just by enjoying herself. In that moment, Meg felt more powerful and more in control than she had in a long time.

How much farther could she push him? What would he do for her if she asked? She stepped forward, reaching out to palm his impressive length, but he snapped up her wrist before she could. "That's enough for today."

The world froze for a moment. Had she been so very wrong? She tried to tug her hand away so she could regain some pride. Maxu held fast.

"There's nothing more in the universe I want, Meg." He used his grip to pull her toward him and ensured she met his serious gaze with a hand on her jaw. "But I can't be gentle with you right now."

Meg stared. His eyes were still fully black, each muscle rigid as if his whole body were clenched. As much as she wanted to push and see exactly what sex with him would look like at that moment, fear held her back. She'd only ever been with one man, and if a six-and-a-half-foot alien mercenary with a huge dick and a raging mating instinct was warning her away, she should probably listen.

"Okay," Meg breathed. He quickly ushered her to the door. "Wha— Now? But I could—"

"It's now or you stay all night." His voice was hoarse.

"Okay, let me just get— Hey!" Meg had been reaching for the pillow she'd come here to get in the first place, but he snatched it out of her hands.

He held it up. "Until I can bury my nose in your cunt anytime I want, this is mine."

Meg blinked at the incredible sentiment wrapped in such a harsh delivery. Words failed her. She was still staring with wide eyes as he activated his door, gently pushed her backward through the opening, and closed it again.

It took a few moments for her brain to kick-start, but when it did, a wide smile broke over her face. Maybe this whole mate thing wouldn't be so bad after all.

16

Sweat poured down his back, his thighs and calves burning with the effort it took to sprint up the vertical side of Nascep Mountain. This was Maxu's third trip up the steep incline, and his lungs were on fire. Still, he pressed on. Anything to forget about the warmth expanding his chest for a minute or two.

He'd intended to break down her barriers and, on the surface, he'd succeeded. She'd been shackled to the wall and made to do exactly what he'd wanted. So why, then, had he come out of the exchange so raw and exposed?

Maxu reached the peak of the mountain and sucked in ragged breaths. He hated feeling this way. Weak. Like if she asked him to drop to his knees before her, he would.

He stabbed a hand through his sweat-soaked hair. Gripping it with his fingers while turning in a circle and relishing the sting. His steps paused when he remembered her kiss.

This emotional overwhelm hadn't felt awful then. She'd asked him about the items he'd collected, and until that moment, he hadn't known specifically why he'd lugged the junk around with him. But when she'd asked with those red cheeks and large blue eyes, the reason had been clear. He'd wanted to keep the information inside, so it was safe, protected, only open to his own judgment, but somehow the words had spilled out. And she hadn't pulled away.

No screaming about how he shouldn't be taking her things. Instead, warmth had lit her eyes and she'd kissed him. And it had been...amazing. Not just the kiss itself but the acceptance of his words. When Meg had pressed her lush lips to his, it'd felt like he was being rewarded for his honesty.

So, did he despise admitting such private feelings to her? Or did he love it?

What was he supposed to do with the little human who had the ability to confuse him so thoroughly that he'd needed to empty his cock three times and then sprint up a mountain just to process his thoughts?

Maxu laughed humorlessly into the warm wind. Anger? Annoyance? *Those* he was used to. But this? This was a new type of puzzle entirely.

One of the two moons was already visible, rising in the sky though the sun hadn't set yet. He'd see her tonight at the party. How should he act? How would she act? Would she regret what had happened in his room?

Even as trepidation made his chest clench, there was something exciting in the air. What if she wasn't unhappy to see him?

He jogged back down the mountain, legs a little shaky now that his adrenaline had worn off. He sped past happy people going about their lives and whispering about the humans. Then he locked himself in his room, used some cleansing foam to get himself clean, and spent the next few hours examining the objects he'd stolen from the Xeric Tower.

Frustration built as he stared at the items, most of which hadn't been added to the sparse directory he'd stolen. There was no context to explain what they were or how they were used. Some were easy to figure out since they were similar to things on Clecania. A golden ring. A ragged shirt. A primitive communicator of sorts.

But others were just too foreign. A purple canister with a sparkling symbol on it hadn't been catalogued yet. Maxu sprayed a small amount into the air and waved a portable chemical reader through the mist, sure it would be innocuous.

He was shocked when the reader flagged the spray as a nonfatal toxic substance. He lifted the canister again, squinting at the small, sparkly Y on the side. *Who'd make weapons that look like this?*

When his translation glass indicated a small rectangle containing even smaller soft pink rectangles was something called bubble gum and seemed to be edible, he held himself back from tasting it for fear it was another disguised weapon, possibly an unknown poison.

Maxu set the items aside, resigned to the fact that it would take longer than he currently had to decipher their uses. Tomorrow, on his ride to the next city, he'd have time to read some of the expansive directory he'd stolen. He only hoped it was more enlightening than today had been.

He dressed and tamed his hair, trying to ignore the creeping doubt whispering that Meg would prefer a different outfit. Then, with his heart pounding in his ears, he stepped out of his room and navigated through spiral hallways and sandy paths until he reached the Zoa Chamber, the location of tonight's party.

The cylindrical building had been constructed around an ancient, fossilized coral climbing hundreds of feet into the air. Taking a deep breath and urging his jaw to unclench, he stepped into the lowest level of the chamber.

The hardened sea plant towered over him, dominating the room. A walkway wide enough to hold twenty people across ran in a spiral around the perimeter of the building all the way to the ceiling, so that the coral remained the focal point wherever you stopped.

He scanned the crowds, eyes gliding upward even though the people on the higher levels were out of sight. His gaze rested on the underside of the walkway about thirty feet up. Somehow, he knew Meg was there. His chest expanded with his deep inhale. A piece of *him* existed, miraculously, outside of his body, and he could sense exactly where she was. The mating instinct was becoming easier to recognize, but it was no less incredible.

With tentative steps, he meandered his way through the party, stopping at intervals to grab a drink or a bit of food. Stalling.

"You look wonderful," a female voice called from his right. Rita and another human, Camille, were there standing among a group of curious Adenelese. Camille gave him a smile and a wave, while behind her the guards Uthen and Atolicy prowled, taking in their surroundings while staying close enough to intervene in case of trouble.

They appeared more on edge tonight than they had before, and Maxu understood why. The tour, while pleasant for some, wasn't calming the growing curiosity of Clecanians. If anything, having a glimpse of the humans only made the people angrier.

There were reports coming in of cities demanding answers from the Tremantian Queen. Why hadn't Earth been reclassified yet? Why wasn't the Queen pushing the Intergalactic Alliance harder?

Apparently, there had been a common misconception that humans were primitive, sheltered, naïve. Seeing them dash through each city, displaying a similar level of intelligence to Clecanians begged the question of why they were still a Class Four planet.

"Have you seen Meg?" Camille asked. He did a double take at her mischievous smile. She and Rita exchanged a knowing look. His spine straightened. Had Meg revealed what had happened between them in his room?

A small boy he hadn't seen before stepped out of his father's shadow and stared up at Maxu with large sunset-orange eyes. "Do you have a mate, sir?" The boy's gaze flicked between Maxu's face and hand where his mating marks were on full display. Maxu clutched his drink a little tighter.

"Yes," he said shortly. He didn't like his private life on display. First Camille and Rita had behaved as if they knew something they shouldn't, and now this curious boy was staring at his hands.

A part of Maxu enjoyed his mating marks, wearing them proudly for everyone to see. Yet another side of him wanted to bury them in his pockets so he could keep them to himself.

The blue marks spanning his hands were great big signs to everyone that he had a weakness. If any of his old enemies saw them, all they had to do to hurt him was hurt her.

"Do you want a mate one day?" Rita asked the boy when she realized Maxu was not intending on speaking again, busy scowling into space.

The boy's nose scrunched. "No." The group chuckled. But then the boy glanced up at his father. "I think my dad would like one, though."

The group chuckled again, but Maxu caught the barest glimpse of pain light the eyes of the Clecanians standing around the two humans.

Life was difficult on this planet. Clecanians were dying out. Estimates had them reaching extinction within three generations. Three.

Mothers were expected to leave their children so they could mother more children, all in the hopes that one day they'd sacrifice enough and could finally rest. Males, like this boy's father, who were lucky enough to have conceived a child, were no longer eligible for marriage. They were expected to spend the rest of their lives raising their child and finding scraps of romantic affection where they could.

And now there was a world with billions who were reproductively compatible. Earth.

Humans not only had ancient Clecanian DNA running through their veins and could have Clecanian children but they could also call mating marks forth. It was easy to see why cities were growing restless.

Resentment settled in Maxu once more, and he stared down at his mating marks. There were so many people on his planet who'd struggled to do the right thing, to sacrifice and hope for a better world. Maxu had never been one of those people.

For so long, he'd been comfortable knowing that Clecania would die out. That, just like everything else in the universe, his species would end. It had never mattered what he did.

Nothing mattered. People died. Planets died. The universe itself would one day die. He'd never seen the point in following the expectations of his people. Best-case scenario, they eked out a few more miserable centuries before the last Clecanian vanished.

But now, for the first time since he'd been young, he felt like something mattered. A renewed hope was rising among people who'd been so worn down. They might have found a solution to all their troubles. Finally, a way out that would alleviate the crushing pressure placed on them all.

But who was he supposed to be in this new world? The male he'd always been? The one he'd come to accept and even like?

Or a new male? One that worked to save his planet and allowed hope to guide his actions. He peered at the boy once again. He'd never wanted children. It'd always seemed pointless and cruel to bring a child into this world, knowing that each generation was one step closer to extinction. All he would be doing was gifting his offspring an even harder life than he'd had. Like forcing someone to burn themselves in order to throw a cup of water on an inferno.

But now? Maybe his children could live in a world on the rise. They could flourish, knowing they'd have choices. That one day they might even have a mate and love. Having a child didn't seem so pointless when he thought about it that way.

The conversation had moved on while Maxu swam in his mind. When he focused on the group once more, he locked eyes with Rita and she gave him a sad smile.

With a silent nod, he drained his glass and continued toward his mate. Did she want children? Until there was a plan to lessen their burden by sharing it with the people of Earth, Meg would feel the same pressure to have children as the other females of his world experienced. Maxu didn't even know enough about her to guess how she'd react to that.

Warm, glowing tentacles of the anemones planted over every spare inch of wall lit the space in gentle neon light. Only days ago, he'd felt like the coral dominating the center of the room. Fossilized and stripped of all potential. But now it was as if he was thawing. Was it just the mating instinct, or was he changing on his own?

Did this new lens through which he examined the world emerge out of nowhere, or had it always been there locked away under layers of bleak pessimism?

The crowd parted ahead of him, and he nearly crashed into a stationary Adenelese male. There she was. Heartbreaking in her beauty. She was smiling, waving her hand, and pointing at the mass of coral, her eyes wide and enraptured. He looked at it again, trying to see it how she did.

He made his way closer but didn't approach her. Despite the things that had happened between them in his room, he'd told her he'd keep his distance, and he intended to do just that. It helped that forcing her to approach him was easier.

There was a whole new world of things he was beginning to want now, but what if she didn't want them too? What if she still didn't want him? What if she never did?

17

⚮

Music floated through the gorgeous cylindrical room, melting Meg's stress away. Many of the cities she'd been to hadn't played music when they had gatherings like this, feeling it was distracting to conversation and connection. But she loved it. The soft, sultry melodies sounded as if they were created with an odd mixture of wind and string instruments.

Meg missed very little from Earth, but lately she'd been missing music more and more. She'd even resorted to singing when she was on her own. She sang quietly so no one would hear since she had a terrible voice, but it made her feel more normal.

In the last few days, the songs that had bloomed in her mind had been sappy love songs, and she knew exactly why, though her feelings were more confused than ever.

"I think our interviews went very well today," Kel, one of the Queen's representatives, said once again. Why was he so interested in confirming that? She studied his eager expression as he nodded toward the group of Adenelese surrounding her, as if hoping they would nod back.

The interview *had* been successful. Meg and the other humans had finally found their footing, knowing which answers were most helpful and which weren't. They'd also figured out how to include harder truths about what reactions humans might have to aliens, while still leaving the people satisfied and hopeful.

"I found Meg's description of ballallies particularly interesting. Could you tell us more, Meg?" Kel stared at her with an expression so keen it almost looked panicked.

Meg had half a mind to hand him her drink so he could calm the fuck down, but she wouldn't call out his weird behavior and embarrass him in front of this group of nice people. "Bowling alleys," she corrected slowly with a polite smile. During the interview, she'd been asked again about how courting worked, and in her explanation of dates, she'd listed a few common activities, including bowling. No one had ever asked for elaboration on bowling before, but the concept of the game seemed to fascinate the Adenelese. "So, at a bowling alley you have lanes and heavy balls." Meg's focus drifted to Daunet, who'd halted two impatient men standing on the periphery of the ten-person group she'd been escorted to.

The appearance of the men wasn't what had her stomach somersaulting, though. In the background, leaning against a wall in a quiet corner, sipping an electric-blue drink and staring, was Maxu. The gentle glowing pinks, blues, and oranges of the wall anemone lit the side of his face, casting the other side in shadow.

The men Daunet had halted joined the group, replacing the ten others who had been there. Whoever they were must've been important, but Meg couldn't focus on anything but the dark, heated expression oozing from Maxu.

When Kel asked her something she didn't catch, Meg held up a finger. "I'm so sorry. I'll be right back." She smiled, dispersing polite nods, then maneuvered past the group.

Her palms sweat as she got closer. He looked unbearably handsome tonight, his skin tinged bronze from the sun. His shirt was a style she'd seen often in Adenelas. A long piece of fabric wrapped across his chest and shoulders asymmetrically, allowing a sliver of his right pec to be seen before cinching at his waist.

Meg smoothed the intricate pleats of her dress as she approached. His eyes never left her, and when she was within a few feet, he finally lifted from the wall.

"Hey" was all she could manage to say.

"Hello," he answered back. They stared for a few awkward seconds.

She wanted to bring up what had happened and ask how he felt about it. Maybe knowing would help her make sense of her own thoughts. But what was she supposed to say? *I'm terrified of being in a relationship with someone because I'm just now finding out who I am and if I'm with you, I might lose that again.*

"What are you doing over here?" she asked instead.

He glanced around the room and then took a sip of his drink. "I'm doing what you asked." His words were a little tight, rough. So different from the gentle way in which he'd whispered to her in his room. Her heart took a step back.

She pushed past his tone. "Would you like to join us?" She gestured to the waiting group of Adenelese, and her focus caught on them for a moment. They all studied her while leaning to speak to each other. Gossips existed on all planets, it seemed.

Maxu frowned at the three men. His green eyes were fixed in place, but she could see his mind working, his jaw clenching and unclenching. He was bothered again, upset, and closed off.

"Is everything alright?" she said after building the courage. "Last night—"

He cut her off. "You better get back to them before your handler keels over."

"Handler?"

He stepped toward the group, waiting for her to follow in a detached sort of way. Her chest hollowed, but she plastered a smile on her face and trailed him, promising herself that after the party was over, she'd force him to sit down with her and have a genuine conversation.

They were greeted by wide smiles and enthusiastic congratulations from the taller of the two Adenelese men as if she and Maxu had announced their engagement. Both newcomers gave her and Maxu a dramatic sweep of their hand, the Adenelese version of a wave *hello* or a handshake. Meg returned the gesture, while Maxu gave a halfhearted flick of his wrist before stuffing one fist into his pocket. Her brows knit. Was she imagining it, or was he hiding his hand?

"Hello, Meg. Calm seas and luck are with us. My name is Galuvin." The taller man with curly red hair, long sideburns, and kind peach-colored eyes said. He pointed to the other man, who could have been Galuvin's much shorter twin, except for the violet freckles covering every inch of exposed skin. "And this is Abrin. We were hoping to ask a favor of you."

"Calm seas and luck are with me as well," she said, almost forgetting to use the preferred greeting in her attempt to ignore Maxu's imposing presence. He was just behind her right shoulder, posture as rigid as a statue. He couldn't have been more distracting if he were doing jumping jacks.

"I'm sure Meg would be happy to grant you a favor," Kel answered for her. The corners of Meg's mouth twitched, almost curling into a frown. She hated when people did that.

Maxu shuffled behind her, and she inched over so he wasn't at her back anymore. She had enough to stress over at the moment without being distracted by his body heat leeching into her spine as he hovered behind her.

"We're part of the Adenelas team who researches fertility, and we were hoping to get a few samples from Meg before she leaves to expand our investigation." Abrin held out a pad with scrolling script. "Perhaps you could have someone read this to you. These are the samples we're hoping to take and what we'll be using them for."

Her fingers were rising when Abrin extended the pad not toward her but toward Maxu. Meg's hand dropped like it had been zapped, her entire body stiffening. An irrational lump inflated in her windpipe.

This wasn't the same as on Earth. They hadn't given her Clecanian version of a husband a medical information sheet because they didn't value *her*. They did it because they weren't expecting someone from a Class Four planet to be able to read their writing yet. It was a perfectly logical assumption.

Knowing this in her mind did nothing for the tears threatening to spring to her eyes, though. She breathed through her nose, trying to get her emotions under control so she could explain she didn't need anything read *to* her without her voice cracking.

Maxu snatched the pad out of Abrin's hand. Meg's heart shriveled a little more.

But then, without a moment of hesitation, Maxu handed the pad to her, glaring at the two men with a stare cold enough to freeze. "She can read it herself."

Maxu spared her only the briefest of glances when she took the pad. She couldn't look away.

"Apologies," Abrin croaked. "I didn't realize."

"Yes, I…I…" Meg stammered, tearing her gaze from Maxu. She cleared her throat. Would they be able to see her pulse beating through her body? Because she felt like she was vibrating in time with her heart. "I can read Clecanian."

It took her a while to comb through the lists of tests they wanted to run and samples they wanted to take, but it wasn't because she had trouble deciphering the words.

Finally, her concentration kicked in and she truly assessed what they were looking for. It seemed alright. A little invasive, maybe, but it was for the good of the planet. It might be a frustrating few hours of answering questions and being prodded, but how could she say no when the information might help?

"I'm interested to hear your thoughts," Galuvin pressed gently.

Meg was about to agree, but then she glanced at Maxu again. The image of Jeremy standing there and theories about how he'd react in the same situation turned her stomach. What would her mate say about this? It was her decision either way, but she was so curious to know what it would feel like to decide *with* a partner rather than having things decided for her.

"What do you think?" she asked.

Maxu gave her a funny look, as if he were confused who she was speaking to.

"I'd like to know," she urged, holding the pad out to him.

He took it silently and read through the information on the screen. His jaw remained welded shut. When he was finally finished, he handed the pad back to her. "I don't see anything that could harm you. I feel the way they asked was disrespectful, and it would be appropriate to offer you compensation for your time as they would any participant in a medical study, but otherwise…"

"Disrespectful?" Meg questioned.

Galuvin, Abrin, and Kel all huffed in agreement. "I've seen no disrespect, Meg," Kel announced with a serious look at her.

Maxu let out a muffled growl. "Of course you don't. You're clearly using this as an opportunity to keep the cities satiated. I wouldn't be surprised if you or the Queen offered the humans up for testing and then made a show of asking permission."

Meg whirled on Kel. His pale face was growing redder by the second. "Is that true?"

"They asked you at the last minute, hoping you'd be pressured into agreeing. Why else wouldn't they have asked the first day? And this contract?" Maxu continued, tapping on the screen with his finger and releasing an ominous chuckle. "If you believed she couldn't read this, then why didn't you bring a translation glass along with you?" He leveled Kel with a cold, accusatory glare. "And why don't you know she can read? Shouldn't you have some knowledge of the humans you're traveling with and what skills they possess?" Maxu crossed his arms over his chest, dipping his head to Meg and cutting everyone out of the conversation. "I think what they're trying to do isn't without merit, but the way they went about it is disrespectful. If you want to do this, you should, but don't let yourself be pressured into it."

Meg looked at Maxu, really looked. Past his dark scowl and bruised knuckles. He was possessive and controlling, but not in the way she'd expected. He was on her side. She blinked at the ground for a moment, working out what she should do with the inexplicable knowledge that her mate was ready to support her decision. A wave of confidence had her lifting her chin toward the researchers.

"Have you asked any of the other humans?" She handed the pad back to them.

Galuvin's gaze flicked to Kel for an instant, and Meg knew Maxu had been right. She'd need to deal with that problem later. "We were going to speak with them next."

Meg didn't know whether to be offended by that. Had they approached her first, thinking she'd be the easiest to convince? Maxu was at her back again, and before she could stop herself, she'd backed up a step closer to him. "I'll do it. But I want you to guarantee that if any other humans in my group are approached, you'll give them a reading glass and you'll offer them the same compensation as any other volunteer would get."

With a slight grumble, the men agreed and gave her a much less enthusiastic swirl of their wrists as they left. She locked eyes with Daunet and found a restrained smile on her face, her eyes landing on Maxu for a moment. Meg could hear her telepathically issued, "I told you he was a good male," as if Daunet had screamed it into her ear.

"We'd better get some more groups in to speak with you before you leave," Kel said, clapping his hands together as if nothing had happened.

"She's done enough tonight," Maxu rumbled, tugging Meg away from the man.

She pressed a hand over Maxu's, peering up at him. "That's alright. I can handle a few more."

His eyes locked on her fingers draped over his. Maxu remained still for a few tense seconds. A slight incline of his chin was his only response. He stepped back.

Kel let out a relieved breath and retreated, gathering a new group.

"You could have asked to be paid as well," Maxu grunted when Kel was out of sight.

Meg shrugged. "I could have." She leaned against the railing dividing the walkway from the enormous coral sprouting through the center of the building. "Honestly, though, I owe it to them. Each city gives us clothes and food and lodging. They throw us beautiful parties. I've been able to see amazing things like this." She gestured to the fossil. "I feel dumb for not offering samples to every city. It's the least I can do."

"How noble," Maxu grumbled, resting both elbows on the railing.

She chuckled. "You say that like it's a bad thing. Won't doing things like this be good for your planet?"

Maxu downed the dregs of his glass and licked his lips, staring out at the coral. "I'm not interested in what's good for the planet. I'm interested in what's good for you." His eyes slid closed for a moment, as though he'd regretted saying that.

Since he refused to look at her, she grinned into the distance instead, swiping glances at him every few seconds as silence stretched between them. "It's incredible, isn't it?" Meg nodded toward the coral. The fossil itself was white and spotted with starburst patterns, but the light from the anemone and the bright moonbeams streaming in from above cast it in an otherworldly glow.

"I don't see the appeal." Maxu tipped his glass at it. "It's useless. Millions of years ago, it may have been a home for countless sea creatures, but now? Nothing more than a rock."

"Useless?" Meg breathed. "It's beautiful, but more than that, it's meaningful. These people built a shrine around this *rock*. It's a shared treasure that bonds them." When Maxu remained unmoved, she clicked her tongue. "I read that every five years the whole city comes together for a holiday, the Zoalin Week. They bring in a bunch of levitation platforms and this special sealant they make from the bones of all the creatures they've caught over that time. Then each citizen coats their hands and they work together to cover the fossil in that paste, to protect it. The youngest put their prints at the bottom to signify their position as the new backbone of the population, and the eldest place theirs at the top." Meg grinned and pointed to the bottom of the fossil. "See. You can tell where the thick, sloppy bits made by children are." Her grin faltered when she caught Maxu staring not at the coral but at her. "What?"

"Before I joined you, you were speaking to a male and his father. They described the Zoa and its history, and you didn't stop them. Why didn't you explain that you already knew?"

Meg eyed him. "How did you even hear that? You were so far away."

"The mating bond has changed many things about me." He stared into his empty glass. "Why let them ramble on about something you already knew?"

Meg chuckled and shook her head. "It wasn't rambling. Didn't you see their faces light up when they were talking about it? Just because I've learned about something or read an entry about it doesn't mean I really *know* it. Listening to that old man try to point out where his son's prints were..." She searched for the right words. "It's like he transferred his love and enthusiasm into me." She shook her head again. Memories of her shabby bookcase back on Earth flooded back to her. Worn-out library-sale encyclopedias and outdated coffee table books full of places she'd known she'd never get to travel to. "Believe me, you can read and read and read all there is to know about a place, but it will never come close to experiencing it."

Brows furrowed in thought and head tilted ever so slightly, Maxu considered the fossil.

"If you really believed dead things like this don't matter," Meg began, voice dropped low, "you wouldn't have collected all those pieces of junk and kept them in your room. To anyone else, my eating glove would be no more than trash."

She held her breath, waiting for her words to settle. At length, the harsh crease between Maxu's brows softened and he faced her. They stared at each other, the air pulsing around them. *Say something*, she wanted to scream.

His mouth opened, then closed. Meg leaned forward.

A group of Adenelese, led by Kel, swarmed, and her attention was torn away. By the time she looked back, his mask of indifference had returned.

Meg spent the rest of the party answering questions, chatting, sharing stories from Earth and listening to stories about the city. She marveled with her visitors about how similar some things were and how very, very different others were. All the while, Maxu remained silent and sturdy by her side. He'd refused to join in the conversation when she'd prodded, but she'd caught him smiling absently down at her a few times, though he always quickly looked away.

Eventually, Rita, Camille, and Tara approached, their guards trailing behind them. "We're supposed to collect you and go to the Med Bay," Tara explained.

Meg turned her back on the women and put a hand in the crook of Maxu's arm. His attention flashed to her. She tugged until he finally bent forward, brows drawn in confusion.

"Thank you for tonight. Really, thank you." She kissed his cheek, then joined her friends. When she looked back, his neck was still bent, frozen in place, and staring after her. With an embarrassed glance over his shoulder, he cleared his throat and straightened, a light blush on his cheeks.

18

❦

Where the hell is he? Meg stared out of the cruiser window, sulking. It'd been two whole days. They'd arrived in and departed from a city, and she hadn't seen Maxu once.

She began chewing on her sore lip, then forced herself to stop. She'd already gnawed on it enough that it looked like she'd painted one half with red lipstick.

What had happened? She thought they'd finally been getting more comfortable with each other, to the point of wondering whether she and Maxu could not only have a cordial relationship or a purely sexual one but a meaningful connection. But then he just ghosted her? After weeks of chasing her down and forcing himself into her life? Seriously. What. The. Hell?

She thought maybe she'd seen him a couple of times, lurking in the back of a crowd or disappearing around a distant corner, but was it just her mind playing tricks?

Was he alright? Was he dead? Did he not know the next city they were going to?

She gnawed at her lip again, gaze falling to her feet as a cruel voice whispered in her mind, *What if I did something wrong? Was I being a know-it-all?*

Had she been too over the top when they'd fooled around in his room?

No man wants a woman who behaves like a slut. Her mother had used that line to get her point across more than once. A flush of shame made her clammy. Had she been too…enthusiastic?

Her fists clenched. No. She had nothing to feel ashamed about. And if Maxu found the way she expressed herself unattractive, then he just wasn't the right man for her and that was all there was to it.

Someone snorted with laughter, breaking Meg out of her spiral. Daunet sat on the other side of the cruiser with a hand slapped over her mouth, appearing appalled at the sound she'd just emitted. Meg tried not to let her jealousy get to her.

They were sharing a cruiser with Tara and Gamso today. Initially, it'd been like pulling teeth to get Daunet to speak at all, but eventually she and Tara had bonded over some famed sculptural artist Meg had never heard of.

The two women now sat on the opposite side of the cruiser, chatting. A grin remained sprawled across Tara's face, while Daunet tried and failed to hold back her own smile.

Meg studied the faint crinkles that appeared around Daunet's eyes, brought out by her wide grin. She couldn't remember seeing those before. Not like this anyway.

How selfish was she? Her friends were practically floating with joy, and all Meg could do was glare at them bitterly. How had she gotten here? A week ago, she'd been determined not to settle down with any man—but especially not a man like Maxu. Now it took all her strength to keep her expression neutral when she thought of him.

One great orgasm and I'm putty. How pathetic.

It had been great, though. She'd never expected to enjoy having her wrists tied up, but, damn, she had. Something about surrendering control like that was liberating.

"Does it feel different?" Gamso, who'd remained silent for most of the ride, was staring at her.

"Pardon?" she asked.

"Being apart from him. I couldn't help but notice he hasn't been around for a few days, and you seem upset. I was just wondering—with the mating bond and all—if you felt anything out of the ordinary."

Meg let out a sigh. Gamso's expression was so curious, so hopeful. "Not more than the usual annoyance I might feel at him taking off without a word."

"Oh." His head turned down, and he deflated in front of her eyes, making guilt spike.

"I mean, I think maybe I'm more annoyed with him than I would be if he were just some guy who disappeared for a couple days." It was a stretch, but it might not be untrue.

Gamso grinned into space at that. "Wonderful."

"I just can't get a good read on him. I don't understand what he wants. First, he chases me down, annoys the crap out of me by always invading my personal space, and then when I want him around, he vanishes." Meg threw up her hands, staring into the blank wall of the cruiser.

"He sounds frightened to me," Gamso murmured with a sad smile.

"Frightened?" Meg had to contain a chuckle. She couldn't imagine anything that could frighten Maxu.

"The males on our planet have to get used to rejection, but we never fully grow numb to it. We spend our whole lives being judged. Did we get good enough grades? Do we have pleasant enough features? Would we make excellent fathers? It's not as difficult as a female's place in this world, but it's still hard." He avoided her gaze. "It takes a toll."

Meg stared down at her feet. He didn't show it all the time, but Meg was sure she'd spotted glimpses of vulnerability behind Maxu's eyes a few times now. Was Gamso right? Was Maxu afraid of rejection?

What a pair they made. Meg was afraid of having a controlling, distant relationship, which had pushed her to avoid them completely. And Maxu was afraid of rejection, which had pushed him to be cold and controlling to hide his insecurities. But she was beginning to see who he really was.

"How do you manage it, Gamso?" What had Maxu gone through? What were all the men of this planet going through every day?

"You learn to expect it. Ignoring the feeling of failure." With a shrug and empty chuckle, he added, "Some males don't mind. They enjoy the challenge of rising to the occasion. Being the best. But some rail against it. Maxu refused to participate in any ceremonies. Every few years he'd break the law to get out of it." Gamso straightened, dropping his head against the seat. "Sometimes I wish I felt that way. We live on a lonely planet. The way Maxu dealt with it was to not be a part of it, to isolate himself even more. I can only imagine how it may crush a male to be rejected by their mate too. It hurts when a female turns you down for marriage, but how could you cope if your fated one found you lacking as well?"

Meg's heart felt like it was being squeezed in a fist. She hadn't often heard people complain about the customs of this planet, the troubles that the uneven balance of genders created. Her heart broke for them. Was that what Maxu was going through now?

She didn't feel guilty for how she'd reacted to learning she had a mate. Her freedom, her goals for herself... The way Maxu had approached her had made it seem like those were all going to be torn away from her at any second.

But she'd come to realize that he was more than the uncaring, temperamental guy he presented to the world. Every time they interacted, he chipped away at her fears bit by bit. Now she had to figure out how to chip away at his.

"Thank you, Gamso," she said. "That really helped. It's wonderful to meet a man who's so introspective. Earth women are going to love you."

She grinned when his brows rose in surprise. The corner of his mouth curled, and he stared at the ground dreamily.

19

Alacera emerged before Meg's eyes, and she sucked in a gasp. Her chest remained expanded as her head tipped up and up and up, taking in the glittering palace where they'd been invited to stay.

Surrounded by a verdant rainforest, the city of Alacera was built on land that was cut through with hundreds of waterways, like a more lush Venice. Except these waterways were all fed by towering waterfalls that spilled over the crescent moon–shaped cliffs—a backdrop to the Alacera palace.

The magnificent building rested at the base of the curved mountain range and was surrounded by a natural moat formed by the water crashing down from above. The vapor rising into the air from the powerful water created a glittering haze strewn with dewy rainbows through which the lapis spires and teardrop roofs of the palace could be seen.

Cruisers weren't allowed within the Alacera city walls, so the group had been ushered onto boats that now floated to the palace through quiet neighborhoods and manicured gardens. Meg studied the intricate way in which the plants had been trained to create glorious flower-capped temples and grinned when a lime-green toad with fluffy yellow wings fluttered between the flowers.

Through her amazement, a twinge of sadness ate at her. What would Maxu say about that creature? Would he lift a sardonic brow and complain about the pest control here or some such nonsense? The thought almost brought a smile to her face. Almost.

The iridescent glimmer of large wings caught in the sun and drew her attention. The Alacera people had wings in a variety of colors, and Meg was transfixed by the cellophane-like material that bathed the area around them in brightly colored light, like the sun streaming through stained glass.

There were many winged races on Clecania, but in Meg's opinion, no others were quite as dazzling as the Alacera. They were mythical fairies come to life. Even the burly soldiers who'd come to escort them to the palace had long, elegant wings that gleamed. One guy kept peering back at the group and shaking out his wings to draw attention to them. Meg had to admit, they did appear a bit more vibrant than the others. Maybe he treated them with the famous Alacera oil harvested from the Ibsi nuts that grew in great vines behind the waterfalls.

They reached a set of stone stairs and departed the boat, towing their floating bags, which had grown in number as the humans continued to collect souvenirs. If Meg was going to buy anything from Alacera, she'd have to do it today.

They were fortunate enough to be visiting during the most important holiday of the city. Meg was beyond thrilled, but it meant that all business would be closed for the next few days.

A statuesque woman approached them, holding a staff tipped with gems. She was dressed in an outfit whose material was more like glossy leaves than cloth. The queen.

For a moment, Meg was surprised to see the woman alone. Didn't all royalty travel with a small contingent of soldiers at all times? But her confusion vanished when an enormous animal prowled forward, planting itself next to the queen.

Lucy hissed, "Is that a fucking lion-bear?"

Camille was the first to get over her shock. "That's a casican," she breathed. "They're the products of thousands of years of domestication. Common pets here."

The casican was enormous. Easily larger than a full-grown bear and just as round and furry. It was a soft brown with pale mint–tipped fur and a wide, fluffy rose-pink mane circling its neck and traveling down its spine.

From the queen's right darted a shaggy baby casican. It let out a collection of squeaks and huffs as it inspected the newcomers. When it got to Meg, it attempted to stand on its back feet and sniff at a printed flower on her pants before toppling over, gripping its toes and trying to stuff a foot into its mouth.

"Are you trying to impress us, handsome?" The cub froze at Camille's words and scrambled to get to her. Her grin was infectious as she stooped to examine the chuffing creature.

"I apologize," the queen interrupted in a melodic voice. "Mafapi is a newborn. She must have gotten away from her mother."

Mafapi just about melted against Camille's fingers as she scratched the cub's round ear. The casican let out a wailing groan and her dark lashes slid closed. With a final reluctant pat, Camille stood.

"Welcome. I'm Rhal, the queen of Alacera." Rhal spread her wings, casting blues, pinks, and greens over the stone walkway, and dipped her head. "I wanted to be one of the first to greet you, but I can only stay for a little while. As you may be aware, Stigalthi Marin begins tomorrow, and there are preparations I need to see to."

Meg's translator stuttered out the closest approximation for Stigalthi Marin it could. *The emptying and filling.*

"Today will be busy for you, I'm afraid. We've organized a large reception tonight. But for the next two days of your stay, you're welcome to celebrate with us in lieu of interviews, as long as you respect our traditions."

"I'm beyond grateful," Rita exclaimed. "This sounds like a beautiful, healing holiday."

"Indeed it is," Queen Rhal answered and lowered her wings.

The queen explained the holiday a little more as she led them to their rooms in the palace. She also not so casually questioned them about the number of humans back in Tremanta, if they were happy there, and whether or not they were prevented from leaving.

Mafapi scurried along next to them. She ran on all fours up toward each soldier, nudging their ankles with her nose. Every so often she'd get distracted by a plant that had crept onto the lacquered stone walkway. She gobbled up any flowers she came across, then bounded back to the humans a proud grin exposing her blossom-stained teeth.

It wasn't until a clipped growl that couldn't be mistaken for anything but the annoyed exhalation of a mother that Mafapi's ears turned down. A full-grown casican growled at her cub from behind a woven vine gate.

Mafapi peered up at the humans with sad wide violet eyes, then dragged her feet over to her mother. With a tsking noise, Queen Rhal used her long elegant tail to scoop up the cub under its arms and plopped her onto her mother's back. Mafapi stretched, already falling asleep as her mother ambled away.

With a kind grin, Queen Rhal bid their group goodbye, and the remaining soldiers guided them the rest of the way.

"We're being housed up there," Daunet pointed at a column that split into three spires near the top like a pitchfork with gleaming mosaic roofs and lush, flowering vines dripping with dew collected from the mist in the air.

"Man, I'm already soaked," Camille half complained, pulling the fabric sticking to her stomach away.

"No wonder they don't use cloth," Tara said, running a hand through her hair until it was fashionably slicked back.

Sophia spun in place, hands raised. "I love it. It reminds me of when my sister and I took a trip to Niagara Falls."

"It's gonna get old real fast," Lucy grumbled, her hair already frizzing.

They reached the base of the tower, but before they stepped onto the spiraling staircase which would take them up to their individual rooms, Daunet and the other guards discussed their schedules for the next few days.

"I'm gonna need to pee every five minutes, I can already tell." Tara crossed one foot over the other, gazing up at the towers impatiently.

Aqueducts and gutters ran over and through every roof, archway, and walkway, ensuring you were surrounded by the calming sounds of bubbling water wherever you went.

Lucy sighed, staring at one archway in particular that had been strung with tinted crystal beads that sparkled in the sun. "God, that would be a good spot for a picture."

As Lucy often bemoaned, the fact that Clecanians weren't overly fond of photography killed her. Back on Earth, she'd made a career of curating posts across social media and contracting out her services to companies to help them do the same.

Heleax and Lucy had gotten into a few arguments about it so far, and Heleax had continued to argue that to truly appreciate a place you had to visit it—if you'd seen a hundred pictures beforehand, then the joy and awe would be lessened.

Lucy argued the opposite—seeing pictures of people or places only worked to build your excitement so that when you finally experience a place you could marvel over how it was even better than you'd thought.

Meg found herself agreeing with Lucy on this. Perhaps travel was more accessible on this planet, but on Earth, pictures had been all Meg had of the world.

When the patrol arrangements had been set up, the women were scanned so they had entry to their doors. Meg requested her print be added to her mate's room just in case he appeared again. The reminder that Maxu was either gone or avoiding her tugged at her heart, dimming her cheerful mood once more, but when she stepped into the spacious suite she'd been assigned, she couldn't hold back her smile.

Aqueducts circled the round towers of her building and emptied into pools inset on the room's balconies. As the pools filled, water spilled over the edge, creating a mini waterfall, and she was delighted to find a thin chute of water falling from the balcony above into her own pool, splashing droplets over the garden planted around the water's edge. Tropical blooms sprouted out of every square inch of dirt.

Gentle breezes rustled their petals, filling the room with a sweet fragrance.

Rather than one elevated mattress, one entire corner of the room was covered in velvety soft petals and moss. She crashed onto the soft bedding, imagining she was reclining in a fairy garden, and stared up at the hundreds of small solar-powered light bubbles floating around the ceiling.

She had the same orbs in her room on Tremanta, the style of lighting being a favorite among many cities, but here the small glass balls arranged themselves into a spiraling design across the ceiling. Some gleamed brightly, while others flickered in and out. The gently pulsing light reminded her of early summer fireflies back in Indiana.

This place was beautiful. Magical. She couldn't push away the thought that it would be the perfect place to spend time with someone you loved. She'd been content to flirt and socialize and explore all on her own, but now that she was alone in her room once again, she ached to share the experience with someone. To marvel at the beautiful surroundings. To lie down while holding someone's hand and listen to the gentle splashing of the water.

She remembered Maxu's stuffy view of the fossilized coral and wondered what he might say about this room. She grinned. "Seems like a waste of water," she rumbled in a silly imitation of him. It was a cruel joke that the mere thought of him scowling made her lips curl.

As she got ready for the party, she sorted through all her emotions, looking past the surface feelings of hurt, fear, and defensiveness that shadowed everything else. In the past three weeks, she'd gone from abhorring the thought of having Maxu as her mate to warming to the idea to all-out daydreaming about the man.

Slowly but surely, Meg was figuring out who she really was and what she really wanted. In her old marriage, she'd backed down and given in far too often. It was safer that way, easier. She'd always been too afraid to push back, and maybe if she'd been more open with her family, with Jeremy things might have turned out differently. It probably would've been a car wreck, but at least she'd have been honest. Instead, she'd allowed herself to wallow for far too long, but not anymore.

The next time she saw Maxu, she'd be prepared. She'd keep her guard up and her expectations low, but if they failed to make a relationship work, she was determined that it wouldn't be her fault.

By the time she and the other humans arrived, the party was in full swing. The Alacera people crowded into a gorgeous sunken space where gentle streams wound through the floors and massive flowering trees glittered with dew. The colored light from the Alacerans' wings combined with the misty air and the calm blue water pouring all around gave the open space the feel of an impressionist watercolor painting of a fantasy world brought to life. Large casicans roamed through the party as well, curling into the sides of their owners and dragging their cubs back with their teeth when they became a little too rambunctious.

Some of their group had gotten used to the constant dampness all around. Lucy, Nirato, and Heleax hadn't. They stood together, complaining among themselves since the rest of the group was too happy to commiserate.

Meg's outfit was beautiful, the party was *beyond* beautiful, but what she loved the most were the artificial wings they'd attached to the back of her dress. Meg and Daunet found a beam of light pouring through the mist and took turns dragging their wings into it so they could admire them.

A delicate shade of green that had emerged behind her lids every time she closed her eyes had called to her when she'd been presented with outfit choices. Her sea-glass colored bodice and skirt paired beautifully with the pinks and purples of her wings. She smiled at the spray of colors glowing on the stone walkway as the light passed through her wings before forcing Daunet to flash hers the same way.

Daunet froze just as Meg clapped at the warm yellows and oranges of her guard's wings. "He's here."

Meg's hands stilled before her chest, her breath hitching.

On some level, she'd known he'd been nearby all along, hiding in the shadows. But tonight, he was letting himself be seen.

No interest in subtlety or playing hard to get, Meg turned in place, scanning the crowd until she spotted him. Though she was still slightly annoyed that he'd disappeared, she couldn't help but grin. He didn't wear wings. His outfit was plain compared to the natural explosions of leaves, petals, and gossamer the rest of them were wearing. But he was still the most striking person in the room.

And he was scowling.

Not an angry scowl—or rather, not angry with her at least. The expression seemed more frustrated than anything else. She took a step toward him, and his body stiffened. Meg stopped. With a frown of her own, she straightened her spine and pushed forward again.

Meg sidled by crowds of cheerful people and stepped around lazy snoring casicans, but when she reached the spot he'd been standing, Maxu was gone.

Exasperation welled in her, though she tried to push it away as a couple of large ethereal men engaged her in conversation. They asked her about Earth, typical things mostly, and she did her best to focus, but half of her wanted to reach out and touch their arms. Laugh a little too loudly at their jokes. Stare for a little too long. Anything to bring her mate out of the woodwork so she could see some evidence that he still cared.

But that wouldn't be fair to these men, especially not since she wouldn't put it past her mate to materialize ready to injure. She shouldn't like the idea of him getting so jealous, but a bitter part of her that wanted him to suffer as much as she had for the past few days bubbled at the notion of him showing a bit of that possessiveness she'd thought she despised.

The golden hour hit, then the moons rose, and as the tipsy Alacerans drained the last of their drinks and trickled out of the party, Meg still hadn't found him.

Both she and Daunet were silent on the walk back, lost in their own thoughts. She was at risk of pulling a muscle in her neck from craning it all night in search of her elusive mate, so she turned her focus on Daunet. For the first time that evening, she spotted the tightness around Daunet's mouth and the permanent crease between her brows.

Guilt crawled up her throat. Her friend was upset, and she hadn't even noticed. Had something happened with Tara?

"Do you wanna talk about it?" Meg asked quietly.

Daunet exhaled a deep breath. "No." Pressure seemed to build in the air around her, and Meg knew she was going to say more even before she opened her mouth. "Tara spoke with one female all night."

Fira. Meg recalled how well they'd gotten along when the woman had helped the humans pick out clothes and attach their wings. Her candy apple red cellophane wings matched her fiery hair and complemented her deeply tanned skin. She'd been kind and open, talking to the humans as if they were old friends, revealing the stresses of her job and discussing how excited she was for the holiday.

"I overheard them speaking of all the natural sights she could explore tomorrow. Fira offered to escort her," Daunet added, voice low with a hint of defeat.

Meg winced. "And you're upset that they might spend time together? It may not be romantic at all, you know." She slipped an arm through Daunet's, locking their elbows.

Her guard turned her face up and peered through the mist that distorted the stars and made them twinkle more than normal. "I have no right to be upset," she whispered. "I've tried to hide my feelings, as I've done my whole life, but I'm now realizing I may end up missing my opportunity by refusing to reveal my wishes to Tara."

Meg was shocked when Daunet faced the ground again and she saw moisture gathering in her eyes. Clecanian women didn't show emotions out in the open like this. They'd been trained not to. While men went to husbandry school to learn the best ways to please their wives and raise children, women went to their own school and learned how not to feel—and if they did feel, how not to show it to anyone else. Meg had never seen Daunet like this. She squeezed her a little tighter.

Daunet's whisper dropped even lower, barely audible over the trickling water all around them. "I think I can feel her just under the surface. Like I could recognize her if I really tried."

"Isn't that amazing, though? I thought you'd say it was a gift from the Goddess."

"But what if it's not true? If I allow myself to hope too much…what if I open myself up and nothing happens?" she asked. "I've buried these feelings for so long now." Daunet winced, a guilty look flashing toward Meg. "I never told you, but I've noticed Tara for a long time now. Since she was brought to the temple. I know more about her than is healthy. I always hoped I'd recognize her. And then when I learned she was going on this trip—"

"Wait, *that's* why you pushed so hard to be my guard on this tour?" Meg chuckled, tsking at Daunet.

Daunet gave her a sad smile in return. "I hope you aren't offended when I say yes, absolutely."

"I told you I wouldn't push you anymore, Daunet, but do you want my real, honest advice?"

"No." Daunet grinned down at Meg's shocked expression. "Not right now. I don't think I could accept it right now," she added, patting Meg's hand. "Just walk in misery with me. It helps."

Meg chuckled, then did just that. They strolled through winding pathways, over small bridges, and towering stone arches, silently bonding over their confusing love lives.

20

Maxu gazed at the retreating form of his mate. His mind was in shambles, his confidence clouded. He'd lain awake thinking about Meg for the last two nights and how she had agreed to testing in Adenelas without pay, even after the way the two scientists had treated her. Seeing her willingness to help Clecania—a planet she didn't owe anything to, despite what she'd said—had even made him consider returning the human items he'd stolen. It was doubtful the researchers could learn anymore from them, but what if they could?

He was going soft, and it was fucking with his head to the point where he didn't trust himself around her. He wanted her desperately, but there was too much at stake. Maxu could remember only one other time he'd felt this clawing greed.

When he'd been a boy, his father had taken him and his brothers to a nature reserve near Tremanta. He'd hiked along behind his family, bored as his elder brother Luka had rambled on about the different animal species living in the forest. But then the most glorious flower he'd ever seen had caught his eye.

Rising out of fluffy black moss, the white flower had glowed in a beam of sunlight breaking through the canopy. Its delicate petals were splattered with fuchsia, and the smell wafting from it had been sweeter than any candy he'd ever had. His family had moved on, not noticing he'd remained transfixed.

It was the first time he'd ever desperately wanted something to be all his, *only* his. So, he'd picked it even though they'd been in a nature reserve and it wasn't allowed. He'd hidden it in his pack the whole way home, then scurried to his room and placed it in a glass of water.

He'd hide in his room, just staring at the velvety petals, smelling it, loving the fact that he had something more beautiful and precious than any of his brothers and no one else could even look at it. But over time, the water had turned cloudy, the white petals wrinkling and growing yellow. The sweet smell had become sour.

In a panic, he'd attempted to plant it outside in the forest behind his house. He'd go to check on it every day, and he could recall the sadness he'd felt when the flower had finally wilted into nothing.

Maxu followed Meg, watching from the shadows as he'd done for the past two days. His temper rose to near anger at how gorgeous she looked. How unattainable, untouchable she was, with her pale green dress and pink wings glimmering in the moonlight. He wanted to take her, hide her, and selfishly keep her brightness and warmth to himself, but he knew he couldn't. So he'd seethed from afar instead. At least if he only watched, he couldn't harm.

He blinked at her retreating back, wondering for the twentieth time what had made her choose the light green color of her outfit. His fingers curled as she disappeared into the tower. *Chase her.*

He clutched a piece of stone in his pocket, and a vile wave of guilt helped keep him planted in place. He'd thought nothing of it at the moment, cracking off an innocuous piece of the coral from Adenelas. The way she'd spoken about the fossil with such passion…if he couldn't have that passion for himself, he'd take a piece of something she *did* love instead.

He'd intended for it to bring him a modicum of relief, but the rough stone only reminded him he had a tendency to take more than he should with no thought of the damage it might cause. He had to remind himself of that every time he found his feet carrying him toward her without his consent.

Keeping his eyes trained on her balcony, he waited for her light to come on. He tumbled the stone more quickly through his fingers when it didn't. A buzz in his arm had him freezing. His heart thundered in his ears. His alarm.

She wouldn't. Not after last time. Would she?

He brought up an image on his communicator and sucked in a shaky breath, his cock already filling with blood. Meg was there, wrists and neck trapped against the wall in his room, but this time she didn't look mad. She looked triumphant.

The stone turned to dust as he closed his fist over it. This female would be the death of him. For once in his life, he'd been doing the noble thing, the right thing by staying away from her, but there was only so much he could take.

He quickly showed his room credentials to the guards waiting outside. Though the steps of the stairway activated, spiraling upward, he took them two at a time anyway.

The breaths he sucked in as he stood outside of his door did nothing to calm him. He needed to just release her and shoo her away before he did something he'd regret. Scrubbing a hand over his face, he steeled himself.

She stiffened as he entered, her eyes going wide. Maxu's gaze lingered for too long on the curve of her breasts as he watched her chest slowly rise and fall as if she were attempting to control her breaths. The cuffs had sliced through her wings as they'd magnetized to the wall behind her. Delicate flaps of fabric hung by her wrists. The sight helped him control the urges pulsing straight from the dark corners of his mind to his dick.

He held up his communicator, making a show of turning off the shock to her collar. "What are you doing here?" His voice was hoarse, his gaze now glued to the high slit running up her thigh. He took a step closer, unable to help himself.

That damn blush was on her cheeks again when he met her gaze. He still hadn't discovered how far down her body that flush would travel. His mouth watered. He hadn't even seen what her nipples looked like. He could look now if he wanted to. She wouldn't be able to stop him.

"I wanted to talk to you. Where have you been?"

"You chained yourself to my wall in order to talk to me?" He chuckled, taking another step closer. There was a seam on the right side of her bodice. It would be so easy to rip.

She swallowed, seeming to gather her nerve. He traced the stubborn line that appeared between her brows. "You never spoke more honestly to me than when I was chained to your wall, I figured..." She licked her lips. "I think, maybe, seeing me vulnerable helps you open up. So, if that's what it takes to get you to talk to me..." She gave a tense shrug. "Quid pro quo."

"A favor for a favor, huh?" he repeated as his translator uttered the phrase in his ear. This was dangerous. She didn't understand where his mind was at the moment.

Large cool-green flower petals were plastered over her bodice, and a matching gossamer skirt wrapped around her waist. The material was almost see-through, the delicate threads as fine as any he'd ever seen. Water droplets from the air clung to the crisscrossing threads as they would on a web.

"What if the favors I want are ones you're not willing to give?" Heat flourished behind his eyes; a sign he was starting to understand meant his irises were going black.

His focus lingered on her delicate neck as she swallowed. "I wouldn't have allowed myself to be shackled to your wall if I wasn't prepared for that," she murmured, skin flushed with red but gaze determined.

A dark laugh bubbled up in him. She thought he was someone else. Maybe he should show her. Just scare her a little so she knew not to pull anything like this again.

He could see her pulse fluttering in her neck as he ran the back of his fingers over the curve of her waist. A bit of white dust on his palm caught his eye. This wouldn't end well.

"You'll go back to your room, and we can talk another time." He lifted the communicator, thumb a hair away from pressing the release.

"I'm married," she blurted.

21

Her pulse rang in her ears as she waited for Maxu to respond. She knew he'd heard her. How could he not have? As soon as the words were out, his whole body had gone still. His gaze remained trained on the controls to her cuffs, but he hadn't released them. A bit of fear curled in her belly. What if she'd read him wrong? What if she'd just locked herself up and worked him up into a rage?

"On Earth," she continued. "I'm technically still married."

His head snapped up, his features covered with something icy and fierce, though she couldn't tell if it was anger exactly. "Hear me, Meg," Maxu growled. "You have no husband. You are not married. And unless you want that male found and gutted, you won't speak another word of it."

"But I want you to understand." Sweat gathered under the metal at her wrists. "I don't consider him my husband anymore. It's been over nine months since I was taken from Earth. We didn't have a happy marriage. But I think maybe you and I could have one. I mean, granted"—she peered at her restrained wrist out of the corner of her eye—"this is a little…unorthodox. But I'm starting to believe that we were put together for a reason."

The tension radiating off his body in the heavy silence felt like a blow. Had she just opened herself up for nothing?

She jumped when he suddenly whirled, presenting her with his back. One hand stabbed through his hair, the other was planted on his hip. He paced away, then stilled, staring out through the sheet of water falling from the roof above.

Meg chewed on her lip as his hand dipped into his pocket and he pulled out his communicator. The tension in her cuffs relaxed, and her throat tightened. *I shouldn't have told him. Stupid. Stupid.*

"I'm sorry for upsetting you. I'll go." She waited for her cuffs to fall away from her wrists, but they didn't. Should she just leave with them attached? He was so still, radiating a dark energy that sucked all the dim light out of the room.

"Come here." His deep firm command fluttered through her and made her shiver, for it was most definitely a *command.*

Her neck craned to peer at the door. She could just leave, but that wasn't why she'd come here.

He slowly rotated, his black gaze lighting a fire under her skin. His tongue flashed over his bared teeth, an impatient lion waiting for its prey to wander within reach.

Be brave, Meg whispered to herself. She kept her eyes locked on his as she took one step, two steps, three steps closer. The cool air licking her skin sparked with electricity the closer she got, until she was standing before him all but vibrating.

His neck remained straight as he stared down his nose at her. "You don't consider yourself married to this…human?" he spat.

She shook her head.

He nodded sharply, as if praising her for answering a rhetorical question. "No. Because you're mine now. Correct?"

Meg's lips pursed. She knew they were just words. Just a statement. Possibly something he even needed to hear, but she couldn't bring herself to say it.

The right side of his mouth curled dangerously, and he gave a small shake of his head. "You want to be vulnerable for me, vahpti? A favor for a favor?"

Meg's lips parted, but her trapped breath remained in her lungs. She nodded.

He hummed out a low growl. "On your knees."

It took her a few moments of internal fighting, but slowly, she sank down, down, down until she was craning her neck up at him. After a pregnant pause, he grinned, all brazen and lecherous and gloating. And damn whatever trauma was doing it but her sex throbbed at the powerful set of his thighs and shoulders as he loomed over her.

"Why have you been avoiding me?" she asked.

The fabric of his pants rustled as he crouched in front of her. With his thumb and forefinger, he pinched her chin, lifting her face. "I think I need to see you a little more *vulnerable* before I can tell you that." His knuckles glided over her jaw, his gaze following their progress hungrily, leaving goose bumps pebbling on her skin. He dipped his forefinger between her breasts and pulled her bodice forward. "How about we take this off?"

Meg lifted a brow in challenge. "Fine."

His gaze held for a moment, as if giving her a chance to change her mind. When she remained silent, his finger moved, tracing the round edge of the fabric over her breast until he stopped at the seam on her side where the garment was fastened into place.

She'd imagined he would rip the petals free. Clean, easy, quick. But what he did was so much worse. Turning his palms over her rib cage, he searched for the hidden pins and clasps holding the leaves in place. The snaps of the fastenings popping open boomed through the hushed space as he pulled them apart. A bolt of heat raced to her pussy with every firm tug of his fingers until she felt the insides of her thighs grow damp and hot.

He'd unfastened the garment completely but hadn't yet peeled it away when his nostrils flared. He stared at the vee between her legs. The black of his eyes seemed to darken. She shivered when he licked his lips, as if he could see through the fabric still covering her.

"No underwear, little human? That's a very dangerous thing to do."

She'd known this would happen. Known it the moment she'd slipped off the thick underwear that shielded some of her scent, tossed them into her room, and dashed up to his door.

"You don't scare me, Maxu." A lightness cut through the intensity of the moment when Meg registered how true that statement rang in her mind. She wanted to see him like this, forceful and dark and rough. But even though her pulse was soaring and she was on her knees in front of a man who was actively attempting to scare her away, she trusted him.

His jaw hardened at that. "Really?" His hands shot out and locked around her wrists. He forced them down to the stone ground and held them there while a subtle *zing* told her he'd locked them in place. He waited for her to answer with a scowl.

She lifted her head and gave him the widest grin she could muster. "Do I smell scared to you?"

A surge of pride went through her when his glare faltered, and he swallowed.

"Why have you been avoiding me?" she asked again.

His fingers pulled the petals covering her torso away. Cool air hit her skin, and her nipples hardened immediately. Any embarrassment she might have felt was soothed under the rolling purr that reverberated through his throat as he traced her ribcage and the curve of her breast with his thumb. "I'm

269

not used to explaining myself to anyone." Before she could answer, his rough palm cupped one of her breasts, and she moaned. "But you're not just anyone, are you?"

Unable to help herself, she squeezed her legs together to relieve some of the throbbing pressure. "No," she breathed.

"Open," he demanded, pointing a finger back and forth between her clenched thighs. She did.

Wrists still held to the ground, her breasts swayed between her biceps as her knees split wide, her ass resting on her heels. He muttered some curse she couldn't make out that made her flush, not with embarrassment but with confidence.

Maxu fell to his knees and leaned his face into the crook of her neck, angling forward until his calloused hand scraped down her stomach. She shuddered again when he traced a finger over her hip bone. His palm cupped her pussy, pressing firmly enough to send sparks exploding through her. She gasped, letting out a small whimper, when his thick forefinger slipped between her lips and delved inside her wet channel.

"You're dripping for me, sweetness." The groan he breathed against her neck was hot. "I suppose I owe you an answer now."

"Please." Meg blinked, trying to concentrate past the knot tightening in her belly.

His head rose from her shoulder, and he watched her face as he spoke, all the while rocking his palm against her with delicious even pressure as his finger stroked inside. "I feel changed by you." His eyes danced over her expression, his breaths coming in deep and even. "You have a piece of me I can never get back. You own it. And all I want is to have a piece of you in return. But I can't decipher you."

Meg's lids slid closed at his words. Finally—he was finally talking to her. All it had taken was her agreeing to be bossed around, bound, and fucked with his skillful hands.

He slipped another finger inside her, stroking lazily but making her knees tremble. He cupped her face with a rough palm, forcing her to look at him again. His brows were drawn, his black gaze studying her features as if trying to work out a riddle even now.

"I don't know how to win you," he growled in frustration. "I heard what you said at that interview yesterday." His fingers had stopped pumping into her, but his palm continued to gently rock, keeping her on the edge but not letting her come. "What are you looking for in a partner, Meg? Repeat what you said yesterday."

Meg licked her lips, though her cheeks were a bit squished from his gripping fingers. Yesterday, in Pesquen, she'd been torn. Confused why she'd been missing a man who, by all accounts, she should despise. And when one of the citizens had asked her what she looked for in a partner, she'd faltered. Every other time she'd given her rehearsed speech about wanting to find a man that treated her like a goddess, but at that instant the practiced response had felt so shallow.

Thousands of memories had passed through her mind in the minute it had taken to answer that question. She'd thought about Jeremy. Her parents. Their marriage. What they'd wanted for her and what she'd wanted for herself. She'd recalled lying in her cold bed, debating whether or not she should get up, wondering if it'd matter to anyone if she did.

Then she'd thought about Maxu, and an answer had come to her. A real answer.

"I want someone who I can grow with. Someone who makes me better."

"I don't know how you're doing it, but I think you're making me better." The harsh lines bracketing Maxu's mouth softened. "Seeing the world through your eyes makes it brighter than it used to be. I've been avoiding you because…I'm not capable of doing the same."

She hadn't noticed when his hand had moved, but it now rested on her waist, his thumb stroking over her ribcage. Meg tried to push through the tightness in her throat so she could explain. "Yes, you are," she whispered. "You're showing me I can speak my mind and argue and fight and be unlikable."

"You mean fight *me*," he chuckled humorlessly.

"Yes," she agreed easily. "Do you like me, Maxu? As a person?"

The warmth that instantly lit his face had butterflies exploding in her belly. "You know I do, vahpti."

"But I bit you and screamed at you and ran away from you." Meg let out a laugh. "I even shot you!" When Maxu didn't seem fazed by the reminders of her horrid behavior, she went on. "My whole life, I've always felt too scared to be myself. I had a personality built for me, and if I didn't fit into that mold, I wasn't worthy of love. But with you…even when I'm being a pain in the ass and making mistakes…you've never made me feel worthless. You make me feel safe. Like I can say the wrong thing and I won't be abandoned or judged. I don't think you understand how liberating that is. I've never had that before." Meg's lips kept twitching downward as tears rose in her eyes. "I want you to feel that way when you're with me. I don't want you to hide from me."

The smile beaming out of him made her melt. She'd never seen it before. She'd seen smirks and grins and cocky flashes of teeth, but never anything this unguarded. A purr reverberated through his chest as he brushed his lips against hers, hands still tight on her jaw. His kiss was slow and languid. Meg sighed as he slid his tongue against hers. Maxu answered her with a groan of his own.

"I think I like you most when you're being a pain in the ass," he whispered, brushing a thumb over her bottom lip.

"Good," she grinned, lifting her face as far as she could with her hands still planted on the ground. "Because I enjoy getting you worked up."

He descended on her again, his lips a bit more demanding than they'd been a moment ago. With a whimper, she wiggled her hands. He smiled against her mouth, then went right back to sucking her tongue. One of his hands traveled to one cuff, releasing it, then to the other. Meg launched herself toward him, throwing her arms around his neck and pressing her naked body to his clothed one.

Maxu didn't topple over, though. He caught her, wrapping his brawny arms around her waist and palming her ass. He shifted so he was sitting on the ground, knees slightly bent, with Meg cradled in his lap. His fingers twisted in her hair, and with a firm tug, he pulled her head back until her spine arched and her breasts were perfectly accessible.

He held her there, just staring. Then his hot tongue landed on her nipple. How did he know just how to swirl and suck and bite to make her breath catch like that? It was unfair. Grasping blindly for his free hand since his other was still clutching her by the hair, she guided his fingers up to the collar at her throat, silently urging him to take it off.

When he did, she snatched it before he could toss it to the side. Maxu pulled away from her nipple, now dark and hard from his unrestrained ministrations.

He eyed the collar clutched in her hand. "Meg?"

"Lie back," she crooned, biting her lip and urging him to recline with one hand to his shoulder. It was like pressing against a wall.

"I don't think so, vahpti." He reached for the collar and missed. She was sure he could've gotten it if he really wanted to, but he became distracted by the jiggling of her breasts as she thrust the collar above her head as high as she could.

He moaned and shoved his mouth into the soft tissue under her nipple. Her toes curled, her hand almost losing hold of the metal as he dug his fingers into her hips and rubbed her sex against his shaft through his pants.

Trying to keep her wits from clouding over by lust completely, she angled her body forward, urging him again to lean back. He growled against her skin, nipping at her neck as he pressed her flush to his body, but he did eventually lie back, pulling her with him.

She tried to sneak the collar to his neck, but he stilled her with one hand on her wrist. Growling a warning, he stared up at her with an adorably stern expression. "Why?"

"Because I want to try new things," she whispered, pressing soft kisses to his firm lips until they softened. "Just trust me."

Inhaling a deep breath that lifted her body, he released her wrist. And waited, jaw tense, gaze suspicious.

She giggled, then placed the collar over his neck. Nothing would happen without his print, they both knew it, but he didn't move to help. "Please," she implored.

A small quirk lifted his mouth, his gaze flashing hungrily. "Beg."

With a grin, she ducked under his jaw and gave the firm muscles of his neck a lick, then a kiss. "Oh, please, please, please, handsome, strong mate of mine." She kissed up to his ear, swirling her tongue around the shell, and almost squealed with pleasure when he shuddered.

He grumbled something she couldn't hear, then lifted his hand to the collar. "Fine, but after you're done with whatever this is, I fuck you any way I want."

Meg's head jerked up and a slow smile spread, a pulse thrumming through her pussy at the thought. "Deal."

22

Maxu's collar sealed to the floor, magnetically binding to the metal buried within. He glared up at his mate as she rose to her knees, still straddling his hips. He didn't like this, being restrained, but the look of pure excitement lighting her features and making her limbs relaxed was enough to make him shut up and deal with whatever she'd planned.

That and the promise he could take control when she'd had her fun. What position would he put her in? On her knees, ass lifted in the air, perhaps. Maxu licked his lips.

Meg's dark hair skimmed her chin as she leaned forward and undressed him. Maxu tried to remain annoyed, but the soft gliding of her fingertips over his bare skin as she opened his tunic had his heart racing in an instant.

Eyes widening, his throat hit the metal of his collar when he lifted his head to watch her slide down his body and kneel between his thighs. Though her blue eyes were heavy with lust, he noticed some trepidation. Her hands shook as she picked at the knot cinching his pants together.

Meg's dark brows knit with determination, and he held his tongue. Her blush lit under her skin, making faint red crawl down over her chest. The color deepened when she worked his pants loose and his cock sprung free.

The widening of her eyes as she knelt naked before him was almost enough to have him tearing off his collar, but then curiosity got the best of him. "Touch me, vahpti."

A tremulous smile flicked over her features before she bit her lip. His dick twitched at the sight. He'd thought she'd reach out, stroke him maybe, but the air froze in his lungs when she tipped forward, planting her soft palms on the ground for stability. She couldn't be planning to—

Her tongue darted out and licked the tip of his dick, and Maxu shouted to the ceiling. He panted, shutting his eyes to keep himself collected and bracing for the feeling of her hot mouth touching him again. This wasn't a normal pleasure. Clecanian females didn't tend to do this. Sex mostly focused on their enjoyment, since the male would find release regardless.

He scrubbed his hands over his face and peered back down at her as far as he could with the damn collar holding him in place. Her broad grin told him she'd appreciated his reaction. "Enjoying this, female?" he growled, but he couldn't hold back a small smile. She was just so proud of herself, and he could scent the arousal flooding her core even now.

She leaned down again, this time wrapping a small palm around the base of his shaft. He hissed and his thighs tensed along with his fists. "Not as much as you." Her mouth was close enough to his shaft that her whispered words buffeted hot air over his oversensitive flesh, making him shiver.

Her small pink tongue licked the underside of his dick from root to tip, and his eyes rolled. "Goddess, help me," he muttered to himself. It took everything in him to keep his hips from bucking when she took the head of him in her mouth and lowered as far as she could go. He couldn't look away.

Panting as if he'd just ascended another mountain, he watched, transfixed as Meg sucked upward, leaving a wet glimmer on the parts of his shaft her mouth had been. He wanted to throw the collar off so he could sit up, get a better view, watch as his mate fucked him with her luscious mouth, but she'd asked him to remain in place and right now he knew he'd give her just about anything she asked for.

She was pumping her lips over him now, picking up speed and making his balls tight with the seed aching to be released. His palms flattened against the floor, then fisted, then flattened again. He needed something to hang on to, so he slipped his fingers into the gap between his collar and neck and squeezed the metal.

His abs jumped under her palm as she scraped her nails down his belly. "I'm going to come, beautiful." His exclamation was half choked warning, half growl.

She sat back, releasing him with a pop. The ache in his dick was an all-out throb now. So close—he was so close.

"Your turn," she grinned.

***

Raw power vibrated through the layers of muscle covering Maxu's magnificent body, but there was a sudden stillness underneath. A flutter of nervousness had her gripping her knees.

He remained in place, two hands clenching his collar so tightly she could see the evidence of bowed metal under his palms. He was sprawled in front of her, his beyond-massive chest roped with muscle, thick thighs tensed, glistening length rigid, and she wanted nothing more than to climb over him and see how difficult it would be to slide the length of his straining cock inside her.

"Are you sure?" His voice was hoarse, clipped. She wondered how much control it took him to ask her yet again, and warmth curled in her chest.

She nodded.

With a creak rather than a click, he undid the metal at his neck and flipped to his knees until he was on all fours. She stared, liquid arousal painting her thighs, excitement making sparks dance in her veins as his eyes slowly turned black again.

She had the faintest urge to run—not from fear but because it looked like he wanted her to. His ravenous dark gaze all but dared her. Slowly, she rose to her feet. He matched her movements, but they felt so much heavier than hers, each of his weighty muscles firm as he straightened.

Meg took a step away. Maxu grinned, his purr roaring to life. She smirked, then took another step. His thumbs skimmed over the tips of his fingers, and he crouched ever so slightly.

Not knowing exactly where she was running to, she spun. In less than a second, he'd caught her around the waist, flipped her onto his shoulder, and stalked to the sunken area of strange bedding.

Falling to his knees, he flipped her off his shoulder and pried her thighs apart. His fingers tightened on the rounded bit of her lower belly as his thumb pressed inside her opening and swept up until it firmly slipped over her clit, already slick with her arousal. The pressure was too concentrated, and she twitched.

Slowly, Maxu lowered to his elbows, his hot breath ghosting over the flesh of her thighs as he moved in. Despite everything that had just happened, heat raced to her cheeks. The direction of his gaze—not to mention his ever-lowering mouth—was undeniable.

Meg's breath trembled out of her. She'd only experienced this twice in her life. Both times had been at her insistence. Neither time had been good. A moment of doubt cooled her lust. This wasn't something men actually liked, not really. Her thighs began to close. Maxu's growl reverberated through the room as his palms slapped down against her inner thighs. She let out a hiss at the pain of the light sting.

His mouth descended on her, and all doubts fizzled away. His tongue delved into her core deeper than she'd thought possible. He stilled, and she held her breath, waiting to see if he'd pull away or make a funny face. Nothing could have prepared her for the purr that rumbled all the way from his chest to his tongue to her entrance.

A yelp, embarrassing in its volume, echoed through the room. She fell back against the sloped curve of the bed and gave in when her knees opened wider. Her body shook, breasts quivering, as he pulsed a finger inside her and rocked the flat, thick part of his vibrating tongue over her clit.

The tops of his wide shoulders hit the backs of her thighs as he squirmed to get closer, ragged groans mingling with his purr. One of his hands came up to squeeze her breast and pinch at her nipple. She rocked her clit against his mouth in time with the warm vibrating swipes of his tongue and couldn't hold back the words bubbling up in her throat.

"Yes, Maxu. Please…that feels so good—" A cry broke free from her chest as his answering groan sent her crashing over the edge.

He remained in place, sliding his fingers through her come and lapping gently at her clit until the absent rocking of her hips subsided. Maxu raised his head, his wild gaze roving over her sweaty skin and spread thighs.

She whimpered weakly as he first licked his lips, rolling them together as though savoring the last morsels of a dessert, then lifted the fingers he'd buried in her and sucked them clean.

Just like that, the embers simmering in her belly blazed back to life. Without a word, he rolled her onto her stomach, then lifted her hips until she was on her knees. Electricity sparked over her skin at the commanding way he forced his thigh between hers and spread her knees wide. His heavy palm gripped the meat of her ass. "I was right," he rasped. "You get pink everywhere."

Meg peered over her shoulder, and her breaths grew heavy. His wide chest rose and fell quickly, his firm abs constricting on every exhale. Matching his black eyes, mussed sections of his dark hair fell over his forehead. Heat pulsed deep inside her core at his insatiable perusal of her body.

His fingers curled around her waist, and the thick head of his dick pressed against her entrance. He held her in place there, though her sex trembled at the sensation of the tip of his cock splitting her wide. Gaze meeting hers, he ran a worshipful hand over the curve of her spine, his shaft pulsing. Meg attempted to wiggle her hips and bury him deeper, but his palm flattened on the small of her back, pinning her in place. "Please, Maxu," she begged. This was torture.

"Are you ready for your mate to fill you, vahpti?" He punctuated his question by pushing into her a bit more, then groaned at her answering moans.

Inch by inch, he filled her. Meg pressed her face into the pillows and tried not to notice the slight pain that came along with the glorious stretching. When he was buried deep, his damp chest came down over her back.

"Fuck, Meg." He slipped one hand between her thighs, and the other wrapped around her shoulders, his mouth pressed to her ear. "You have a magnificent cunt. Hot and tight. Delicious."

Meg preened, stretching her back against his chest like a contented cat. Her neck arched toward his mouth, reveling in his dirty praise.

His fingers slipped in light circles around her clit, applying just the right amount of pressure to make her wet and gasping. Maxu began moving inside her, sliding in and out slowly at first, but gaining speed with each one of her breathy moans. Powerful quads slapped against the backs of her thighs, forcing her forward until she collapsed onto her stomach, his devilish fingers still working even though his hand was trapped between the bed and her hips.

His knees pivoted her legs farther apart as he pounded into her. The pulsing of her heart echoed through her body and emerged in her core as a deep throb growing hotter and hotter each time he buried himself in her.

Heavy and slick with sweat and the warm moisture in the air, his chest weighed her down, while his arm clamped around her shoulders kept her held in place. She'd never experienced anything close to this. Not just the mind-numbing electricity of her climax building even now, but the connection of it. The way Maxu was all out fucking her from behind but still somehow managing to make her feel like he was treasuring the moment.

In her mind, sex had always been either depraved or wholesome. Shameful or virtuous. No in between. But this was both. It was dirty, tender, rough, and attentive all at once. Meg breathed out strangled yeses on every one of Maxu's thrusts.

His mouth pressed against her temple, nose burying in her hair, and he inhaled, releasing a loud purr. Her toes curled as the vibration of that sound pulsed from his cock to the walls of her core.

The yeses were gone, her breath trapped in her lungs as she waited for the crest of her orgasm to break over her.

"That's right, vahpti. Come. Come all over me." His harsh, hissed words against her skin were more than she could handle, and she came. She cried out, head going dizzy from lack of oxygen.

A proud, vicious growl built in volume as his thrusts grew deeper and more frantic. Meg was still trembling from the intensity of her climax, and his powerful, driving hips only elongated her cries until he slammed into her, shoving her collarbones against his forearm, and roared into the empty room.

She was too hot, too oversensitive to feel his semen filling her, but she noticed the tickle of it as it dripped out from her clenching sex. Maxu's lips trailed kisses over her shoulder between panted breaths. He kept himself buried inside her but shifted, pushing his upper body up so he could continue his progress down the center of her spine.

"Don't," she breathed. "I'm all sweaty."

A rumbled chuckle was her only warning before he gripped her hips and licked a long line up her spine to her neck. His nose nuzzled her ear, and he exhaled a hot "Mmm."

Meg flushed with pleasure even as she teased, "You're so weird."

When Maxu slipped out of her, she tried to rise, but he pressed her back down with a firm hand to her lower back, then sauntered away, muscular ass flexing with each step. When he'd disappeared into the bathroom alcove, she frantically attempted to smooth her tangled hair and wipe at her face to remove any rogue makeup.

"I like you rumpled."

Meg let out a short shriek and flailed onto her back. He'd been quieter than death on his approach.

He grinned down at her as her cheeks heated, then took a knee before her clenched thighs. With a single raised brow directed her way, she opened her legs. He took his time wiping away his seed from her ass and her pubic bone where it had dribbled, then tossed the cloth away.

Sitting back on his heels, he just stared at her for a moment. Sex was over, the haze of lust that lowered inhibitions and modesty gone with it. Now she was just…naked. Sprawled out before him for his clear-headed inspection. She wanted to shove her legs back together, but she forced herself not to, biting her lip again instead.

His stare went on for so long that she finally broke, sitting up so she could curl her knees into her chest. "What are you doing?"

His brows furrowed angrily, but he didn't try to stop her. "Searing your body into my mind so I can think of you when I fuck myself later tonight."

Warmth and a tendril of hurt curled together in her belly at his words, until she remembered that Clecanian couples didn't normally share rooms. He probably expected her to return to her own bed.

She smiled tentatively. "I could stay too…if you wanted."

"You mean sleep here? With me?" His expression hadn't shifted.

Meg squeezed her knees to her chest more tightly. "I mean, I can go if you'd rather. I just thought—"

She squealed as he dove, tackling her flat to the bed.

Hours later, Meg awoke to the faint trickling of water. The bright moon shone in through the open balcony, casting cool shadows over Maxu's sculpted cheeks. She was lying on her stomach, her preferred position for sleeping, and he was next to her, half his body draped over her back.

Their skin was covered in either sweat or condensation from the air. She didn't know which, and she didn't care. His thick bicep stretched across her upper back, while his tree trunk of a thigh weighed down her ass.

She shifted her arm a fraction, and he grunted, pulling her under the side of his body more tightly and resting his chin against her forehead. Meg fell back asleep with a grin on her face and the sexiest man she'd ever met holding on to her for dear life.

23

Maxu had spent the silent time before dawn lying as still as a statue, forcing down the constant threat of a purr as he watched Meg sleep. Lush curves and soft skin nestled under his body had greeted him when he'd opened his eyes. He'd gaped, mind still fuzzy with dreams of his mate, and wondered whether she was really there resting peacefully in his arms.

Over hours, he'd watched as dew had collected in glistening droplets on her skin. He'd jealously followed their progress as they'd broken and slipped down the graceful curve of her back.

The sun rose on the horizon, painting the world in pink and gold, yet the view didn't come close to making his heart ache as much as it did when Meg winced at the light and curled into the darkness of his chest.

The muscles in his right arm were screaming, but he refused to lower his hand. It was blocking a small portion of the sun, and he'd sooner face the Goddess's wrath than allow the offending rays of the morning to wake his female before she was ready.

A flashing light from the glowing orbs on the ceiling indicating a visitor made Meg's brows draw together. He ground his teeth, glaring toward the door as if he could injure whoever it was just by staring hard enough.

The flashing lit up the room again, this time accompanied by a gentle tinkling sound, and Meg's lids eased open. What would her reaction to waking up with him be?

From her spot on his chest, she tilted her head up to look at him. Her gaze then traveled to his lifted hand. Back to his face. A weight lifted from his shoulders when she grinned, rolled onto her side, and draped an arm over his waist, pulling herself flush against his chest and yawning.

There was no helping it anymore. His purr roared to life in his chest. Maxu felt her lips curl against his skin. He dropped his hand, cupping the back of her head, and lowered his chin to her scalp.

The lights on the ceiling flashed again and a loud ping echoed around the room. His purr morphed into a growl.

"What time is it? You should get that. It's probably Daunet." Meg's voice cracked, and another yawn broke through.

His fingertips tightened around her head for a moment before he extricated himself, swiped a blade from his bag, and stomped to the door, fully nude. Annoyance was plain from

Daunet's harsh brows and pursed lips as his door slid open. She scanned him up and down, eyes landing on his knife.

"We need to leave. The Stigalthi Marin begins soon, and Meg needs to get ready."

"I'll escort her," Maxu snapped.

Daunet shook her head. "That's not how this works."

Maxu opened his mouth to argue, but Meg's palm landed on his elbow.

"It's okay," she said with a sleepy smile. "I'll go get ready and see you down there, yeah? Oh, can I borrow this?" She spread her arms, showing off one of his cloth shirts. Before he could command that she remain exactly where she was, she'd lifted to her toes, hooked a hand around his neck, and tugged him down for a kiss. His mind blanked. He still hadn't recovered when she pulled back, brushed a bit of unruly hair off his forehead, and all but skipped away from him.

The door slid closed in front of his dumbfounded, stark-naked frame. After he'd recovered, he raced to get ready. Washing in the foam shower, fumbling to clip the hidden stays of his water-repellant clothing, and dashing down the spiraling stairs.

Impatiently, he waited for Meg and Daunet to emerge from the tower entry. His skin itched, and fresh floral scents rising from the surrounding blooms were putrid to his nose. They didn't smell like her. His limbs stiffened. *He* didn't smell like her anymore either. Like an idiot, he'd washed her away.

Finally, she appeared, a ball of light from the darkness of the covered entryway. His heart picked up speed. Her clothing was simple today. A flowing purple dress made of the same gossamer fabric as her skirt last night. The hem of the garment brushed against her upper thighs as she walked, smiling and laughing with Daunet.

Her skin held a fresh glow this morning, and he marveled to think he might have helped put it there. He would not fuck this up. His fingers fidgeted. *I won't,* he repeated to himself as he stalked toward her. The warmth that lit her rich blue eyes when she spotted him almost halted him in place.

"Glad to see you clothed yourself."

The glare he directed at Daunet's comment melted into a witless grin when Meg whispered, "I'm not."

Meg slipped her hand into his, sending a bolt of electricity up his arm, then tugged him along. They strolled toward a wide series of platforms raised at the base of the largest cascade. The area was crowded with Alacerans. Their excited, grinning faces and jittery wings built the tension in the air. The first stage of the Stigalthi Marin was about to begin. Sweat slicked Maxu's palms. He should speak to Meg before the festivities began. Say something memorable and important. Something to impress upon her how meaningful last night had been to him.

Jumbles of words clamored in his throat, but before he could decide how best to order them, Meg gave his hand a squeeze and went to greet her friends.

After pressing a kiss to Meg's cheek, Rita walked up to him with a grin.

"You two are getting along, I see." Rita's lips spread wider.

Getting along? Did that really embody what he felt? He could only grunt in agreement.

"Is there anything that you need from me before the event starts? Human questions? Relationship advice? Better ask now."

Maxu had never enjoyed relying on others, but this past week he'd relied on Rita heavily. Without her intervening and pushing them together, he wouldn't have the most incredible female he'd ever met grinning over her shoulder at him right now. "You've done enough," he rasped.

The tone of his words hit his ears, and he rushed to soften it. "I mean, you've done more than enough. I don't expect we would have gotten here without you. I'm forever grateful."

Rita smiled, gazing up through the light mist at a rainbow. "It's been a fun project, to say the least." With a dreamy sigh, she patted him on the shoulder and floated away, lifting her hands into the damp air and swaying.

As more Alacerans piled onto the platforms, the space between bodies lessened until Meg was being gently jostled from all sides. Enough.

He stomped forward, pleased to see startled Alacerans jump out of his path. It took all his effort to nudge and not shove a tall male away when his wing accidentally scratched Meg's shoulder. Maxu moved in behind her quietly, not wanting to interrupt but needing to keep a protective few feet of space clear around her.

"There you are." Her upside-down grin pulled a small smile from him when she tipped her head all the way back and gazed up at him. "Try to have fun today, okay?"

His insides bubbled when she lifted to her toes, tipping her face farther back. Did she want him to kiss her? In front of all these people? Tremantians didn't often show affection in public like this, but the idea that he could essentially stake his claim for all to see was too tempting to pass up. He obliged, kissing her from the odd upside-down angle, keeping her chin propped up with a gentle hand at her jaw. It took a moment for her lids to open after he was done.

From the corner of his eye, he saw Alacerans—male and female—giving them a disgusted look. He ensured Meg was facing forward again and couldn't see him before snapping his teeth at the pair. They scuttled back a few feet.

Queen Rhal parted the crowd with her contingent of casican protectors and stepped onto the dais raised above the rest of the platforms. She explained the ceremony, he assumed for the benefit of the humans.

Maxu's immediate response to the feverish murmurs spreading through the crowd was an eye roll, but then he caught sight of Meg's rapt gaze. She was so excited. He knew in that moment that he'd participate in earnest to make her happy.

A countdown began, the crowd cheering as the seconds dwindled down. Engineers braced themselves on either side of two massive levers and waited for the go-ahead.

Meg's pulse thrummed wildly in her neck. He hesitated for a moment before placing his hands on her upper arms. Her smile twitched wider, though she still counted down with the crowd. She scooted back until her back rested on his chest, and his purr started up.

The countdown ended, and the engineers pulled on the levers. The world seemed to hold its breath for a moment, all eyes turning up toward the towering beginnings of the Alaceran falls. Distant roars of rushing water echoed through the silent space, and then it appeared, spewing over the sides of the mountains and crashing into the lake surrounding their viewing area.

The dams had opened and now a year's worth of collected water pounded down from above, soaking the crowd with sharp pinpricks and throwing the world into a deafening misty dreamworld.

For a moment all other noise was drowned out, but then one by one the Alacerans began to wail. They shrieked and cried and roared, tendons straining and wings expanding with the effort. Meg raised her hands to the spray of falling water, lifted her face to the sky, and screamed. Her knees bent as though she were squeezing every bit of oxygen she had out of her body.

Closing his eyes, Maxu roared to the sky as well. When he glanced back at Meg as he sucked in a breath, her face had changed. Her eyes were squinted shut, her mouth no longer holding the hint of a smile. Skin red and blotchy, she shrieked with all her might, releasing something he couldn't see.

Clecanians, casicans, and humans bellowed as one until their voices were cracked and raw. All the while, the water pouring in from all sides filled the aqueducts above them and spilled over, drenching them. It tumbled over archways and cascaded down the turrets of the castle, obscuring the sky in a thick, humid fog that cocooned the participants and helped them to release whatever they'd been holding inside. Maxu allowed himself to do the same.

Defensiveness, anger, resentment, hurt, loneliness, worthlessness. The feelings retreated from his body, riding on the waves of his bellows.

At long last, the water slowed and the cacophony of the crowd died with it until the engineers locked the dams into place and all the noise that remained was a ringing in his ears. The waterfalls became no more than a trickle.

He glanced down at Meg, who was grinning serenely, eyes closed as she basked in the quiet. Even the sounds of the crowd's harsh panting faded until silence reigned, almost painful after the earsplitting cacophony from a moment ago.

They were frozen. Standing motionlessly together and bathing their souls in the sacred hush of the forest. Maxu closed his eyes. The gentle sounds seemed to echo through his mind: slow, steady breaths; the light whistle of the breeze and rustle of leaves; droplets of water hitting stone; his own beating heart.

He suddenly noticed the softness of the warm air as it brushed over his skin. The heavy smell of wet earth and damp stone. And the loveliest scent of all, Meg. Warm and sweet. At some point, her hand had come to rest in his. He squeezed her palm. She squeezed back.

Everything else faded away, and in that moment, he felt a bond he never had before, not just to Meg but to everyone standing close by just as astounded and in awe as he was.

His gaze found Meg, and his chest expanded. She was soaked, her dark hair plastered to her cheeks. He brushed it away from her face. She leaned into his palm, causing his heart to crawl into his throat. No one spoke—and they wouldn't, not for the next five days, until Stigalthi Marin was over.

Meg shifted on her feet, removing pressure from his hand which she'd been gripping. He distantly realized she'd been using him to stabilize herself. Hanging on to him to keep herself upright as she let all her own buried heartaches go.

Maxu thought of the flower he'd picked as a child again, and something in him shifted. He'd assumed that by keeping her with him, he'd be no more than that greedy boy who'd ripped something perfect from the earth—the very thing that had made it grow—but what if he could be what fed her?

What if he could provide the support and nourishment she needed to thrive?

Maxu was a male who could acquire anything, yet that ability had never once made him truly happy. But now? He'd be what she rooted to, and he'd devote his life to providing her with everything she needed to bloom.

24

Meg had never realized the quiet could be so loud. She didn't feel restricted or bored by the fact that she couldn't speak. The lack of words was almost liberating. There was no expectation to say the right thing or act any specific way. All around her the Alacerans oozed calm. After the downpour this morning, the world seemed less heavy. The lack of waterfalls made the once-misty air clear and bright. The paths were dry and warm under her bare feet. And the hot sun baked the exposed flowers, filling the city with a sensual fragrance.

The humans, their guards, and Maxu spent the day roaming the city and enjoying all the sensory areas erected for the holiday. A winding pathway had been filled with a sound art installation. The shaded arched treetops were strung with glass ornaments that clinked together. Water collected on the spire ornaments and dripped onto thousands of floating crystal plates below. The only way Meg could describe it in her mind was to imagine that the tinkling echoes all sparking together were the sound version of fairy lights.

She and Maxu hid in dark areas, stealing kisses as they strolled through other sound gardens, one of which was formed from thousands of reeds sliced in such a way that when the air flowed over them, their hollow centers whistled and they all knocked together as if they were a natural orchestra being conducted by the wind.

The group ate incredible food and used wide, expressive eyes to communicate how delightful it was. They touched and hugged without restraint as they felt the soft fur of casican cubs and dipped their feet into the cold velvety water of a bubbling stream.

They spent the late hours of the afternoon helping the famous Alacera perfumers gather dried, fallen petals and sorting them into steel bins where they'd be boiled and condensed to create gorgeous scents. Meg practically salivated over the sultry fragrance of a cluster of warm yellow blossoms as she dumped them into a pot. For the rest of the day, Maxu would chuckle at her every time she lifted her fingers to her face and inhaled the slowly fading scent.

After dinner, citizens of the city migrated to enormous fire pits set amid circles of padded seating. They laid down together as a group and stared up at the twinkling sky, listening to the pops and cracks of the fire while the heat licked their skin. Maxu's body radiated warmth next to her, and though they hadn't spoken all day, he captured every ounce of her attention without even trying. His mere presence made her pulse with awareness. A zing shot up her thigh every time their legs brushed, and after the fifth time, she could've sworn he was doing it on purpose.

A few people, Sophia and Rita included, took part in a sensory-heightening drug that was being passed around. Meg was surprised to find she had no interest. More and more often, she found herself happy just as she was. The experience of taking drugs like that had always intrigued her, but she wondered if that might have been because she used to be so uncomfortable merely existing in her skin.

The world was beautiful now. *She* was beautiful now. Real and vibrant. It felt as though she was a part of the universe. Functioning in it. Changing it. Having an impact instead of being dragged along as an afterthought.

Now that words weren't in the way, it seemed other barriers had been broken down as well. As she and Maxu had ambled back to their rooms, she'd looked over her shoulder to find Gamso, not Daunet, trailing them. When she'd raised a concerned brow toward Gamso, he'd nodded over to a small fire blazing under a stone archway heavy with dark green vines. Beneath it sat Daunet and Tara, silently holding hands.

Maxu paused at Meg's door but didn't let her hand drop from his. He stared down at her. His dark lashes and deep-set eyes made his sea-green irises even more breathtaking in the dim hallway light. The lines around his mouth were back. His gaze flicked to her door, his brows drawn in a look of indecision. His grip on her hand firmed infinitesimally.

Heat slipped over her scalp and neck when she understood he was waiting to see whether she wanted to retreat into her room alone. She checked over her shoulder to make sure Gamso had gone. In a move that would've gotten her called some foul name by Jeremy, she dipped one hand to the impressive bulge between Maxu's thighs. He hissed at the contact, and the sound had her inflating with confidence.

He stole her breath when he swept her into his arms and sprinted up the stairs two at a time until they emerged in his room. Once inside, he took his time unlacing her dress, keeping his eyes locked on hers, and succeeding in scorching her from the inside.

The waterfall splashing into the pool on his balcony had disappeared when the dams were drained. The round tub of water was calm, reflecting the silvery-blue moons on its glassy surface.

Her dress pooled around her ankles, and he let out a long sigh. Hooking his thumbs into her underwear, he slowly crouched, dragging the material down her thighs. Then he rose, his rough palms skimming the backs of her calves, knees, thighs, ass, until he straightened to his full height, a foot taller than her at least. She shivered at his largeness, his heavily muscled frame looming over her.

Biting her lip, she backed away from him with slow deliberate steps. Though she was completely naked and he was fully clothed, she felt no vulnerability. If anything, she felt ruthless, wicked. How provocative must've her backlit figure appeared to make his cock strain against his pants like that?

The soft earth sinking under her feet told her she'd hit her target. She turned and lowered into the pool, then beckoned him forward with a crooked finger. He remained still, rubbing the center of his chest with the heel of his hand as his gaze devoured her. He took one step toward her before halting and dragging a collection of clinking bottles out of his pocket.

Maxu stooped before the pool and placed each small bottle on the ledge, eyeing her to see her reaction. She couldn't hold back her goofy grin. Somehow he'd gotten his hands on a selection of perfumes. But how? Shops weren't open today.

She sent him an admonishing look, with her brow furrowed, complete with fists on hips. She pointed to the bottles, then tipped her head to the side, obviously asking about how they'd been acquired. Maxu used one hand planted on the ground to leap over the arranged bottles and splashed fully clothed into the water before her.

One hand glided to her lower back and hauled her lower body flush to his; the other slithered into the hair at her nape. Any reprimand she'd had in mind slipped away as she stared up into his sly, grinning face. He held her wide gaze for a moment, his fingers scratching against her scalp, then shrugged. If there was a more unapologetic movement, she couldn't imagine what it was.

Meg couldn't help the exasperated smile pulling at her mouth. She'd need to speak to him about his kleptomaniacal tendencies when they could actually talk again. He tugged her head to the side and kissed the bared curve of her neck, sending sparks skittering down her spine all the way to the top of her ass.

When he moved away to undress from his wet clothes, she studied the delicate glimmering bottles. Picking up the first one, she uncorked it, tipped it on her finger, and dabbed some on her wrist. It smelled heavenly, like roses and honey. She turned with her wrist held out so Maxu could smell, and she had to keep from swallowing her tongue. He was naked and wet, the pale markings covering his body glowing in the moonlight.

How could a man be so beautiful yet look at her with such unhinged hunger, like he wanted to devour her whole, then spit her out and fuck her senseless? His long, strong fingers gripped her palm as he pulled her wrist toward his nose for inspection.

Meg held back a chuckle when his lip curled. He dunked her arm underwater, washing away the perfume. She pursed her lips and tried a different bottle. This one was sweet, like a warm sugary baked good, but he plunged her arm under again, unimpressed. Three more perfumes, three more thumbs down.

She picked up the last citrine-yellow glass bottle and started to uncork it, but he stopped her. He tugged the perfume out of her hands, setting it back on the stone ledge of the pool, then closed in, crowding her until her back was pressed against the edge.

He ran his fiery gaze over her body, following the progress of his stare with his fingertips. Meg sucked in a deep shaking breath as his thumb just barely brushed over her nipple, making it pebble instantly. Chirping insects and the swish of water as his wet hand ran up her spine were the only sounds in the room.

The hard length of his shaft rested against her belly, the head reaching her ribcage in a crude domineering display that had her pussy throbbing with heat. His gaze darkened, his fingers clenching her ass harder than the gentle pressure he'd been applying before.

The water swirled as he hoisted her out of the pool, propping her on the edge. Her mind raced, wondering what he'd do. Simply adjust himself and pound into her right there? Flip her over his shoulder and carry her to the sunken sleeping area?

She shivered, the air chilling her damp body. But her sex was hot and the liquid arousal leaking from her core warmed her inner thighs. Maxu wedged himself between her knees, their faces at the same height from her elevated position, and without warning or preamble, he dipped two fingers into her slick channel.

She whimpered, head falling back and chest arching toward him. But his fingers were gone as quickly as they'd delved into her, and she snapped her head up to face him. A devilish grin spreading over his face, he eased her wrist toward him, rotated it upward, and slid the two fingers that had just been inside her over her pulse point. He lifted her newly perfumed wrist to his nose and inhaled a long rumbling breath, lids slipping closed in bliss.

Meg could've come right then and there. So strange, so unlikely, so fucking hot.

She pounced, flying off the ledge to wrap herself around his body like a damn monkey. He caught her with a deep chuckle. Meg was burning up from the inside, impatient to feel Maxu's cock buried in her aching, empty core.

When she rotated her hips, aligning their slippery bodies so she could sink onto him, his humor vanished. He peeled her away, flipped her onto her belly, and locked one hand around her nape, forcing her upper body flat against stone, dirt, and fluffy flowering bushes. In one smooth stroke, he entered her from behind. She cried out, her toes slipping along the slick floor of the pool as she tried to find purchase. A purr and growl mixed and echoed through the room, creating a sound that was so perfectly Maxu, equal parts soft and hard.

The indelicate sound of water sloshing over the edge of the pool and splashing over her back was buried under her moans. His clutching palm was almost painful on the back of her neck, his hold allowing him to use her shoulders for leverage as he thrust inside her. It wouldn't take long for the tight ball of flame in her belly to explode. She was primed for him, turned on by every scowl, every snarl, every smile he granted to no one but her.

He tugged her toward him enough to make a gap for his hand and reached over her hip, fiddling with her clit as he rammed against her ass. She wanted to scream out his name, spur him on, something, but they weren't supposed to speak, and the sinful slap that vibrated through her body whenever his skin met hers was music in its own right.

She came, her back bowing off the ledge even as her upper body remained pinned in place. It took all her effort not to scream, though from this height any noise she made would be carried away on the wind.

His driving hips pistoned faster now, welding her thighs flush against the wall of the pool. She'd have bruises on the front of her hips where they were being shoved against the ledge, but she didn't care. She turned her face in the dirt, delighting in the gruff rasps and groans he breathed out with each upward thrust. Maxu's hand moved to wrench her face up and to the side, and just as he slammed into her and tensed, his mouth landed on hers. She gladly swallowed the strangled moans that accompanied the pulsing of his shaft as he came. He shuddered above her, collapsing onto his elbows.

His hands slid over her forearms until they found her fingers clenched around handfuls of dirt. He forced them open, then laced his fingers over hers, squeezing and making his blue mating marks almost glow in the dark room.

Maxu lifted her, pulling her back until she was submerged to her shoulders in the water, his half-hard shaft still deep inside of her. Without a word, he produced a bottle of foam and ran the slick hydrating liquid through her hair, washed her shoulders, massaging the knots away unhurriedly. Meg's lids slipped closed as she let him take charge. With sure guiding hands, he maneuvered her around the pool, cleaning and massaging every inch of her body until she was half-asleep, pleasantly sore in all the right places, and pliant everywhere else.

After quickly cleaning himself off as well, he swept her out of the water and carried her to the bedding. They collapsed, wet and sated. This time, he didn't hesitate to pull her in close. She laid on her stomach while he threw a thigh over her back and a heavy bicep over her shoulders.

They drifted to sleep listening to the soothing chirps and croaks of Alacera. Though it was terrifying to acknowledge, Meg knew her heart had already run away from her. Maxu might hurt her or betray her, but he had a piece of her now, and there was no getting it back.

25

"This place is so metal." As one, all eyes turned to Sophia. The aliens stared with confused tilts of their head, while the humans held back snorts of laughter.

Camille cleared her throat. "We haven't spoken in hours since leaving Alacera and that's the first thing you say?"

Sophia grinned and pointed at the imposing city of Vrulatica in the distance. "Well, it is! Both figuratively and literally. I'm mean, damn."

When Maxu's rumpled expression was still furrowed in confusion, Meg explained. "Metal is a kind of music from Earth that is very…hard and intense, I guess. It's tricky to explain without a song."

Her head swiveled when Sophia softly sang some lyrics to a rock song she vaguely recognized but couldn't place. Heavy metal had never been huge on her playlists.

"You know, I followed Metallica on tour once. Lars made a divine cup of tea." Rita's gaze went hazy as she daydreamed about the drummer.

Lucy and Sophia stomped over, their interrogation only beginning.

Meg chuckled, then stared at the city again. Sophia wasn't wrong. The sharp spikes of the gleaming charcoal tower rising in the sky were striking. Vrulatica was built in the center of a red desert, over an enormous metal ore. Vrulans were known for their impressive metalworking, and it showed in their forged dark spires and columns.

Heat waves shimmered off the monumental tower sitting amid the blood-red sand. All that metal baking in the sun. How did the citizens not have constant burns or punctures from bumping into the sides?

Though they'd settled here to control the mining and export of the vast metal ore beneath the sand, the same qualities that made the metal so prized for delicate use in electronics also meant that in great quantities like this it created a dead zone. The group's cruisers couldn't pass through the area, so they'd been instructed to wait at the edge of the city for transport.

The sun blazed down on them, but Meg felt as though there was a cold spot at her shoulder. Maxu had been off for a while now, retreating into a broody quiet place, his muscles stiffening with each inch closer to Vrulatica they drew.

Though she tried not to let his odd mood—or his refusal to acknowledge he was in any particular mood—irritate her, it did. For the last day and a half, they'd done nothing but have sex. Glorious, feverish, rough fucking that had left her sore, exhausted, and delightfully sated.

They'd slept as often as they could in between, which had usually only resulted in a few hours of rest before one or both of them had been coaxing the other awake. Meg didn't know if the worn-off spell of silence from Alacera was making her worries worse than they should be, but she was viscerally aware of how much of a stranger Maxu still was to her.

How could she feel so close to him, like she knew his soul, but not know what foods he liked to eat, what his past relationships had been like, what his goals for the future were? Their relationship was happening in the wrong order, and it was throwing her.

She peered up at Maxu and found his gaze distant, the muscles of his jaw tight. *We'll get there*, she told herself. She slipped her palm into his. Relief warmed her chest when he squeezed tight, as if pacified by the contact. Yes, they'd get through this. She was just being impatient.

A hollow clicking roar echoed through the sky and lifted the hairs on her neck. From far in the distance, specks in the blue sky neared, growing larger and larger with each second.

Meg's breath stilled as the silhouette of massive, winged creatures sharpened into focus. They were bright white with shaggy hair that fell over their long-limbed bodies. The hair vanished at their hands, feet, faces, and tails, revealing thick gray scaled skin and deadly white claws. Their snouts were scaled as well. With slits for nostrils, razor-sharp teeth, and sloping foreheads, they reminded her of an odd mix of dragon and dog. Something out of a nightmare.

"I'm not riding one of those things," Lucy whispered, staring in horror as the thirty-foot-long monsters spread their enormous spotted wings against the wind to slow for a landing. Gravel jumped off the ground when the creatures touched down, sending shockwaves up Meg's shins.

They emitted the same clicking sound as they stood in place, waiting to be commanded by their riders. Their wide eyes were cloudy, as if they were reflecting the stormy sky, even though the heavens were a painfully bright blue today. Antlers rising from their skulls were pointed and cast in metal. These were not the velvety, rounded things on Earth deer. These antlers were weapons used to gore enemies in battle.

Meg shivered. She was always desperate to try new things, but even she hesitated to get within twenty feet of the monsters. The largest of the creatures stepped forward, its four-fingered hands flat on the dirt. Its rider dismounted, sliding to the ground, then walking toward them as if the ten-foot drop had merely been his first step.

He was tall and powerfully built. Meg couldn't make out much more than that since he was covered in metal-plated black clothing and a dark silver mask. However, she could see he had eerie glowing eyes. Bright gold shone through slits in the mask like beams of light from the darkness. Sophia had been spot on. This place was *very* metal.

"Welcome, humans. We're thrilled to have you here." The man's voice was cool. Not at all *thrilled*.

He aimed a gloved hand at a collection of bowl-shaped objects about the size of a round hot tub. The outside was overlaid with intricate lacy metalwork and spotted here and there with bright silver-and-gold paint. Chains formed a net cradling the underside, and Meg realized what they were.

"Please have a seat. The king and Guild are waiting to welcome you tonight at the—" The man's mask, aimed at Maxu, froze. Maxu glared back with a stiff spine. A tense silence pulsed in the air. Finally, the armored man spoke. "Does he know?"

Know what? Meg's eyes jumped between the Vrulan and Maxu.

"He does not," Maxu answered in a cold voice.

"I'll need to escort you to him first. Your human can join the others."

"His *human* will stay with him," Meg's voice cut through the thick animosity more loudly than she'd intended. The creature at the Vrulan's back let out a clicking growl and shuffled in place.

The glowing, golden light of the armored man's eyes landed on her. His head tipped toward their clasped hands, and Maxu's hold twitched, curling slightly as if he were trying to hide his marks. Pain lanced through her.

"Very well." Cape whipping in time with the man, he spun, used his weapon-tipped tail to climb the rungs of his beast's harness, and waited.

Whispered arguments ensued as the guards tried to get the humans to seat themselves in the metal bowls. Nirato dragged a hissing Lucy forward, her heels leaving ruts in the sand, but Meg's focus was all on Maxu.

"What's going on?" she whispered.

He guided her toward one of the bowls with a hand at her back, his stony gaze never leaving the Vrulan proudly mounted behind the gold-plated horns of his beast. Maxu helped her climb into the deep well of the bowl where a circle of red, cushioned seats lay, then hoisted himself over.

Daunet had been confident enough to allow Maxu to act as Meg's guard in Alacera, but it seemed the uneasy buzz in the air made her nervous since she, too, joined them in the bowl.

Once they'd strapped themselves in, the creatures came to life, stretching their wings. Using the reins of their antlers, the riders guided the beasts.

"What have you not told me?" Daunet snapped to Maxu as one creature scooped up two looped ends of a chain in one hand and hoisted a shrieking Lucy into the sky. "If there's an increased threat to my charge that I need to be aware of, you—"

"I wouldn't allow Meg to come here if I felt she'd be unsafe," he snapped back. Meg tried unsuccessfully to hold in a squeak of pain as his grip on her hand tightened with his mounting unease. His face fell, and he dropped her palm like it had scalded him. He took in a breath, shoulders rigid. "Any conversation that needs to be had will be had with my mate first."

Daunet opened her mouth, ready to argue, but was cut off when the jolt of their carriage being lifted in the sky captured her attention.

What was going on? Why was he so closed off all of a sudden? The wind whipped through the open air of their transport, howling and making conversation impossible.

Meg caught Maxu looking down at her and saw worry lingering behind his stoic expression. What was he hiding from her?

26

Maxu hadn't been back to Vrulatica for fifteen years. At one time in his life, he'd considered the city a second home. He'd taken numerous jobs from King Sikthand and a few other high-ranking members of the Guild, and after a while, he'd found himself connecting with the Vrulans and their way of life.

They were different. Cut off from the technologies they worked so hard to bring into existence. Vrulatica was not only known for its craftsmanship and export of metal but was also credited as the most effective protectors of the Choke—the dry desert to the north that saw nary an inch of water per year by design.

The magnetic interference of the Askait ore under Vrulatica had resulted in a blind spot to the north that planets across the universe knew existed. Whenever marauding intruders were feeling bold, they'd exploit the blind spot, landing unseen by Clecanian border defenses in the desert and spreading outward to pillage surrounding cities.

Over decades, the Clecanians had devised a plan to deal with the chink in their armor. In addition to ongoing patrols that were sent out from the cities surrounding the Choke, Vrulatica, the city downwind, was in charge of seeding their clouds so no rain fell once the clouds passed their borders.

Trained riders flew winged malginash through storms, pouring chemicals into the clouds and forcing them to drop all of their precipitation into an aqueduct controlled by the city. When the clouds passed over the Choke, they were dry. Plants, animals—nothing could survive out there, including their invaders.

But the Vrulan way of life had created a harsh people relatively cut off from the rest of the world. In between storm seasons, they enjoyed their lives drinking and carousing until the toil of the rains began. Maxu had found camaraderie with many of them, including the king, who had employed him as his personal mercenary.

Until the day Maxu had been sent away.

When Daunet had revealed Vrulatica would be their next stop, Maxu's insides had frozen solid. He'd debated demanding they not go, but if nothing else, Vrulatica was an incredible sight, full of incredible things. A place even *he'd* marveled at. His mate would love it. He couldn't keep her from this experience just to avoid unpleasant memories. The king would just have to accept he was there.

Meg's soft hand curled over Maxu's tight fist and, as if her touch had the power to melt him, his forearm relaxed. Would she judge him for the time he'd spent here and the things he'd done? He could have gone his whole life without telling her about certain chapters of his past. He'd intended to. But now he found he didn't want to.

Maxu wanted Meg to know everything, if only so she could accept everything. He didn't want to have to choose his words carefully for the rest of their lives, stepping around difficult topics forever so as not to reveal some unfortunate event he'd been party to.

Maxu wanted the kind of relationship she'd described. One where she knew the good and bad. He didn't need her to like the worst parts of him or approve of them, just accept them and confirm that she wouldn't be scared away.

Careful not to squeeze, Maxu allowed her probing fingers to slip into his palm and closed his hand around them. He wasn't used to his newfound mating strength yet, and he was certainly not used to the exploding emotion that expressed itself in his body without him realizing.

Raising his gaze to her, he spotted her wind-chapped cheeks and scowled. He pulled her face into his chest, recalling the first time he'd ridden a malginash.

The Vrulan sky was a beautiful—yet hostile—place. Cold, harsh, and dry. The first time he'd accompanied Sikthand on a storm seeding, he'd been in awe of the cloud chaser's skill and the malginash's ferocity as they dove through hail and bolts of lightning, milking the clouds of every ounce of moisture they contained.

His hold on Meg's skull tightened as a high offshoot tower of the castle came into view. The rest of the malginash glided far below, toward the reception hall in the middle of the fortified tower. But their carriage rose, soaring to the private landing of King Sikthand.

The king's landing bay was wide, just like the others, and malginash nests crowded around its entrance. But unlike the other bays, this one was fortified with a gate. Electrified, thick metal bars crisscrossed over the entry.

Drabik, the king's confidant and Maxu's one-time friend, forced his mount to hover in front of the gate, awaiting admission. After a few moments, the bars lifted.

Their malginash rose, depositing their carriage onto the extruding platform before landing itself. Daunet jumped out first, then Maxu. Face pale and hands shaking, Meg gripped their outstretched palms and clambered out.

Wind whipped her hair over her eyes, but she didn't brush it away. Her shaking fingers stayed sunk in the flesh of Maxu's arm. "I didn't know I was so scared of heights." She laughed weakly.

"Only Vrulans are used to this height, vahpti."

"At least it's cool up here." She forced a smile, wide gaze searching every inch of the dark receiving room. The center of the ceiling arched inward as if it were dripping down and formed a point above an enormous roaring fire.

"Wait here," Drabik commanded, prowling away while tossing a large piece of minata wood toward his mount, who chomped through it, devouring the metal-rich sap inside.

Meg peered up at him expectantly when the male was gone. He pulled her away from Daunet, far enough that the glowering guard wouldn't be able to overhear.

It wasn't that he didn't trust Daunet, it was that the guard was annoyingly law-abiding. Similar to his disciplined brother, Auzed, who'd been Daunet's commander for a while. Over Maxu's life, he'd learned not to discuss illegal things in front of people like that. It made them uneasy.

"I don't know what you'll hear, but my past hasn't always been something to be proud of. Sometimes people who have hired me have dug their own graves yet blame me, the spade."

Meg's brows were furrowed, her gaze flitting over his features. She didn't understand yet, but she would.

The muscles of his back unclenched when she lifted a hand to his arm. "Are you sure you're welcome here? Will you be safe?"

"You're mated." A deep voice rang through the room, making everyone turn. Sikthand stood in the towering arch entryway, his pale silver eyes glowed. He was covered up to his chin in black, but Maxu was surprised to see the king's face remained uncovered. Sikthand preferred to keep himself shielded, always wearing his armor and crowned mask. Either rage or anxiousness had pushed the king to rush here.

The bright silver of his eyes was just as uncanny as Maxu remembered. Sikthand's pale white jaw tipped down, gaze narrowing as he stared at Maxu's hand still resting on Meg's cheek. He'd hate him for having found Meg after what had happened with Japeshi.

"I am."

Meg's gaze was wide as she beheld the king, a slight hint of sour fear wafting from her, contaminating her lovely scent.

He understood Meg's reaction. Vrulans were severe in all ways. Their hoods—the colored triangle of skin that spread from their temples to their chin—were usually intense hues of metallic black, gold, or bronze. The hood combined with their glowing eyes always gave their faces a shrouded, treacherous appearance, though most of the Vrulans he knew weren't like that at all.

Sikthand's coloring made him even more chilling, though. A stark white chin and hair to match contrasted with his inky-black hood and bright silver eyes.

Maxu pulled Meg to his side, taking a step in front of her. Sikthand's narrowed gaze leveled on his. "Out of everyone. You?" the male hissed, the sharp words bouncing around the cavernous space.

"If we're unwelcome, we'll leave."

"*She* is not unwelcome. *You* are," the king spat.

Maxu's fists balled. "What happened was not my doing."

"That's untrue and you know it."

They seethed at each other, this argument having already been played out over and over without resolution. Sikthand was a good king. Fair and firm. He was a soldier and a legendary cloud chaser. The first to soar into the harshest of storms. The first to sacrifice. The first to bleed if needed, and his people respected him for it. But he had his troubles, and they haunted him, hollowing him out until only duty remained.

"Sikthand," Maxu called, calming his voice and stepping toward the man. The king flinched at the familiarity of the name. "She's my mate. I won't leave her. You can understand that."

Sikthand's scowl grew venomous, his fangs flashing. "I *can't* understand though, can I." If not for the empty space in the room carrying sound, Maxu might not have heard him.

Daunet, who'd been silent and poised with a hand on her weapon until now, stepped forward, spine straight, chin raised. The picture of a perfect soldier. "Can I have your guarantee that my charge will be safe? That all the humans will be safe while we're here? I don't know what this male has done to you, but I will not allow—the Queen will not allow her delegation to stay in a place where they're treated with hostility."

Sikthand stared unblinkingly at Maxu. The only sign he'd heard Daunet at all was the familiar scrub of his thumb over his fingertips.

Finally, a cold mask worked its way into place on his face. "You have my word." His silver eyes slipped to Daunet, then rested on Meg. "But I'd like to have a private word with you."

"I go where she goes," Maxu growled.

Sikthand tipped his brow up, holding Meg's wide gaze. "Your guard is welcome to join us, of course."

"I'd like my mate to be there," Meg argued, stepping to the side of Maxu. Her tone was firm, though her words were as polite as they could be, considering she was speaking to a powerful king. The brave set of her jaw and the quick reassuring glance she darted to him were the only things keeping Maxu from pulling her behind him again.

Sikthand scowled. "Let me be clear. Either we speak or I throw him into a cell for the remainder of your visit. Be parted for an hour or days. Your choice."

Fury blazed to life at the mere threat Sikthand might separate them, and Maxu took a step toward the male.

Suddenly, Meg was in front of him, her pale hands pressed to his chest. His narrowed gaze remained locked on Sikthand, who sent him a taunting smirk in return. The male was goading him. Maxu knew it even as his Traxian side rose to take the bait.

"Stop. He wants an excuse to lock you up—can't you see that?" Meg whispered, trying to pull his attention to her with a hand tugging at his nape.

"It may be worth a few nights in jail to draw some of his pishot blood," Maxu snapped.

Sikthand flashed his fangs. His shoulders rounded and his tail flicked behind him, the clawed armor scraping against the stone ground in challenge.

"Maxu!" Meg finally succeeded in drawing his gaze down when she clasped both sides of his face. "It's not worth it to *me*." Her voice dropped low, and she gave him a coy smile. "Are you telling me you'd rather land a punch and wake up in a cold cell than wake up in bed with me?"

He wrapped his palms around her wrists and released a gruff sigh. He met Sikthand's scowl with a frown of his own. She was right, as always, but how could he let her go off with someone who despised him?

"Are you worried he'll hurt me?" Meg whispered.

After a moment, Maxu grumbled, "No." He gazed down at his mate and pushed past the tightness in his throat. "I'm worried he'll hurt *us*." Meg's brows rose at that.

There were sensitive topics he'd wanted to broach with Meg, but if Sikthand spoke to her before he could...

No. Sikthand wouldn't hurt her. But he'd do everything in his power to plants seeds of doubt in his mate's mind. To poison her against him.

"It's okay." Meg ran her palms over his forearms. "I understand you have a past. Nothing he says will scare me off. I'm going to meet with him, let him spew whatever crap he wants, and then we can talk about it. Trust me."

Maxu pulled her into his chest and inhaled her scent. Two glorious days. That was all they'd had before the shadows from his past had come back to tear his happiness away. Perhaps it was what he deserved.

At length, Meg pulled away. "I'll be back before you know it."

"Follow me." Sikthand swept a pale hand toward Daunet and Meg. To Maxu, he sneered. "You stay with Drabik."

Even before Meg was out of sight around the corner, Maxu felt her absence. His gut was hollow. His anger simmered back to life. This was the right decision, yet he couldn't keep himself from setting off after her.

The soldier with golden eyes stepped before him, blocking his path. Maxu's fists balled.

"Heed your mate. Sikthand's hatred of you has only festered with time. This punishment is mild compared to what he'll do if you give him a reason." The male raised his mask, Drabik's familiar golden eyes and bronze hood revealing themselves. He hadn't changed at all.

Maxu recalled when Drabik had argued with his own king in Maxu's defense. Though the soldier remained loyal to Sikthand, Maxu would always consider Drabik a male worth trusting, someone far better than him.

"Let me show you to her quarters. She'll be escorted there when she's done."

When she's done, Maxu blustered. Done with whatever manipulation his old friend had in mind.

***

This was bullshit.

For the last fifteen minutes the king had trailed around the large room, pouring himself a drink and reading through papers. Not once had he spoken to them. And now? Now the asshole was sharpening a wide axe on a spinning whetstone.

Arms already crossed, teeth grinding, Meg began tapping her foot on the stone floor. She aimed a furious glare at Daunet, hoping for a commiserative eye roll, but all she got was a warning head shake.

Meg huffed. What was the king playing at?

Finally, after he set down his razor-sharp blade and picked up another, Meg had had enough. "Excuse me, but if you'd rather not speak to me right now, I'd like to leave."

Without even glancing up at them, the king rasped, "You will stay."

"What's the point of us sitting here if you don't plan on speaking to us?" Meg blurted before Daunet could still her with a hand on her shoulder.

The scrape of sharpening metal rang through the silence before he answered, never taking his eyes off the rhythmic back-and-forth swipe of his blade over the rotating stone. "The point...is to torment your mate. I don't need to speak to you for that to occur."

Meg rose to her feet. "Why do you hate him so much?" she demanded.

"He tortured and killed my wife." Sikthand's voice rang hollowly through the room. His armor-clad tail flicked behind him, the only sign he was affected by his words.

"That's…" Meg breathed in a shaky inhale. "Maxu wouldn't do that."

The king released a cruel laugh. "He wouldn't do what? Torture? Kill? Kill a female? He's done all that and more— and not only to my wife." His glowing eyes finally met hers. "That's why you simply being in here with me will rip him open. I do not lie, and your mate knows this. He'll sweat and shake and crumble knowing that the worst I can do is simply tell his innocent human the *truth*."

A swallow lodged in her throat. Was Maxu capable of those things? She'd known he'd been a mercenary and he'd told her he wasn't proud of some things he'd done, but… Meg's chin lifted. "I'm sorry you lost your wife, but I don't believe you. What you're saying may be a truth, but it's not the whole truth."

That got his attention. A dark scowl descended over the king's face, and he stood. Daunet matched his movements.

"And if he really did do all those things you say, then why wasn't he already in jail? You're the king, after all. The only thing I can think is that you must have given him permission. Maybe even hired him. Am I right?" It was stupid to keep speaking, but Meg couldn't seem to stop.

The flash of outrage in his eerie eyes told her her guess had been spot on. This asshole was a hypocrite who'd hired Maxu to harm. It didn't make it right, but it made her uninterested in hearing another word from him.

Her mate might've had a past she didn't like, one she'd need to learn how to accept in time, but that was something she and Maxu would work through together. She wouldn't give Sikthand the pleasure of knowing he'd spooked her—even though, in truth, he had.

27

Meg forced herself to act normal. *Look at the people talking. Lucy's saying something—focus on her so it seems like you want to be here. Listen to their questions, dammit. What if they get to you and ask something related, and you weren't paying attention?*

This interview was turning out to be a constant battle. She'd known Maxu was a mercenary. She'd known he liked to set booby traps and steal things. But she hadn't realized how dark his life had been. And worse still, Sikthand had kept her sequestered in their "meeting" right up until the interview had started, so she hadn't even been able to speak with Maxu.

He was in the crowd. She'd spotted him as soon as they'd been led into the stepped seating area. One glimpse and she could see the misery sprawled over his features despite the indifferent mask he wore. What did that look mean?

Without being able to talk to him and hear his side, her mind was spinning, presenting her with the worst scenarios it could dream up. What if he had truly been a monster earlier in his life? He wasn't that person *now*. At least...she thought he wasn't. But how well did she really know him?

Should she just move on and forget about it? Should she move on only if he seemed regretful?

It didn't help her anxiety that the Vrulatica interview was more complicated than normal. The citizens weren't as harsh as the people had been in Kitibard, but their questions were laser focused on one topic—the Tremantian Queen.

"Next question, please," Malinu prompted tentatively, gesturing to Meg, whose turn it was to respond. So far, Malinu and Kel had had to answer just about every question themselves as each subject had focused on plans for the Intergalactic Alliance.

A man with dark brown skin and an obsidian hood clapped his metal plated knuckles together—their version of raising their hands. "Why has the Queen refused to acknowledge the questions she's been asked? She's been silent for days now."

Though Malinu had indicated Meg would answer the next question, the man was focused on the Tremantian representatives, knowing full well they'd be the ones to respond. She couldn't blame the Vrulans for their frustration. The political nonanswers both Malinu and Kel were spewing would've made her annoyed too. What *was* the Queen doing?

Were Malinu and Kel refusing to give concise answers because they weren't allowed? Or because they didn't know?

Meg's lips thinned in sympathy, and she peered over her shoulder with raised brows at Malinu, who'd released an almost inaudible groan. "As I've said, the Queen is organizing her plan in such a way as to release it to the entire planet at the same time. She's hard at work, focused on getting her arguments ready for the leaders' summit next month. Once Clecania's rulers come to a consensus, more information will be dispersed. Until then, let's remember that we have humans here already." He grinned, but she noticed sweat beading on his forehead. "Isn't there anything that you'd like to know about them?"

Another man with gray skin and a bright silver hood shot to his feet, his knuckles clanging together as an afterthought. "What could these humans possibly know?" he yelled, gesturing to Meg. She clenched her jaw. "They come here, and you force them to only talk about silly things," he continued. "Our planet is dying, and we want to know what your Queen is doing about it, not listen to this female describe outdated sky machines." His hand lifted to the air to emphasize his point.

Meg straightened, her chin lifting even as heat rose to her cheeks. Well, what the fuck had she been supposed to say? They'd asked her how people got around if they didn't have wings, flying creatures, or cruisers, so she'd explained what an airplane was. Perfectly reasonable.

Some of the other Vrulans hissed at the man speaking and threw her pitying glances as if she were just a poor, dumb human who didn't deserve to be singled out. Her lips remained pursed when the man himself muttered a quick apology to her before launching back into a rant directed solely at the Tremantian representatives.

Rude.

Meg sat up straighter, blood running cold. Oh no. He'd been rude to her. She searched the crowd for Maxu. He wasn't about to attack that guy for aiming an impolite jab her way out of frustration, was he?

She spotted him, and a funny mix of attraction and nervousness swelled. While every other pair of eyes was focused on the humans or the Tremantian representatives, her mate's blazing stare was directed squarely on the male still arguing with Malinu. Muscles tense, he gnashed his teeth silently, then a terrifying smile lifted a corner of his mouth. Shit.

Sikthand is going to throw you in jail if you so much as step on a bug, you dummy! Look over here, she silently urged. Come on.

"Meg, what is the most popular Earth metal?" Malinu asked the question slowly as though he already had and she'd missed it.

She turned back to Maxu and saw him staring at her. Everyone was as they waited for her answer. How the hell was she supposed to know what the most popular metal was? "Uh, actually Sophia really knows more about that stuff than me. Sophia?"

"What?" Sophia's eyes were wide as she stumbled to answer, but Meg was already focusing back on Maxu now that she had his attention.

Vaguely, she heard Sophia in the background awkwardly listing metals. "Gold, uh, silver, platinum. Mm. Oh, tin! Uh, let's see…"

Meg narrowed her eyes at Maxu until she had his full attention. She gave a brief shake of her head, jaw clenched.

His brows furrowed.

She checked to make sure no one was focused on her, then glanced at the curt silver man, then back to Maxu, raised her brows accusingly, and shook her head a bit more firmly. For good measure she mouthed the word no, realized his translator couldn't read lips, and covertly crossed her arms in her lap to make an X.

His brows softened, shoulders dropping. He relaxed back in his chair, crossing his arms over his chest. He'd understood, but he wasn't happy about it. She lifted her brows again, this time in a silent question.

He sent a glare toward the man, who was clearly unaware of Maxu's simmering anger, then looked back at her. At length, he gave her a tight nod of ascent.

Meg relaxed. *Focus on the interview*, she prodded herself, recognizing that she hadn't heard a word of what had been said in the last five minutes.

Realizing they were fighting a losing battle, Kel and Malinu devoted the rest of the time to answering the Vrulan questions as best they could, which wasn't saying much. Meg got the impression they truly didn't have answers, which only piqued her curiosity. She peered over to Camille, who was sitting next to her.

Leaning close while the crowd was occupied with mining any nuggets of truth they could, Meg whispered, "This is wild. None of the other cities have been this intense about this stuff before."

Camille lifted a brow, her gaze ping-ponging between Kel and a bronze-eyed female glaring from the stands. "It doesn't surprise me, with what happened yesterday."

Meg tipped her head, wracking her brain, but couldn't remember anything out of the ordinary. "What happened?"

With an eye roll, Camille shook her head. "Your head is always in that reading pad, but you don't read the news posts?" Camille gave her a playful grin. "Or maybe you were too *busy* to read anything at all yesterday."

Meg's face heated, recalling the long bouts of writhing under Maxu she'd been engaged in yesterday when she should have been exploring the city and immersing herself in their culture.

Camille leaned in a little closer. "The city of Merinta announced they've cut off all trade to Tremanta until the Tremantian Queen steps down as the Clecanian Intergalactic Alliance ambassador."

"Oh my God," Meg breathed. She furrowed her brows, trying to work out what repercussions that could have. "They manufacture most of the solar tech, don't they? But that won't be a huge blow right away. Most places have all of that built into the sides of their buildings, no?"

Camille nodded. "From what I've gathered, the fear is that other cities will follow suit. I mean, imagine if Gulaid shut down trade. Or here? No more tech being made with fancy Askait metal?" She clicked her tongue. "If I were the Queen, I'd be coming up with a new plan and fast. This little PR tour clearly isn't working. I wouldn't be surprised if she cut it short, to be honest."

Meg sat back, suddenly understanding how out of touch her description of airplanes had really been. She didn't blame that guy for being annoyed.

28

When the interview turned interrogation was over, the humans were guided into an enormous feasting hall. Long communal tables were set up in rows. Rowdy metal-garbed Vrulans drank and ate, the glittering jewelry that studded their ears and lower jaws clinking from all directions.

Meg watched the table across from her, alternating between feeling exhausted, numb, and worried since Maxu hadn't appeared at the dinner yet. An older man and a beautiful young woman with a gold-plated piece of jewelry covering the bottom half of her jaw laughed at something the man said. The effect of the sculpted metal malginash jaw piece covering the woman's chin made it look like her lower mandible was that of the animal itself. When she grinned, it was fierce and powerful and oh so creepy.

Reigning above it all on a dais were the king and six other people, his Guild. Meg didn't know exactly how they worked together. Either the king had final say and the Guild was included in every decision, or the Guild had final say and the king oversaw the Guild. In any case, no one was more of a spectacle than King Sikthand.

He was the only one in the room wearing a mask, his shining silver eyes glowing from beneath the slits in the black carved metal. Unlike the other masks she'd seen, antlers sprouted from the head of his, the fine silver protrusions glinting in the firelight.

Elbows on the arms of his weighty seat, one hand clasping a large tankard, Sikthand oozed authority. Every so often, he lowered the flexible jaw of his metal mask and took large swigs before raising it up again.

Had he done something with Maxu? Locked him up or commanded he not come? Meg's toes curled in her shoes.

"Do you think he's trying to intimidate us with that getup? Or does he always dress that way?" Sophia whispered, matching the direction of Meg's gaze.

He was covered in black from chin to toe. Even his bright white hair was bound and covered by his helmet. His width was made larger and more imposing by rigid sheets of metal that ran over his collar and tipped into points at the ends of his shoulders and elbows.

"I wouldn't be surprised by either answer," Meg commented distantly.

For the majority of their dinner, he'd unnerved the women at her table by focusing on them. She supposed it made sense. After all, she was the person in the city he hated *second* most.

The rest of the invited Vrulans didn't seem to notice their king's brooding, though. Perhaps this was his normal state.

Citizens continued to visit the humans, greeting them by dropping a gift onto their laps and asking them to walk in a circle around the perimeter of the room. It was odd to see such a simple, innocent custom in a place that felt so harsh, but Meg liked it.

A short stroll through a partially hidden route around the large room where you could talk and nobody would interrupt you. It was a wonderful way to meet someone without becoming stuck in a never-ending conversation. She'd kill to take a walk around the room with Maxu right now. Damn! Where was he?

Meg pushed the tankard filled with a weaker version of mott away.

"What is going on with you?" Tara asked from her left. "Is it Maxu again? It's like hot and cold with you two, I swear. Can you just get it together?" Sophia chuckled across from her.

Meg had already had a shitty few hours. She was confused and tired and annoyed that all she wanted at that moment was to go for a silly walk with Maxu and ask him what circumstances had led him to murder the queen. Maybe that was why she blurted, "I don't want to hear it from you. I see you and Daunet haven't been talking."

Not at all offended, Tara lifted a brow and gave Meg a once-over that communicated "watch it," better than words ever could. "Not that it's your business, since *we* haven't been making our relationship everyone else's problem," Tara began, causing Meg's neck to go hot, "but Daunet is…upstanding and hardworking, and I respect that. When she's ready, I'll be ready."

"Just like that? That easy?" Meg sighed.

"Yeah, that easy. I told her how I felt. After a little prodding, she did the same, and we came up with a plan. Done and done. I don't mess around when I like someone."

"Must be nice." Meg didn't feel guilty about her bitterness. If she told them the whole story, she knew they'd feel differently about the supposed unnecessary drama that was her and Maxu's relationship, but she didn't feel right disclosing what Sikthand had told her. She didn't want for anyone to look at him differently when he wasn't here to explain himself.

"Just tell him how you feel like I did," Tara urged.

"And what did you tell her, exactly? That you've been dreaming about her ass in that blue dress since Cribus?" Sophia chuckled, drinking deeply from her tankard. "Leave Meg alone—she's fine." Her ex-tattooed, horror movie–loving friend was besotted with the aesthetic of Vrulatica, not at all creeped out by the terrifying malginash or the muted color scheme seemingly inspired by the lyrics from "Paint It Black."

Tara pursed her lips and tipped up Sophia's cup as she drank so it splashed over her front. "No, asshole. I told *you* that in private. I told *her* that I noticed how well she took care of everyone and asked who took care of her." A sheepish smile forced its way onto Tara's face. "And for good measure, I *also* told her how much I dreamed about her ass in that dress."

Meg and Sophia laughed, Sophia patting down her wet chest with a cloth. Tara glanced over her shoulder toward Daunet, who stood with shoulders back, hovering by the table. The guard noticed Tara's attention and quickly looked away, but Meg saw the faintest hint of a blush light on her cheeks, and something gooey broke open in her chest.

A warm breath by her ear made her jump and squeak out an embarrassing sound. "Just me, vahpti," Maxu's voice whispered. She slapped her palms against the table, heart still racing.

"Would you stop doing that?" she snapped, face heating at the few chuckles rising from the Vrulans. "Where have you been?"

"Walk the room with me?" he asked, holding out a hand. As if the last few hours had never happened, her heart sped up and a wide grin split her face. Meg savored the warmth and strength of his large hand as she let him pull her up.

The Vrulans shot glances toward them as they walked, leaning their shoulders together to whisper about the miraculously mated couple. Their glowing gazes were so focused on Maxu's hands that he stuffed them into his pockets.

She bit the inside of her cheek. "Why do you do that? Are you ashamed of them?"

Maxu stopped mid-step, and she was forced to halt as well. He'd found himself a typical Vrulan outfit, black with formfitting leather-esque cloth and a stiff-shouldered cape that climbed up his neck and made his muscled frame appear even larger. Over his thighs, arms, chest, and abs were decorative plates of metal. Not quite armor, but not quite *not* armor. God, she wanted to just forget about today, pull him into a dark corner, and feel the hard metal of his outfit crush her against a wall.

His hands emerged from his pockets, and he brushed them over her arms. She regretted the metal detailing of her long-sleeved shirt preventing her from feeling the rough warmth of his hands, even if the interior gel layer of the garment kept her temperature perfectly consistent.

"I don't like *others* seeing them." A muscle in Maxu's jaw pulsed before he continued, urging her to keep walking forward. "When Sikthand saw them today, the first thing he did was take you away from me. They're a sign to every enemy that a piece of my heart exists outside my body."

Meg bit her lip to hold back her smile. Then she shook her head to clear away the fluttering hearts that had filled it. "Wait, we need to talk about what happened today."

They rounded a hidden corner, and without a word, he swept her against a wall. With one slap of his palm to a sculpted malginash tail spike, a door slipped open, and he silently pulled her inside.

"What are you doing? Daunet's gonna kill you. And me."

"I told her I'd be taking you off her hands for the evening," he said, pulling her down a narrow hallway behind him. Faint light glowed in the distance, and she couldn't help the thrilling beat of her heart, or her grin.

They emerged in an open landing bay where Debrik waited, holding the reins of a shaggy malginash whose fur was grayer than the gleaming white mounts they'd rode in on. Meg stopped, dragging her heels, but Maxu pulled her forward as if she weighed nothing.

"Get in the carriage, Meg," he demanded, pointing at the metal bowl sitting before the beast.

"No." She watched on, horrified, as Debrik held out the reins to Maxu. "Do you know how to ride one of these? When was the last time you were even here?"

"Quickly, or I'll get in trouble," Debrik barked with an impatient jangle of the reins. Suddenly, the creature let out a keening, clicking sound, its nose rising to sniff the air. It spun in place until it faced Maxu.

The malginash emitted a small screech and pounded toward them. Meg tried to pull away from Maxu's hold again, and he let her. The creature whined a little louder, clumsily jogging over to Maxu and knocking Debrik in the head with its wing. The man grunted in annoyance and rubbed his scalp.

"Hello, beautiful," Maxu crooned as the beast came to rest its head against Maxu's chest, face down with its deadly charcoal antlers bracketing his body. He scratched the long hair on the creature's neck and let his cheek rest against the top of its head. "I missed you too."

Meg's insides fluttered at the unexpectedly affectionate display.

"A love story for the ages." Still rubbing his head, Debrik whispered out a curse and lifted a dismissive hand. "You deal with her, then; I'm heading back to the party. You owe me," he added, pointing a finger.

Maxu grinned, his eyes slipping closed as he stroked the creature under its chin and their purrs synced together. He pulled away, lifting its head to his face. "Shall we go for a ride?" he asked. The malginash seemed to rejoice, hopping on its front feet and waddling to the edge of the platform while stretching its wings.

He held his hand out to Meg. "Come on. I want to show you something."

Meg's mouth was open, and she stared between him and the malginash. "I don't know. It's terrifying enough with somebody who drives these every day. I'm not sure we—"

Before she could finish her sentence, he'd thrown her over his shoulder, dumped her into the bucket, locked a belt around her waist, and whispered for her to hold on.

When she finally righted herself, it was too late. He'd thrown himself onto the mount, reins in hand. A little more jerkily than the malginash this morning had, Maxu's mount grabbed the rings of Meg's carriage and swept her into the sky. She shrieked as the creature dove and her body went weightless.

29

Meg kept her head buried below the rim of the carriage and cursed over and over in her head until they finally came to a jarring halt, her bowl hitting the ground and rocking in a circle until it finally stilled.

She poked her head up, hair a mess, eyes watering from the wind, and found Maxu showering the malginash with praise for the fabulous job she'd done.

A little disgruntled that this creature was stealing her mate away, she half climbed, half tumbled out of the carriage, landing on velvety soft red sand.

Maxu mumbled something to the creature, pointing to a distant hill topped with strange traffic cone shaped trees. Meg rose from the ground. She brushed sand off her pants as she readied to berate him for tossing her into a metal bucket thousands of feet in the sky, but then she spotted a crackling fire. Blankets, pillows, and drinks were laid out around it.

A small smile tugged at her lips. The gentle crunch of sand sounded as he neared. One look at his nervous, hopeful grin and all her annoyance dissolved.

With a feigned pained sigh, she asked, "Maxu, did you kidnap me for a date?"

"Yes." He nodded without any hesitation.

"I suppose I won't leave." She sent a teasing grin toward him, and he sucked in a large breath, smiling down at her. "But we need to talk about—"

"First look at this," he interrupted before spinning her around by her shoulders. Meg's eyes went wide.

The city loomed in the distance, but it wasn't the image of the ominous tower glittering with blue light and reflecting the white moons that made her gasp. It was the clouds.

They were fluffy and clustered together and…green. Their interiors lit with neon-lime explosions. The sight was unreal, magical.

"What is it?" she asked in a hushed voice.

"Cloud chasers. They're seeding them. See?" He leaned down and pointed toward a fluffy cloud passing over one of the moons.

Through the glow of the bright light, she could see small dark figures silhouetted. Explosions colored the cloud in an acidic green. "It looks like fireworks or lightning."

"They're bombs of sorts. It's the easiest way to disperse the chemical over a wide area. They add dye so that the riders can see where they've already treated."

She let Maxu guide her away while keeping her eyes glued to the incredible sight. He eased her down onto the blanket surrounded by pillows, wrapped her palm around a bottle of mott, then, with a chuckle, lifted it to her lips for her. She couldn't look away. The clouds were *green*. They were sparking. It was…amazing.

"I wanted to give you something too."

Her attention slowly locked on to his words, and she tore her gaze away. "Give me something?" She set the bottle down, shaking her head. "Wait, wait, wait. We need to talk about Sikthand."

"Let's do this first. Then we can talk," he pushed, fishing in his bag.

"You're stalling!" she exclaimed.

He sat up straight, clutching a balled piece of trash in his hands. "I'm stalling," he agreed. "But I brought you this because I think it's yours."

That left Meg at a loss. He lifted the balled-up paper, holding it out to her. She tilted her head at it, eyeing the trash.

At her confused look, Maxu explained, "I read in the directory that humans prefer gifts wrapped in paper."

Despite the seriousness of this morning, despite the fact that her mate had done things in his past she shuddered to think of, she had to bite her lips together to keep from bursting out laughing.

He furrowed his brows. "Not right?" he asked, staring down at the paper ball. "It didn't seem right, but I didn't know…"

"I'm sorry, I'm sorry," she said, sucking in a deep breath. She took the paper ball out of his hands. His eyes were wide and there was a nervous stiffness to his lips as he watched her try to unwrap the thing without letting it tumble to the ground.

"Is this another thing you stole from my room back in Tremanta? Because taking my stuff then giving it back to me…isn't…exactly…" Her face fell, heart stilling when the item came into view. She couldn't breathe. Tears sprung free, flowing down her cheeks without warning as she ran her fingers over the smooth surface of her iPod. She turned it over, checking for the familiar nicks, and sucked in a choked sob when she found them. She slid her thumb over the dull scratches.

"How did you get this?" she whispered, hardly able to get the words past the lump in her throat.

"I broke into the tower where they keep the human items they'd recovered from the bunker sites. I thought I smelled the faintest hint of you on this and took a guess. Right?"

She sniffed, a watery laugh coming out of her. "Right."

His chest puffed with pride. "I had to take you far enough away from the city so we could use it. It wouldn't work too close to the ore."

Meg's eyes shot up to his, her brows knitting. "Use it? But it's broken. It was broken before I was abducted. And how could we get it to work anyway? We don't have a charger or headphones or anything."

"I gave it to a friend to repair. It's one of the reasons I was gone for those two days. I didn't know what it was when I found it, but my friend was able to figure it out. He gave me this." Maxu reached into his bag and produced a flat piece of tech that he clipped to the back of the iPod, then lifted a couple of sound orbs, turning them on and letting them float in the air. Their gentle light pulsed as they waited to play music. "He assured me this would work."

"I don't... What do I..." She pressed the Menu button, fully expecting the old screen that had survived with her for decades to remain blank, but it lit up. She sucked in another laughing gasp.

"Show me what you like," Maxu coaxed, gazing at her trembling smile as if it were his favorite drug.

Meg's grin faded. She set the iPod down on the blanket. "I love it. I do. I want to listen to music with you. I want to show you all my favorite songs and see what you like." Gripping his hands and, making sure he looked her in the eye, she pressed on. "But you need to tell me what happened here. Sikthand said—"

Maxu squeezed her hands. "I know what he said." His throat bobbed with his slow swallow. "Are you sure you want to hear these things, vahpti?"

Meg forced herself to nod.

He sighed, his eyes sliding to the sand, then back to her. An air of resignation settled over him. Jaw tensing, his spine straightened. "What do you want to know?"

***

Maxu clenched and unclenched his jaw as he waited for Meg to ask her questions.

"The king...he said you tortured and killed his wife," Meg began tentatively, failing to hide a wince.

This conversation needed to happen. Maxu knew that. But he didn't enjoy not knowing how Meg would react to his past. He ran a tongue over his teeth, eyes lifting to the sky for an instant. "Is that what he said? It's true in part," he grated, watching her reaction. Her lips only twitched.

"My job wasn't always pleasant, vahpti. I was paid to retrieve things, and sometimes, those things weren't physical items. They were secrets." Meg's shoulders tensed as he spoke, and his muscles bunched in time with hers. "Sikthand employed me for many years and was obsessed with learning everyone's secrets. Do you understand what I mean?"

She let out a small breath through her nose. "It means you hurt a lot of people while you worked for him."

Maxu didn't love hearing it in those words. They weren't untrue, but...it was a job. It wasn't as if he'd gotten into mercenary work because he was a sadist. He'd simply made himself jaded when it came to certain things.

His moral standards had grown into existence slowly. Small seeds planted in his heart after moments of regret. They'd grown over time, spreading through him until he'd found himself turning down projects that had seemed like they'd weigh heavy on his soul.

But when he'd been here? Maxu had been angry at the world. Resentful of his place in it. He'd let himself sink into that bitterness for far longer than he should've. That period of his life had been dark, but he didn't exactly regret all of it. He'd matured here. He'd learned which parts of himself to accept and which to keep reins on.

"He hired me to find out many things. Yes," Maxu agreed.

Brows knitting, Meg asked, "So he hired you to...question... his wife?"

"Japeshi." Maxu shook his head. "She was a cloud chaser and a friend. Beautiful, funny. Sikthand was smitten. So when his eyes changed with preliminary recognition, he rejoiced. We all did. They married, believing the recognition would come, but the captain of the cloud chasers, Sikthand's uncle, wasn't convinced."

Maxu's lips slammed shut. Even he winced, recalling the slithering trepidation he'd felt when Urganish had come to him with a fat stack of credits and his suspicions.

Maxu swallowed. "Urganish hired me to question her."

Meg raised a hand to her mouth. "Oh no."

"I learned she'd been tricking Sikthand with help from his personal medic. She'd admitted to drugging him and allowing her lover to inject his eyes with a special powder. They use it for tattoos here. The particles are inserted under the skin and then various magnetic devices are used to draw in a design. The cones of the powder are so miniscule they're invisible to the naked eye when turned on their side, but when they're pulled straight? All she'd had to do was activate a magnet in her pocket and she could make his eyes turn black. She admitted to plotting to kill him, leaving her as the undisputed queen since she'd been his mate."

"How did she die?" Meg's knit brows were wary, but at least Maxu could breathe knowing that was where his regretful involvement had ended.

"I relayed everything I'd learned to my employer, Urganish. He, in turn, told Sikthand. The king was forced to send both Japeshi and his vile medic to an off-world prison planet. News of their deaths came only a few months later. Sikthand was…shattered. The female he'd thought of as his mate was dead. He transferred the hurt of that betrayal onto us. Urganish was banished from the city, and I was asked to leave."

"But why? She was plotting to kill him, and you exposed her."

"Because I lifted the veil from his happiness," Maxu explained. He'd had years to think through Sikthand's anger, and his mind had always come back to this conclusion. "He thought he'd finally surrounded himself with people he could trust. His uncle, me, his new bride—and in one fell swoop, he learned all of us had been hiding secrets of our own from him. It didn't matter that Urganish and I had done it to help him. I think part of him felt he could've been happy if the illusion hadn't been stolen from him, that perhaps in time, she would have developed true feelings and admitted everything."

She didn't speak, and a lump formed in his throat. He tried to swallow it. "I've never claimed I was good, Meg." Her gaze lifted to his. "I didn't care about anything. People, honor, my family. All I wanted for so long was the thrill that came with reaching the goal I'd set for myself. Solving a problem. Acquiring the thing I was after. Learning the secret they didn't want to divulge. Those accomplishments were the only things that brought me any peace. Everything else was irrelevant."

Her brows were pained, her mouth thinned as she listened to him. She stared at his face, taking in his words, yet he felt transparent, as if she were weighing his heart even now. "Did you stop doing that kind of work after you left here?"

"I stopped doing it without good reason. Without solid proof. Only when I knew there was no other way."

"Would you ever do it again?" she asked, her breathing deep.

He was about to say *no*. The word was almost out of his mouth, but then a thought hit and he stopped himself. "Meg, if I thought you were in danger...if you were taken... If anyone ever tries to hurt you, I will do *anything*."

Meg chewed on her lip, brows furrowed. Maxu couldn't manage to exhale as he waited.

Finally, she looked back up at him. With a tight smile, she breathed, "Okay."

His brows lifted, his eyes zooming over her features. "Okay, what?"

Meg sucked in a long slow inhale and lifted her shoulders as if lost for words. "Okay, I accept what you've said. I don't like what you did, I won't lie about that. But I don't think you're the same person you used to be, so I'm choosing to move forward." She sent him a small smile. "I think I struggled with it at first because we're doing this out of order."

Maxu inched closer. His mate wasn't appalled. She wasn't trying to run from him again. "What do you mean, out of order?"

She took a sip of her mott and gave him a half smile. "We became mates, then we had sex, and *now* we're getting to know each other. Except we're starting with the bombshells. Er…the big stuff," she corrected at his confusion. "That's not how it works on Earth. We start with the little things like learning each other's favorite music, but we" —she gestured between them— "we've admitted our worst secrets first, and it's tripping me up. I know you, but I also don't know you at all," she finished, offering the bottle of mott to him.

How could he be so lucky? His chest was tight as he stared at Meg, a green glow from the seeded clouds illuminating her dark hair. Understanding, gorgeous, smart—she was everything he'd ever wanted and everything he never knew to wish for.

"I'll tell you whatever you want to know, vahpti."

"I want to know *everything*. That way, when you reveal things to me like you did today, they aren't as shocking because I'll understand them within the context of your life. I won't spiral into a default crisis mode. At least, that's my working theory for now."

That was all she wanted?

Maxu didn't understand his mate, but perhaps she was right. If she needed to hear about all the trivialities of his life to feel connected to him, then he'd reveal them all.

Gripping her around the waist, he hauled her forward until her legs were draped over one thigh. "I was born in the city of Tremanta, the fifth child of my Traxian mother."

Meg grinned up at him before resting her head on his chest.

30

As the rolling green clouds cleared and twinkling stars appeared in the blue velvet sky, Maxu described his whole life. Meg listened with an absent smile on her face. She loved the way his words reverberated through his chest, thrumming against her cheek.

Every bit of information he revealed was a puzzle piece, and as he told her more and more, the pieces finally began fitting together. His mother had died when he'd been too young to remember her, and his father had had a difficult time spreading affection between his six children. Though Maxu didn't admit as much outright, it seemed as though he'd grown up very lonely.

It made sense he was so closed off and distrustful. He'd been relying on himself for so long, it was no wonder he didn't care about anyone else. Meg kissed the underside of his jaw when he described the one temporary marriage he'd participated in and how awful it had made him feel.

When he couldn't think of anything else to say, he asked about her life, and she told him everything, matching his raw honesty with tough admissions of her own. He wasn't pleased with what she had to say—especially not the bits that involved Jeremy—but when she broke down while admitting how scared she was of Earth opening contact with Clecania, he wrapped his arms around her and squeezed her close.

The warm cocoon of his embrace eased her worry. When Clecania made contact with Earth, she'd let her parents know she was safe. She even felt confident allowing them to have a relationship with her, but it would be on her terms this time. Whether they chose to accept that would determine how much a part of her life they'd be.

"I never want to lay eyes on them," Maxu growled when she explained this.

Meg sniffed, wiping away a tear. "They aren't bad people. I think they really believed they loved me in their own way. They're just misguided, too focused on what they've been told and too insecure to question it."

"You mean their religion?" he rumbled, recalling what she'd described concerning their ties to the Evangelical church.

"It's not religion that's the problem. Religion is a healing thing, and it's used by so many people to spread happiness and love. But it's like anything powerful, I guess. It can be used as a weapon too. My family and many of the people in my small town used it to control others. And Jeremy," she sighed. "He's just a product of it. I hope one day he'll start thinking for himself. Maybe me going missing will push him to grow up. I doubt it. He didn't really want to be married. That's why I never felt much guilt about moving on when I was brought here."

"He's a fool," Maxu growled. "He'd trample a brenti, then curse it for hurting his foot."

Meg peeled herself away from Maxu and stared up at him with a confused grin. "What?"

His warm gaze roved over her body as she reclined on one hand. Goose bumps sprouted across her skin. "It's a saying from my mother's home planet." Eyes riveted to the slice of skin showing at her belly, his large palm curled over her waist. "Brenti are creatures that flatten themselves over small pools of water. They're spiny on top, so they hurt to step on. But Traxia is a very dry planet and finding a brenti means finding water. It's a blessing." His eyes lifted to her and grew warm with affection. "It means he's a pishot who didn't recognize the gift he'd been given."

Meg smiled at that.

"I will not make the same mistake, vahpti," Maxu rumbled, tightening his grip on her waist.

"Good." Meg's chest was tight, her lips twitching. With a laugh, she added, "I don't get why you still call me a bug, though."

Maxu's face split, and he chuckled, pinching her chin with his thumb and forefinger. "You will always be buzzing about my head, vahpti, and I wouldn't have it any other way. Do you know what happens to the animals that have lived with vahpti for years when the insects die?"

Meg sat up, bringing her face close to his, and gave him a playful smile. "No. What?"

"They go mad." He flashed his white teeth, eyes softening as they lingered on her mouth. "They grow so used to the sound that when it's gone, the silence is unbearable. That's how I would be without you. The world would turn off and I wouldn't be able to handle it."

"That's so messed up," she cried, all but swooning at the morbid idea of animals and their pests. How was he able to make something like that so romantic?

With a great exaggerated sigh and a sarcastic roll of the eyes, Maxu gestured to her, then himself. "Now you understand what it feels like to have a mate."

She shoved against his shoulder, laughing and only managing to push herself back.

He lifted the iPod to her. "Play something for us now."

***

Maxu's chest was permanently expanded, warmth seeping from every pore. His mate was with him. He hadn't scared her away, and he was confident he *couldn't*. She was a fierce female.

Meg played him song after song, explaining the words when his translator couldn't communicate their meaning, and sighed out a sweet sound of contentment when the thing she called a playlist ended.

While he fed the fire, she relaxed into the blankets. He stared down at her, loving the way her short, dark hair fell around her face. She bit her lip and grinned up at him. As though daring him to pounce, she slowly spread her bent knees wide and licked her lips. Maxu needed no more invitation.

He fucked her in the moonlight until she was sore and wrung out, then used his mouth to make her come until her legs were shaking and she was kicking him away with her feet on his shoulders.

Then he dragged her naked body into his arms, shielding her back from the cold with his body warmth, and whispered Vrulan folk tales into her ear until she drifted to sleep.

His whispers didn't stop, though. He told her how smart and confident and capable he found her to be. How incredible she was. If he said it enough, perhaps it would leak into her subconscious and overshadow the harm her family had caused.

He whispered all the things she should've been told her whole life, hoping the words played out in her dreams. And before he shut his eyes, he admitted how deeply he loved her.

31

The sun had risen early, already charring his back from its intensity. He'd swept a blanket over them both, but the heat was becoming unbearable. Meg's body was beaded with sweat. She fidgeted in her sleep more and more until, finally, she woke up.

She ripped the blanket off them, trying to breathe in fresh air but scrunching her nose to find it dry and boiling. Maxu rested on his elbow at her side and swept his fingers through the sweaty, slick skin between her breasts. "I think it's time to go, unless you'd like to stay a little longer." He gave her nipple a pinch.

She chuckled, blindly swatting him away. "Please. I need to get somewhere cool."

He cleaned up as she cursed, trying to get her discarded outfit on over her sticky skin. When she was finally dressed, he whistled to call his old mount, Urio, over from the feast of trees he'd sent her to. Within minutes, his friend was there chuffing and bowing her head, expecting scratches on her neck. He obliged.

She was old now, retired from seeding duty yet still so full of life. He missed her. Maybe more than anyone else. She'd been faithful for the few years they'd ridden together. It'd torn something in him to leave her, but she'd thrived. She'd danced through storms until a stray bolt of lightning had hit her wrong. Then she'd settled, had some pups, and now nested with her mate on a low platform, spending her time munching on minata trees and snapping at her disobedient younglings.

He loaded Meg into the carriage more gently this time. She winced as she sat. Glancing up at his questioning stare, she explained, "Sore." A light blush stole over her cheeks, deepening the sun-pinkened color a shade.

Maxu couldn't bring himself to feel too bad. He mounted Urio and ascended. The wind was cold and harsh against his skin, reminding him again of the first time he'd flown. Up here, the wind was alive and visceral. Urio glided on its currents, showing him the unseen life that existed above everyone's heads.

They landed, and before sending Urio off, Maxu pressed his forehead to hers, promising they'd ride together again before he left.

This platform was one of the many hidden spots in the tower that Maxu had discovered during his time here. Sikthand had shown him many of the secrets of the tower so he could spy more effectively. Both red from the sun and disheveled, Maxu was glad he recalled the hidden routes through the tower walls. He could guide his mate to her room without needing to expose her to any scrutinizing looks.

They meandered through the cramped, hidden walkways until they were at the exit nearest her floor. She let out a small yelp when he pushed her against the wall, surprising her with a kiss before they emptied into a public hallway.

"We're almost to the room." She giggled. "Keep it in your pants. I haven't even brushed—"

A steady pulse ran through the metal walls, making them both freeze.

"What is that?" Meg gasped. "Is it an earthquake or something?"

"A call to action," he answered with furrowed brows. "They send vibrations through the metal when they want soldiers to assemble, but...there was no storm. And" —he pressed a hand to the wall, feeling the pattern of the call— "this isn't the right rhythm."

They'd flown far enough from their spot on the edge of the ore that he would've seen any approaching clouds. So, why were they calling soldiers together?

Unease raced over his skin. Meg noticed. "What's wrong?"

He faced her, thinking fast, and shaking his head at the ground. "Something," he answered slowly.

He pulled her in the opposite direction, racing through secret halls and cubbies he'd used while under the employ of the king and arrived at a small crawl space left in the walls of the Guild antechamber.

Maxu was too large to fit into the awkward curled space above, more muscular than he'd been when he'd lived here. But Meg would be able to squeeze up into the right spot and peek out through the crisscrossing spears of metal that provided a hidden view.

"Meg, I'm going to lift you up. See if anyone's out there," he whispered. Without hesitation, she nodded, determination hardening her features. If he weren't nervous, he might have beamed at her. He lifted her by her hips, then switched his hold to her feet until she was leaning against the curve high above, pressed between metal.

Silent minutes passed. He was about to climb up there and bring her down himself when she finally gently tapped at the metal to signal him. Her face was pale, her expression drawn as he lowered her to her feet. "They're not letting us go," she whispered.

His brows drew together. "What?"

"I couldn't hear much and it was only a couple of people talking far away, but I think the king decided to keep the humans locked up here."

"Why?"

Vrulans weren't the type of people to make rash decisions. Sikthand wasn't stupid. He wouldn't hold a royal contingent from Tremanta hostage for no reason, even if it contained humans.

Meg's shoulders jerked up. "I don't know. They didn't say."

Maxu's jaw firmed. He kept Meg close, navigating his way back through the secret maze of passages until they were at the same loading platform they'd left minutes before.

"What are we gonna do?"

"Leave," he rasped. He dragged Urio's saddle back from where he'd discarded it.

"Leave? We're not leaving. What about my friends?"

Maxu had known this would be a point of contention for her. His shoulders stiffened. "I don't know why this is happening, Meg," he said, frowning down at her from his full height. "But I do know that I can get you away. Once we get to Tremanta, we can send reinforcements."

"No," Meg said, stomping her foot. "They're holding them here for a reason, and I'm betting Tremanta already knows. What would be the point otherwise? I'm not leaving without them."

Maxu groaned, sucking in a calming breath. "You're getting in that carriage and we're leaving. I won't hear more about it."

"No," she repeated, a small crack in her voice.

He ignored the pain stabbing through his chest, focusing on the saddle instead. She stomped up to him, wrenching at his shoulder until he met her eyes.

"You're a man who can find anything, right?" she asked, determination tensing her mouth. "That's what you told me.

Well, this is me, your mate, the person you say you'd do anything for, and I'm asking you to find my friends." Maxu just started shaking his head when she added, "Please."

He froze, his face lifting to the ceiling, his eyes scrunching shut. With a growl, he threw the saddle against the wall.

32

Hours later and Meg was sore and tired and hungry. They'd crawled through old malginash feeding troughs, shimmied between sharp unpolished metal beams, and eavesdropped on dozens of conversations. They'd learned that the king was holding the Tremantian party hostage until the Queen stepped down as Intergalactic Alliance representative, but they still hadn't figured out where Meg's friends were.

Their rooms, which had been their first stop, were empty. No guards even patrolled the area, leading Maxu to believe Sikthand had moved them for some reason, though he couldn't understand why. If the humans were being detained, why force them to leave their rooms? It wasn't like they could fly a malginash to the ground.

The only answer they'd been able to conceive was that Maxu's absence might have spooked Sikthand, forcing him to hide the women away. Maxu disagreed with that guess, though, claiming the king knew him well enough to know he'd never put his life—or more importantly, his mate's life— at risk to rescue a group of humans from mere detainment.

Meg's stomach rumbled loudly, and she squatted down, trying to muffle the sound against her knees.

Since agreeing to rescue her travel companions, Maxu's energy had shifted to something she hadn't seen before. He could be aggressive, charming, sweet, ill-tempered. But the cold efficiency with which he'd guided them through the hidden maze of Vrulatica was new.

He didn't complain or curse when the narrow passages bit into his chest. He didn't slow to eat or drink, though he made sure *she* did, feeding her the scraps he'd packed to bring to the desert. He didn't even appear tired, though they'd spent most of the day searching. Was this what his life had been as a mercenary? Detached and focused at all times.

They crouched in place, awkwardly stuffed together in a crack between walls that opened into a private bathhouse. Meg's legs burned from her weird squat, her toes cramping. At the end of all this, she'd at least come out with a newfound respect for spies everywhere.

Though Maxu hadn't revealed any fear and anxiety he might've had, Meg noticed a tense twitch in his jaw. Something was bothering him, but as they waited to pounce on a Guild member they'd followed into the bathhouse, she forced herself not to ask.

Another hour passed in which the Vrulan official socialized and gossiped out of earshot. Meg was about ready to tear her hair out when the male moved in close, taking his time redressing and straightening his tunic.

Like a shot, Maxu flashed out from the darkness, wrapped a hand around the man's mouth, slipped a blade to his throat, and dragged him back into the shadows before anyone had noticed. Meg backed up as quickly as she could as he dragged the Vrulan back, scraping his own elbows against the walls so badly bits of metal chipped off. Finally, they emptied into a wider bit of the passage that was embedded far enough into the city walls that they wouldn't be overheard.

Meg stayed out of the man's reach as Maxu had forced her to promise, but she faced him and when he caught sight of her, his dark brows furrowed. The Vrulan's bronze gaze rose to the small cubby they'd tucked themselves in, and she could tell he was unfamiliar with the area.

"Where are the humans being held?" Maxu questioned, holding the knife tighter to the man's throat to punctuate his words. The Guild member hissed against Maxu's hand. When her mate uncovered the man's mouth, his lips remained stubbornly sealed.

"Tell us where they are," Meg demanded. "Do you all really think this will make the Queen step down? She won't. Not for a few humans and their guards."

The man remained silent, his throat bobbing against the edge of the blade.

Maxu's forehead tipped down. He ran a tongue over his teeth. When he looked back up, his stern gaze hinted to her she wasn't going to like whatever he said next.

"Take a walk down that passage, Meg." He tipped his head in the direction they'd come from. The fingers wrapped around his knife flared and tightened again.

She glanced between the two men, cold understanding turning her stomach to lead. "No...you can't... It's not right."

The man's gaze flashed into focus, lids widening.

Maxu let out a restrained growl. "We need to know where they are. This male knows and won't tell us. What do you suggest we do instead?"

"Not torture him," she hissed, throwing her hands into the air. But even she had to admit she had no other ideas. It wasn't like they could just push this guy back into the hallway and try again. She could admit she'd been willfully naïve about what they were planning to do once they'd finally caught one of the Guild members they'd been hunting, but this?

Maxu softened his voice. "I'll be fast, sweetness. He isn't trained for this. He'll break quickly."

Fear was making the steel-gray hood of the man's face paler and paler.

Maxu's head tipped toward the man almost too subtly for her to catch, but then he raised a brow and she understood.

"You've grown jaded to torture, though. Too many years spent getting information through pain has left you with a skewed sense of how much pain is enough. The things you do now…they're just cruel." Meg curled her lip in disgust and wrapped her arms around her waist as though suddenly chilled to the bone. "It's like you enjoy it or something."

A tic manifested in the Vrulan's eye as they spoke. His throat bobbed more frequently.

Just a little more.

"Like you said," she plodded on, "this is just a politician. He's not a soldier. Do you really think it's fair to pull out his fingernails or whatever it is you're planning? It's barbaric. Can't you just punch him or something?"

The man attempted to stifle a whimper.

"We're in a hurry, love," Maxu said softly, mimicking the appeasing tone of someone trying to convince their partner to fix their hair more quickly. "Pulling out fingernails won't work." The man's shoulders relaxed for a moment before Maxu added, "It needs to be far more painful than that if we want to get out of here before morning. Sticking slices of metal *under* the fingernails would be a better option."

The politician trembled as Maxu pointedly studied the small enclosure.

"What?" Meg asked, hands on hips.

"Now that we're standing here, I think this space might echo a little too loudly."

"They're in the old forum," the man burst out, breath shaky. Meg held her own smile back as she watched an evil grin split across Maxu's face.

371

"Why's Sikthand keeping them there? What's the point of this kidnapping?"

Sighing in defeat, the man spoke. "There's been news going around the world that the Queen has humans hidden in Tremanta. Thousands of them, all asleep in pods."

"That's ridiculous!" Meg snorted. "She doesn't have anyone hidden. Why would he believe that?"

"It came from a reliable source. One of the Tremantian envoy."

Meg sucked in a breath. One of their envoy? But…it was a lie. It *must* have been a lie. There were a few humans who were still asleep in pods because the technicians hadn't been able to crack the encryption for their controls yet, but there were maybe six pods, not thousands. The Tremantian Queen sometimes did things that Meg didn't fully understand, but she wasn't the type to do this. Time and time again, she'd fought for them. Kept them from being forced into marriages. Provided safe housing and given them a certain amount of leeway while keeping them safe.

No. If somebody was spreading these rumors, they were either stupid or had an agenda, and the timing told her the latter was far more likely. But who?

Licking his lips, the man whispered, "Everyone thought you'd fled. The king assumed you'd heard the news, took your mate, and ran. You could leave now. Let me go."

Veins popped along Maxu's fist as his grip on the blade tightened. He watched Meg, a muscle in his jaw ticking.

Brimming with irritation, he let out a deep groan, then using a hand at the man's nape and his body weight's momentum, he spun them both, slamming the Vrulan's head into the wall.

Their captive crumpled to the floor. Maxu cut a swath of fabric off the man's cloak, bound his hands and mouth, then flipped the blade, stowing it in a pocket on his side.

He stared down at the slow rise and fall of the unconscious Vrulan's chest. "He'll wake up and cause us problems."

"You're not killing him," she argued. "Where's the old forum?"

He let out another sigh, hefting his bag over his shoulder. Face tipping to the ceiling, Meg watched Maxu's mind work, his gaze flicking over the metal as if plotting a course.

"We have a few stops to make first, vahpti. I have a plan."

33

Whispers floated up to the ceiling where Meg and Maxu were sprawled on their bellies. The short crawl space above the circular forum was dusty and stifling from the heat rising off the central fire. Meg's body was protected, but every time the bare skin of her hands accidentally touched the metal, searing pain made her hiss.

They reached the round grate in the ceiling disguised as an artistic metal overlay, and Maxu peered through the small carved holes. He laced his fingers into the grooves of metal and twisted.

Meg lifted a hand to her mouth. The hot steel must've been burning his hands, but he didn't even wince. Ever so slowly, he rotated the panel without a creak or scrape to be heard.

As soon as the panel was out of the way, Meg snatched up his hand, exposing his palm. A shudder ran over her—angry red welts covered his fingers. She kissed his palm, shooting an apologetic smile at him. Maxu silently kissed her hand in return, then his mask of determination was back in place.

He dipped his head through the opening and scanned the room. From her vantage point, Meg could see a few soldiers stationed around the perimeter, but not many. Maxu had expected that, arguing it was more likely they'd be sent to patrol the halls outside once they'd disarmed and disabled the Tremantian guards.

Tugging forward a long coil of rope they'd stolen from a malginash-handling storage cupboard, he passed one end to her, fed the other through a ratcheting winch, and activated the magnetic base. The winch cemented into place with a hollow clank. They froze, staring at each other, and listened. Had anyone heard?

When no ruckus from below sounded, Maxu nodded. His body stiffened, eyes roaming over her mouth, lips thinned. She knew he didn't want to leave, but he had to. Their plan relied on him. She gave him an encouraging nod and smile.

"This is splitting me in two," he whispered. Cupping the back of her head, he pulled her face alongside his cheek. His mouth brushed against her ear. "I've fallen in love with you. Neither of us can die until I've forced you to fall in love with me too."

Inflating like a balloon, she beamed at him. "I knew I loved you the moment you chose not to torture someone for me."

He smirked.

"And if I'm honest," she rested her palm on his chest, "long before that."

Lifting her hand to his lips, he inhaled her scent. With a tight nod, he crawled away.

Her heart was thundering in her throat as she waited. There were six soldiers she could make out. From the looks of the bloodied and bruised Tremantian guards sprawled over benches, they wouldn't be much help. She prayed they'd find their second wind. If not, Maxu would have to fight everyone all on his own.

Gaze darting between all twelve captives, Meg finally spotted Daunet almost directly beneath her. She debated dropping something small onto her head to get her attention, but it was too risky. They were already lucky that the ceiling was so heavily ornamented that they could remove a person-sized hole in it and not be noticed.

She didn't dare stick her head out, so the only view she had was of the envoy below and part of the far wall. Suddenly, one soldier did a double take across the room. He didn't yell, but he took a step to the side and dipped his head left and right.

Shit. He must have noticed a guard had gone missing. Maxu had planned to take them out one at a time as quietly as possible until he was spotted.

"Tivi?" the male called. A soldier walking close by straightened, hand moving toward a sickle-shaped blade. Suddenly, something flew at his head, knocking against his helmet and laying him out flat. The other guard stared in disbelief for a long moment before springing into action. He began to shout for backup, but Daunet had already pounced.

She slid across the floor, swiping up the fallen sickle blade, and brought it down with a loud clang, connecting with the soldier's own raised weapon.

Shouts from somewhere below and behind Meg rang through the room, making her blood turn to ice in her veins. Meg tossed the rope down to the floor and dipped her head out.

"Tara! Sophia!" she yelled at the two women closest to her. They whipped around, searching.

Tara spotted the rope first and looked up. "Finally." She grinned up at Meg for a moment before bolting toward the guards and other humans.

Heleax limped over, pushing Camille and Rita ahead. Rita grabbed the rope, while Heleax wrapped it around her thigh to keep her stable. "Just hold on," Meg shouted, getting into position so she could use her body weight to pump the winch ratchet.

She pulled up and threw herself down over and over, lifting Rita slowly but surely. Her knuckles burned as they rubbed against the floor. Breathing grew difficult in the dense, humid air, but she kept going until Rita's gray hair popped through the round opening.

With a wince when her hands touched the metal floor, Rita hauled herself into the ceiling space. Meg didn't waste time checking on her, throwing the rope down again and readying the winch.

"Now," Rita called, watching the ground so she could direct Meg.

"What happened?" Meg wheezed, ignoring the burning pain spearing from her knuckles to her shoulders.

"They bombarded us. A small army barged into our rooms, fought off our guards, and dragged us here this morning. They kept asking questions about some hidden women. We told them we didn't know anything, but the king wouldn't accept it."

Rita reached out just as Camille's arm stretched in and planted on the metal floor.

"Fuck," she screamed, dragging herself through the opening, then waving her arms. "That's fucking hot." She blew on her scalded palms as Rita and Meg dropped the rope once more.

Camille shuffled over to Meg when she noticed her labored breathing. "Let me take over for a minute."

Meg didn't have the strength to argue, spots already dancing in her vision from the heat. She crouched over the opening instead and watched Sophia and Heleax working to strap an unconscious Nirato to Lucy so both could be lifted together.

Rita groaned and joined Camille at the winch. "This one will be heavy."

When Sophia gave a thumbs-up, Meg panted, "Okay, go."

Rita and Camille used their combined body weight to work the winch, grunting with the effort. After painfully slow minutes, they lugged the unconscious guard and Lucy through the opening.

The sounds of fighting ebbed, but the metal of the tower rumbled ominously. Meg's hands shook as she untied the knot affixing Nirato. "That has to be an alarm."

"Hurry," Camille shouted through panted breaths. Lucy joined her at the winch.

Uthen helped support Tara, who'd somehow injured her shoulder. As soon as Uthen crawled in, though, he collapsed onto his front, blood running from a crack on his head. When the rope dropped again, Kel and Malinu glanced around the room with wide eyes.

"Where's Sophia?" Meg breathed, switching off with Lucy and Rita at the winch as they lifted Kel.

"She's making it difficult for the soldiers to fight. Girl picked up a sword and started swinging. She was pretty good too. Mostly, though, she knows the soldiers have strict orders not to hurt any of us, so she keeps putting herself in the way."

"Damn," Meg hissed. It was brave, but it was stupid. "And Gamso?"

"We haven't seen him. We've been asking. I hope the king isn't hurting him." Lucy crawled over Uthen and Nirato, checking their pulses, and then helped pull Kel into the cramped space.

"Shit," Meg panted, feeling the skin peel from her knuckles. "It was him. Someone from our group told Sikthand that the Queen had humans hidden all over. That's why he believed it."

Tara froze, her face reddening. She glared in Meg's direction.

"That little shit," Rita wheezed. Tara moved to bump Rita out of the way, and she shrugged her off. "Don't be dumb. Your shoulder's busted from trying to bash your way out."

Meg didn't have the breath to comment on Rita's swift personality change, so she just lifted a brow.

"It's been a long day," Rita grunted when she caught her looking.

"May I?" Kel gestured at the winch, and Meg immediately moved aside. He might have been a timid politician, but he was also a large Clecanian man. He began pumping the winch and had Malinu climbing in in half the time it had taken Meg.

"Maxu is gone," Malinu coughed. "There's one soldier left, but Heleax and Sophia seem to have him handled. Daunet and Atolicy are covering the door to take out nearby guards as they filter in, but I'm sure more are on their way as we speak. Soon they'll be too many."

"Maxu's heading to a landing bay to get our transport ready," Meg explained. "We need to meet him there." They'd just dropped the rope again when someone let out a yowl of pain.

Daunet appeared below, hefting Atolicy over her shoulder in a fireman carry. She grabbed the rope, wrapped it around her forearm, and used her other arm to keep the male steady as they lifted her.

Meg's brows furrowed. "Damn. I didn't realize my guard was Superwoman."

"Well, this isn't really the time, but…" Tara shot Meg a wide grin. "She's feeling a little stronger today."

It took Meg's tired brain a moment to catch up, but then her gaze locked on to Daunet's hands. Bright blue mating marks were visible under splotches of red blood. "Congratulations," she shouted.

Sophia and Heleax appeared below a dangling Daunet and smiled up at them. Malinu and Kel were working the winch without breaking much of a sweat.

Meg yelled down to Sophia, who was still clutching a crescent sword. "I heard you're pretty good with that thing. You never told us you could fight."

Sophia grinned, flipping the sword in an impressive little twirl. "Ten years of LARPing have proved surprisingly useful."

"What's LARPing?" Lucy whispered.

The group all took fistfuls of Atolicy's clothing and dragged him through the opening. Meg pointed to the curved passageway which they'd crawled through. "We need to drag the unconscious folks through there so we can run as soon as Sophia and Heleax are up."

Daunet lifted herself through the ceiling as if it were no more difficult than exiting a pool. She'd heard Meg, though, and without needing anymore direction, she grabbed Tara and began dragging Atolicy toward the exit. Lucy and Camille worked together to drag Nirato.

Kel rushed to grab Uthen, leaving Rita, Malinu, and Meg grappling to drop the rope for Sophia. When it hit the ground, Sophia tossed her sword to the side with a clatter and locked her arm around the rope.

Malinu began ratcheting. She lifted a few feet off the ground, when a flash of silver hurtled through the air, severing the rope and embedding into the side of the metal wall with a crunch. Sophia dropped, landing on her back with a painful thud before curling into a ball on her side and gasping to get breath into her lungs.

Meg dipped her head through the opening and saw King Sikthand standing tall, eyes blazing, and his thick arm pulling back from his impressive throw. Soldiers streamed in, parting around him while he remained still as a statue.

Heleax must have realized he was outnumbered, but he crouched in front of Sophia anyway, weapon raised. Sophia finally regained her breath and rolled onto her back. "Run! I'll be fine."

Meg's vision spotted, a ringing in her ears. She hadn't crawled through filth and slimy rodent nests and put her mate's life on the line just to leave someone behind, but before she could think of an alternative, Daunet was dragging her away with her newly acquired matehood strength.

Sound slowly came back to her. "We'll come back. We'll come back for them," Daunet assured.

Meg sucked down the lump in her throat, trying to steel herself the way Maxu did, hardening her heart. She could let herself feel the guilt later. Everyone waited in the hall, gasping and bruised. Their expectant gazes helped Meg see things more clearly.

She had to be strong. She was the only one who knew the way out. Maxu had made her walk the path three times over before they'd crawled into that ceiling. They'd get Sophia back, but Meg couldn't help everyone else if she was stupid now.

With a deep breath, she pressed through to the front and led the way.

They were slow moving as they took turns lugging the unconscious guards through narrow spaces and hoisting them over half walls until, finally, they emerged in the landing bay that she and Maxu had taken off from the day before.

Her mate was waiting for them astride Urio. He let out a visible breath of relief when he saw her, his whole body slumping forward until his head hit the back of Urio's mane. He pointed to the two carriages, and they piled in.

"Anyone else?" he shouted, eyes fixed on the end of the hall. Meg's mouth twitched, tears welling. All she could do was shake her head.

Meg held up one of the many long-barreled cannons that they'd piled into the carriages. "They'll probably chase us. Shoot at them with these." She showed them how the cannons worked and then ran over to the other bucket, clambering in. When they were all strapped and armed, Maxu guided Urio forward until she gripped their chains, and they lifted into the night.

***

Never in Maxu's life had his body felt so eviscerated. He'd fought as long as he could until the soldiers had numbered few enough that he'd been confident the Tremantian guards could take over. Then he'd gone against every instinct shooting stabbing pain through his body. He'd left.

His mate had been crouching alone in a boiling metal ceiling, trying to lift eleven people into the air, and he'd left her there. He'd wanted to vomit with each step. Even now, when she'd appeared, his body had exploded, relief spreading through his limbs as a jolt, electricity skittering over his skin. And they weren't even free yet.

The most impressive force Vrulatica had was its riders. If Urio didn't make it to the cruisers in time, there'd be no escaping. Maxu dove for the ground, gliding just high enough for the carriages not to scrape through the sand.

He heard shrieks below, and his heart stilled. He peered over his thigh and found Meg pointing a gun into the sky, dark hair flying around her face. Formidable.

Three malginash were on their tail, diving in a way he was unable to with the added weight of the carriages. Meg waited until they were close, until it would affect the creatures most, then fired.

The tubes of cloud seed weren't used as weapons in Vrulatica, which meant they hadn't been guarded. Almost too easy to steal. As the green chemical exploded into the air, creating a wall of sparks and thick green fog, the malginash gaining on them were forced to rear back.

It was only a second's hesitation, but it was enough. The creatures swerved, diving through the fog, only to be met with another explosion.

He thanked the Goddess that Sikthand needed the humans alive, otherwise they would've been shot out of the air within seconds. Their escape plan had gotten them a few minutes' head-start, and as they zoomed closer to the cruisers, he prayed it was enough. An explosion to his right had Urio swerving. A malginash had attempted to intercept, guessing their direction, but one explosion had stopped him.

Maxu guided Urio lower and lower until the carriages clanked onto the ground, dragging violently through the sand. He brought the creature to a stop before the cruisers. Fumbling with the ties holding his legs to the saddle, his burned fingers having lost sensation, he finally unlatched himself and jumped down.

He swept his palm over Urio's neck, whispering his thanks. The group was already half piled into the largest cruiser. He scooped the last unconscious guard over his shoulder, dragged an argumentative Meg along with him, and loaded them both into the cab.

"Stay in here, or I can't focus on making this work," he growled at Meg.

She stayed put, but she glared outside toward the conscious members of their group still shooting bombs into the sky to buy them time.

The resonant clicking roar of the approaching malginash boomed outside. Maxu plugged in his override device and ripped off the metal sheet hiding the cruiser's manual dials.

"Get in," he bellowed to the others. They dove inside, piling on one another, while Daunet brought up the tail, backing in and sending a final bomb into the sky before the door closed.

He forced the cruiser to lift into the air faster than the old safety protocols allowed. The cab shuddered as a malginash crashed into its side, the screech of gilded antlers against metal made his brain pulse angrily.

Maxu threw the controls as high as they could go and barely managed not to tumble backward when the ball jetted away at a speed faster than any malginash could match.

He watched their progress on the cruiser map and lowered the windows once he felt they were far enough away from Vrulatica not to need shielding. The scenery zoomed by underneath as only a rush of color. When greens, browns, and reds dissolved into solid blue, he finally let out a breath of relief.

The tension in the cab was palpable. Kel and Malinu were scrunched in a corner on the floor, while Rita and Camille tended to the injured guards, digging through the cruiser's emergency pack for a healer.

Maxu's own body vibrated when he gave his mate a once-over and found her shaking, tears building in her bloodshot eyes. When the autopilot was reengaged, he lifted Meg from her seat, then collapsed back with her on his lap. He clutched her head to his chest and forced himself to remember to breathe as her tears leaked through his torn shirt.

Eventually the heavy breathing settled, adrenaline leeching away and leaving them all in puddles of exhaustion.

Daunet took in steadying breaths, then used the cruiser communicator to connect with Tremanta. They all waited in silence. No answer.

No one dared to speak. The cruiser belonged to the Tremantian envoy. The communicator should've been registered to connect directly. But it wasn't.

Daunet tried again, a different line this time. After a small eternity, a quiet "Hello" rang through the space.

"Metli, this is Daunet. We've gotten free from Vrulatica, but we need reinforcements. Two of our group were left behind. One human and one guard. Are soldiers already on their way? What's the Queen's plan for dealing with Sikthand?"

Silence pulsed through the cab. Maxu's fingers tightened around Meg.

"Metli," Daunet barked.

"Don't come back," Metli whispered.

Over the years, Maxu had come to know Metli rather well. They despised each other, yet he always had begrudging respect for the female and her unbending will. Her fierce loyalty was a testament to their city, even if he felt it a bit misplaced at times. Never once had he heard the wobble in Metli's voice that he heard now.

The sob she released on a breath had Maxu's throat going dry.

"The Queen is dead."

Epilogue

"Hurry—it's starting soon," Tara yelled over her shoulder. She sat with Daunet's hand clutched in hers while Daunet rubbed slow circles over her arm.

Meg settled into the seat next to them, but Maxu didn't sit. He paced behind their backs, occasionally stopping to flatten his palms on Meg's shoulders before pacing again. Meg sipped some of the mott she'd gotten for herself so she'd have something to do, but her stomach was too tied up in knots. The liquid settled in her throat.

For the last week, they'd been hiding out in Maxu's safe house. After their escape from Vrulatica, they'd come to an agreement that this would be the best place to wait until they knew more. Thank God her mate was the cautious sort, having built this place years before on the chance he one day might need to hide from angry ex-employers or victims from his past.

From what the group could gather, the Queen had been assassinated. The question remained, by whom? There were too many suspects. Angry politicians across the planet who'd wanted her resignation. Insurgents hiding in plain sight who hadn't appreciated her razing their operations, or Insurgent members looking to regain their foothold in power.

They'd had some limited communication with Maxu's brothers, along with a few of his seedy contacts across the planet, but no one seemed to know much. It felt as though the world was holding its breath until the interim queen, Vila, could ascend.

And now, in only a matter of minutes, she would.

Her first address would be broadcast to cities around the world. No one knew exactly what she would say, but whatever it was would set the precedent moving forward. Meg, for one, was terrified.

Atolicy and Nirato were patrolling the perimeter of Maxu's fortress, while the rest of them crowded around the projection cube where the image of Vila would be displayed in real time.

"This is much too fast," Malinu muttered for the thousandth time. "New Queens don't ascend until a vote with the entire council has been taken. Kel and I—"

"They're claiming we're dead or lost, you know that," Uthen grumbled. "They don't have to wait for you if they think you aren't coming back."

Camille sat with her elbows on her knees and fidgeted, picking at her nails while staring intently at the space where the holographic projection would emerge. "No, he's right. Something's up. This all feels wrong. Vila always had it out for the Queen. I wouldn't be surprised if she'd planned this all herself."

"Doubtful, considering the Queen was her mother." Kel, who'd taken to cleaning Maxu out of his mott supply, shrugged at the open-mouthed stares of everyone in the room.

"What?" Tara asked.

"Kel," Malinu admonished.

"What?" Kel shrugged. "The Queen gives up her name and all her family—past, present, and future—for as long as she reigns. She paints her hands and becomes the mother of us all. But she's dead now." His voice cracked a little. "What does it matter if they know?"

Lucy opened her mouth, about to say something, when Vila materialized in the center of the room. She looked exactly as Meg remembered—lean, stoic, dressed to perfection, yet now she wore a lavender robe. The Queen's colors. Her eyes, the regal lift of her chin. Meg couldn't believe she hadn't seen the resemblance before.

Maxu's heavy palms came to rest on her shoulders as they waited for Vila to speak.

"We've suffered a loss," she began, staring ahead. "Our Queen was tragically killed one week ago. No words can fill the void she's left."

Lucy snorted from across the room. "I don't trust that bitch for one minute," she hissed. Harsh *shushes* echoed through the space. She crossed her arms over her chest.

"We won't rest until we find her killer, but at present, our world is in crisis. This is a time of change, and I know our Queen would understand the shift in focus. As named successor, I'm ready to take her place. For the first time in a hundred years, her name shall be spoken, and mine shall be locked away until I've either stepped down or moved to my next life. Nabiora Vilafina, you ruled with benevolence and grace, and you'll be missed."

Vila's lips thinned ever so slightly as she stared into the distance, allowing a moment of silence. "Nabiora was fair and kind. Perhaps to a fault."

Whispered curses echoed around the room as the tone of Vila's address shifted.

"She sacrificed in a way that made sense in the moment. She kept the humans safe. She kept them happy. But she did so by awarding them freedoms that not even her own people possess."

Meg's breath caught in her chest.

"The humans of Tremanta were not required to engage in marriage ceremonies. They weren't required even to socialize with the public, though it's been proven they spark recognition wherever they go. Through study, we've learned that humans come from Clecanian stock. Their ancestors are our ancestors. Yet we don't treat them as Clecanians. We don't hold them to the same standards. Is that not an insult to them? It's no wonder we've struggled to draft an argument strong enough to support the reclassification of Earth. How can we argue humans are equal to us in intellect and ability if we don't treat them as we treat each other? If we don't have them abide by the same laws we abide by?"

Maxu's grip on her shoulders was growing too tight. Meg lifted her hand, resting it over one of his. He moved away, resuming his pacing behind the long built-in seating that divided the kitchen area from the sunken communal room.

"As my first action, I decree humans will be subject to our laws." Vila paused there.

Addresses like this weren't given in front of live crowds on Clecania. They were projected from a private location, but the pointed pause and arrogant lift of her chin made Meg's insides roil. It was as though she were holding for the invisible hoots of applause to die down.

"Furthermore, I feel in this time of upheaval and transformation, our cities need to come together. Only united can we move forward with the heavy task that will be acclimating a Class Three planet to our existence. For that reason, I've decided to disperse the humans. Unmated Earthlings will be sent abroad to reside in cities across the planet. Not temporarily on a tour but permanently. There's no reason that Tremantians should have more of a chance to recognize a mate than anyone else."

Vila kept talking, but Meg could barely listen. Everyone in the room began murmuring, their anger building in volume until they were shouting into the air.

"'Disperse them'? As if they're airlifting goods to cities in need. We're people!" Lucy shouted.

Tara gripped Daunet's hand a little harder.

"So, if we're unmated, we're just gonna be sent off in the hopes we get recognized somewhere? With no say?" Rita shot to her feet. "I'm in a loving relationship, but I doubt they'll care about that."

"We're not going back, that's for sure." Camille laughed humorlessly, nail firmly between her teeth. She glanced up to Maxu. "You can't drag me out of here."

Maxu kept pacing but lifted his hands, palms forward. "You'll hear no argument from me."

Ice crystallized over Meg's spine. Vila was making it seem as if she were merely holding the humans to follow the same rules as everyone else, but that was absolute bullshit. The rest of the world would see that, surely.

The new ruler went on, talking about specifics, outlining her plans for the leaders' summit, and reminding her audience that a new ambassador needed to be elected. But Meg was done listening.

Sophia was still trapped in Vrulatica. Guilt clawed Meg's insides with every day that went by without a plan to break her free. But now...?

What about all the women left in Tremanta? What about the ones still asleep in their pods?

Meg staunchly believed that the old Queen had been in their corner. Now? She didn't know who was fighting for them now.

The energy of the house was somber after that. Maxu's guests wandered around like ghosts, making food and not eating it. Sitting, then immediately rising. Rita spent most of her time asleep, the events of the last week smudging out the confident, dreamy happiness that always clung to her.

Meg curled into the sheets as Maxu did his final patrols of the snowy mountain where he'd built his safe house. When he got into bed behind her, silently pulling her against his chest, she closed her eyes, forcing her mind to go blank.

"We'll be okay, vahpti. Vila's actions won't stand."

Meg gnawed on her lip, stress causing a headache to build between her eyes.

He gave her a little shake, then pressed her back into the bed and gazed down at her. "One day, things will be normal again. I promise you."

"You don't know that." She smiled at him anyway, loving the certainty in his deep voice.

"I *do* know. You won't be happy until your people are safe. And the only thing I want is for you to be happy. So, I know.

If I must steal every single human and hide them away or ferry them back to Earth, I'll do it just to see you glow again."

Warmth spread through her chest, and she allowed herself to feel a moment of bliss at his words. She stretched up and kissed him. "I wish it wasn't so hard for you, sometimes," she admitted, curling her leg over his hip. At his furrowed brows, she explained, "The mate bond. I know you feel this drive to fix everything and make me happy because of it. It seems unfair. It makes me feel that your life with me will always be one big chore after another."

Maxu's naked chest expanded against her side as he stared down at her. "Since the moment I breathed you in back in Vondale, I've found joy in the world in a way I never have before. Even in dark times, like these, I still see beauty in places it never used to be. That's because of you." He swept her hair behind her ear. "I'm using you, love. Using you for your light and your morality." His hand skimmed down her bare back. He palmed her ass and sent her a wolfish grin. "I'm using you for your body." His touch softened. "And your warmth, your smiles, your tears, your mouth." He added with a soft kiss, "It's only fair I make up for all my greediness by devoting my life to you. You don't just make me happy, Meg, you make me alive."

Silent tears fell over Meg's cheeks, tickling her ear. She smiled, sucking in a small sob. "I suppose it's a fair trade, then," she said with a long-suffering sigh and a roll of her eyes.

Maxu chuckled, his hand on her ass squeezing as he used his body weight to roll on top of her.

"Have I told you I love you yet today?" she whispered, brushing her hands down the powerful muscles of his back. The purr started up in his chest almost instantly.

"Not yet in words today."

"I love you," she breathed.

His purr vibrated through her whole body as he whispered back, "I love you."

About the Author

Victoria Aveline has always enjoyed immersing herself in a good romance. Alpha males are her weakness but, while possessive dominating heroes have always been titillating, she craved something more. So she decided to create a world in which devastatingly sexy men could be aggressive and domineering but still bow down before the matriarchy.

Victoria lives with her husband, dogs, and about sixty thousand badass honey-making ladies. When not writing or fantasizing about future characters, she enjoys traveling, reading, and sipping overpriced hipster cocktails.

www.victoriaaveline.com

Made in United States
Orlando, FL
07 September 2023

36797458R00243